HONOURING THE
STRENGTH OF
INDIAN WOMEN

FIRST VOICES, FIRST TEXTS

SERIES EDITOR: WARREN CARIOU

First Voices, First Texts aims to reconnect contemporary readers with some of the most important Aboriginal literature of the past, much of which has been unavailable for decades. This series reveals the richness of these works by providing newly re-edited texts that are presented with particular sensitivity toward Indigenous ethics, traditions, and contemporary realities. The editors strive to indigenize the editing process by involving communities, by respecting traditional protocols, and by providing critical introductions that give readers new insights into the cultural contexts of these unjustly neglected classics.

1. *Devil in Deerskins: My Life with Grey Owl* by Anahareo
2. *Indians Don't Cry / Gaawiin Mawisiiwag Anishinaabeg* by George Kenny
3. *Life Among the Qallunaat* by Mini Aodla Freeman
4. *From the Tundra to the Trenches* by Eddy Weetaltuk
5. *Honouring the Strength of Indian Women: Plays, Stories, Poetry* by Vera Manuel

HONOURING THE STRENGTH OF INDIAN WOMEN

PLAYS, STORIES, POETRY

VERA MANUEL

KULILU PAⱵKI

Edited by Michelle Coupal, Deanna Reder,
Joanne Arnott, and Emalene A. Manuel

Introduction by Emalene A. Manuel

Afterwords by Michelle Coupal,
Deanna Reder, and Joanne Arnott

UNIVERSITY OF MANITOBA PRESS

Honouring the Strength of Indian Women: Plays, Stories, Poetry
© Vera Manuel 2019
Introduction © Emalene A. Manuel 2019
Essays © Michelle Coupal, Deanna Reder, and Joanne Arnott 2019

23   22   21   20   19   1   2   3   4   5

University of Manitoba Press
Winnipeg, Manitoba, Canada
Treaty 1 Territory
uofmpress.ca

Cataloguing data available from Library and Archives Canada
First Voices, First Texts, ISSN 2291-9627 ; 5
ISBN 978-0-88755-836-8 (PAPER)
ISBN 978-0-88755-576-3 (PDF)
ISBN 978-0-88755-574-9 (EPUB)

Photographs courtesy Manuel family, unless otherwise noted.
Cover design: Mike Carroll
Back cover image: Shain Jackson
Interior design: Jess Koroscil

Printed in Canada

The University of Manitoba Press acknowledges the financial
support for its publication program provided by the Government of
Canada through the Canada Book Fund, the Canada Council
for the Arts, the Manitoba Department of Sport, Culture,
and Heritage, the Manitoba Arts Council, and
the Manitoba Book Publishing Tax Credit.

Funded by the Government of Canada | Canadä

DEDICATION
BY EMALENE A. MANUEL

I'd like to acknowledge my daughter Nukinka. Vera was her champion and she always believed in Nukinka and her storytelling. She is a founding member of Storyteller. Acknowledgements and appreciation to my nephew Rainbow who Vera helped raise and brought with her on the Constitution Express to Europe. Thanks to Constance Brissenden and Larry Loyie for connecting us to get the ball rolling to get this book published. Great appreciation to Deanna Reder, Michelle Coupal, and Warren Cariou. I first met Michelle over the phone and we had a great conversation about Vera's work and then I met Deanna and Warren later on and we just had the best working relationship. Although it is what Vera and I had hoped for, it was hard because of still feeling the loss and they offered warmth and support. I've learned a lot from Joanne Arnott for starting and maintaining Vera's tribute page. She's been Vera's closest poet sister and I am glad that she was able to come to Cranbrook and go through Vera's writings with me. I wouldn't have been able to do this without her. Thank you to Jill McConkey and all of the other editors and publishing folks at University of Manitoba Press who have helped make this possible. Thank you Ariadne Sawyer and the poets at World Poetry Café. I'd like to thank those who have influenced Vera's creative and training work. I would like to express deepest gratitude to Vera's family, colleagues, and fellow poets/writers/trainers: Rod Jeffries, Jane Middelton-Moz, Shawn Middleton, Loretta Todd, Kamala Todd, Debra Wingo, Jann Derrick, Joyce Johnson, Nicola River, Suzy Goodleaf, Wanda Gabriel, Mary Kay May, Margo Kane,

Lee Maracle, Tonya Gomes, Kimberly Tootoosis, and Anthony and Daloras Lee. I know there are many others whose names I may have missed but know that Vera greatly appreciated you in her life. There are also those whose support and encouragement over the years have undoubtedly shaped her writing. In particular these are Beth Cuthand, Louise Mandell, Stuart Rush, Pauline Douglas, Dianne and Tatsuo Kage, Bessie Brown, Catherine Blackstock, Elizabeth Mackenzie, Joyce Johnson, and Jackson Crick. Most importantly, on my sister Vera's behalf, I'd like to dedicate this book to all of the women and their relatives who she has worked with through her training, facilitation, and drama therapy. She loved her work and you were her greatest inspiration. I also dedicate the book to the remaining siblings of my mother, who, more than anyone, understand and take these stories to heart. I deeply appreciate my sister Doreen and my brother Richard. I thank Chief Malu Maseelah for her unwavering support and encouragement. Greatest love and appreciation to Ktunaxa relations. Additionally, I thank Kulilu Pa‡ki's adopted family who she loved like her own and would dedicate this book to all of her nieces, nephews, and grandnieces and grandnephews. You were the reason why she worked so hard and were the hope that it offered her for the future. You are the future. Finally, I dedicate this book in loving memory of our mother Marceline Paul Manuel. I miss you with all my heart but am reminded of you throughout every page.

CONTENTS

AFTERWORDS

EDITORS' NOTE

Much of the impetus for this collection is a combination of efforts inspired by Vera Manuel. While in graduate school, Michelle Coupal began teaching *Strength of Indian Women,* and her students, Manuel's readership, urged Michelle to bring this work back into print.[1] Michelle then called Deanna Reder to discuss whether she was interested in collaborating on this project and Deanna shared that she had been holding several scripts that were generated by Manuel's dramatherapy groups, and was uncertain what to do with them.[2] Michelle then contacted Larry Loyie and Constance Beresford (now Brissenden), whose press, Living Traditions, had first published *Strength of Indian Women;* Constance then put us in contact with Vera's sister Emalene Manuel.

As we began working together in earnest, we had the opportunity to speak with Métis poet Joanne Arnott, who had befriended Vera in her last few years of life and worked with her to select poems for publication. Excited by this other Manuel project, we decided to join efforts. We contacted the First Voices, First Texts series at the University of Manitoba Press precisely because the series publishes works by people, like Vera Manuel, who historically did not receive the kind of support and recognition they deserved.

As we worked together and were looking for other unpublished plays, we discovered that Emalene had protected her sister's archive. In the summer of 2016, Joanne visited Emalene at her home near Cranbrook and collected files from Vera's old computer and took photos of any materials that seemed relevant. Among the papers, we found rough notes and chapter outlines for an incomplete novel, as well as short stories, that seemed to have been produced for 1987 creative writing classes, with notes in the margin and comments throughout by both Vera and an unnamed teacher. We then worked with Iñupiaq research assistant Rachel Taylor who, as part of the research project The People and the Text, transcribed the hard copies as we sorted through comments and integrated only those changes approved by the author herself. Together we developed an editing practice based on the following principles: while we tried to change as little as possible, we corrected typos and we standardized punctuation in the interest of clarity. We did not change colloquial speech patterns or any other major redrafting of Manuel's words.

Our hope is that Vera Manuel will be recognized as a writer who was ahead of her time and who made profound contributions to our understandings of Indigenous trauma and healing. We hope that she will finally find the wide readership that she hoped and worked for, and that her readers can learn from her teachings long after she has gone.

INVITATION

One of the reasons we did not include several of the jointly written plays by Vera Manuel and the other participants of the Storyteller Theatre in this book is the complication this brings to the discussion of authorship and in gaining permissions from all the contributors. We would like to invite the participants in Vera's collaboratively written plays to contact us to discuss the possibility of future publication and of bringing some of those plays to a wider audience.

ACKNOWLEDGEMENTS

We would like to express our deep gratitude to Vera Manuel for her work. We would also like to thank her sister Emalene for agreeing to share Vera's archive with the rest of us. Michelle Coupal would like to thank the Social Sciences and Humanities Research Council of Canada (SSHRC) for funds supporting the work undertaken in preparing this manuscript and for the support of her broader research on teaching trauma and Indian Residential School literature, which helped to bring this project to fruition. This research was undertaken, in part, thanks to funding from the Canada Research Chairs program. Michelle would also like to thank Deanna Reder for her helpful suggestions on her afterword and for her ongoing mentorship. Michelle is grateful to her research assistant, Daimen Tokiwa, for transcribing one of the plays. In addition, Deanna Reder would like to thank SSHRC for funding The People and the Text project that supported some of the research in this volume, such as Joanne Arnott's research visit to ʔaq'am and Cranbrook. Deanna would further like to thank her amazing research assistants Sandie Dielissen, Patrick Canning, and especially Rachel Taylor, formerly of *Redwire,* for their careful transcriptions of the many documents, and Margery Fee for her careful editing suggestions. We extend our gratitude to Larry Loyie and Constance Brissenden for their help in contacting the Manuel family in the early stages of this project. A special thank you is owed to Constance for providing us with the images used in their 2018 republication of *Two Plays About Residential School,* which includes Manuel's play *Strength of Indian Women* and Cree survivor

Larry Loyie's play *Ora Pro Nobis, Pray for Us.* Joanne Arnott would like to thank Emalene, for conversations, friendship, and support. Sandy Scofield, Loretta Todd, Lee Maracle, Maria Campbell, Garry Gottfriedson, Joyce Johnson, Ariadne Sawyer, and Art and Doreen Manuel have also assisted and supported Joanne in understanding Vera's works and the context within which they arose. Sandy Scofield was also able to provide text to poems that Vera wanted to include but could not locate.

HONOURING THE STRENGTH OF INDIAN WOMEN

INTRODUCTION

BY EMALENE A. MANUEL

TRADITIONAL INTRODUCTION OF SELF

Ki'suk Kyukyit
Hu qaklik Emalene Manuel
Kakiklik 'aqlsmaknik nini Kucinqac Palki
Hu nini Ktunaxa ts Secwepemc
Hu qaki kaxi Aqam

Good Day
My name is Emalene Manuel
My traditional name is Moving Up Camp Woman
I am Ktunaxa and Secwepemc
I am from the area near Cranbrook, BC.

It was in December 1988, the day that our mother Marceline Paul Manuel passed on to the spirit world, that Vera (Kulilu Pa‡ki, Butterfly Woman) and I started the real work to establish Storyteller Theatre. Our mother's role of storyteller in our lives came about when she arrived on our doorstep in Los Angeles a few years earlier. She had responded to an urgent call from me informing her that

Vera was in trouble and in jail in Palm Springs, California. We had been stopped for a broken tail light and they had her name on file for failing to appear in court as a witness. The case was connected to an old boyfriend who had passed away many years previous. Because Vera had never received the notice to appear, this was the first she had heard of this. I told my mom that my stepmom had informed me not to call back as she was concerned about what people would think. Mom had told me bluntly and sternly, that she would take care of it. She informed our eldest brother Bobby what happened and said that she was going to turn to her American Indian Movement (AIM) family and they would help. Bobby responded immediately with an airline ticket for her to LA. For us, that was the beginning of our journey back home.

Our mother had been a part of a renaissance and she joined in the movement with great vigour. It was as though she had been waiting for it and when it came, she was ready. She told us stories of how it was for her in those early days of reawakening. She had gone back to receive her adult upgrading and her first job was working for the Department of Indian Affairs (DIA) in Victoria. One day she said that she was walking down the street and she heard the drum. Her heart racing, she ran in the direction where the drumming and singing were coming from and hurried up an incline in the park. When she got to the top and looked down, she spotted a group of young people dressed in traditional shirts seated around a big drum singing. She remembered way back to the last time she heard this and she thought out loud, "you've come back." She walked down to join them and introduce herself. A few days later, she was sitting in her cubicle at work at the DIA and she heard voices raised in the front office and she went to see what it was. She saw some of the young people from the park moving to tak on the floor. One of them announced that they were there to take a place on the floor. She felt her feet moving, one in front of the other, until she reached some of the familiar faces and they moved aside to make room for her on the floor.

What does it mean to be storyteller? Our mom had gathered her adult kids around her during her last twenty years. In our absence, she had found a newly awakened spirit and became a woman who we didn't really know growing up. When we returned, we started to get to know one another all over again. More importantly, we started to begin to know who we were for the first time.

In 1988, when I was 33 and Vera was 40, we were left with the responsibility of carrying the stories that our mother had shared with us. Our mother had painted vivid stories about her experience in the St. Mary's Residential Boarding School in Cranbrook, BC. Much of her storytelling took place while travelling to and from traditional gatherings in the US and Canada. Many losses, internal turmoil, and unanswered questions brought these stories to life. In 1987, we lost a beloved young family member to suicide. Throughout the months that followed there was a rash of suicides within neighbouring communities. Having just returned home from Los Angeles, we hadn't experienced this kind of loss one after another within a close proximity of kinship relationships and connections. We became numb and stopped going to funerals. Then the following three years brought the biggest blow of all—the losses, in yearly succession, of our beloved mom, our dad, and our grandmother Kupi. We were dizzy with grief.

Vera had been contracted to write a play about family violence for a youth conference. She had drawn much of the ideas for a play called *Song of the Circle* (1989) from our experience with our mother and the strength that she'd instilled in us. It was important for the both of us to retain ownership of the story as we knew that we had a responsibility to protect it. I would learn later in film school that Hollywood productions sign contracts where writers retain no rights over their writing. They in fact lose ownership of ever having any say as to how it is represented. These are the kind of questions that have been since scruitinized by Indigenous research but at that time hadn't been thought about. As a result, we almost lost this story. Luckily, we sought legal counsel of a close ally and avoided a catastrophe. This is when we started to develop our ideas around decolonizing our thinking about storytelling. We were talking about what kind of storytelling we were doing. We were interested in not using Western terms to describe our work so that wouldn't limit us or others' perceptions of what we were creating as we wanted to decolonize our Western minds to imagine what and how our ancestors did story and how we could draw from that for dealing with life today.

Vera was co-owner of Ancestral Visions: People for Wellness and Development. Within this company her role included training, facilitating healing groups, research writing, curriculum development, cross-cultural and awareness training throughout Canada and the United States. She worked mainly with intergenerational trauma and unresolved grief related to the residential school. Additionally, she facilitated healing workshops for youth using drama, mask making and other creative processes to explore the impacts of shame as it relates to sexual abuse trauma. Two of these youth workshops were presented in the Ktunaxa territory and in the Secwepemc territory. She was a distinguished keynote speaker at many local and international conferences. She worked with Merritt Friendship Center in conjunction with Nicola Valley College (accredited) to develop curriculum, and she also presented and facilitated processes specifically designed for frontline workers to gain skills in working with trauma survivors. She worked for the National Native Association of Treatment Directors where she was the co-writer of a Family Systems training manual and a sexual abuse manual and program, presenting in communities through Canada and the U.S. She worked with Round Lake Treatment Centre as writer and director on four training videos, focused on family systems for youth. She wrote and co-wrote and contributed to several training manuals, journal publications and two CDs, "Lonely Like a Child" and "LA Obsession Song" (for Wayne Lavallee CD), and "Justice" (for *Redwire Magazine*'s CD for youth). She additionally co-scripted the film *No More Secrets* (Round Lake Treatment Centre, 1996, produced by Loretta Todd), and she scripted *Voice—Life* (Healing Our Spirit, 1995, produced by Loretta Todd). Vera was mentored by Jane Middelton-Moz, Bea Shawanda, the family counsellor Elaine Story, MSW, RSW, and the psychodramatist Debra Wingo, MC, CGP.

Vera was contracted through Helping Spirit Lodge Society (2004–2005) to do storytelling work with women from the Choices Program. It was a welcome change as she was diagnosed with pulmonary fibrosis in 2004 and this gave her the chance to be closer to home. The program was exciting, innovative, and forward thinking and it involved working with twelve participants over a six-week period. It involved developing a process to look at deep and meaningful truths. It was called the Drama Therapy Program. I fortunately finished film school in Scottsdale, Arizona, in time to be the production manager and also put my new skills to work and excitedly filmed the program. The participants were phenomenal in the storytelling, involvement, and transformation but much of it was Vera's many years of experience, knowledge, and care in storytelling, trauma treatment, political astuteness and self-work. One thing that her mentors believed in was the importance of "walking your talk" and honesty. Vera showed this over the years and it was a strong point that she brought to her work and to our family. That's one of the major differences between Euro-Western models and our own Indigenous Knowledge Systems models. The programs ran for several weeks and the end result of each group was a public event where the community was invited to come and witness the story. It was an incredible turnout every single time. There was an immense feeling of support and involvement from the families, community members and leaders in the community.

An example of our different systems of knowledge which we had become familiar with is that Vera's credibility was questioned by the organization's non-Indigenous therapist. She wanted the organization to let Vera go because she said she didn't have the experience or credentials to be doing this kind of work. The organization, Helping Spirit Lodge Society, stood behind Vera and confirmed that Vera's credentials were more than most people working in our communities and they wanted to develop a program that was by our people for our people. We were fortunate that they were so clear about how colonialism works and the need to hold space to develop our work from our own Indigenous knowledge and story ways. We recognized that many wouldn't have been able to stand up so strongly and we hold our hands up to them for their vision and leadership.

As Vera moved towards adapting storytelling into her training work, she included the process we developed in order to create *Strength of Indian Women*. It also worked the other way as well. She brought her training experience into the Storyteller experience. The process was one of using story to find meaning for our internal pain in order to create truth in the world and also to create space for articulating that truth. After our mother passed on Vera started to work on the stories that sprung out of our need to reconnect with her and as the following losses left us further unbalanced, story served to cement our history and shifting roles firmly in our heart.

One thing that our mom said repeatedly is that whatever you do in life it is for the People. Our dad was often gone when we were growing up and he, of anyone, showed us this lesson by example. This is also evident through the stories as they are laid out throughout Vera's life work. Stó:lō scholar Jo-ann Archibald (2008) explains that "storywork" begins when we become aware of the importance of teachings and wisdom that have been passed on to us: "One must be ready to share and teach it respectfully and responsibly to others in order for this knowledge, and its power, to continue. One cannot be said to have wisdom until others acknowledge an individual's respectful and responsible use and teaching of knowledge to others" (3). At the time we started our storywork to pass on the stories that our mother had shared with us, we decided that it was important to emphasize decolonization. We actually asked the questions as we were building our ideas about relationships, story, accountability and leadership structures within the group. Someone can say that they are working from the cultural teachings but what kind of experience or understanding do they have of that culture or knowledge? We were posing questions like researchers, although not knowing that is what we were doing. Vera was establishing some really strong alliances through her training. Over the years the initial group went its separate way but we had the experience that I think influenced the later pieces of work which were the poetry-spoken word workshop performances and the drama therapy witnessing work. We had no idea what a big job we had taken on and how much we were going to learn. In fact, this learning has continued over a lifetime.

After we first mounted *Strength of Indian Women*, Vera started to see what a huge undertaking it was on so many levels but she was also gaining experience and knowledge through her training work and mentorship. Nonetheless the work was daunting and sometimes after we'd get a booking, she'd say that she felt like putting the play on the shelf and never looking at it again. It was a big responsibility and very painful, frustrating, and emotionally exhausting at times. Some of the lessons that we came across are outlined here. Although it was a huge responsibility and there were so many challenges to learn to overcome, we were also greatly rewarded as we overcame each obstacle.

We were invited to the 1992 Healing Our Spirit Worldwide Conference in Edmonton and it all came to a head around the issue of alcohol abuse and we got really hurt. That could have ended our work right there, but my sister was invited to stay behind afterward to attend ceremonies. She came back and we talked and realized that we could only take others as far as we'd come and we had some serious decisions to make. We had to look inward and dig deep. What came out of it is that we were more clear about drawing the line and asking for help in doing that. It was a process. Among other things, we created a contract that included an agreement of sobriety from the time you sign on with us until after we had our closing meeting after returning from the performance. Vera asked Jane Middlelton-Moz, who was mentoring her and others, for support. We were forever thankful for the guidance and prayers.

Vera discussed the process in a panel discussion for Indigenous playwrights at the Miami University in Oxford, Ohio, in 1999. She mentioned our experience with theatre venues when we asked if they could close down their bar during the intermission; sometimes it was done and other times they wouldn't do it. We had to think about working with a story about one of the most horrendous experiences in our history and the aftermath and then having an intermission when everyone's running out the door and having a drink. We were concerned for ourselves and the others who were participating in the story and showing respect for wherever they are in their journey. We weren't very popular sometimes. Some of those who were working with us thought that we were going too far. As a result of us setting these non-Western parameters, we were viewed as not professional theatre storytellers. We prioritized decolonizing methods and didn't fit or measure up to Western standards for funding purposes. It meant that we were marginalized as a theatre group. We believed that we had something special that we were developing and we had an idea of documenting the process of what we were doing but we were spread thin with having to do all of the work as well as rehearse and fill in for any role if we weren't able to get enough people to mount a performance.

I don't believe we ever turned down an invitation to bring our stories to a conference or a community. That is, of course, until Vera's health made it impossible for her to travel any longer. In the last year of the Choices Women's Group, she had canisters of oxygen that we'd load into the trunk of her car. Vera was so committed to her work that after I did some research to find out the options, she traded in her old canisters for a newer, lighter model so that gave her more freedom. We were sad when we had to quit doing the program as we suspected it was exactly what is needed within our community. She really wanted to mentor someone who had previously taken her trauma training advanced workshops but that wasn't meant to be. She did continue to attend every poetry reading that she was called to after that. I wondered sometimes because I knew it was difficult especially as she neared her final years and the truth in her stories became stronger. She told me that it was a waste of time and energy if she wasn't going to tell the truth.

The idea of Story-Truth-Telling or 'Akaminki (the Ktunaxa word for "telling the whole story" and derived from the word *akamin*, which means circle) is embedded within all of these texts and is written to emphasize women's voices and to re-install Indian women's roles within this genealogical timeline. There are so many places where women even contribute to the erasure of women's voices within the colonial program. It also is upon us to look at how colonialism has impacted us to hold our men relatives up at the expense of women. If we want to compete for a respected space within the eyes of colonialism we must behave like a man or, more specifically, behave like a white man.

Within this context Vera and I had hoped to create a nurturing women space but also a space where women can be strong and resist the need to smile or succumb to Christian hegemonic pressures. I'm thinking of a previous version of a story that my mom, Marceline Paul Manuel, had entrusted to me about an experience that she had early in her marriage to my dad, George Manuel. A version of this story is also written in my dad's book *The Fourth World*. As my mom told this story to me, she said that my brother Arthur had to have his tonsils out and they couldn't afford it. The Indian Affairs was trying to push Indians to pay their own medical bills and go back on their agreement. She said that everyone was getting upset because no one could afford to pay their own medical bills. Dad was telling her he was worried about what would happen. She told him they are just trying to get away with not paying for our medical and that after all that they've done pushing us back and taking all of the best land, forcing us into boarding school. She was very angry and she told him, "go to that meeting with that Indian Agent and get mad!" She said, "Don't ask him, tell him and yell." She said, "Go straight to the desk where he is sitting and throw your fist down on the table and yell at him and tell him, 'No! We aren't listening to you!'" In my dad's book, he gives all the credit to Dr. Treloar (106). He only makes mention of my mom as calling him to let him know "the Indian agent had called a joint meeting of our Neskainlith Band and the neighbouring Adam's Lake Band on the question of medical costs" (108).

There is no doubt in my mind from knowing my mother all of my life and from the stories that she has passed on to me that it is true what she had told me about my great-grandmother Sophie Williams. I understand by her stories about great-grandmother "Sope" and great-grandpa "Semo" (see "That Grey Building") that they had instilled in her this strength to stand up to colonialism and encroachment of our Indigenous Knowledge ways and homelands and that she said these words "and some" to our dad on a continuous basis. It is also true that she struggled in her lifetime, as we all do, from the impacts of the boarding school but we are also complex and creative people and although we struggle to be heard and articulate meanings some have been gifted with vision and story. The intention isn't to discredit our dad's work but rather to shed light on how story shapes how we accept what is the truth. When it is erased, it in effect erases that person or people. In a way it is as though our mother never existed or, in the case of warrior resistance, that we didn't have true warrior resistance stories or that they existed only as something to look back upon but doesn't serve a valid, crucial place in the world today.

Through Kulilu Pa‡ki's (Vera's) writing, her beautiful writing, she will return again and again. These writings have come to life. Part of these stories came from the streets. They speak of and have felt the pain of all of these women. We were and are these women. We felt the lifelong insecurities that tugged and tugged at our soul. How does it happen that we grow up needing so much that it's impossible to share that space because that empty hole inside of our souls are massive? Yet we try to love each other. We try, yet we have spaces inside of us that are so tender that one little bump on the road and we are torn into so many scattered pieces. Regret, she had said, is useless and I have come to know the meaning of these words. Had I known that her life was nearing the end there would have been no vacant regretful spaces left behind. But look at me. Look at me here trying to work as hard as I can to show how sorry I am. Full of regret and heartache. Full of stuffed and stifled tears.

My niece Dayna told me to write to her. She told me that I have a story to tell. She reminded me that her auntie Kulilu Pa‡ki had said that in order to write we must get in touch with our heart. We must feel the tears. My tears let loose from eight long years of holding back. Eight years of holding back a lifetime. What is it that made us so close? What is it that seals us to one another as sisters, twins?

I remember "L.A. Obsession Song" when you excitedly told me that the words just poured out onto the page like a melody. Our time together in L.A. was parties and bar scenes. It was careless, intense relationships. It was living on the edge and watching each other's back. I remember times when we felt and seemed to be millions of miles away from our family, community and culture. I remember after you were released from jail in Indio County, our mom had arranged for us to fly home for a visit. We decided for some reason to travel home at separate times. We both told one another, "if I don't come back within a month, know that it's probably against my will and please come and get me." Both of us went home and returned to L.A., but it was only a short few months that we returned home for good.

I remember one time, we were sitting in a café in L.A. talking about our crazy city lives and how so many things had spiraled out of control. I was twenty-one and Vera was twenty-eight. It was 1976. One particularly troubling time stands out when we were talking and sharing our hopes and dreams. Vera was saying that she wanted to be a writer. I was telling her that she was smart enough to do that, but I didn't think that I was smart enough to attend college. I told her I felt sad and that one day she was going to move on and do great things and she would leave me behind. She told me in that reassuring way that older sisters do that that would never happen. She said that one day I would find what I wanted to do.

At that time, we were also talking about how crazy and reckless our lives had become. We were also being impacted by a fear that was spreading around Los Angeles as several women had turned up missing. It had touched close to home for us as one of our young and vibrant friends had turned up mysteriously dead. There was talk about how she might have been murdered but no real knowledge about what happened, only that she was seen with a certain questionable character and now she was gone. Her funeral was the first city funeral that we'd ever attended. We met her family. We had wondered as to why she had chosen the crazy life that we knew, rather than this seemingly serene upper middle-class life that she came from.

Looking back, after we'd returned home, we recalled how we felt at times like we were being watched over. Like those times that something had reached over and pulled us out of harm's way. Then too, the final return home, which was swift and insanely sudden. Only a few short weeks earlier we were making pacts to rescue one another from being taken back to the reserve against our will and the next thing we knew we were flying just as suddenly back home, never to look back. What seemed odd then doesn't seem odd anymore. It only seems like a bigger design of life that spans back to the beginning and is observed and intricately woven throughout some of these texts. These were the final years in L.A. and the early years after our return home that inspired my sister's poetry pieces like "Addictions," "Lies," and "Life Abuse of Girls." These were the years that she also wrote "The Storm." I remember how excited she was when she told me, "I had a dream. It was so real. I wrote a poem. It just fell out onto the page!" Looking back at these times of her expanding awareness materializing through exploring layers of complex truths, she reminded me of the birthday when Snake and I appeared down the end of our block with big smiles on our faces carrying her dream writer's roll-top desk, in red.

Song of the Circle is Vera's first play. It's a role that Michelle Thrush and Byron Chief Moon played over the span of about three years (1989–1991). It was first mounted for the twentieth annual Union of B.C. Indian Chief's conference, in August of 1989, with Sophie Merasty as the Elder, Anmah. The experiences outlined were drawn from our own experience of family violence while growing up and the impacts that it had on our subsequent relationships. It was also very closely drawn from our late mother's cultural teachings for the role of the Elder. Vera had started being mentored as a trainer and would later collaborate and co-write the training manual *In the Spirit of the Family,* which drew upon Family Systems Theory, which was at that time believed to be most closely aligned with Indigenous Knowledge Systems. Vera took part in a process of storytelling with Family Systems Therapist Elaine Story in order to emphasize the aspects of Indigenous Knowledge Systems' credibility as a therapeutic model. This was exciting work as it was in line with our ideas of valuing our First Nation's oral tradition as it supersedes Western ideas of theatre.

By the time that *Strength of Indian Women* was first mounted at the Women in View Festival at the Firehall Theatre in Vancouver (approximately 1991), both Vera and I were in counseling and we had both started to talk about the sexual abuse. We had actually started this process in 1987, the year before our mother passed on. Mom had actually taken part in an important group family therapy session where I had disclosed being sexually abused as a child. This was a significant breakthrough for us and opened the way for us to be able to continue the direction that we did after her passing. I also started looking at my own experience in the boarding school, but it would be many years before I would look at my experience as a street kid and runaway. We were starting to put the pieces together and to understand the deep impact of the church in our lives and to the ongoing colonialism in Canada. We were witnessing it first hand as an Indigenous Theatre company that was resisting the status quo. Vera was quick to recognize that while we were struggling along trying to make ends meet, non-Indigenous theatre companies were accessing Indigenous funding and creating credibility within our own communities as experts in the field of theatre and "healing." Vera also pointed out to me that they were setting a precedent impossible for us to meet, being they were set by non-Indigenous standards.

During this time, we also received questions to our own credibility as to whether we even measured up to "professional" standards due to our non-mainstream ways and our interest in redefining Euro ideas of theatre and storytelling. Even still we did have Western creditable performers who really wanted to support and work with us as they recognized, understood, and supported what we were doing. One particular show stands out as Gordon Tootoosis (Cree and Stoney) had taken on the role of Anmah in *Song of the Circle* in an out of town venue. We had changed the Elder character to a male character in this one instance. We all learned a valuable lesson from him. There was a young man working with us who was strongly influenced by Western models and was speaking out of turn and being insolent. It was wearing on all of our nerves as it went against our philosophies and our ideas of decolonizing Western theatres' thinking and behaviour. Gordon was very gracious but said that he had to stop everything and set something straight. He talked about how long he'd been working in this field and how he understood what he is there for and how he believes in what we were aiming to do. He emphasized the importance of the story that we were telling and the need to respect one another while preparing and that we have a chance to do something better. I'll never forget that because he was the living example of resurgence of Indigenous Knowledge Spaces within colonial theatre structures! Although we didn't know those exact words at that time it immediately opened up our vision and shifted our space to prioritize our ways. I found myself drawing from his spirit many years later while performing in *The Ecstasy of Rita Joe* at the Firehall and having my own Gordon Tootoosis moment and setting the record straight. Why do we have to be demeaned and have to prove ourselves within Western standards even within our very own spaces and within our very own stories and sometimes even among our very own Indigenous people or "so called" allies who ought to know better? We had many struggles along the road to decolonizing theatre and we had many teachers. He was one though that stood out in his strength, vision and integrity and our group appreciated his wisdom, clarity and undeterred honesty.

All of those who we worked with throughout the years contributed greatly to the overall strength of the work. I only wish that we could have documented this while Vera was still alive. We thought it would be possible if I went to film school and we were excited at all of the possibilities when I completed my studies. That is when we documented the drama therapy program but still something was missing. It became very challenging at this point partly due to the fact that it was a change in career for Vera due to her health. She was supported by family and friends in making the decision to stop travelling. That was a very painful and scary time as she loved working as a trainer. I'd asked her one time about the risk involved in working in communities sometimes when leadership or people in power would aim their anger at her for facilitating the truth. She told me that if she didn't go then maybe no one would go and that wasn't a choice at all and that if the Creator wanted her to be there, that is where she was going to be. It's hard to think that these are the kinds of things that some of our strongest and most needed leaders have faced, while the colonial machinery continues on in many ways uncontested.

During our first performance Byron Chief Moon (Blackfoot) and Michelle Thrush (Cree) took on the roles of James and Mary in *Song of the Circle*. It was my first experience working with these layers of depth of stories. This was to become Vera's signature throughout her life as a poet, playwright, storyteller, director and trainer. It was something familiar that rose out of the deepest places of despair and hardship that wove its way throughout our earlier lives that gave her that instinct and ability to not only bring people to that place but to also assure them and maintain focus. With years of training she only got better but she told me one time not long before she left us, "I have a gift. I'm good at this. It's like this is what I came here for." It was something that I grew to count on throughout the years. It was magical, but it was also an honour to work among some of the best talent and gifted storytellers in Indian country. Murlane Carew (Mi'kmaq/Celtic) joined us with many years of mainstream theatre experience. She had one of the most complex characters in Mariah. Mariah's character also is one that Vera described as "just falling out onto the page." Just as the writing of Mariah's character appeared so too did the storyteller of Mariah. It was amazing to watch Murlane work at developing Mariah. It's like she could look inside Vera's mind. Vera would give her direction and before our eyes Mariah would materialize. It was a bit unnerving but we were all happy when Murlane came to Storyteller Theatre. It was like, okay, Mariah is here. She also brought additional strength in her long-standing sobriety and helped us to stand firm, once we had made that commitment ourselves. This was when Vera had come back from the Lethbridge experience with a message from Elders that we had to make some changes.

We finally saw the contradiction and compromise that we were making in not being clear enough to set parameters and understanding what the responsibility of leadership meant. It was so hard to make that decision and to ask the questions deep inside. It's actually one of the most devastating questions to ask, a question that no one else is asking or that hasn't been done before, the question that makes you feel like you are alone and everybody is going to hate you. What makes it harder is when you have one foot on the other side. Those ones among us who had clearly made that decision of sobriety made that transition much better and Murlane wasn't advertising it but she lived a sober life. She was also going on regular auditions while working in a women's transition house.

Marianne Sundown (Cree) and Pineshi Gustin (Anishinaabe) played the role of Eva. Both brought their strong presence to the role of Eva and also brought their strength and tenacity to Storyteller. Pineshi is a brilliant painter who also currently does digital search and rescue and spends her time scouring satellite photos for lost planes. All those who came to Storyteller in their own capacity were greatly appreciated. Thank you for being a part of this journey and remembering my sister Kulilu Pa‡ki and helping to develop this work and realize this vision. I am thankful for all of those involved in believing and working to bring this book together.

Over the years it turned out that the core group did the Storyteller work but also gravitated towards social service jobs. We started to form our vision and model. I had started working as a community support worker (1991) and later became a school-based family support worker and counselor (1994). We managed to move towards careers that would allow us significant time off in order to travel and rehearse. We had a core group. Since Vera's passing, I've gone on to receive my undergraduate degree, Bachelor of Social Work (BSW), and more recently my Master's in Education. All of this with the focus of developing our lifelong work and realizing our dreams and hopefully at long last being able to articulate and challenge all of the colonial credibility structures and doubters.

We were fortunate to work with Samaya Jardey, who took on Sophie Merasty's role as Lucy. We were sad that Sophie was moving on because she was a phenomenally talented actor. She didn't only carry the talent of generations in her DNA but she also had that depth of life experience that made you compelled to drink in her translation of that feisty character of Lucy. Samaya was this tall slender model beautiful woman and we were all curious how she would define Lucy but it was amazing to see her transformation. She was an ongoing developing cultural leader among her Skwxwú7mesh people and later also became involved in the growing developments in dialogues on the residential boarding school issues. Our sister Doreen joined us for a couple of performances of *Strength of Indian Women* and took the role of Eva for one performance and Agnes for a couple of out of town venues. She described honestly the experience of getting to the depth of the story and the early place where she was in her own wellness. She revealed the amount of vulnerability that the work involves, "I had to tell Vera to stop ringing the bell. I was remembering how it felt to be a little kid playing in the boarding school playground. For a while we could forget about it and just play. Then that bell would ring and you'd remember that you were in a prison."

The honesty and depth of this experience of the bell rang true for all who were involved and witnessed. We had a focus of wellness but also were developing a firm grasp of resurgence in Indigenous Knowledge Systems through storytelling.

I remember one time when we brought *Strength of Indian Women* to the Carnegie, Vera did what she often did. She described me in the opening as her twin. She said we were just like twins and that throughout our life we had come to many turning points together. She acknowledged that many times we could have perished in that crazy life in Los Angeles but that the spirits were watching over us because we had an important job and we had to survive that life so we could tell the story of what we had been through and what we had seen. She said it's as if we came into this world for that reason to accompany each other through life and to do this work. That is what I felt too! We saw things in a certain way and we had experienced the worst of it and we were compelled to use story to change it. She always used our experience to lift others up, to respectfully guide and role-model, and make room for the voiceless. It was and remains throughout life a primary goal as although we had attained much by way of speaking we still on other levels struggled to be heard.

There is so much that we wanted to say about the voice and the voiceless. This is a theme that is prominent in *Strength of Indian Women* which is witnessed by Sousette's daughter Eva of the telling of the secret. Additionally, "Woman Without a Tongue" prominently attests to the question of subalternity. Gayatri Spivak's essay "Can the Subaltern Speak?" discusses the idea of speech and stirs debate that this question evokes. We had thought about this in terms of our own voice and the voices of the women portrayed throughout many of the writings. More recently I had decided that it is true that no, the subaltern cannot speak, because our Indigenous societies are layered upon by generations of colonialism and genocide, intended to silence resistance to anything that has potential to pose a problem or trouble the colonial program. In this environment one or two voices don't pose any problem because they are quickly silenced. Even the resistant thought is squelched by a most stern look or ignored into submission by its gatekeepers.

I'd like to differentiate between upholding protocols and keeping secrets. The voice that we had been looking at through the Storyteller work hasn't been so much to do with speaking about secrets that we know as cultural protocols of things that we need to be respectful and mindful of but rather speaking that involves forms of silencing and oppression that appear to be consensus. It has actually been very carefully orchestrated silencing. These are the thoughts and questions that this story truth telling work has looked at and set in motion so many years ago.

I'm glad that Vera's writing was relentless throughout all of the twists and turns that life brought her, especially towards the end. It was told to me that during her final hour friends and family spent time at her bedside reading her poetry and playing her recitations, her final last calling out to the world through her spoken words.

One time she had gone to a psychic reader in the north and I had asked her to ask a question for me, about the direction of my life. The reader told her, "I get the feeling that she is very gifted in the arts like a singer or something like that." And she paused. "I get the feeling that somehow you help her in this?" At which point Vera blurted out, "Yes, I write plays and she acts in my plays!" Yes, Vera was true to her word of many years earlier, when she told the young twenty-year-old me that she'd never leave me behind and that I'd just have to find what I really wanted to do! I really miss her. My eyes sting as I write this as she has moved on, for now. Well, Vera, I've found what I really want to do. Through this lifetime of work is a legacy and the many generations ahead to look towards.

My daughter Nukinka started coming to rehearsals when she was seven years old. We were talking about things to do with generational abuse and the role of the church and how it impacted on what we knew about our culture. We talked honestly about how we grew up with violence and alcohol abuse and that we didn't want that to be the future for the next generation. We were wondering how much children and youth should know about our horrendous history. Much of the determination and vision that we held to are contained within the stories passed down to us by our mother of the fearsome way that she protected our cultural practices and our homeland. They are contained in our DNA. I believe this is why those who came together as Storyteller answered that call. I think it's that call that makes it impossible for some to turn away. Some of us crave decolonizing spaces. Even still there are also those who crave only the appearance of the same.

This is the kind of environment that Storyteller makes possible. I called it in my Master of Education thesis "Story-Truth-Telling" and 'akaminki, which means in the Ktunaxa language "to tell the whole story." Nukinka used to be a part of many of our working groups and rehearsals. She'd sit behind the flats throughout the performance and we all were excited the first time someone forgot their lines and we heard her little voice whisper their lines perfectly from backstage. She was so important to the work and keeping that focus and hope for the future that Vera wrote a role for her as Suzie in *Strength of Indian Women*. Nukinka went on to get one of the best child agents in Vancouver when she was sixteen (1998). She got a role in *Millennium* Season 2, *Anamnesis* and a mini-series called *Dragon Boys*. She went on auditions for several years and continued working with Storyteller but eventually stopped going on auditions. Many of the roles that she got were street kids, sex trade workers and alcohol and drug addicted youth. She went on to work for Children of the Street Society and Young Bear Lodge Society and worked as a lead storyteller at Storeum in Gastown. Vera also included her in co-presenting for youth trainings. She was mentored in the best way possible through all the People who were part of Storyteller, especially Vera. The word the agent used to describe her work was "honest" but she also said that there had to be much more emphasis on First Nations writers, producers and directors because there was not many roles out there for girls who looked like her.

One of my favorite poems in this collection is "When My Sister & I Dance." It didn't happen easy. It wasn't like in a popular story book where teachings all line up in a neat row. No, but once again, this was a passage that we entered into together, true to the nature of Vera's twin analogy. Our mother had gathered us up and we came plummeting back to our homeland, but she was patient, gentle and kind. She never reminded us of our shortcomings or belittled our addictive lifestyle. She told us stories. She gave us teachings. She saved her biting commentary for those special occasions when nothing else would do. In looking back, I realize that she was catching up for lost time. She was preparing us. In our absence, she had adopted others and had nurtured a lengthy circle of relatives. Many of these traditional relations became our lifelong family. It was during these times of learning to understand ourselves that we entered the dance circle and Vera got to wear the white buckskin dress that she'd carried with her for all of her growing up years away from home. It was kind of an awkward time in learning to feel comfortable in these ceremonial settings. It was new, but it also felt like home as Vera shares through both "When My Sister & I Dance" and "When I First Came To Know Myself." I like the honesty of Vera's writing in that she doesn't merely describe the journey as someone who has grown up with the teachings, but she captures that feeling of the struggle and pain of wearing something that has borne witness to a hard life. She captures this reality in her poem, "When My Sister & I Dance":

This dress and I have travelled
A long way together,
As far away as the city
And back,
There are tear stains
From those times
I've held its softness
To my cheek
And wondered
Who am I?

PLAYS

STRENGTH OF
INDIAN WOMEN

AUTHOR'S NOTE

A tremendous responsibility is attached to telling the unresolved grief stories of First Nations people. Words have power: They cause us to feel the emotions of the story they are telling. Stories about the abuse and helplessness of little children in residential school are true stories. Because of this, they are the most difficult to write. I didn't make up the stories told in *Strength of Indian Women*. They came from pictures my mother painted for me with her words, words that helped me to see her as a little girl for the first time. Each time we staged a performance of the play, I mourned that little girl who never had a childhood. I mourned the mother missing from my childhood, and I gave thanks for the mother who became my loving teacher in adulthood, who had the courage to say the words I longed to hear, "I'm sorry I wasn't there to protect you when you were a little girl." Other stories came from feelings attached to the little knowledge I held of my father's experience as a survivor of residential school and a tuberculosis sanatorium, a world of violence and isolation. Finally, the character Mariah, and her experience, I believe, came from the ancestors. She spoke in a voice I had never heard before and wrote every word and cried her tears.

The responsibility we hold in passing on these stories is to role model a healthy lifestyle for our children, who are always watching us for direction. When we share our life stories, we must create a safe place for those who come to listen, in order not to hurt ourselves or others. Creator: I say, thank you; and thank you, Nupika, for this lesson.

DEDICATION

To Marceline Paul (Woman Comes Up Singing, kyuwakał haqłuk pałki) and George Manuel, Mariah Manuel, Mary Paul, Terry Paul, Annie Capilo, Pete Clement, Ida Dick, Marlene, Minnie, Addie, John, Jean, and all the other survivors of residential school who gave permission to share their stories. And to all the children of survivors, the healing generations committed to undoing the damage: Bob, Art, Bev, Richard, Arlene (Ku¢inqa¢ Pa‡ki), Doreen, Martha, George Jr., Ida and Ara. And to all the generations of hope for the future: Rainbow, Nukinka, Mandy (Kanahus Pa‡ki), Niki (Mayuk Pa‡ki), Neskie, Ska7cis, Claudia, Esteban, Anita Rose, Angus, Raven Rain, Luke, Samuel, Jordon, Dayna, Geni, Desiree, Corinna, Evan, Aaron, J.W. Rivers, Jamie, Adam, Misty, Nigel. And to all the children.

EDITORS' NOTE

Strength of Indian Women was first published in *Two Plays About Residential School* by Living Traditions in 1998, pages 75–119. In 2018, it was republished by Indigenous Education Press.

ABOUT THE PLAY

Strength of Indian Women by Vera Manuel was first staged by Storyteller Theatre at the Women in View Festival at Firehall Theatre, Vancouver, British Columbia, Canada, in January 1992. The original cast included Carol DeEscobar Hoof (Agnes); Kutcinkaats Pathkey Arlene Manuel (Sousette); Nuhkinka Swinwen Uktht Mountain Melanie Manuel (Suzie); Penishe Gustin (Eva); Denise Lonewalker

(Mariah); and Sophie Merasty (Lucy). At the time, the play was directed by Joyce Joe, produced by Viola Thomas, and the soundscape was engineered by Russell Wallace.

Over the years, *Strength of Indian Women* has toured Canada and the United States, with Vera Manuel directing. The cast has included Vera Manuel, Ku¢inqa¢ Pa†ki, Arlene Emalene Manuel, Nulikinka Swinwen Uktht Mountain Melanie Manuel, Marianne Sundown, Murlane Carew, and Samaya Jardey.

Special thanks to the Canada Council; Canadian Native Arts Foundation; Women in View Festival 1992; Healing Our Spirit Worldwide Conference, Edmonton; Women & Wellness Conference, Saskatoon; Alternatives 1993 Conference, Scottsdale, Arizona; International Native American Women's Conference, Polson, Montana; Healing Our Families and Communities Conference, Wisconsin Dells, Nicola College, Wisconsin; National Association for Native American Children of Alcoholics (NANACOA); Campbell River Band, British Columbia; Narrative Therapy Conference, Vancouver; Justice Institute of British Columbia; Mandell Pinder Barristers and Solicitors; Cambie Group; Jane Middelton-Moz; Rod Jeffries; Judalon Jeffries; Ska-Hiish Holdings; Pauline Douglas; Louise Mandell; Jeanette Armstrong; Elaine Story; Diane and Tatsuo Kage; Michelle Thrush; Byron Chief-Moon; and Herman Edward.

CHARACTERS
Sousette, an Elder, the peacemaker
Suzie, her thirteen-year-old granddaughter
Eva, Sousette's daughter, in her mid-thirties
Lucy, an Elder, dark-skinned, strong and cantankerous
Agnes, an Elder, a flashy dresser with a lively personality
Mariah, an Elder, light-skinned, shy and nervous

All scenes in *Strength of Indian Women* take place in the living room of a house on a reserve over the course of three days.

Ktunaxa words used in the play: Nupik'a/the spirits; Titti/ Grandmother. Actors may substitute these words in their own language.

ACT ONE
SCENE 1

All scenes take place in the living room of a house on a reserve over the course of three days. Music fades into a darkened stage. Scenes of residential school are projected on the back wall. The room is simple, with a couch, two armchairs, a coffee table, a kitchen table, and two kitchen chairs. Someone is asleep on the couch. While the last slide is being projected on the wall, Sousette enters the room. She is wearing a nightdress and has just woken up.

It is early morning, just before dawn. Sousette, an Elder, always wakes up early. Her light is the first to go on in the reserve. But first, she putters around her front room in the dark. This is her favourite time of the day, before anyone else is awake. She knows every inch of her beloved home by heart; she doesn't need the light to see. She is trying to be quiet, though, so as not to wake her granddaughter, who is asleep on the couch. She is searching for something, digging through tins and bags beside the couch, searching among the books and magazines under the coffee table.

SUZIE: What are you looking for, Granny?

SOUSETTE: Oh, no, don't wake up. I'm trying to be quiet. I'm looking for pictures . . . of some girls I used to know.

SUZIE: It's still dark. What time is it?

She turns on the light, yawns, stretches.

I'll help you look, Granny.

SOUSETTE: You go back to sleep. Ah, here they are.

Suzie, a tall, awkward thirteen-year-old, wanders off, dragging her blanket behind her. She is at that age of being almost a young woman but in many ways still a child. Sousette sets her picture aside and from her crouched position by the coffee table gazes lovingly at her grandchild. Suzie almost bumps into her mother, Eva, who is a stern, serious woman in her mid-thirties.

EVA: I hope you're not going back to bed. It's time to get up.

SUZIE: Aw, Mom.

EVA *sternly*: You should get some wood in, and help me start getting breakfast.

SOUSETTE: Eva, let her sleep a little bit longer.

Suzie exits into the bedroom.

EVA *with slight animosity*: That's not what you used to tell me. You used to chase me out of bed in the middle of the night.

SOUSETTE *surprised at her outburst*: She's going on a fast for two days. She'll need her strength . . . and all our love.

EVA *a bit ashamed of her emotions*: I'll get some wood.

SOUSETTE: I brought a whole pile in last night.

EVA: You should let Suzie do those things—she's young.

SOUSETTE: That's how *I* stay young. Here are those pictures I was looking for.

She motions to Eva to come sit beside her and hands her a picture.

I can't see without my glasses.

Sousette searches in her bag for her glasses while Eva describes the picture to her.

EVA: It's a bunch of little girls. Lots of them, standing in front of a big grey building. There's a priest and a nun standing there with them.

Sousette puts her glasses on and takes the picture.

SOUSETTE: That's the school I was telling you about, St. Eugene's Residential School. That building still stands there. All our cheap DIA houses are falling down, but that building still stands there, reminding us. How old do you think these girls are?

EVA: They look younger than Suzie, about eight or nine. A few of them look older.

SOUSETTE: I was looking all over for this picture. I wanted you to see it. You were asking about Lucy. I'm going to show you a picture of Lucy when she was a young girl. She was a really pretty girl. See, there's Lucy there.

EVA: Lucy? A pretty girl? Yeah, she sure was, but she don't look like that today. What happened to her eye? And that arm that's all messed up?

SOUSETTE: Joe Sam did that to her. Joe was her husband, and he was real mean. He died long before you were born. He nearly took that eye out, and he broke that arm so many times it never would lie straight again. He was so jealous. She never did nothin' for him to be jealous about. She only had that one baby that wasn't his, and she took such good care of his babies, the ones that weren't hers. She always loved babies. She was a good mother.

EVA: Sure does sound like he was mean.

SOUSETTE: He'd be in jail today if he was still alive. Every time he got drunk, he beat her. I don't know what made that man so mean.

Except he never would let her forget about that one baby that wasn't his.

EVA: Wasn't there a story that she had a baby in residential school?

Sousette looks uneasy, but she nods.

EVA: Whose baby was it?

The silence is broken by a loud noise, the sound of a bucket and some tools being dropped. Eva is startled but Sousette is used to these interruptions and grand entrances. Lucy, an Elder who looks very strong and fit in her gumboots and work clothes, enters loudly. Her voice is startling in the early morning quiet.

LUCY: I stopped by to see if you wanted to go across the road with me. I'm gonna fix that little bit of fence that's falling down by Joe's grave. Huh! You got company. I better get to work before it gets too late.

Lucy begins to hurry away.

SOUSETTE: Lucy, I told you Eva and Suzie were staying for a few days. Lucy, come back here, I'm talking to you. We're having Suzie's coming-of-age celebration, she's going to become a young woman. You come back later today. You are going to help, aren't you?

LUCY: Yeah, yeah, yeah. I've got lots of work to do. I'll come back tomorrow.

SOUSETTE: No, Lucy, you come back today. You help us with Suzie. She'll be real disappointed if you're not here.

LUCY: I have to go now. It's getting late. I've got lots of work to do.

She exits.

SOUSETTE: She doesn't have anything to do—she's just pretending she's busy. She spends all her time in that graveyard visiting her babies . . . and Joe.

EVA: She scared me, sneaking up on us like that. Do you think she heard?

Sousette silences her with a motion.

SOUSETTE: She says she's deaf.

Sousette sits down and picks up the picture again.

SOUSETTE: I've thought about it a long time, and I talked to the others. We decided you need to know everything, about the school and about us. You need to know because of Suzie. It's her history too.

Eva is grave, and respectfully silent, listening.

EVERYBODY suspected it was the priest who did that to Lucy. Not just Lucy. Other girls had babies too. Lots of babies buried behind the school, buried in the schoolyard. She never would talk about it though. That baby died anyway, same as all her other ones. She had fourteen babies, all of them by Joe except for that one baby. Her daughter Angeline was the one who got killed in that car accident last winter. She was the last one. There's no one left, just us. We're all the family she's got.

EVA: Oh, Mom, that's sad. Why did she marry Joe, when he was so mean to her?

SOUSETTE: She had no choice. It was arranged by her people. He was a widower with small children and she was pregnant with no husband. It wasn't easy in those days for a woman to get by on her own. Joe never had an easy life either. His parents died when he was a baby and he was passed from relative to relative, nobody really wanting him. Musta been someone hurt him real bad when he was little. The way they used to beat those boys in that school, it's a wonder they didn't all turn out mean.

Sousette focuses her attention back to the picture.

SOUSETTE: Can you pick out which is me? Right there. The pretty one.

EVA: The one with the nice haircut, eh?

SOUSETTE: That's my bowl cut. I still wear my hair like that sometimes, when I get tired of braiding it. (*Both women laugh.*) And this other picture here is of me in that white buckskin dress.

EVA: Mom, you were so beautiful. Is that the dress Suzie's going to wear for her feast?

SOUSETTE: That's the one. The deer hides were brought from the hunt by my grandfather, and tanned and sewn together with beads and shells by my grandmother. I was a girl like Suzie when this dress first came to me. I can still see my grandmother. "I made this special for you," she said, and she slipped it over my head. It was so soft. She took me outside to show Grandpa. He told me a story about the hunt, that the deer just stood and waited for him, like they knew they were offering up their lives for something special. They made me feel special.

Sousette is far away as she speaks, as though she has gone back to that time. Eva is very quiet and still. She doesn't want to break her mother's concentration. Sousette picks up the picture of the girls again and continues. As she speaks, the light fades, and a slide of the picture of the girls in the school lights up on the back wall. Mother and daughter talk quietly in the background.

You know, out of all these girls there must only be a handful of us still alive. Most of them died—pretty violent too . . . alcohol, suicide . . . murder. This one here, her name was Annie. She got murdered in the city. She was Agnes's friend, and Agnes was my best friend. Here's Agnes here.

EVA: That's Auntie Agnes? Yes, she still looks like that. She's got a bowl cut too.

The women laugh. Blackout.

SCENE 2

Late afternoon of the same day. Suzie and Sousette sit on the couch unpacking the white buckskin dress that Suzie will wear at her celebration feast after her fast. Suzie is dressed in a long, flowing ribbon dress and moccasins. She has special paint on her face. She is waiting for her aunties to take her to the lodge. She is excited about her fast, and especially about the celebration feast. Eva is on the floor packing a small bundle for Suzie, consisting of her medicine, smudge, a cup of water, a towel, and a light blanket.

SUZIE: Granny, it's so beautiful.

SOUSETTE: We have to be careful with it. Some of these beads may be loose. I'll get your mom to repair it before you put it on.

She holds the dress up to Suzie to see the fit.

SUZIE: How old is this dress, if it was made by my great-, great-grandmother?

SOUSETTE: I was nine when I first wore this dress, and I'm sixty-seven now.

EVA: That would make it fifty-eight years old, and if we take good care of it your daughter will wear it to *her* feast.

SUZIE: Did you wear this dress, Mom, at your feast?

EVA *sharply*: No, I didn't have one.

SUZIE: But how come?

SOUSETTE: I suppose that was my fault. We quit having coming-of-age ceremonies when your mom was a girl. People were afraid of Indian ways back then.

SUZIE: Was that sad for you, Mom?

EVA: No, I didn't know about those things then, so I didn't miss it. (*Eva softens.*) But I always wanted this for you. You'll make up for the feast I never had.

A light knock on the door. Sousette answers it.

SOUSETTE: Why, Mariah, come in. What have you got there? Let me help you, that box looks heavy. Suzie, the aunties are here, they're just pulling up. You better hurry. Don't forget your bundle. Come and give me a big hug.

Sousette sets the box on the coffee table and gives Suzie a hug.

SUZIE: I'll see you in two days.

SOUSETTE: I'll be down to visit you later. You listen to the aunties and do everything they tell you.

SUZIE: I will.

Suzie gives Mariah a hug. Mariah stiffens slightly. She is not used to touches and hugs, but she loves Suzie and pats her on the cheek.

Hi, Granny Mariah. Bye. Will you come later too?

Mariah nods.

EVA: I'll be down there as soon as I can too. Don't worry about anything, the aunties will take good care of you. And if you need to know anything, you just ask. They can tell you everything you need to know. Are you excited?

Eva's and Suzie's eyes glisten with tears and excitement.

SUZIE: Yes, yes, yes.

EVA: Hurry, hurry, hurry. You better go.

Suzie exits. Eva goes to the table and sits down to make bread. She is silent and unobtrusive, dutiful and listening.

SOUSETTE: Isn't this wonderful, Mariah? Our little baby girl is all grown up.

MARIAH: I brought jars of canned peaches for Suzie's feast. I canned them in the summertime. I was hoping we could talk. I haven't been sleeping very good again. Every time I close my eyes, I see something. I was hoping you could give me more of that medicine.

SOUSETTE: I've been so worried about you. Why don't you let me take you to that person I was telling you about? This medicine I got here, all it will do is help you to sleep. It can't take care of the real problem. It can't take care of what's troubling you in your heart.

Mariah nervously tugs at a gold cross that hangs from a chain around her neck.

MARIAH: I can't. I can't go there, Sousette. I can't go against the church like that.

SOUSETTE: Mariah, it's not going against the church. This person I'm telling you about is a very spiritual person too, and I can't believe the things she does is anything against the church. She's a very respectful and very kind and loving person. She knows about dreams, Mariah. She knows those kinds of dreams that haunt you. I wish you would trust me on that. You know I'd never do anything to hurt you.

While Sousette and Mariah talk, Eva is working. Lucy enters, silently this time. Mariah's back is to her, so she can't see her.

MARIAH: I know, Sousette. Maybe if I pray on it, I'll know what to do. I'll leave it up to the Lord. He'll tell me what to do.

Lucy's entrance is suddenly dramatic and loud. Startled, Mariah tries to hide behind Sousette.

LUCY: Oh Lord! What is the Lord going to do now?

Lucy chuckles to herself and mocks Mariah. Mariah stays as far away from her as she can. Sousette attempts to calm Mariah, while coaxing her not to leave.

SOUSETTE: Lucy, quit that now. Mariah, come back. At least wait until I get your medicine. It'll only take a few minutes to prepare.

LUCY: Why you wasting good Indian medicine on her for? You know she don't believe in it. Besides, the Lord might get upset, and heaven knows what He might do to you. He might strike you dead.

Mariah is at the door by this time and crosses herself. She is horrified at what appears to be a blasphemous comment by Lucy. Lucy, pleased with herself and the reaction that she's getting from Mariah, snickers and chuckles all the way to the couch, where she continues to carry on, mocking Mariah's sign of the cross.

SOUSETTE: Lucy, will you sit down and be quiet? This conversation has got nothing to do with you.

Sousette speaks soothingly to Mariah. As she speaks, Lucy sneaks up to Mariah behind Sousette's back and yanks at her shirt, then hurries back to the couch. This last action by Lucy unnerves Mariah, who promptly heads for the door. Sousette follows her.

SOUSETTE: Come back later. I'll have your medicine ready for you by then. And don't mind what Lucy says. Honestly, I don't know what gets into that woman sometimes, but you've got to stand up to her. If you raised your voice to her once, she'd leave you alone.

MARIAH: I'll come back later, after she's gone. Do you think she'll be gone by then?

SOUSETTE: You come back whether she's here or not. You stop running from her. Maybe she'll leave early, although it's hard to get her out of here once she gets started.

Mariah exits. Lucy is still chuckling to herself. She's had great fun at Mariah's expense. This sums up Lucy's character. There are not many people who can get close to her or who are not intimidated by her.

SOUSETTE: Why can't you leave her alone? You just do that because you know she's timid, and you make fun of her religion because you know it's something she cares deeply about.

LUCY: I'm just getting back at her for the residential school.

SOUSETTE: And you think it wasn't hard for her in there too? If you only knew.

LUCY: Yeah, it must have been really hard being the favourite. You should hear the way she talks about the place sometimes. You'd think it was the Newcastle Hotel and we were royalty, the way she describes it. That's probably the way it was for her, but it sure wasn't that way for us black Indians.

SOUSETTE: Oh, Lucy, your bitterness is going to eat a hole right through you. Be quiet a minute. I've got to prepare this medicine, and you know I must have only good thoughts while I'm doing it. Sing with me that song that we always sing so well. It's a good strong song.

LUCY: One more thing about that medicine. Do you think it's a good idea to be giving it to Mariah?

SOUSETTE: Lucy, think good thoughts, and I really want to hear that song. Think of something happy, Lucy. It always sounds much better when we're happy. Think of Suzie in the lodge, and all the things that she's learning to become a strong young woman.

LUCY: Okay, you fix the medicine and I'll help you sing.

As Sousette and Lucy sing, all the grief seems to drain from Lucy's face. She becomes calm and peaceful. When the song finishes, they are silent, lost in their happy thoughts, until Lucy spots the picture of the girls in residential school on the coffee table in front of her. Immediately, her agitation is renewed.

What's this? Who are all these kids?

SOUSETTE: That's us in the residential school. Eva, come and show her the ones we picked out. She hasn't got her glasses so you have to point them out for her.

Eva approaches cautiously, bringing a tray with a pot of tea, cups, milk, and sugar.

EVA: This is Mom, and this one is Agnes, and that's you, I think.

LUCY: That's not Agnes. She didn't look like that. I don't think I'm in this picture.

SOUSETTE: Sure, Lucy, that's Agnes. She's standing right next to me, and Annie's standing on the other side of her, and you're standing down here.

LUCY: Huh? Maybe it is, I don't know. Here.

Lucy hands the picture to Sousette, who props it up on the table. Lucy ignores Eva's attempt to serve her tea and starts poking around in the other things on the table.

EVA: I brought you a cup of tea, Lucy. What would you like in it?

Eva looks helplessly at Sousette and sets their tea down, careful not to get too close to Lucy.

SOUSETTE: You have to talk really loud when you talk to her. Sometimes she pretends she's deaf, especially when she's not wearing her glasses. She uses lots of cream, like me, and put four spoons of sugar in there.

EVA: Do you need anything else here? If you don't, I'm going to work on my beading. I want to get Suzie's moccasins done before Agnes gets here. She's bringing a cape, so I want to make sure everything is ready for Suzie's feast.

SOUSETTE: You go ahead, Eva. We'll drink our tea and visit.

Eva sets her beading supplies out and begins to work. She always keeps herself busy, the way she was taught. Lucy is upset and makes like she's going to leave.

LUCY: What? What? Did she say Agnes is coming? Is that what she said? I don't want to be here when she gets here. Agnes! Huh!

SOUSETTE: Sit down, Lucy—she's not going to be here for some time. Stay and visit. Besides, you two should bury the hatchet. Try to get along.

LUCY: You know where I'd like to bury that hatchet.

Sousette is skilled at soothing Lucy's ruffled feathers. She coaxes Lucy to stay by tempting her with Eva's bread. Lucy is still standing and is not going to give in too easily.

SOUSETTE: Hush now, Lucy, come sit back down and relax. Eva is going to cook some bannock. She could even make some fry bread with strawberry jam. You'd like that, wouldn't you?

LUCY: Well, okay, I could eat some fry bread. I'm not very hungry, though—but I guess I could eat something.

Lucy is almost lulled into forgetting about Agnes, but suddenly she remembers some real or imagined slight and becomes agitated all over again. She jumps out of her chair and begins her harangue.

Just as long as that Agnes don't start telling me what kind of an Indian I should be, when she comes, like she's some kind of expert or something. Talking about First Nations, and what was that other one ... Aboriginal. Just because she travels around the country doesn't mean she knows everything.

Lucy sits down close to Sousette and speaks in a conspiratorial tone.

I wonder if those people she talks to know she used to be an alcoholic, and a prostitute? Used to live down there on skid row. If it hadn't been for us who took her in, she's still be down there.

SOUSETTE: Hush, Lucy. What makes you so hateful? You know Agnes has worked hard for what she's got, and she deserves to have a good life. She's never said a mean word to you, or about you, and I'm sure if you wanted to travel around, she could set it up for you. She's always been generous that way. Anyway, she's never tried to hide what's in her past, and people love and respect her for that.

Lucy turns away abruptly. She hates it when Sousette defends Agnes.

Come on now, Lucy. Let's talk about something else. My daughter, Eva, she goes to college, and she's doing some studying about Indians. She's gathering lots of material and I told her that the best person she could talk to in the area was you, that you know everything about the history around here.

LUCY *puffs with pride*: I guess I do know the history probably better'n anyone. I probably could travel around too and talk about the history. I'm probably the only one who could talk about it seein' as I'm the only one who never left from around here. I've lived here all my life, you know. I never went off to the city, not once.

SOUSETTE: That's what I told Eva: "The best person for you to talk to would be Lucy Sam." Hey, Eva, isn't that right?

Eva sets her beading aside and pulls out a notepad she always keeps close by. She sits attentively, respectfully.

LUCY: Your daughter, she doesn't speak Indian though, huh? I couldn't tell it to her all in English. It's too bad she doesn't speak Indian.

SOUSETTE: I know, but I could interpret for her, and she does understand some.

LUCY: I guess I could sit down with her some day, if she tells me what it is she wants to know.

EVA: I'm really interested in anything about the residential school.

Lucy stiffens and moves close to Sousette.

LUCY: Did she say the residential school? I could tell her some things about that, but she can't write it down, not all of it.

She turns her attention back to Eva.

There's some things that you shouldn't write down. There's some things that I shouldn't tell you.

Eva puts her notepad away.

SOUSETTE: But we agreed that we have to tell them sometime, Lucy. That's their history—they have a right to know.

LUCY: Hmmm. What're they going to do with it? Sell it?

Eva flinches. Sousette is dismayed.

SOUSETTE: Lucy! It's her birthright, and it's part of her education. She's been going to school and coming back here every summer for a long time, to get an education. You have to give her credit for that.

Lucy whispers conspiratorially to Sousette.

LUCY: You want to tell them everything? What about the priest? What about what he done? You want that they should know that?

SOUSETTE: They know more than we think they do, and we made a promise that we were going to tell them everything. I know it's hard, Lucy, but we must.

When Eva speaks, they both jump, as though they'd forgotten that she was there. Her words are gentle, yet strong and determined. She is not afraid of the truth.

EVA: Tell me what? What is it that you're afraid to tell me? That he molested little girls?

The old ladies cover their eyes and Lucy turns away, her back to Sousette. Sousette approaches her cautiously, weighing every word. Eva sits very still, drawing in every word, and rocks gently, cushioning them softly against her heart. These words, she knows, are sacred. Flute music begins.

SOUSETTE: You know, Lucy, in your heart you know why Agnes went off to the city and became what she did. She didn't have any people to go home to—they all died of smallpox, or else they were drinking. She had no one but us, and we weren't much for helpin' one another back then. I remember the day she and Annie left. I went down there and saw them off at the Greyhound. I already had two babies, and all I had was five bucks.

I slipped it into Agnes's hand and I made her promise to write to me every day. She didn't want to take the money, but I wouldn't let her give it back. She cried, and she said I was the only family she had. Annie, she was just anxious to get on the bus and get out of town before her uncles discovered she was gone.

It must have been hard for Annie, being the only girl in that family of men . . . and all that drinking. I stood there and watched till the bus was out of sight. I was thinking I'd never see those girls again, and it was like losing a piece of myself. If it wasn't for them, I don't think I could have survived that school. Agnes was my big sister.

LUCY: I was one of those girls who got caught with Agnes when she ran away. It was her fault we got caught. She was too soft-hearted. One of the other girls, Monika, she went and fell down and hurt herself, and Agnes wouldn't leave her behind. Nobody wanted to go on without Agnes, so we all waited there until they caught up with us. I've always blamed her for that beating.

Gregorian chant begins. Lucy stands and moves slowly to centre stage, gathering her strength.

If it wasn't for that priest, I wouldn't have even run away. It was the first time he ever got me alone. The older girls always warned me never to go alone with him, but I was on dorm duty and Sister sent me to get sheets from the storage room, and he was waiting there. He rubbed his tongue all over my mouth before he let me go.

Gregorian chant ends.

Agnes found me throwing up behind the stairs. She cleaned me up, then she told me she was gonna run. She said some others were gonna go with her. And if I wanted to, I could go along. It didn't take me long to decide to go along. We almost made it over the mountains when they caught us.

Lucy is weary. Disappointment in her body, she moves back to the couch to sit down. She speaks with a sense of betrayal.

Our own people brought us back.

Sousette sympathizes briefly with Lucy, then stands and moves to centre stage to tell the rest of her story.

SOUSETTE: They made us clear away the tables and chairs in the cafeteria. There was Mariah, Julia, Helen, Molly, and me. We didn't know for sure what was going on, but we heard somebody saying they had caught the runaways and they were going to punish them. They sounded the bell (*a handheld bell rings three times and flute music begins*) and called us girls to stand in a circle in the cafeteria.

I saw the Sisters bringing you in, one at a time, holding you down so you couldn't get away. I heard your screams and cries, and I heard that whip slicing through the air, cutting through your flesh. We tried to close our eyes, but those Sisters standing among us forced us to open them and look. The whole top of my dress was soaked with tears.

Sousette moves back to the couch and sits down, holding the tears to her chest. Lucy stands to deliver the rest of her story with all the power she needs to conjure up the image and destroy it.

LUCY: They took turns whipping us. When one of them would get tired, another would step in. They were harder on Agnes because they said she was the ringleader, and because she wouldn't cry. I wanted to tell her to cry, so they would stop, but she wouldn't cry.

The priest was yelling at her, "Cry! Cry! Cry!" But she wouldn't. Then I noticed a trickle of blood running down her leg, and when she fell, it smeared on the floor. She had started her period, started bleeding, and still they wouldn't stop.

Lucy returns to the couch to sit down. She is weary and broken herself, at this moment.

They broke her that day.

The lights begin to fade. A slide of girls in school is projected on the back wall. The women continue to speak as the stage fades to black.

SOUSETTE: They broke her body, they broke her heart, but they never broke her spirit. Agnes's spirit lives inside each one of us.

LUCY: It was my cousin Julia who told me Agnes was on the skids. She hit the skids real hard after Annie was murdered.

SCENE 3

Evening of the second day of Suzie's fast, and everyone has gone down to be with her. The Elder Agnes is sitting at the kitchen table with her feet propped up, sipping a cup of tea, and reading the newspaper. She has Eva's beadwork in her lap and every once in a while, she stops to look at it. Her bags are all around her, on the floor and on the couch. She has made herself right at home. Sousette enters first, followed by Lucy and then Eva. Lucy almost bumps into Sousette, as Sousette stops abruptly, surprised to see Agnes at her kitchen table.

SOUSETTE: Well, are you a sight for sore eyes! Look at you, you look great.

Eva is struggling to get by Lucy, who has stopped dead in her tracks and refuses to budge.

I didn't see your car. I had no idea you were here. Lucy, look who's here.

Sousette firmly moves Lucy out of the way and pushes her toward the couch. Lucy stares in disgust at Agnes's bags on the couch. Eva finally makes her way over to Agnes.

EVA: Aunt Agnes, you're finally here. I was beginning to worry that you wouldn't make it. We just came from making an offering at Suzie's lodge, an offering for her fire.

AGNES: I wondered where you were. My car broke down, but I woulda gotten here even if I had to hitchhike. Lucy, just push those things out of your way.

Lucy bends down and sweeps everything into a heap onto the floor, then practically steps on them as she sits down. Sousette shakes her head.

EVA: Auntie, are you hungry? I'm cooking your favourite stew.

AGNES: And I smell bannock. You know your auntie always shows up here hungry. Let me get out of your way so you can do your stuff. The moccasins look great. Let me move over here and settle down beside Lucy.

Agnes moves over to the couch, bringing her newspaper, the moccasins, and a few of the bags from the floor. Lucy does not want Agnes to sit beside her, so she spreads herself across the middle of the couch. Sousette starts to get up to give Agnes her chair.

AGNES: Now don't get up, Sousette. I'll just settle here beside Lucy.

Agnes squeezes herself in beside Lucy, who is forced to move over, disgruntled.

LUCY: Ow!

EVA: I'll bring your tea. What do you want in it?

AGNES: Just a tiny bit of sugar. I'm trying to cut down, and no cream please—I have to watch my figure.

LUCY: I'll have another cup of tea too, Eva. Double cream and five sugars.

SOUSETTE: That must have been you, with your car broken down by the Band office. Lucy said she thought she saw your car over there earlier.

AGNES: Can't sneak nothing by Lucy. She did see me, or pretended not to see me. I was waving away. Didn't you see me waving at you?

LUCY: Now, I can't be noticing everything that's going on, can I? Lots of people wave at me that I'm too busy to notice.

AGNES: Anyway, that was me. This tea is good, Eva. It's Labrador tea, isn't it? I tasted this when I was up in the North.

Lucy raises her cup in mock salute to thank Eva.

SOUSETTE: Where were you this time?

AGNES: I just got back from two weeks in South Dakota.

Agnes is a flashy dresser. She shows Sousette her turquoise jewellery. Lucy studies her with disdain.

And three weeks in the Territories. My, I sure have been gone a long time. But tell me, how's our little girl doing?

SOUSETTE: Suzie? This is her second night. She's doing good. You'll be proud of her.

AGNES: I always am. I'll go down at sunrise so she'll know I'm here. I brought her the most beautiful cape. It'll go well with Eva's moccasins. By the way, when I came in earlier it was pretty dark but I saw someone sitting on your back porch. I called out, but whoever it was left in a hurry. I couldn't tell who it was in the dark.

Lucy makes a mocking motion of the sign of the cross, indicating that it was probably Mariah.

SOUSETTE: That must have been Mariah. She always comes to visit me late at night, but I doubt that she'll come in, with so many visitors. She usually only comes when I'm here by myself.

LUCY: That Mariah, she's always sneaking around like that. She's never sociable. She won't even talk to me.

Lucy gets up and noisily crosses over to the table to get more tea.

If you ask me, I think she's crazy.

SOUSETTE: Nobody asked you, Lucy. I've heard the way you taunt her.

LUCY: She still thinks she's better than us.

Lucy hates it when Sousette defends someone. She takes it as a personal affront. Noisily, she throws sugar into her cup, pokes around Eva's cooking, and stirs her tea loudly. No one pays attention.

AGNES: It's funny. I never thought she'd come back here to settle. I thought she'd stay her whole life in the city. If she doesn't get along with Indians, it sure must get pretty lonely for her here.

SOUSETTE: She had her grandma's place left to her. That's where she grew up, until they shipped her off to school. That place sat empty for a long time. She sure fixed it up nice, but yeah, she does get lonely. (*Glances at Lucy.*) Some people are pretty unfriendly around here.

LUCY: She doesn't really belong here.

SOUSETTE: She belongs here. She belongs here every bit as much as you and I do. You'd be surprised how much knowledge that woman has. Her grandmother taught her good.

AGNES: Wasn't her grandmother a medicine woman?

SOUSETTE: Yes, and she was a strong woman. I have a feeling that Mariah inherited that strength, and some day she's going to find that out. I think Nupik'a guided her back here. I think she came back to teach us something.

Lucy returns to her seat noisily. Before she sits down, she retorts.

LUCY: Well, she can't teach me nothin'.

SOUSETTE: Yeah, that probably would be hard to do. Now, Eva, you keep an eye out for her. She probably won't come tonight, but she will come tomorrow, when Suzie finishes her fast. She promised. Take her this medicine, and ask her, as a special favour to Suzie, and me, if she would come in and sit with us, so that she's here when Suzie comes out. Suzie asked that all her grandmothers be here to help her dress for her celebration.

Eva takes the medicine and carefully puts it in a pouch at her waist.

EVA: I'll keep it close to me, so I'll have it when I see her.

Eva returns to the table and continues beading.

AGNES: I wouldn't mind getting to know her. I remember her from school, but we were never friends. The Sisters never allowed us to have too much to do with her. I wonder why that was?

LUCY: She didn't have too much to do with anybody, being a pet like she was. Anyway, if her grandmother was a medicine woman, how come she had a half-white granddaughter?

SOUSETTE: Being Indian, Lucy, is more than just the colour of your skin. There were reasons why Mariah was kept separate. I pray that she finds the courage to talk about it some day.

LUCY: What? What is it? I know everything that went on in that school. I never heard nothing.

SOUSETTE: You don't know everything, Lucy. Maybe there *is* something Mariah can teach you.

As Lucy and Sousette talk, Agnes's attention is drawn to the picture on the table.

AGNES: What's this picture here? Sousette, you kept this picture after all these years? I can't believe this is how we used to look. Let me see if I can recognize who these other girls are. There's Lucy, that's me, and Sousette. Is that really you? You must have just got your hair cut. It looks like you have a bowl on your head. And who's that other one there?

Lucy pokes her finger at the picture and gloats.

LUCY: That's your friend Annie.

AGNES: Yes, it is, isn't it? Look at her just smiling away, looking like she didn't have a care in the world. Annie. She was always smiling. No matter how rough things got, she always had that big smile on her face.

LUCY: I'll bet she's not smiling now.

AGNES: Oh, I don't know, I'll bet she is. At least, that's the way I want to remember her. That's exactly how she looked the last time I saw her, all sparkly and bubbly, in her red dress that kinda hung offa her shoulder, with sequins and glitter all across the front. Annie was real pretty, you know, even without all that glitz . . . but she sure liked to dress.

Agnes is far away, in another time and another place.

We were hanging around the Zanzibar that night, trying to make some money offa these loggers that just pulled into town.

Lucy draws away from Agnes abruptly, as though she's afraid she's going to catch something. She is visibly shocked and disgusted.

LUCY: Agnes, how can you talk about that? Don't it make you shamed?

Sousette, always fascinated with Agnes's life, brushes Lucy away as if she is an annoying fly.

SOUSETTE: Hush, Lucy, be quiet.

Sousette turns her full attention back to Agnes.

AGNES: Ashamed of what, Lucy? That we made the best use of the only assets we had? Annie and me, we didn't know any better and we were just trying to survive. We left here with just that little bit of money in our pockets.

We thought we'd find work, but nobody wanted two Indian girls fresh off the rez, at least nobody who'd pay an honest wage. You try makin' it in the city when you got nothin' and nobody to back you up. When you're hungry, or thirsty, you just sell whatever you can just to get that few bucks. Annie and me, all we had was each other. I'da done anything for her, and I did.

She was sick, real sick, and they wouldn't let her in the hospital. I thought she was gonna die. I went down to the corner to see old man Bill. I knew he was sweet on me, always givin' me the eye when his wife wasn't lookin'. I told him my friend was dyin' and I needed help.

He promised me he would, if I let him. It wasn't hard. I just closed my eyes and did what he said, and I didn't think about it. It wasn't much different from those times at school with Father. After the first time, it just got easier to close my eyes and think about how I was gonna spend all that money. I'd moan and groan now and then, pretend I was havin' a good time. Just like that, it was over.

Bill kept his word. Annie got better and she and I took to the streets and bars together. Mr. Bill, he was my best customer. He was still there for me when Annie got killed. That was such a long time ago but I remember it like it was yesterday.

Agnes gets up and moves to centre stage, into the spotlight, as though she is back there standing under a streetlight.

That night at the Zanzibar was hookers' convention night. That's what we called it when those loggers got into town. We'd been waitin' all week, and by the time Saturday night rolled around we barely had enough money for a cheap bottle of wine to keep our heads together. We knew we were lookin' good. I had on my long black dress, the one with the slit up the side, and Annie, of course, she wore her red dress. We came strolling into the Zanzibar that night turnin' heads all the way, and we knew we were goin' to be real busy.

By midnight I'd already made close to a thousand bucks, but I was pretty tanked up. This big white man was trying to get me to go with him, but I didn't want to go any more and he started gettin' crazy on me. He was all up in my face when Annie came along. When she told him to leave me alone he got real mean, talkin' about how he'd already spent lots of money on me, buyin' me drinks and all, and how I owed it to him.

She tried to calm him down, then she said she'd go with him. I argued with her, but she called her friend over and told him to get me home in a cab. You know, the last thing she said to me was, "Agnes, you can have the money. I just don't want you to get hurt. I can handle him. You go home. I'll see you in the morning."

She was just tryin' to look out for me.

They didn't find Annie for a whole week. I went crazy day and night lookin' for her. She just never came home. When they found her, she was all beat up. You couldn't even recognize her, except for that red sequined dress.

I stayed drunk after that. I can't remember a time when I ever felt so alone or so sad as that time. I know Bill called you, Sousette, and you came to get me.

The lights rise as Sousette stands and goes to Agnes.

I know you all chipped in to send Sousette to get me, and I thank you for that. You all saved my life back then.

Sousette gently leads Agnes back to the couch.

SOUSETTE: And today you have a beautiful granddaughter who is about to become a woman in a very special way.

Sousette gently helps Agnes come back to herself. Eva brings a fresh cup of tea and Lucy is quiet for once.

AGNES: You know, sometimes when I'm travelling in the city I still see young Indian girls, just like Annie and me, standing around street corners, hitchhiking, jumping into strangers' cars, and it breaks my heart to think of what must have happened to those little girls. You know, the Creator left me alive for one reason. It could just as easily have been me that got killed. Somebody has to talk about it. Somebody has to tell the truth about what happened to all those little girls. I figure the Creator saved me because he knew my big mouth would come in handy some day. Still, it's hard to talk about the things that people are so afraid to hear.

LUCY: We didn't all turn out like that though. Nobody told you two to go runnin' off to the city.

AGNES: And did stayin' here make your life any easier, Lucy?

LUCY: At least I wasn't a prostitute.

AGNES: You were just a battered wife. I wouldn't have traded my life for a life with Joe Sam.

LUCY: If I were you I'd be careful of how I speak about the dead.

SOUSETTE: Now, come on, settle down you two—don't fight. Let's have some of Eva's stew. Eva, bring Lucy a piece of that fry bread and some stew. Agnes and I, we'll help ourselves.

Eva gets busy serving up food. Sousette stands and picks the picture up. The lights begin to dim.

There isn't a single one of us in this picture who's had an easy life.

LUCY: Except maybe Mariah, and Sophie, and Joannie, all those teacher's pets with their light skin.

Blackout.

ACT TWO
SCENE 1

Late afternoon the next day, when Suzie will finish her fast and the ceremony and celebration will begin. There is an air of excitement. Sousette, Agnes, and Lucy are bringing all the pieces of Suzie's outfit together and making sure everything is ready. Sousette lays the dress out across the chair, Agnes brings the cape, and Lucy holds the moccasins and hair ties.

AGNES: Sousette, that dress is so beautiful. That's the one that was made by your grandmother? The one you wore when you were a girl?

SOUSETTE: The same one. I dreamed about this day, before Suzie was even born, and Suzie dreamed about it when she was just a little girl. She said, "I'll be wearing that dress and all my grannies will be here, in this house"—me, you Agnes, you Lucy, and Mariah. But Mariah's not here, and soon Suzie will come and Mariah won't be here.

Sousette is clearly disturbed.

AGNES: There's still time. Maybe Eva will convince her to come.

SOUSETTE: She won't come with so many people in my house.

Eva appears at the door holding Mariah by the arm. Mariah looks like she is about to flee, but Eva has a firm grip on her. Sousette quickly clears off the chair and offers it to Mariah, while waving Agnes, and especially Lucy, back to the couch. Agnes moves so that she is sitting between Lucy and Mariah. When Mariah is seated, Eva takes the dress and accessories from Sousette and lays them on the kitchen table.

SOUSETTE: I'm so glad you've come, my friend. This is a special day for all of us, and it will even be more special for Suzie now that you're here. Can I get you anything?

MARIAH: No, Sousette, I've come to talk. I want to thank you for the medicine and thank you for sending Eva to invite me in. You know I have a hard time with so many people, but I know you've been waiting a long time to hear me say what I'm going to say here today. Perhaps you would like to sit?

SOUSETTE: Yes, I think I will. Do you remember Agnes?

Mariah nods to Agnes but won't look at Lucy.

MARIAH: I get afraid to talk. All my life people tell me, "Be quiet, shut up, don't say nothin'." Even the old people before used to tell me, "Don't tell stories—if you attack the church you make hard times for everybody." Now I'm old, and I keep my mouth shut, and still we have hard times. It's gettin' harder and harder, Sousette. It's gettin' harder and harder for everybody.

I don't know why the Lord guided me back to this place, or even why I should still be livin' and all those other women are dead. I keep askin' the Lord every day, what is it that I need to do, and I hear nothin', just those dreams that won't allow me a decent night's sleep.

I know there are those of you who believe I don't belong here. For most of my life, I've wanted to believe that too. It's always been so easy for me to leave here, and to turn away from the side of me that's Indian, except it's like turnin' my back on the only human being who ever truly loved me. My grandmother, who was Indian, told me once that it was not going to be easy livin' on the edge of two worlds, and I see that now, when my eyes are opened, that this has been true.

When I walk in the Indian world, I hear them tauntin' me.

"Teacher's pet, teacher's pet, hey little white girl, whatta you doin' 'round here? Are you a 'Wannabe'? One of those Bill C-31 Indians?"

And when I walk in the white world, I hear them tauntin' me.

"Little Indian squaw, why don't you go back to the reservation where you belong? Hey, Pocahontas, you wanna come home with me and be my little Indian princess? You're not really one of them, you're almost white."

Well, almost is not good enough. I've come home to find out who I really am. I knew who I was when I was a little girl livin' in ka Titti's house, before they took me away to school. I knew who I was when she would light the juniper and guide my tiny hands over the smoke, pulling it up over my hair, across my heart, and down the rest of my body. She would turn me in a circle, always to my right, and she would tell me that the Creator gave me as a special gift to her, to watch over for a time. That, at that time, I was the most perfect and precious being, there was no doubt. I believed that with all my heart. What I seen in that school shocked me into silence, and disbelief in everything that was good. But it was not the Lord that did that. I know that now. It was people just like you and me.

Gregorian chant begins.

I saw that girl, Theresa, refuse to stop speakin' Indian, refuse to quit praying to Nupik'a. I saw her always encouragin' others not to forget they were Indian, and I admired her strength and the depth of her determination. While no one else spoke to me—I had no friends, you see—she would always stop to give me a kind word, and I grew to love her like the older sister I never had. I saw her challenge them repeatedly, daring them to do what they finally did to silence her. I saw Sister Luke, hate and venom spewing out of her mouth, "You dirty, savage Indian!" and threw that girl Theresa down two flights of cement steps, and I said nothin'.

The hand-held bell rings three times.

My screams were silent and my agony all consumin'. I saw murder done in that school, and when they wrapped that broken body and sent it home to the mother, tellin' her it was pneumonia that killed her little girl, she unwrapped her and, runnin' her grievin', lovin' mother's hands across the bruised face, shoulders, legs, and back, discovered the neck was broken, screamed out in agony, "Why? What happened to my baby?" And I said nothin'.

The hand-held bell rings three times.

I saw little girls taken in the night from their beds. I heard the moans and groans, and the sobbin'.

Shut up, shut up, I said. Glazed eyes, ravaged and torn bodies returned in a frightened, huddled mass beneath the sheets. And I said nothin'.

The hand-held bell rings three times.

"You're a good girl," they often told me. "These girls are bad. They need to be taught a lesson."

I saw a baby born one night to a mother who was little more than a child herself. I saw her frightened, dark eyes pleading with me to save her child, and later on, when the grave was dug and the baby lowered into the ground, I said nothin'.

The hand-held bell rings three times. The Gregorian chant stops.

When my grandma died, I was only nine and I had no one. At Christmas and summer holidays, no one came to claim me, so they became my family. They stroked my light skin and brushed my brown curls and told me I was almost white. They pampered and spoiled me, and there was not a place in that school where I was not welcome. I had special privileges, and because I was so good at saying nothin' I became one of them. Father put this cross around my neck, and he cried and wished me well, made me promise to come back and visit.

Mariah walks toward the door, then stops.

I walked away. Never looked back. Not once. For a long time after that, I couldn't pray, and for years I believed in nothin'.

Sousette does not want Mariah to leave. Gently, she calls after her.

SOUSETTE: Mariah, what do you believe in now?

Mariah turns back, her face radiant.

MARIAH: I believe what my grandmother told me, that I am the most perfect and precious being in all of creation.

AGNES: And you are, Mariah, you're magnificent.

LUCY: Ah, you're still crazy.

SOUSETTE: I understand what she means, Lucy.

AGNES: So do I. Mariah, won't you come back and sit with us?

LUCY: Well, then, you're all crazy.

Mariah comes back at Agnes's coaxing and then sits. Eva brings her some tea.

SOUSETTE: Maybe we are, Lucy. That school made us all a little crazy, even you.

Everybody laughs except Lucy.

SOUSETTE: It was so long ago it hardly seemed worth talking about. I figured I could just forgive and go on, but Eva and Suzie, they opened my eyes.

Sousette looks affectionately at Eva.

Eva, my little girl, she lost a lot too. When they started to talk about residential schools, and even started an investigation, I didn't want to be involved. I thought we'd be better off to just keep the past behind us. When young people came to ask me about residential school, I wouldn't tell them nothing. I said it was a good place for me. Then one day, Eva, she opened my eyes.

The light dims. Eva moves into the spotlight. Sousette pulls a chair just to the edge of the spotlight. All other action freezes as the memory begins.

EVA: How can you say it was a good place for you? How can you lie like that? I'm so sick of hearing about residential school. I'm sick of reading about it. I'm sick of hearing about how you all suffered, from everybody else but not you. What about us? What about me and how I've suffered? Does anybody care about that?

Do you remember how you used to beat me, Mom? Do you even remember the bruises? Do you remember the ugly things you used to call me, and all the times you left me alone? I wouldn't have cared, if only you loved me. Do you even know what that means, love? Every time I go to hug you, you stiffen up. Do you know that you do that, Mom? Do you know how that makes me feel? And now I'm doing the same thing to Suzie. I push her away, Mom. I call her stupid, and I hit her, and I don't want to.

Tell me again that residential school was good for you. Talk to me more about forgiveness, so I can get angry. At least when I'm angry I know that I'm alive. I know that I'm feeling something. The rest of the time it's like I'm frozen.

Sousette is bent over in pain. She barely whispers.

SOUSETTE: But Eva, I do love you.

Eva crumples to the floor, the revelation of her mother's love too much to bear.

EVA: No, you don't.

Sousette speaks more forcefully this time.

SOUSETTE: Yes, Eva, I do love you. I never meant to hurt you.

Eva, if you hug me now, I won't stiffen up, I promise. Please forgive me. I'll make it up to you, if only you'll forgive me. I'll start talking about it. I'll tell you everything that happened to me, so you'll understand. We'll help one another to understand.

EVA: Oh, Mom, I'm so sorry.

Sousette and Eva sit on the floor. Sousette rocks Eva as though she were a little girl.

SOUSETTE: It's okay. Hush, hush, it's okay.

Blackout.

SCENE 2

Evening of the same day, very close to the time when Suzie will return. Sousette and Lucy are sitting on the armchair and couch. Agnes is helping Eva peel carrots and potatoes. They are filling up a big soup pot. All the women are dressed in their best traditional dress.

AGNES: There. That should about do it. Do you need any more help?

EVA: No, everything is done now. By the time this finishes cooking, Suzie will be here.

Agnes moves to the couch.

Here, Auntie. Here's another pot of tea. If you don't mind bringing it over, I'll bring the sugar and milk.

Agnes gives Eva a warm, affectionate, one-arm hug.

AGNES: I don't mind at all. You're a good little worker, you know. I'm proud of you.

Eva beams, and so does Sousette.

LUCY: I'm gettin' hungry.

Eva brings her a plate of cookies.

Here, Auntie, I don't want to spoil your appetite.

Agnes reaches over to grab a cookie, and Lucy moves the plate, allowing her to take only one.

AGNES: Yes, sir, that school never taught me a thing about being a mother. My babies—I had two of them—got swooped up by Social Services a long time ago, and I never saw them again. When I sobered up I tried to get them back, but it was tough. I remember them, though. I'll always remember their sweetness.

SOUSETTE: Maybe they'll come looking for you, Agnes. That's happening more and more nowadays . . . kids come looking for their parents. I wouldn't be surprised if they just showed up here one day.

LUCY: How would they even know where to find you, when you're always runnin' around all over the place?

AGNES: Well, if they came, Lucy, I expect you could tell them where I am.

SOUSETTE: Hey, do you remember how we used to get sick in that school?

AGNES: I remember getting sick and my neck swole up.

SOUSETTE: I don't know what that sickness was, but our neck used to get really big. It must have been hundreds of kids died of that sickness.

AGNES: One time, mine swole up so big I could hardly get my dress zipped up. I thought for sure I was gonna die. In fact, that's what Sister Rose told me, that I was gonna die. I was terrified to go to sleep, just in case I didn't wake up.

LUCY: Is that why you didn't die, because you wouldn't go to sleep?

AGNES: No, Lucy, I think it must have been your prayers that kept me alive. We spent so much time praying, some of those prayers must have been for me.

SOUSETTE: Did I ever tell you about that man I met in Creston when I was in my twenties? He asked me right out if I went to St. Eugene's. When I said yes, he asked if us kids used to get sick a lot out there. I told him about that sickness with our throats, and you know what he said?

Agnes and Lucy listen attentively.

He said he worked in a factory back then that supplied flour to that school. He was the one who sewed the sacks after they were filled. He was told to keep them St. Eugene sacks separate. Before he sewed them up he was to add a scoop of some white, powdery material to each of those sacks. You know, in those days you did what you were told and you didn't ask questions. One day his curiosity got the best of him and he asked what that powder was. The next day he was out of a job.

AGNES: Did he think there was a connection?

SOUSETTE: He seemed pretty sure that something wasn't right.

No medicine could cure that sickness once it took hold, at least no medicine that they would give us, Indians. They were always sending kids home in those bags. One time, one of the girls from here died, and they put her in a bag and slung her over the back of a horse; they had to tie her down so she wouldn't slide off. They made me and this other girl bring her back to the reserve. It took us all day to get home. We were just little girls then, and I remember we were riding through the bushes and we got into a fit of giggles because that other girl, she was watching Molly—that was the name of the girl who died—and she said, "Lookit Molly's head bouncing up and down. I wonder what she's thinking?" Gee, we musta been crazy just laughing at her like that. These old men came along from our village and they really bawled us out.

The women can't help but laugh at this memory. Suddenly the mood changes, becomes sombre. The lights dim. Sousette gets up and moves to the centre spotlight.

When my neck swole up, Sister sent me to the infirmary right away. When I got to the room I noticed there was another girl there. Her name was Sarah. I tried to talk to her, but she told me to pretend to be asleep or someone would come and bother us.

Sound of two girls.

SOUSETTE *as a girl giggling*: What're you doin' here, Sarah? Are you sick too?

SARAH: Be quiet. When he comes in, keep pretending you're asleep. Sometimes he just goes away.

SOUSETTE: I didn't know who she was talking about, but I pretended to be asleep until I got so tired I almost did fall asleep. Then I heard someone talking, a man's voice. I peeked out and I could see Father LeBlanc.

MAN'S VOICE: I come to visit you again, Sarah. Huh? Who's that in the other bed? What a nice surprise! It's Sousette. I think I'll visit her first. You don't mind, do you, Sarah?

SARAH: She's asleep. Maybe you shouldn't bother her. She's real sick.

SOUSETTE: He just ignored Sarah. I kept my eyes closed tight, hoping he'd go away. I felt the weight of him lean against the bed as he knelt down. At first I thought he was going to pray over me, so I just lay still. Then I felt his hand under the cover, touching me, down there. I tried to push his hand away—really, I did.

MAN'S VOICE: No, Sousette, you just lie still.

SOUSETTE: He kept feeling around, and I kept pushing his hand away. I started to cry because I didn't want him doing that, and he told me to be quiet. But I couldn't stop crying. Finally he got mad and left.

MAN'S VOICE: I'll go over to Sarah. She's not scared. She's not a crybaby like you.

SOUSETTE: I shut my eyes and covered my ears. I tried not to listen. It made me sick to hear that. And Sarah, she didn't say a word. Didn't make a sound. Didn't even cry. He must have done that to her a lot. Do you remember how she was always sick, always in the infirmary? She finally died too. That was probably a relief for her. She suffered so much.

The lights slowly fade. Eva goes to her mother and gently leads her back to her chair. She tucks her shawl around her shoulders. She is full of tenderness, and Sousette is grateful. Eva stays close to her mom.

After that time, I wouldn't lie in the infirmary when I got sick. I'd get a whole bunch of coats, and I'd pile them in the toilet, and I'd sleep there. It sure was cold, but I didn't care. It was better than going through that with Father.

I couldn't stop him forever, though. One day he just did what he wanted with me, and oh, how I've hated him. He did awful things to us. I sure used to hate getting sick. I still do. Whenever I get sick now, I gotta be half dead before I'll go to bed. Isn't that right, Eva?

Eva smiles and nods.

I used to think that I was the only one that happened to, so I took my anger out on everybody. Then other women began to speak up. Even my mother, before she died, said the same thing happened to her. And my Eva, I couldn't protect her. I was too busy running away.

Sousette is very sad. Eva reaches over to take her hand.

EVA: But you taught me how to keep Suzie safe and how to celebrate her becoming a woman.

AGNES: That's right. Suzie will turn the whole world right side up again, the way it was meant to be, and we'll celebrate.

EVA: When I hear your stories, I feel so lucky that you're one of the handful of girls who did survive. I can't imagine what my life would have been like without you. Even when you weren't there, you taught me something. You taught me how to get through tough times, and how to survive. All of you went through so much. Someone should write about it. They should make a movie about how you survived. I feel real proud sitting here among you. You're just like old warriors.

AGNES: Maybe you'll write that story, Eva. You sure must get an earful sitting around with us old ladies.

LUCY: I don't mind being called a warrior, Eva, but I'm really not that old.

AGNES: Oh, Lucy, you're falling apart like the rest of us.

EVA: Suzie's here. I'll help her with her things. She'll be so pleased that you're all here.

Sousette gets the dress and holds it tenderly. Agnes gets the cape and hands Lucy the moccasins and Mariah the hair ties. They all stand, waiting expectantly. Suzie bursts through the door wrapped in a beautiful Pendleton blanket. Her hair is wet; she has just come from a swim. Eva carries her bundle. Suzie hugs each of her grannies long and tenderly, starting with Sousette.

SUZIE: Thank you, Granny. I had the most beautiful time.

To Agnes:
I dreamed about you in the lodge. I saw you dancing on the mountain. I'm so happy you're here.

To Lucy:
Granny Lucy, you're always here for me, always.

To Mariah:
Granny Mariah, I prayed for you to be here, and Nupik'a brought you.

To Eva:
Mom, I need to get dressed right away. The People are waiting.

EVA: Let's hurry. We've got lots of celebrating to do. Agnes, help me with the blanket. Mom, you can bring the dress.

SUZIE: Next I'll need my moccasins.

LUCY: Come here, my girl. Put your feet up, I'll put them on for you.

Lucy puts on the moccasins while Suzie visits with the others.

SUZIE: Aunt Agnes, there was an eagle flying around the lodge every time I came out to take a swim.

AGNES: Now, that's a good sign. Did you see anything else?

SUZIE: I saw the two little deer that came to Great-grandpa when he was hunting for the hides for this dress. They came right inside the lodge, and they talked to me.

SOUSETTE: What did they say?

SUZIE: That I was going to have a long life, and that my daughter will some day wear this dress.

AGNES: Another good sign. Lucy, hurry up. Can't you see? Let me help you.

LUCY: Get away. The moccasins are mine. I'm just about done.

Lucy finishes. Suzie stands up so Agnes can put the cape on.

AGNES: Now, you gotta bend over 'cause you're too tall for me.

SUSIE: Oh, Granny, what a beautiful cape.

AGNES: It's just perfect for you. Mariah will do your hair. It's still wet so it will be easier.

Eva moves a chair over for Suzie to sit, and Mariah begins to braid her hair.

EVA: It's so short, Mariah. She just got it cut. You might have to struggle with it.

MARIAH: It'll be fine. Bring me some water in case I need to wet it.

SOUSETTE: Suzie, while Mariah is doing your hair, I'm going to explain to you what will happen at your feast.

Everyone is waiting for you. Nothing will begin until you get there. Your mom and your Granny Agnes will cover you with the blanket again. The blanket is a gift from your great-granny Marceline. We'll surround you when you come in to the hall, and the aunties who helped you will lead the way, and some will fall behind. There's an arbour built of spruce and cedar in the middle of the hall. All the medicine people will sit inside this arbour.

We'll lead you to the very centre and we'll remove the blanket and place it in a spot set aside for you to sit. There will be an honour song and a special prayer, which we'll all stand for. When this is done, all the women will make the victory call. Do you remember how that's done? Agnes will show us.

Agnes makes the victory call. All the women join in, laughing.

When you sit down, the chief will come with all the dignitaries to congratulate you. You'll invite them to sit with you to eat, and you'll gift them for being there to witness this great day.

SUZIE: How will I know what to give them?

SOUSETTE: We'll stay around you all the time. We'll help you to know who gets what and how things will happen. We are there, just like old buffaloes surrounding the young, to protect you.

LUCY: Oh, now I'm an old buffalo.

AGNES: Well, there are worse things, Lucy.

The women laugh.

SOUSETTE: We'd better get going.

Eva and Agnes wrap Suzie in the blanket. Lucy carries her bundle. Mariah brings the medicine, and Eva trails behind with the pot of soup. As they leave, an honour song begins. The room darkens behind them. Exit to blackout.

SONG OF THE CIRCLE

AUTHOR'S NOTE

Song of the Circle is a story about abuse. It is the story of James and Mary and the baby they are trying to raise beneath the shadow of their haunted pasts. Their future becomes only a reflection of their painful childhood memories. James seeks relief by hanging out with his buddies and drinking, while Mary is left alone with the baby and the memory of her mother's tragic death, which she lives and relives until she too becomes a victim of her own circumstance.

James's grandmother, Anmah, too is haunted by a terrible secret that she has kept hidden for seventy-five years. "We never told anyone," she said, "what difference would it make now for me to tell?" And it is through the telling of this secret that the healing begins. The strength emerges in the form of the grandmother's healing song and the knowledge she carries—the answers she holds for the future generations to come.

Song of the Circle is a story about abuse, yet it is also a story about healing. *Song of the Circle* depicts purification; the time that we,

Native people, are in right now, as we strive and search for healing and spiritual growth. The hope is that we start with this small circle of healing, and from this circle other circles will grow and continue to grow, until it stretches across this entire continent and beyond so that all our people are joined together in strength, dignity, and health.

CHARACTERS

Mary, a young woman in her late teens or early twenties
James, a young man in his late teens or early twenties
Anmah, an Elder and James's grandmother
Baby or Sherida, an infant, Mary and James's daughter
Beatrice, Mary's mother
Roy, Mary's father

SCENE 1

The scene opens on a small rundown shack beside the railroad tracks, at the edge of a small interior town.

The story begins with the sound of an old truck approaching from a distance. It is very noisy as it approaches and screeches to a halt. Doors open and slam shut. A young man, James, walks towards the house, balancing a box of Pampers between two bulging paper sacks of groceries. He is followed by a young girl, Mary, who continues to scold him all the way into the house. She carries an infant and a plastic bag bulging with baby things. Grandmother follows slowly behind them carrying her own stuff in her personal bundles and bags. They all go into the house and in a few minutes the young man, James, emerges and sits on the porch. Mary comes out after him and attempts to coax him out of his moodiness.

MARY: James, your grandmother was just trying to get you to slow down. You know you make her nervous when you drive so fast.

JAMES: I don't want to talk about it! How long is she gonna stay here? When is she going home?

MARY: She's just staying until baby gets well. James, why can't you be nice to her? She's always helping us out. She only came because I asked her to. I wouldn't have to ask if you stayed home and helped me.

JAMES: Oh yeah, now it's my fault that the baby's sick.

MARY: James, I didn't say that. I only meant . . .

JAMES: Why is it everytime I come home it's always something?

MARY: James . . . James . . . I don't want to fight with you. I'm just glad you're home. I just want us to have a nice time. I want to cook us a nice supper tonight and have us all together, like a family.

JAMES: I'm not gonna be here.

MARY: James, you just got back!

JAMES: Well, I'm going out again. It's too crowded here for me.

MARY: You just want to go drinking. That's all you ever want to do, drink and hang out with your friends. You may as well not even have a family!

JAMES: Well, I've never said I wanted one, did I?

MARY: You don't mean that, James. I should just go away. I should take my baby and leave you and see how you like being alone.

Grandmother comes out of the house carrying her bags and her bundles. She struggles past the couple in the direction of the forest and then she turns back to speak to James.

GRANDMOTHER: You should be careful what you wish for. Do you think the air doesn't have ears?

JAMES: Don't talk to me about all that mumbo jumbo stuff. You know I don't believe that.

GRANDMOTHER: James, I am talking now. You believed in something once. I hope that you find what it is that you lost, for Mary and for yourself, but most of all I wish for that child in there. If I had you when you were a baby things might be different. *(James turns from her.)* I can't talk to you when you're like this, but you're always like this lately. You should go out there *(points towards the mountains)* where there is nothing but you and the sky and the animals. You could find what it is you lost. Take care of yourself. You know what to do. Everything is here. You just have to make up your mind and do it.

JAMES: Granny, I can't listen to this stuff now. I'm tired *(buries his head in his arms)* and sick.

GRANDMOTHER: This is the time to listen, James. This is the time when you need them the most, you know. *(She stoops and begins to gather up her bundles.)* But I'm tired too. I'm very tired. *(Begins to walk away, Mary jumps up and goes after her.)*

MARY: Granny, you don't have to go. He didn't mean anything by what he said.

GRANDMOTHER: I have to go, Mary. I need to go sleep in my own bed, and anyway, he's home now. You take care of that baby. Just keep her warm. She'll be okay. *(She continues walking, mumbling half to herself, half to Mary.)* There's nobody to feed my chickens. They'll be hungry by now, and my dogs, poor Hippie, and oh oh, they're gonna be wonderin' where I am. Sure hope they don't eat my chickens.

Mary returns to the porch and sits near James.

MARY: You should have at least offered her a ride home. *(She speaks very quietly without reproach.)*

James slides his arm around her without looking at her. He doesn't want her to see the shame and misery that he feels. Mary is momentarily surprised by this act of tenderness and tries to catch a glimpse of what he is thinking.

JAMES: She'll be alright . . . she'll be alright.

Lights fade to blackout.

SCENE 2

The scene opens on the house. It is now morning. The story begins with the sounds of a radio being turned on and switched around until it settles on a tune by Waylon Jennings called "Good Hearted Woman." This is followed by a new report of doom and gloom in Indian country.

Mary comes out of the house and settles down on the porch step. She is a sad, wistful girl, who appears apprehensive while at the same time she struggles to give the outward appearance that she is happy.

Noises persist from the house: the unmistakeable sound of a chair scraping back on the floor, heavy footsteps, the radio being switched off, dumped in the sink. Mary winces, glances back towards where the noise is coming from, shrugs her shoulders, and goes back to enjoying the sunshine.

When James comes out of the house, she is unaware at first that he is there. Suddenly she turns and notices him. He visibly withdraws. His shoulders stiffen, and his face becomes expressionless.

MARY: Oh . . . hi. How was your breakfast?

JAMES: It was alright—friggin toast was burnt. Again.

MARY: It's a nice day today. Do you remember when we used to go down to the lake, just you and me, and we'd walk, sometimes for hours, and talk about life? Do you remember that, James? Well,

I was thinking baby's old enough now. Maybe we could go down to the lake like we used to.

JAMES: Don't think anymore, those days are gone! I need a clean shirt.

MARY: I started soaking them this morning, but if I hang them out now, they'll be ready by noon.

JAMES: Well, I don't need it at noon. I need it now! I told you last night I need a clean shirt this morning.

MARY: You didn't tell me anything. You just came home and passed out.

JAMES: Don't tell me I didn't tell you. I remember telling you I have an interview today and I needed some clean clothes.

MARY: You have an interview? That's great! Maybe today is the day you're going to get it!

JAMES: Yeah, you'd like that, wouldn't you? Then you'd finally have yourself a supporting husband, instead of one you have to support.

MARY: James, I didn't mean it like that.

JAMES: Yeah, right.

MARY: James, we need to talk.

JAMES: I don't want to talk anymore. I'm tired of talking. I've got things to do, interviews to go to. I don't have time to talk.

MARY: Yeah, right. Maybe they're interviewing down at the bar. Is that where you've been putting in your application?

JAMES: What do you mean by that? What are you trying to tell me?

MARY: Just forget it.

JAMES: No, I'm not going to forget it. Everytime I come home you're always naggin' at me about somethin'.

MARY: When you do come home?

JAMES: Don't get sassy with me.

MARY: Last night when you phoned, you said you were at the American Bar and that you were coming right home. Well, when you didn't come, I went over there looking for you, and everyone I talked to said you hadn't been there all night. James, where were you?

JAMES: You went down to the American? I told you never to go into that bar. What the hell were you doing there?

MARY: I want to know where you spend your time. Who are you spending it with while I sit at home every night and wait for you. Who were you with?

JAMES: It's none of your business who I was with. I told you never to go to those bars.

MARY: James, are you cheating on me?

JAMES: Where do you get these crazy ideas? It's from sitting around watching those silly soap operas all day, isn't it?

MARY: Just tell me, is there someone else?

JAMES: Maybe there just is! It's better than coming home to you and your nagging, and that crying every night.

Mary sinks to the porch step, visibly wounded, and starts to cry. Her misery is very visible.

JAMES: Mary, there's no one. There's nothing wrong. Mary?

MARY: Get away from me. Don't touch me.

The baby starts to cry. Mary gets up and moves towards the door, James is turned away from her. She spots the bucket of shirts and impulsively kicks the bucket over off the porch.

MARY: There are your clean shirts!

She exits into the house. James exits and the truck can be heard screeching away.

SCENE 3

Mary comes out of house carrying the baby and a bottle, rocking her and shushing her. She is still very sad, hurting at the thought of James cheating on her.

MARY: It's the loneliness that I fear the most. That's why I can't leave. At least with James and you, baby girl, I'm not completely alone. But, I might as well be. The loneliness, it creeps up all around me, especially at night. It's so thick I can feel it, like it's smothering me. It's like a disease. But why won't it kill me? Where did it come from? I wonder, was I born with it? Inherited from my mother? Oh my poor baby girl. Don't you ever grow up to be like me. I'll always remember Momma, on hot summer nights, sitting on the steps of the house, watching the cars go by on the highway like watching her life slip away. Waiting. Always waiting for Dad to come home. Oh yes, I remember Dad. He always came home angry, but he wasn't always like that, but he never spoke to her either. I was just a kid when Momma finally left for good. I guess she just got tired of waiting; how she struggled and struggled to keep us together, to feed us, clothes us, to protect us. Worry lines on her face. Welfare lines. Shame and ALWAYS, ALWAYS that loneliness. I'd lie and watch her from my bed at night, sitting there at the kitchen table alone with her bottle, staring out the window. Waiting, waiting for the darkness to begin. All the while I'd be praying, hoping that this was the night that she'd just go on to bed when it got dark. But then she'd get up and bring the mirror. It was just a broken piece of glass. She'd balance it between two books and the sugar canister. Then she'd stare into it for a long time, touching her face here and there, touching the lines. Then she would comb her hair. She had such long beautiful hair, and she'd put on the lipstick from the one good tube that she never allowed Katrine and I to play with. Oh God. Her eyes, she had such sad lonely eyes. I've tried to forget them, but sometimes, sometimes I catch glimpses of those same DESPERATE GRIEVING EYES when I'm pacing around the house WAITING ... WAITING for James to come home. I'd try not to let him see them. I'd close them, try to turn away. "YOU STOP LOOKING AT ME LIKE THAT," he'd say. She always came to the doorway before she left, and I'd lie there with my eyes tightly shut so she wouldn't know I was awake. As soon as the door closed, I'd jump outta bed and run over to the window to watch her, looking so alone on that dark street. I knew she was heading up to the bar. I wanted to stop her. I had to stop her. I tried but ... "Momma ... don't go. Please stay home. Please."

As Mary speaks, Beatrice enters and mimes the words that Mary speaks.

Mary is so overwhelmed at the end of her speech that she forgets the baby she is holding in her arms. It is baby's cries that force her back to reality. She exits into the house while trying to quiet the child.

MARY: Stop crying, shush, oh ... why are you crying all the time?

SCENE 4

It is early evening. Once again the radio is on, and there is more news predicting doom and gloom in Indian country. Mary turns the radio off, then emerges from the house. She circles the yard, looks down the road to see if James is coming yet, glances at her watch, then sits down on the porch. Soon a truck is heard approaching and Mary waits expectantly for James to emerge. When he does appear, it is obvious he has been drinking, but he is not drunk. He starts out in

*a jovial, playful mood and Mary tries to humour him, but she has
played this scene too many times before. Suddenly he is angry, at
first only verbally attacking her. Then physically he becomes abusive.
Mary never fights back. In her memory, when these scenes begin, she
always visualizes the fights between her mom and dad, and she easily
identifies with the victim, her mother.*

JAMES: Well, look who's here. Are you waiting up for me? Isn't
that sweet. C'mere, give me a kiss.

MARY: James, stop it. James, your breath stinks.

JAMES: Well, you never usta mind before.

James takes another swig from a mickey that he has stashed in his pocket.

WHAT's the matter with you, you mad at me?

MARY: No, no, I've been waiting for you.

JAMES: Well c'mere. So, what's happening on *Edge of the Night*?
Tell me, who's cheating on who? And what's that other one . . . oh
yes, *All My Children*. Whose husband lost their job today?

MARY: James, you're talking nonsense.

JAMES: Naahh, c'mon. I really wanna know.

MARY: I washed and pressed your shirts so they're all ready
for tomorrow.

JAMES: So, what's happening tomorrow?

MARY: Well, I thought . . . maybe . . . if you got that job.

JAMES: That's the good news I got for you. Darn. I wanted it to be
a surprise.

MARY: James, I'm so happy for you. You did get the job.

JAMES: No, I didn't. That's the good news. Now you can have me all to yourself, all day . . . everyday . . . for the rest of your life.

MARY: James, I'm sorry.

JAMES: What's there to be sorry about, Mary? I thought that would make ya happy. You're always complainin' I'm never home. Well, I'll be home all the time now.

MARY: I was talking to Darlene today. She said her husband went down to put in an application at that new construction site. She thinks they're still hiring.

JAMES: Well, good for Darlene's husband.

MARY: I made you some supper. I'll go in and heat it up.

JAMES: You're not leaving me. Sit down.

MARY: James, the neighbours. Let's go inside. C'mon.

JAMES: I don't care about the neighbours.

MARY: James, let's just go and talk inside. Please.

JAMES: I don't care about nobody. I don't care about the friggin' neighbours.

I don't care about you. I don't . . .

MARY: I hate it when you're drunk. You remind me of my father!

Roy and Beatrice appear from offstage and their interaction plays out to the side of Mary and James.

ROY: So you hate me, do you?

BEATRICE: No, I only hate you when you're drunk.

JAMES: Come on, I'm not drunk.

MARY: Just leave me alone!

JAMES: You're my wife, c'mon, dance with me.

MARY: No, stop it, James. You're going to wake the baby!

ROY: I don't care about the kids. Wake them all up.

BEATRICE: Mary's been sick all day. I just got her to sleep.

JAMES: Give me a kiss. You're my wife. You have to give me a kiss.

BEATRICE: Stop it, Roy, Get away from me. Why don't you just go to bed?

MARY: Stop it! James, stop it!

JAMES/ROY: Don't you go ordering me around.

MARY/BEATRICE: You're scaring the baby. Why don't you just go away?

Mary runs into the house, pursued by James, as Beatrice exits the stage, pursued by Roy. The fighting continues inside the house. The baby is crying loudly, and in the background the sounds of other children crying. Suddenly James bursts from the house. He is distraught and his only thought is to get far away as quickly as he can. He misses the step on the porch and falls flat on his face. He jumps up and continues running towards the woods. Suddenly, the voice of the grandmother can be heard above a rise in the wind. On a high note that is struck, she whispers, "James." The baby stops crying, and except for tiny whimpers the set becomes silent.

SCENE 5: JAMES/GRANDMOTHER

The scene opens with the shadowy figure of James huddled up against a tree stump. An anguished cry is heard, coinciding with the piercing sound of a Loon, and the flutter of startled birds taking flight.

JAMES: Oh God, oh God. What have I done? Oh Mary, I'm so sorry, I didn't mean it. You just stand there and let me hurt you like that. What am I gonna do? I know you're gonna leave me. I can't live without you, Mary. You're all I've got. Mary, please say you'll forgive me.

But she never says nothing. She just lays there, all broken up, lookin' at me with those eyes. TALK TO ME MARY. She won't even move. She just lays there staring like . . . like she's dead.

The boy breaks down sobbing to himself, then he cries out again, and again the piercing, mournful sound of the Loon can be heard echoing off the lake.

JAMES: She told me she was gonna leave me and all I could think of was to make her stay. I wanted to beg her, but I couldn't even say it. All I could do was hit her. I was just trying to make her stop. What's the use of living? I don't wanna live anymore.

James has sunk way down and is so deep into his misery that the clear cutting sound of the Loon echoing off the lake startles him, and he sits bolt upright. He knows his granny is close by. He can feel her, visualizes her running through the woods searching for him, and with his last bit of strength, he calls out to her.

JAMES: Granny. . . . Na aah! Na aah! I'm here.

The grandmother appears and runs towards him. Then she stops, shocked by his appearance and the depth of his despair. She gathers her strength calling on the spirits for help. Then she kneels close to him and touches him, coaxing him back to the living. All she knows is that she heard him say those words "I want to die. I don't want to live anymore," and she knows he means it.

JAMES: I kept hitting her and hitting her. I wouldn't stop, even when she fell. Why? I love Mary. Why do I hurt her like that? She's like my mom. She's so much like my mom. I remember her before she went away. I'll always remember her. She never used to fight back either.

By this time the grandmother has prepared herself, and she has
prepared a smudge and medicine, protection for her and her
grandson. She wants him to keep talking. She encourages him with
little gestures, little phrases in Indian, as she moves the healing smoke
all around, purifying him so the spirits can help him.

JAMES: My mom and dad, that's all I remember about them—his
angry eyes and my mom never fighting back. Then, they'd both
leave. First, she would go. I'd watch her tiptoeing around the house.
After he'd pass out, stuffing things into a paper bag, sneaking out
the door. I'd want to stop her. I'd want to go after her and beg her
not to go, beg her to take me with her, but I couldn't. Then HE'D
wake up and look in all the rooms for her, and pretty soon he'd
go too. They'd leave us kids there crying, and I'd be scared. And
then . . . and then . . . you'd come, Granny, and take me home with
you until she came back. Then I can't even remember when. She
NEVER came back. Mary's just like her. She's gonna leave me too,
and she's never gonna come back. I KNOW SHE KILLED DAD.
She killed him because he couldn't live without her. How could she
do that??? How could she go away and just never come back?

GRANDMOTHER: James, Mary is NOT YOUR MOTHER. She's
young and mixed up, just like you, but she is not your mother. You
were a young boy, *nistal*, when your mother left you. And I tried to
make up for that, but I know I never could. I should have kept you
all together. I should never have let your brothers and sisters go.
You lost too much. (*Grandmother pauses to think carefully about*
what it is she must say.) I should have made you talk about it, way
before this, James. We should have talked about it. When I came
and took you, you were ten years old, but you were still like a
newborn baby. You didn't know nothing but how to be afraid. You
were dirty, your clothes were dirty and your body was so skinny
because nobody ever fed you. And still you were scared to come
with me. How much of that do you remember, James? (*As she*
speaks, James continues to sob quietly, with periodic outbursts of anger

and frustration.) And all this time, we've pretended it didn't even happen. I know that was wrong. (*Pauses. She needs time to think about what she is saying.*) Your life didn't begin when you were ten. It began before you took your first breath, and there was nobody to care for you. It wasn't their fault either.

Once again the grandmother stops to think about what she must say.

Do you know where you come from, James? Do you know who you are? Did you know that your great-great-grandfather was Nisqutam? Do you know who he was? Everyone, even from far away, they knew him. He was a great man. Who remembers him today? That's who you come from, James. And your Utxmix Nuhkinka. If it was not for her, we would not have this land that we have here today.

With great tenderness, she bends to lift James's face up toward the sky, and she wipes it gently with a rag and some rose water from her bag. For too long, she has held many secrets in her heart, and she knows now it will take strong medicine to make her grandson want to heal. Quietly, she puts the articles back in her bag and moves away from him.

All the forest sounds are now silent. Expectant. Waiting for the grandmother to begin. James is startled by the silence and thinks for a moment that his grandmother may have left him. He raises his head and looks around, and then sees her sitting not far away on a stump. She doesn't look at him, but the instant that she speaks James feel her rage emanating from her past.

GRANDMOTHER: Aiyee Nupika, I have grandchildren and great-grandchildren and I thought I'd gone through the worst of it, but this, THIS (*indicates James*) is harder than anything I've ever done. What is happening Nupika? Where is the laughter for MY grandchildren, and MY great-grandchildren? I am an old woman waiting to die and I remember this pain, when it first came, like it was yesterday. I was a young girl up in the mountains and, at that time, I knew nothing but love and happiness. Then the priest came and took me away and I never knew that kind of happiness again. It was only a dream. I thought I dreamed being happy. After that I thought my grandparents and my mom and dad didn't want me. That's why they sent me away. We never talked about it, but all us kids, I know that's what we thought. We didn't know what we were doing so wrong.

Extremely bitter and scornful.

They taught us so much. Teaching. Teaching. Teaching, everyday. How to work hard, how to pray—to their God. How to sew and bake bread. AND FOR ALL THAT THEY TAUGHT US, DO YOU KNOW HOW THEY MADE US PAY? (*She directs this comment to James and laughs bitterly.*) With our language. They took our language and the Nupikas. They took them away too, and our land. All this land that used to be ours, that fed us, and clothed us, and gave us all the love we ever needed. They took that too, so we could learn to cook and pray IN ENGLISH, but they never taught us how to care for our babies.

James has never seen his grandmother so incensed. It almost frightens him to see her so worked up. He starts to rise to go to her, but she stands and with a slight movement she motions him away. The sounds of the birds and forest creatures begin again. The Loon loud and shrill, breaks the silence, as she begins to speak again.

GRANDMOTHER: I became a woman in that school, before I knew what being a woman was, and it made me shamed. I never forget that. In my mind I was still a girl, but my body was becoming like a woman's. And one night he came for me in the dorm and I had to go with him. I knew he would come someday. The older girls used to talk about him. We never told anyone. Most of them are dead now and I'm an old woman. What difference would it make now for me to tell?

Why? Why? Why? All these years I've asked myself why? Why did Nupika let that happen TO ME?? When I left school I was no longer young. I felt all used up and I hate everybody for it. I was so ashamed. I married a man who didn't care for me, and I had children and I never knew how to care for them. I don't even remember their childhoods, because I was trying to forget.

Now her attention has turned back to James. She is spent. The storm replaced by a great sadness.

It took your father's death to finally wake me up. I loved your father, I loved all my children, but I never showed them. I never knew how to love them. It broke my heart when your father took his life. I found him there, you know. I touched his lifeless body and I remembered every moment we spent together—from that first time he lay in my arms, a tiny baby boy that I wanted so desperately to love. When he died, part of me died too. Then you came into my life. The first time you let me hold you close inside my arms, something came back to life inside. Nupika gave me a second chance, and I've tried to give you all the love that I never gave my own children. More than anything in the whole world, all I ever wanted was for you to be happy.

Now the grandmother and James move close to one another. It is as though a great wall has been torn down between them and they are hungry to touch and be close. She has opened up a door inside him and all the fear, pain, and anguish comes pouring out. All that he has kept hidden and locked inside is set free by this one gift that his grandmother has given him the gift of truth that he has waited so long to hear.

JAMES: I've always listened to you, Granny. I've always heard and took everything you've said close to my heart, but I've never known what to do with it, until now. All these things you tell me, I've wanted to ask, but I've been afraid. I've never let anyone in here, Granny (*indicates his heart*), and it's been so lonely.

GRANDMOTHER: I know . . . I know, James.

JAMES: I want to know about my dad and my mom. I want to know everything that happened. There were times I've struggled trying to remember what my mom looked like.

When I was little, I used to think if only I could remember what she looks like, maybe she would come back, but she's never going to come back, is she, Granny?

GRANDMOTHER: I don't know, James. That is something only the Nupikas could tell you, but I do know she loved you. She didn't go away because she didn't love you. It was so much more than that. They were such hard times. She used to tell me, "If anything happens to me, Anmah, will you take care of my boy?" I have pictures of her and your dad, James, locked away in my trunk. Some afternoon, real soon, you come over to the house and I'll show them to you and we'll talk. I'll tell you everything you want to know.

JAMES: I'd like that. Yeah, I'd really like that. (*James is suddenly serious.*) I'm scared, Granny. I'm scared for Mary and for what is going to happen now. I don't know if I could stand being alone if she goes. I feel as though I've been in a nightmare for so long, and that I've woken up, but now I've discovered that the nightmare is real and I'm afraid of what will happen next.

GRANDMOTHER: James, YOU COULD NEVER BE ALONE, and if what happened today has the power to wake you up, then that is all the power and strength you need for now to do what you have to do. Whatever happens with Mary, it will only be the beginning for both of you. THE NAPIKAS HAVE COME BACK, JAMES. They've been back for a long time, waiting for us to wake up. Whatever will happen from now on, it will be in the HANDS OF THE NAPIKAS, and you must trust that that is the way of our grandfathers.

Look around you, my grandson. Look all around you. Everything you see here is yours. All these beautiful gifts that the Creator has given to you. Listen to the Loon, my grandson. That is your spirit. Listen to the trees and to the little animals. They all have messages for you. Listen to them, James. Don't just listen with your ears. Listen with your heart. Listen in between all the things that you hear. Listen with every part of you. ALL THAT PAIN that you feel inside there. TALK TO THE GREAT SPIRITS. ASK THEM to come and walk with you. TALK WITH THEM. Sing with them. SING WITH EVERYTHING YOU HAVE INSIDE YOU. You'll see THAT THERE IS NOTHING THAT THE NAPIĶAS CANNOT DO.

As the grandmother speaks all the sounds of nature join in to help her give life back to her grandson. She doctors James in the ancient way that she knew so well. She asked all the bad spirits to leave, pushing them out of him with her breath and her gentle hands. She talks to the spirits in her own language, so they will be near to help her grandson. When she is done she helps James to his feet. He is shaky, weak, but his spirit is strong and wanting to come out.

JAMES: Thank you, Granny, and (*James looks around him*) thank you, Nupiĸa. I feel strong, Granny, but at the same time my body feels strange and I have so much in my head right now. I think I need to be alone for a while, to walk and think about what you have said here today. Can you go to Mary, Granny? It is only you and the Nupiĸas that can help her. I know that now. And my baby girl, will you see that they're both okay? Tell them, tell them I'll be back soon. I'll be okay, Granny, I promise you.

As James goes to leave, the grandmother calls him back to give him one last message.

GRANDMOTHER: Grandson, use all the gifts that the creator has given TO YOU, James. Soon you will see that life is for living. And YOU, James, YOU are part of the circle.

James walks off into the woods and the grandmother silently waits until he is out of sight. Then she thanks the spirits. They are all old friends to her and she calls out to them by name. She asks them to stay close to her grandson, because he is like a newborn baby now. Watch over him so that no harm comes to him. The grandmother, when she is alone, speaks to the spirits in her Indian language.

SCENE 6

Slowly, the grandmother makes her way over to the house, she is very weary. She is old and it has taken almost all her strength to help James. Then she hears the baby, crying in the house. She rushes over and into the house, and as the sounds of her comforting and tending to the baby are heard, the cries become less frantic and eventually stop.

Mary comes out of the house with her suitcase and sets it down. Slowly and with great pain she sits down on the step and starts to cry. After she has finished tending to the baby, the grandmother comforts Mary like she is a baby too, saying soothing words in Indian.

MARY: I want to leave but I can't. I'm so afraid. What am I going to do with my baby all by myself? I can't leave. I can't leave... Momma here.

GRANDMOTHER: Mary, your mother's dead. Mary, let her go. It is your life that you must think of now.

MARY: I remember. I remember the last time I saw her. It was nighttime, like it is now. She was getting ready to go out. Oh, I can't think of it now. I musn't think of it now.

GRANDMOTHER: Talk about it, Mary. If you talk about it, it will stop hurting so much. You keep hanging onto it. Don't hold it in there any longer. Mary, Mary—let it go. (*End sentence in Indian.*)

By her words and understanding, the old lady has now given Mary permission to talk about that which she has always been afraid to even think about, and for Mary, it is like a torrent being released, as it all comes pouring out of her, all the guilt that she has held inside her for so long.

MARY: It was dark, and I didn't want Momma to go out that night. I was scared. All day I was scared, but I knew she always went out on the weekends. She always did but, just this once, I kept begging her to stay with us. All afternoon, I kept asking her until she got angry with me. Momma never got angry with me, but that day I couldn't leave her alone, and she yelled at me to stop whining around. I stood by the window all that night waiting for her. Katrine wanted to wait up with me too, but I kept picking on her until I made her cry and then she went to bed. It was so cold. I had the blanket wrapped around me and I kept staring down at the road. I couldn't see her. I couldn't see anything, but I kept thinking I did. I would stare and stare into the darkness, hoping she was there. Then I saw a movement up the tracks, and at that same time I heard a train coming. It was Momma walking on the tracks. She kept slipping off the rail and she'd get back upon it again. I kept thinking Momma, don't play on the tracks. Then I realized she couldn't hear the train. I don't know why she couldn't hear it. It was so loud. I started screaming at her: "Momma . . . Momma . . . the train . . . Momma . . . look behind you, Momma . . . the train" and then I couldn't see her anymore. I don't remember running down to the tracks but I didn't have any shoes on and I remember the cold. There were men running from the train. They were trying to stop me, but I had to help my momma. They wouldn't let me go to her. Oh Momma . . . Momma . . . why couldn't you take care of yourself? I couldn't take care of us all the time.

GRANDMOTHER: Mary, it wasn't your fault. You did the best that you could but you were only a child. (*Soothes her until she is calm.*) How many years have you held on to that memory? How it must have tortured you, yet you never cried. You never called for help, but how would you know? You are so young. You should have never stayed in this house. So many times I wondered why James never took you away from here. You could have gone to live at the village. It would have been good for you to be around people.

MARY: He used to ask me to move down there but I wouldn't. I couldn't leave. I felt closer to Momma here. I felt I had to stay near her. I don't understand where she went. What happens to people who die like that? I couldn't bear to think of her alone somewhere and suffering. Momma never liked to be alone. Maybe just being here for her I could help. I could . . .

GRANDMOTHER: Mary, what about your life? Your life now, and the life of that child who needs you? Your mother is on a different road now and she too has a journey that she must complete. She needs to travel on to that place where she can rest. She has finished her time here, but she'll always be there for you. Pray for her, Mary. Pray to her, for your happiness. She would want that. But you have to let her go. You must. I see things in this house, Mary. There is so much that you must do. All your mother's personal things that you have stored in those boxes. You can't hang on to them, Mary. They belong to your mother. Just keep one or two things, special things to pass on to your daughter. But the rest of it has to go. Oh, but you don't know. No one has ever told you. Let me help you, Mary. Let me help you to let her go.

The old grandmother sits quietly for a while.

Look at that blue sky. We are going to have a good summer. We are going to be happy. (*She looks at Mary as she says this, and smiles.*) Rosebushes, wild rosebushes . . . they must grow where you come from, somewhere down by a river. Here, I'll show you what the branches look like.

Grandmother slowly gets up and looks around where she put her bag, mumbling to herself.

GRANDMOTHER: Where are you ? Now, where is that bag? Under here. Heyyy, what are you doing under there? Ah yes, here it is. Have you seen these before? You must have seen them.

MARY: They have pink flowers? With big petals that fall off when they die? I saw a lot of them down there by the lake, with the little thorns on them. They're really sharp, aren't they?

GRANDMOTHER: Mmmmhmmm, yeah, that's the ones. You take those and you put them in with your other stuff. I could do that for you, if you want. And you boil some up and wash everything down. You too. You bathe in it. I'll show you. I'll tell you how. We'll make it better. You'll see.

MARY: I want things to get better. I really do. I want so much for my baby. Sometimes, I look at her, and she is so beautiful. And I get so afraid that she'll grow up like me. I don't want that for her. I want it to be different. James and I, we're no good together. It seems like we can never stop fighting. We can't even think of anything good about each other anymore. I've been thinking. I've been thinking for a long time that I should take my baby home, and make a good life for her. I've been phoning home. I've been talking to my dad.

She says this last line with determination, but is also a little afraid about what the grandmother will think.

GRANDMOTHER: (*indicates that she is pleased*) Heyyy . . . this is good, Mary. How is Roy doing?

MARY: Well, he's not drinking anymore, not for two years, he says.

GRANDMOTHER: Sometimes, Mary, it is only your family that can give you the strength. You need to go on, no matter what has happened between you.

MARY: I had a hard time talking to him at first. I think I've always been a little afraid of him, but he's trying so hard. I can tell. He told me all about how it was to quit drinking. It was pretty hard for him. He sounds different now. He talks to me about things he's never talked about to me before. It's getting easier and easier to talk to him. He wants me to come home. He's been working on our house for the last year. You know my dad used to be a carpenter. He used to make some really beautiful things. He wants to see baby. He said he'd never thought about being a grandfather. And that it felt good to him. I've been so lonely. I don't know about this, but I called him early this morning and I asked him to come get me and baby. He said he'd drive all day and be here by tonight. I'm afraid. I don't know if I can go?

GRANDMOTHER: Mary, you know in your heart what is right for you and your baby. Listen to your heart. You do what you believe is right, and don't worry about what anyone else may think about it. Don't worry about James. He's got lots of work to do and I think he's ready to begin. He's not gonna be alone, you know. He's got brothers and sisters he hasn't spoken to in years, and he'll always have me. I'm not going anywhere for a long time.

MARY: Well, I don't know if I could just leave him. I keep thinking if I stay just a little longer, things will get better, but they never do. I HATE IT WHEN HE HITS ME. Hate to see myself like this. I WANT IT TO STOP.

GRANDMOTHER: Heyyy Mary, you have a strong voice. You should speak that strongly all the time. You tell him what you want and how you would like it to be. I know my grandson, he'd listen to you. You could go or you could stay. You have many choices, but they are your choices, Mary. I think I see James coming now. Isn't that him way over there? You know if your dad's gonna get here pretty soon? I think I'll put on a pot of meat and start getting that baby ready for a long trip. You sit right here and you wait for James. You talk to him now.

MARY: But what will I tell him? What if he's still angry? He'll be really mad when he sees I'm leaving!

Mary in a panic makes a hurried attempt to hide the suitcase behind the chair.

For the first time the granny's laughter fills up the space around them. It is a kind laugh though, a gentle sound of one who understands Mary's turmoil so well. Then she is suddenly very serious.

GRANDMOTHER: You know, Mary, that somewhere inside there, there is a STRONG WOMAN who has the spirit of a WARRIOR. Now is the time for her to come out, Mary. Put your woman spirit away and let your WARRIOR SPIRIT come out, and you'll know what to say. The words will come. You won't be afraid.

Mary sits on the porch, then gets up and walks around. She is anxious and nervous. She pulls the suitcase out, then pushes it behind the chair again. James walks slowly to the house. He is cautious and nervous too.

JAMES: Hi (*he winces at the sight of the bruises on her face*). Are you okay? I'm sorry. I'm really sorry, Mary. (*She turns away from him.*) I don't blame you if you don't believe me. (*He sees her suitcase behind the chair.*) I knew you would leave. I hoped we could talk and I could make you believe that things would change and that we could go on and pretend that none of this ever happened. Or maybe I could promise you that it would never happen again and you would believe me. But it's too late for that now, isn't it?

MARY: I know what I am doing is right, James. What happened tonight must never happen again. Our baby shouldn't have to grow up watching that kind of thing. I love her too much for that.

JAMES: I love her too, Mary. I've never realized how much until today. I keep wanting to promise you that it will never happen again.

MARY: I wouldn't believe you, James. NO! I couldn't believe you. There is too much work for us to do. I'M going to change, James, and then I'll know it will never happen again. I AM going away, so I can begin to make a life for myself, and for our child. A HAPPY LIFE. James, if you are serious about what you are saying, you'll catch up to us someday, and THEN maybe. I don't know, we'll have to just wait and see what happens

James moves to touch her to make some kind of physical contact.

MARY: But right now, I don't want you to touch me. Please don't make it any harder on me than it already is. When I am gone, talk to your grandmother, James. Listen to her. You are so lucky to have one that is so wise to love you. She is not a silly old woman. She is not any of those things you say she is when you are drinking. She has lived her whole life through the worst of it. She is much wiser than you and I could ever be right now.

JAMES: I know that, Mary. I think I've always known it. There is so much that I want to tell you and I feel that there is so little time. I really listened to her today. I really heard what she had to say. She talked to me about my parents and about my life before I came to live with her. Things I've never really wanted to think about. I've never shared them with you. Maybe I can learn to share them, someday? She raised me, you know. I have so many memories in my childhood of her. I know I'm lucky to have her. I don't know why I've been running away from her. I guess I thought I was growing up and didn't need her anymore. She taught me a lot, when I was a kid, when I used to listen to her. I'm going to let her teach me again, Mary. I will learn. I promise I will.

MARY: We'll both learn, James. We'll learn together no matter where we are.

Mary moves to get her suitcase from the porch and James helps her.

JAMES: How will you manage, Mary? If you tell me where you're going, I could send some money. I'll go down to that construction site in the morning. I know I can get a job there. You'll need some money for the baby. Maybe I could come and visit, later on, well, if you wanted me to?

MARY: In time, James. I just need a little time. I called my dad today. I called him this morning, because I knew this morning that I was going to go. He said he'd leave right away, so I think he'll be here anytime now. He's quit drinking, James, and he fixed up our house so there's room for baby and me. He's wanted me home for a long time. He even said you could come, if I wanted you to, but, well, maybe later. I want to go home, but still I'm scared. Look James, there's a truck turning off the highway. That could be him. It probably is. I'm scared, James, and I didn't want it to be like this.

JAMES: It'll be okay, Mary. I know we're going to need this time. And . . . and I know your dad. He'll take good care of you.

Mary is deeply moved by the understanding and support that his reply demonstrates. She has never seen him in this light before. For the first time, she moves over to him and reaches out to touch his shirt, which is torn and dirty.

MARY: James, your shirt is torn. Just a second.

She goes into the house and returns with an armload of James's shirts, clean and pressed. She gives them to James. The grandmother comes to the screen door to watch, then comes outside to greet Roy.

MARY: James, here are your clean shirts.

Roy is very nervous as he approaches the house. Mary is nervous too. They haven't seen much of each other for about eight years, and the last time Mary saw him, he was still drinking. He goes to her, and almost goes to embrace her, but touches her arm instead. Roy carries with him a brown paper bag containing dried salmon and a piece of cloth, gifts for the grandmother.

ROY: It's good to see you, Mary. You look so different, you're all grown up.

MARY: Yeah, well . . . it's been a long time.

They are both extremely uncomfortable and unsure of themselves. They try to look at each other but can't quite connect yet.

MARY: Dad, this is James. I don't think you remember him, do you?

ROY: No . . . well, I don't remember if . . .

MARY: Of course not, we were just kids, when when you were here, but you remember Granny Anmah, don't you? And . . . and . . . oh yeah, the baby, your grandchild.

As Roy and the grandmother greet each other, Mary slips into the house to bring the baby out for Roy to see.

Roy crosses over to greet the grandmother and to give her the gifts he brought.

ROY: It's good to see you, Anmah. You're looking good.

GRANDMOTHER: Hi, Roy. What is this? (*looks in the bag*) OOOHHH, dry salmon, ah. I never get that, hardly anymore. Gee, that looks good. I'll have to save it.

ROY: I brought you a box of it in my truck, Anmah. I dried it myself. You eat that one. We had a really good catch this year.

GRANDMOTHER: James, dried salmon, this used to be your favourite.

— 97 —

As James crosses over to her and they taste the salmon, Mary comes out of the house with the baby. She hands her to Roy, who is very awkward and unused to having a baby in his arms.

MARY: We named her Sherida. She's so tiny, isn't she? It used to scare me to hold her too when she was first born. And James still can't. Oh well, she is so little, huh?

GRANDMOTHER: Is this your first grandchild, Roy?

Roy indicates with a nod that it is.

ROY: It's been a long time since I've held a baby in my arms. It is kind of scary.

GRANDMOTHER: You'll get used to it. It'll just take a little time. They sure like to be held, so you'll get plenty of practice.

MARY: Do you want me to take her now?

ROY: No, it's okay. I could sit down.

GRANDMOTHER: Here, you sit here. You must be tired after that long drive. I've fixed you some food, and I'll make us a pot of tea, or do you drink coffee? You take a little rest before you head back.

ROY: No, tea's fine. Don't go to any trouble, no trouble at all.

As grandmother goes in the house, Mary tries to follow her to help.

GRANDMOTHER: Mary, you sit down and visit with your dad. James, you come help me.

SCENE 7

Roy and Mary are settled down on the porch. He is holding the baby. They are still uncomfortable with one another. Silent, wondering what to say, then they both start speaking at once.

MARY: Did you want me to hold . . .

ROY: She makes me remember when you were little.

They both laugh self-consciously, then Roy hands the baby to Mary.

MARY: What were you going to say?

ROY: Well, when I was holding that baby girl, it reminded me of the first time I held you. I guess, I was pretty nervous back then too.

Mary, with a shy smile to Roy

MARY: Did you used to hold me a lot?

ROY: Well, not a lot, but I used to. You were smaller than Sharon? Shar? What was her name again?

MARY: Sherida.

ROY: I'm going to have to remember that. It's different, but pretty.

MARY: Yeah, you are. I was smaller than this?

ROY: You were born too early, you know?

MARY: Really? I didn't know that. (*She laughs.*) Here. (*She hands him the baby again.*) Do you remember a lot from when I was little girl? I don't remember anything.

ROY: (*Finally looks directly at Mary.*) Yeah, I remember a lot. We used to spend a lot of time together. When you were little, you always wanted to come with me wherever I went. Do you remember that? I did used to take you, that is, before the drinking got too bad. You were always my little girl. Until you grew up. You grew up too fast,

Mary. You grew up too fast for me. Then I didn't know how to talk to you anymore. I guess I yelled at you a lot, instead.

MARY: (*looks surprised*) What do you mean, Dad?

ROY: It was OUR fault. We didn't know how to care of you kids. You needed so much. Sometimes it was a big struggle just taking care of ourselves, just getting from one day to the next. Then when we'd go drinking, I'd even forget we had kids. I'd want it to be just the two of us, like it was before. Your mom, she'd start crying as soon as she had too much to drink. I couldn't stand listening to her cry, so I started leaving her at home, and we'd fight. I don't blame her for leaving me. I sure wasn't much. I haven't been much of a father for you.

JOURNEY THROUGH THE PAST TO THE FUTURE

CHARACTERS

Kokum At'su, Elder, grandmother, and the storyteller of the village
An-Gull, Elder, talks to spirits, sister of At'su
1st Child (Niska), 2nd Child (K'azba), and 3rd Child (Key-le-la),
representing the children of the village
Willow, Manny, Raven, Statum, and Sage, adults of the village
Other villagers
A priest, Indian Agent, and two Royal Canadian Mounted Police
(RCMP) officers
Woman and Man arguing, and their child
1st Child, 2nd Child, and 3rd Child, neglected and
hungry children
Social Worker and Mrs. Williams
Mark and Salena, today's children

Speaker, begins and ends the play with acknowledgements and
words of celebration
Four drummers

WELCOME

SPEAKER: We want to acknowledge the People whose territory
we are on, and to say thank you to the Squamish, to the
Musqueam, and to the Burrard [now Tsleil-Waututh] people for
being so kind and generous to allow us to be here to perform for
you today.

*Four drummers enter and position themselves downstage centre in
front of curtains.*

WELCOME SONG

FOUR DRUMMERS: Traditional Song

*As the curtain opens, the four drummers move right into the scene
onstage.*

BACK IN THE DAY

*It is late afternoon in the village of the People. There is a camp fire
downstage centre. Small clumps of people are busy with everyday
work. At stage left, two men are busy at the river pulling their net
in and removing the salmon. Two women are close by cleaning the
salmon, cutting it up, and hanging it to dry in the wind. A small
group of Elders sit together upstage closer to the left and visit, enjoying
each other's company. Two women are situated upstage right, picking
berries. A child stands close by helping and enjoying the berries. Other
women sit and weave downstage right. They are very concentrated
on their work. Children are situated throughout this scene, some
helping, some playing. Children are welcome everywhere, and when*

a child approaches the adult stops what he/she is doing and greets them. It shows that the whole community is organized around the children who are the centre of The People's lives. It is a peaceful scene of abundance and contentment. The People are waiting for the person who is fasting to come down off of the mountain. This is a very sacred time.

1ST CHILD (NISKA): Kokum At'su, would you tell us a story?

The 2nd Child dances around in excitement.

2ND CHILD (K'AZBA): Yes, yes, Kokum At'su. Please tell us the story of the birds that flew to the sun.

Kokum At'su is very happy to be with the children and gets up to move closer to the fire. The children continue to dance around her in excitement. The mothers move forward to sit near to their children and to calm some of the younger ones down.

KOKUM AT'SU: You never get tired of hearing that story, do you? And Kokum At'su never gets tired of telling it.

She laughs in happiness as the rest of the People gather around her. The Elders sit around the circle behind the mothers. They always stay close by in case they are needed to help with the children. The men move around the outer circle as protectors.

But first I'm going to sing a song. You could even sing with me if you wanted to. Here's a rattle.

She hands a rattle to the nearest child.

You can all help me to sing.

3RD CHILD (KEY-LE-LA): I want to sing, Kokum At'su.

1ST CHILD (NISKA): Me too, I've been practising.

KOKUM AT'SU: You can all sing with me. That would make me and the spirits very happy.

She laughs along with the children.

SONG

After she finishes the song, she turns her attention to the children and begins to tell the story.

KOKUM AT'SU: Now, do you remember who flew to the sun?

3RD CHILD (KEY-LE-LA): Three birds flew to the sun.

1ST CHILD (NISKA): They wanted to bring back the gift of fire to the People.

KOKUM AT'SU: Yes, yes, my little ones. You are very smart. First the Ptarmigan flew way up into the sky, but he only managed to make it halfway, and then his feathers began to change colours. This was the gift especially given to the Ptarmigan to help him to change the colours of his feathers so he could not be seen.

2ND CHILD (K'AZBA): Then the crow flew.

KOKUM AT'SU: The crow got all the way to the sun, but then what happened?

1ST CHILD (NISKA): He turned all black just like the night.

KOKUM AT'SU: That's right, and he is still black, just like the night, today. Then the third bird to fly to the sun was the Eagle, and he was the one who brought back the gift of the fire which is really the gift of life. We can see this in the spots of the Eagle when he spreads his wings and flies way up high.

3RD CHILD (KEY-LE-LA): *Mussi,* Kokum. That is my favourite story.

2ND CHILD (K'AZBA): *Mussi,* Kokum.

1ST CHILD (NISKA): *Mussi,* Kokum.

KOKUM AT'SU: Now I could really use a cup of tea. I am really thirsty.

She barely gets the words out of her mouth and Willow appears with some tea and bannock.

Mussi Cho. I was wishing for a piece of that bannock too. I'm getting very hungry waiting for my sister to come down off that mountain.

She eats the bannock with the same enjoyment as the tea.

She better come down soon or there won't be any bannock left, and that stew is smelling really good. Is that the moose that Statum got?

WILLOW: He got two. He was very lucky that day.

MANNY: He knew we needed moose meat for this feast.

RAVEN: Tell us how you got them. He said they came right to him.

Statum smiles and is very pleased to have been able to provide for the feast.

STATUM: I prayed to them and they came right to me. I talked to them, and they know this feast was important. They gave up their lives without a struggle and we all thank them for that.

RAVEN: Where did you go hunting?

STATUM: Way over on the other side of that mountain. It was a good day's walk.

SAGE: There is lots of salmon too, Kokum.

RAVEN: The river is full of salmon this year.

SAGE: We don't even need a net. They just jump into my arms.

Kokum At'su laughs loudly. An-Gull comes in.

KOKUM AT'SU: Is that my grandson telling stories again? You're almost as good a storyteller as your Kokum.

Statum goes to An-Gull and helps her to the stage. An-Gull enters from stage right. She is returning from a vision quest. She is the one the People have been waiting for. She is accompanied by her helper. The children run to greet her for she is greatly loved by the children and all the People. They make a place for her by the fire, next to Kokum, her sister.

KOKUM AT'SU: Bring some sxúsem juice and that special tea to help her break her fast.

Nula and Sage bring the juice and tea and she indicates to them to set it down near her.

AN-GULL: If the People don't mind, before we go any further, I have an important message that I must tell the People.

She stands up and the People grow silent and listen.

I had a vision during my last night there. An old man came to me. He said he was from around these parts a long time ago. He said he came back because he knew a great change was going to come. He told me to look towards the east, and when I looked I saw these ghost men coming. They were painted all white. Some of them were in black robes, and they carried something black in their hands. They were moving very fast. It felt like they were running right through me. There were lots of them, and I got afraid for you, my beloved people.

Then the old man told me we could not stop what was coming. He said that those ones coming were going to bring great destruction. Lots of people were going to die—many, many people. But he said it was important to tell our people not to lose heart. We must never forget the good things in our lives, and we must always talk about the good things so they don't get forgotten. Someday our young people will lead us back to the beginning again.

After he spoke, the Thunder Beings were making their way across the sky. They were so loud that they woke me.

She sits back down.

I was impatient to get back here to you, my people. I wanted you close. I wanted to feel you all around me, and I felt a great loneliness inside.

She reaches out, and she and Kokum join hands and pull the children close to them. The People all join hands and hold each other up.

A strong clear voice begins to sing The American Indian Movement (AIM) Song and the People join in.

As the light slowly fades, we hear the song and see the People in silhouette until the light is gone to blackout.

REFLECTIONS OF THE PAST

TAPE RECORDING: *It is now 100 years later for the People and residential schools have just been introduced. The People have been struggling with the settlers moving onto their land and their food gathering places, making them harder to get at. Diseases have also wiped out huge populations of the People.*

Now the residential schools which bring about the loss of the children is a much deeper more agonizing loss to the People.

Scene opens with people in the same position as they were at the end of Scene 1. On either side of the People is a figure of the R.C.M.P. The People appear to be frozen and attempting to hang on to their children.

A priest and an Indian Agent enter from the sides. The Agent reads from a legal-looking document to the People.

INDIAN AGENT: It is now the law that children between the ages of five and 18 must now attend the residential school. We have come to gather up all the children and take them with us. It is against the law for you to try to stop us, and we have brought reinforcements to help us to uphold this law. If you resist in any way you will be sent to jail until your child is in school.

There is immediate chaos among the People as they attempt to hold on to their children. The men are held back by the R.C.M.P. A child, representing all the children, is taken away.

In the chaos, the People are left in isolation, fear, rage, grief—this is indicated in body language as they scatter to different parts of the stage, symbolizing a community starting to come apart.

Many Elders die.

There is a graveyard to indicate the many deaths at stage right.

Alcohol abuse becomes common. This is choreographed through dance.

Men unable to fulfill their roles become depressed and idle. Men are alone and angry. The fishing nets blow in the breeze and are empty and useless.

Women become powerless and lose their roles as mothers and wives. There is great distance in relationships with husbands and children as they struggle with their grief.

The land base continues to grow smaller as people are herded onto reserves and forbidden to go to their traditional food gathering places. This is choreographed symbolically.

People from upstage right will enter dramatically wearing white masks and move the People to a small section of the downstage left.

The People use their bodies to indicate their frustration and grief. In this small space, they continue their lives of isolation.

There is loud drumming that turns into thunder and lightning and even greater chaos.

Blackout.

NOTE: archival photos of chaos, slide show of Residential School.

LIFE AS WE KNEW IT

Scene begins with song, "Took The Children Away." Spotlight upstage centre to girls simulating a group picture of residential school (lined up as in a box system). A nun stands among the girls. Song plays up to, but not including: "the children came back." A scrim hangs at downstage right where scenes of destruction for the family will be played out. As girls exit the stage at both stage right and stage left the spotlight moves to the scrim.

First scrim scene is a man and woman fighting over money. Alcohol is involved. They are fighting over a purse, tugging it back and forth.

WOMAN: Give me that. That's my purse.

MAN: What did you do with that money I gave you?

WOMAN: I bought food with it. We got to eat.

She gets the purse away from him and his anger increases.

MAN: You better give me that money if you know what's good for you.

WOMAN: No, you're just gonna drink it up.

Man slaps her and she falls to the sound of a child crying in fear. He grabs the purse, finds the money, and exits to the sound of a slamming door.

She slumps over in despair, and a child comes to hug her, but she pushes the child away. The child cries out and then just whimpers. She yells at the child to shut up.

Blackout.

The second scrim scene is about children being neglected and abandoned, and having to fend for themselves. Light comes up on the scrim to three children huddled together. Another child can be heard crying, which fades down, but stays in the background.

1ST CHILD: Shut up, stop being a crybaby.

2ND CHILD: I think he's hungry.

The crying stops. The 3rd child gets up, as if to look out a window.

3RD CHILD: When is Mom and Dad getting home? I'm hungry too.

The 2nd child simulates standing on a chair looking in cupboards.

2ND CHILD: I'll see if there is anything up here.

1ST CHILD: There's nothing in the fridge.

The 2nd child hands a small bag to the 3rd child.

2ND CHILD: See what's in there.

3RD CHILD: It's biscuits. Uh oh, some of them are mouldy.

2ND CHILD: We can pick that off.

1ST CHILD: Baby fell asleep, finally.

3RD CHILD: Yuck!

2ND CHILD: Shut up and eat your biscuit. Pretend it's bannock.

1ST CHILD: Yeah, with baloney.

2ND CHILD: Shshsh.

Blackout.

Third scrim scene opens with a social worker speaking to a mother about apprehending her children. The mother is angry.

SOCIAL WORKER: Mrs. Williams, we told you if you left your children alone one more time we were going to apprehend them. So we've come to do that.

MRS. WILLIAMS: You can't just come in here and take my children.

SOCIAL WORKER: I've asked Mr. Martin to put the children in the car right now.

Children can be heard crying.

CHILD: Mom, Mom . . .

MRS. WILLIAMS: Stop it! I won't let you take my children.

She struggles with the social worker.

SOCIAL WORKER: Mrs. Williams, the police are also outside and they will arrest you if you make trouble.

All the fight goes out of the mother's body. The social worker exits and she is left alone.

Blackout.

Spotlight now comes up to downstage left. City scene in background. Some youth stand on a corner venting frustration and anger at the struggles in their lives. Spoken word, freestyle, hip hop.

Blackout.

ONE DAY AT A TIME

This scene takes place in the present day. It is late afternoon in the village of the People. We see a village that vaguely resembles the village in Scene 1, only this village appears empty—people stay in their houses and away from each other—and neglected. Two children play near the deserted fishing nets. They are digging in the sand with sticks, and one has a small plastic shovel. The child with the stick is poking it into the ground. Kokum sits by the fire with her back to the children. She is remembering back to the day when the whole community was so alive.

MACK: Hey, what's this?

He tries to push the stick in further, but it breaks, so he gets another one, and tries to make a bigger hole.

SELENA: Whatcha got, Mack?

MACK: Quick, Selena, bring a shovel. There's something down here.

Selena brings her shovel over, and Mack tries to grab it, but she quickly puts it behind her back.

SELENA: I can do it.

MACK: Okay, go ahead.

Selena shovels until she gets tired, and hands it over to Mack. She almost loses interest, and then Mack sees the top of a box.

MACK: See, I knew there was something in here. Help me pull it out.

SELENA: What is it?

MACK: It's a big box of some kind.

Mack is very excited as he struggles and struggles with the box.

MACK: C'mon, Selena. Don't just stand there. Help me.

Selena gives a good yank and it comes out as they both fall backward. Mack gets up and pulls at the box until it opens. Selena watches in anticipation.

Mack pulls out a button blanket, and Selena helps him to hold it up.

He looks into the box, and is about to take more stuff out, but Selena cautions him.

SELENA: No, Mack. We'd better ask Kokum.

They struggle together to put the blanket back into the box, and struggle with it over to where Kokum sits by a fire.

MACK: Kokum, Kokum! Look what I found!

SELENA: Mack found it but I dug it up with my shovel.

MACK: Yeah, Selena helped.

They lay the box down in front of Kokum, and as Mack opens the lid, Kokum is amazed when she sees the blanket.

Kokum cries out, for she believed that everything had been lost.

KOKUM AT'SU: Oh, my little ones, it is what we have lost so many, many years ago.

She lifts a drum out and some other sacred items.

All the medicines of our people. It has been buried here all this time, and I thought it was lost. I am so happy.

She gives the children a hug, and kisses them on their cheeks, and begins to weave a story for them.

A long, long time ago when An-Gull had a vision, she told the People that the white people would be coming to this land, and that our people would have a hard time. We didn't want to believe the destruction that would come, but it came anyway and we began to lose our land.

The children's mother comes and joins them. She is the child that was taken away to residential school, and she is very protective of her children because of her suffering. She sits and listens, and one by one people come out of their homes and listen to Kokum At'su.

And we began to lose our children. Then we lost the language and all our sacred medicines, so the People began hiding the medicines so it wouldn't all be lost. Someday, the children will want to return to culture and our traditions, and we need to hide it for them, so they have something to carry on.

All the remaining backstage actors enter. All the People have gathered around and it is a community again.

Statum helps An-Gull walk.

The spirits told us that the young people would lead us back to the beginning, and I believe that time has come.

She reaches out and gently strokes Mack's and Selena's hair.

You've done a good job. You've done something great for the People. You have brought us together again.

The children gather. Kokum At'su hands them the blanket. Kokum holds up the drum.

Call all the People to sing with us.

Kokum sings a special song that brings the People together once again.

As the song ends, a slide show begins of current community events that show everyone coming together. These pictures of the People bring hope for the future. They are positive pictures of the communities, and the children, and families thriving and growing.

As the slide show continues, the People begin to recreate their lives and their community:

Two people take down the net and begin to repair it.

An adult and a child pick berries together.

Button Blankets and other kinds of ceremonial blankets are brought out.

Medicines are brought out (simulate smudge).

An Elder teaches children the language and culture (re-claim role).

Some people are weaving and some are beading.

A person addresses the audience in the language and another translates what is said. Basically, what she says is as follows.

SPEAKER WITH KOKHUM AT'SU AS TRANSLATOR: I am so happy that you have come to join us in our celebration. We, as a people, have much to celebrate today. We have had many tough times, but I won't dwell on that. It is more important to look forward and to be grateful that our people were so strong and determined to survive. I am proud of you, my people. I hold up my hands to you. This song, the "Women's Warrior Song," is an acknowledgement of our strength. Aho!

Everyone joins in with the "Women's Warrior Song."

Scene ends with whole community as one.

ECHOES OF OUR MOTHERS' PAST

How our mother's pain from family violence impacts us and all future generations.

CHARACTERS
The storyteller/poet
Four masked women
The singer
Angie, Celeste, and Marie, three young girls
Claire, Angie's mom
Laura, Marie's mom
Carol, a thirteen-year-old girl
Anne, Carol's mom
Angie, Celeste, and Marie as adults
Hallie, adult woman in the same support group as Angie,
Celeste, and Marie

Carol, as an adult, in the same support group as Angie,
Celeste, and Marie
Sarah, Marlene, and Haven, three mothers
Four storytellers (Tamara, Sherry, Lorraine, and Peggy)

SCENE 1: IF WE TELL THE TRUTH

*Bare stage. Four masked women stand across the stage, their arms
lifted as though searching for answers. Slowly they move towards
each other and join hands in a semi-circle. The storyteller is at stage
right, the singer on stage left. The singer beats the drum softly as the
poet speaks.*

STORYTELLER: If we tell the truth about our mothers, it won't be
the end of the world.

The masked women cover their eyes, mouth, ears, heart in fear.

The roof won't cave in on us. We won't all die. No, please listen.
Hear me out.

They move back into a listening pose.

Telling the truth about our mothers doesn't mean we don't love
them. It means that we can learn to love ourselves. When we tell
the truth about our mothers, we can finally tell the truth about
ourselves and then maybe, maybe . . .

They all look toward the poet with interest.

. . . we will learn how to love our children the way they need to be
loved. Wouldn't that be the best gift to give for everyone?

*The women begin to slowly take their masks off, testing it at first to see
if it is safe.*

In time, we must also tell the truth about our fathers, and our
grandfathers, and our uncles—the ones who hurt us.

Women cover their faces again and move their bodies into poses of fear and vulnerability. Make sound.

Singer sings a soft, soothing, healing song, and slowly they stand again. They remove the masks and sing with singer, "Oh Great Spirit."

Don't worry. It's a story that will come in its own time. Our mothers and our grandmothers will give us the courage to tell that story. This time they will believe us.

Put masks in bag.

SINGER: With this song, I want us to create a sacred space for mothers and daughters to begin to re-connect our lives again.

Singer begins to sing the sacred honouring song softly, and then more loudly after the women have all spoken.

MASKED WOMAN 1: The truth is not meant to dishonour you, my mom. It is meant to build a bridge between us after I've run so far away from you, since the womb, where you once held me under your heart.

MASKED WOMAN 2: The truth is not meant to hurt you, Mom, because in spite of everything that happened, I still love you and believe you did the best you could.

MASKED WOMAN 3: Mom, the truth will help me to know what I need to do to reach my daughter before we lose each other. I feel she hates me in the same way I once told you that I hated you, and I love her so much.

MASKED WOMAN 4: Mom, the truth will help me to know what I must do to raise good sons who love, honour, and respect women—sons who will honour and protect their wives and daughters—sons who will speak up against violence against women.

Singer leads and everyone joins in the honour song for mothers.

Semicircle.

Blackout.

SCENE 2: WHAT THE CHILD REMEMBERS

Three little girls sit on the steps of a house (use three milk crates). Angie, at centre stage left, holds a bouquet of dandelions. Celeste, at stage left, wears pants and a baggy shirt. She carries nothing, but sits so still, her attention focused on a spot way in the distance. Marie, at stage right, holds a precious drawing in her lap. She is very proud of it. Spotlight is on each girl as she speaks and others freeze.

ANGIE: See—I picked these for my mom. That's why I'm late. She's gonna be so happy. They're so purty and yellow, and they smell like fresh-cut grass.

Mom enters, angry. Angie happily reaches up behind her to pass the flowers to her mom, who slaps them out of her hand.

CLAIRE (ANGIE'S MOM): Where have you been, you stupid girl, and get those weeds outta here. Don't leave a mess. Pick them up and get rid of them.

Angie is scared of her mom's anger, and can't understand what she did wrong. Quickly, she picks up the flowers, and as her mom strides away, she tears them up and throws them away. She cries.

Get in here and wash these dishes and take care of your little brother. I'm going to town. Hurry up, you lazy good-for-nothing girl. Snap to it. I don't know what I'm going to do with you, if you don't smarten up. If you wanna cry, I'll give you something to cry about.

As Angie hangs her head, the other two girls taunt her.

CELESTE: You're gonna get it! Ha ha ha! Those are dandelions, dummy.

MARIE: Dandelions aren't real flowers.

CELESTE: They're weeds. You gave your mom weeds.

ANGIE: What did I do wrong? I don't know what I did wrong.

Angie exits backstage. Celeste begins to pace and stops at front stage left.

MARIE: I thought she was gonna play with us. She never gets to play with us.

CELESTE: Awww, forget her. With so many brothers and sisters, who's got time to play?

MARIE: Her mom never lets her do anything fun.

CELESTE: Guess what? I told my mom last night about Dad touching me.

Marie is upset, tries to cover her ears.

MARIE: (*gasps*) Shshsh! somebody might hear.

CELESTE: I had to tell someone. It's getting worse. Now, he's sneaking into my room at night. Even with my sister right there, he tries.

MARIE: What did your mom say?

CELESTE: She slapped me and told me to quit lying. She slapped me real hard.

Celeste rubs her cheek at the memory and angrily brushes her tears away.

MARIE: My mom hit me when I told her about Uncle Dan. She said he could never do something like that, 'cuz he's a minister and I'm just a stupid girl. After that, Uncle bought us some groceries, and then he bought me some clothes. That made my mom happy.

Celeste sits down beside Marie.

CELESTE: Dad gives me money.

MARIE: Did your dad just start bothering you?

CELESTE: Nah, it's been going on a couple of years now.

MARIE: I don't remember a time when he wasn't touching me.

Celeste reaches over to take the picture from Marie, who lets her see it, but hangs on to it with one hand.

CELESTE: What do you got there?

MARIE: I made it for Mom for Mother's Day. Isn't it pretty? Wait here. I'm going to go give it to her, then we can go play.

Marie goes into the house (backstage)

Mom! Mom, look what I made you.

LAURA (MARIE'S MOM): Isn't there enough clutter around here? Here, get that outta the way. I'm trying to set the table. You should try to help out around here. All I do is slave away for you kids, and you give me nothing but grief. Go get cleaned up. Your uncle Dan's coming for dinner. Go on! Get outta here! I can't stand the sight of you sometimes.

Marie runs out of the house and sits back down beside Celeste.

CELESTE: So how did she like it?

MARIE: She liked it, but it was just a stupid drawing. Do you wanna play jacks?

CELESTE: Sure, I'll go first.

MARIE: How come you get to go first?

CELESTE: 'Cuz they're my jacks.

*The girls hop and skip their way off the stage, laughing and playing.
As they leave, Angie comes back out of the house struggling to carry
a baby that she feeds from a bottle, as she stares wistfully after her
two friends.*

ANGIE: "Hush little baby, don't you cry." Sammy, stay where I can
see you. Jamie, quit hitting your sister. Bailey, you come back
here right now. If Mom sees you in town you're gonna' get it, and
it won't be my fault. Bailey, why do you always go runnin' after
Mom? Don't you know she'll come back eventually? Now kids, be
good so Mom will come home and not be mad. "Hush little baby,
don't say a word. Momma's gonna, buy you a mocking bird."

Blackout.

SCENE 3: BECOMING A WOMAN

*Anna, an older woman, sits at a table (stage right front) holding a
brush in her hand, and watches her daughter admire herself in the
mirror (stage left front). She looks tired and her disappointment
about life is written on her face and in the droop of her shoulders.*

*Carol moves to stand centre front stage. She is awkward and shy in a
pretty new dress.*

CAROL: I'm thirteen years old today, and I notice that my body is
beginning to change, and the boys at school have started to notice.
There are a few of them that I kind of like, but I don't want them
to know that. I'm going to the school dance tonight, and my mom
is going to brush my hair.

*Carol sits down on a stool in front of her mom, who has been tapping
the brush impatiently, and is a little rough when she begins to brush
her hair.*

Ouch, Mom.

ANNA: Well, how did it get so tangled? Don't you brush it every day?

CAROL: I try to. Well, I did this morning.

ANNA: Oh, you did, did you? "Well, I did this morning." (*Mocks her.*) You're always trying to sound so cute. Sit up! Pull your dress down! Your dad's watching you from the kitchen. He might not even let you go out. He doesn't like you hanging around with those boys, just being a little slut.

Anna suddenly yanks Carol's hair, and shoves her violently so that she ends up on the floor. Carol is clearly terrified of her mom's anger.

CAROL: Mom? Mom, stop. What did I do?

Slowly, she gets up and stands in front of her mom, who won't look at her.

Mom, whatever I did, I didn't mean it. Mom, please don't be mad at me.

ANNA: Whore, get away from me.

Carol stifles a sob. She is deeply hurt. She moves back to stage left front, and leaves Anna slumped at the table.

CAROL: I think my mom was jealous of me because my dad was always touching me. She had so many babies because they didn't use birth control, and she never got to be young and carefree. I learned to cover up, by always wearing baggy clothes, and I never trusted men because of what my dad did, and I never trusted women, because my mom never protected me from dad. She knew what was going on and she just got mad at me, not him. I always thought it was my fault, but I know it wasn't. He knows he did wrong because years later he apologized to me. She drank herself to death and died in an accident. Even at the end she called me to come and rescue her, and I live with the guilt, because I couldn't help her, after she turned her back on me so many times. I never married. I have no children and I keep to myself. I stay alone because I don't trust anyone.

Carol sits on the floor, pulls her knees up to her chin, and watches her mom. Her mom lifts her head, and they look at each other from that great distance, which neither of them can bridge. Anna stands up and turns toward stage right, and stares off into the distance as if looking for something. Her full back is toward Carol.

This is how I remember Mom—always looking back, to somewhere in her past. She never, ever saw me. I was forever reaching for her and she was never there.

Blackout.

SCENE 4: MOTHERS LOOKING BACK (DANCE SCENE)

Theme is about the generational impacts of wounded mothers, and how this wound is passed from generation to generation by mothers who are always looking to their past for what they did not get; consequently, they are unable to give to their own children the love, support, encouragement, and nurturance that is needed to help them in their lives. It is as though the umbilical cord is never severed, as each generation holds onto the traumatic and abusive stories of their mothers, which is tied to their own life experience. The more they pull away and isolate, the stronger the tie becomes until it binds them into their own prisons of loss and destruction.

Blackout.

SCENE 5: BEING MY MOTHER'S DAUGHTER

CHOICES PROGRAM SINGLE WOMEN'S GROUP MEETING and WOMEN MAKING HEALTHY CHOICES... says the bannered sign on the wall. Five women enter the room and make themselves comfortable on cushions and stools. They each have coffee cups and a notepad, and are part of a women's group come to debrief a speakers' bureau they just attended that just hosted a speaker who spoke about healthy relationships.

CELESTE: Wow, what an awesome speaker. I learned so much.

HALLIE: Yeah, I actually feel like I'm finally on the right track, and that there's hope.

As the other women settle in, Angie studies the sign on the wall. She's feeling a little disgruntled.

ANGIE: Oh, yah, nothing like this big sign to advertise that we're all a bunch of single losers.

MARIE: Hey now, I never consider myself a loser just because I don't have a man. In fact, I think it's healthy, considering my track record.

ANGIE: That's true. I guess I'm just feeling a little sensitive after listening to that speaker talk about healthy relationships, and realizing how little I know.

CAROL: Sometimes I find it a relief to be single after what that man put me through. All those put-downs, insults, and negative thinking really wore at me. Listening to that speaker was inspiring.

CELESTE: You know what really blew me away? When she said that women have a right to say no to a man and that a woman's body is her own. Try telling that to my ex.

HALLIE: Oh, god, I can relate to that. I used to spend my life sitting in bars waiting for someone to buy me a drink, and at the end of the night I'd always feel obligated, like I couldn't just get up and walk out of there and go home, which is what I wanted to do. Learning to say no was hard for me.

CAROL: Yes, having control over our own minds too. You know, like having a right to our own thoughts and opinions, and not having to always cave in to a man. I'll tell you what, I sure never learned that from my mom. She was like a doormat to my dad and that's what I thought I had to be.

MARIE: I guess that's why I'm single today, because I don't trust nobody, and I especially don't trust myself to not always be giving in and allowing myself to be taken advantage of. I hate that feeling afterwards of being used.

ANGIE: When I was a little girl working like a slave, caring for my brothers and sisters, and feeling alone, I dreamed of all those things she spoke about: a man to love me, a beautiful home where I'd feel safe, lots of babies so I won't be lonely. I wanted it all. Mostly, I wanted to feel loved and respected and happy. I wanted a man I could talk to, someone who would listen and who would give a damn. Well, that didn't happen, although I did get my beautiful children. He was a mean man. He never had a single one of those qualities that that speaker spoke about. How come I didn't know that when I met him? I often wonder where I went so wrong.

MARIE: You know what I think? I think we get what our mothers taught us from their life experience. My mom never stuck up for me when I was a kid being abused. It was like she knew, but she just pretended it wasn't happening. I've learned to never trust women or men, and to always doubt myself. Even today, I wonder sometimes did that really happen with Uncle Dan or did I make that up? When I became a prostitute, I knew every time I got paid that this is what that sick pervert taught me, and my parents supported that. Well, I don't know if my dad knew, but I know my mom did. It makes me wonder what happened to her when she was a girl. Who violated and disappointed her?

CAROL: I used to never give a damn about my mother or what she thought. Never wanted nothing to do with her, but lately, since

I've been having all these problems with my own daughter, I'm beginning to wonder about her. I realize that I know so little about her and the kind of life she must have had. I can't even think of her as a young girl.

CELESTE: My ex treated me like a prostitute. It was sick, the things he expected me to do to please and to feed his fantasies. I started to drink just to put up with it for nine years. He abused me, and it never occurred to me that I could say no. That's the way we girls were raised, and that's how we saw our mothers treated. It's wrong and it's got to change for our daughters' and for our sons' sakes. They don't deserve to see their mother treated that way. That's why I finally left.

Cell phone rings, and Hallie struggles to find it in her bag.

HALLIE: I'm sorry. I'm sorry. I thought I turned it off.

She looks at the call display.

It must be Christie, my daughter. She's the only one who calls me on this line. I have to answer it.

She moves away from the others to speak, but they stay silent, listening as well in concerned support.

Hello, hello, Christie. What is it now? What's the matter? Why are you crying? Oh no! Where are the kids? Where are they holding you? I'll be right there. Yes, I said I'll be there. Yes, right now.

Hallie hangs up and stands in stunned silence.

ANGIE: Hallie, are you okay?

HALLIE: No, no, I'm not. I never see my daughter for months at a time. She tells me she hates me and wants nothing to do with me, yet, when she's in trouble, I'm always the one she calls. She's down at the cop shop. Got picked up for being out in the streets, and her kids are somewhere. I'll have to find them before Social Services does. I can't do this. It's not fair. I'm trying so hard. And she's not.

CELESTE: Yes, you can. You must. This is what we have to do for our kids when they need us. Their lives aren't that much different than ours were, but we're working on it, and eventually they will see that, but right now she needs you and you need to be there for her the way your mom wasn't there for you. I could come with you.

CAROL: At least she called you, Hallie. It's you that she needs and wants. She knows she can trust you to always be there for her.

ANGIE: Carol's right, Hallie. I'll come along too. You shouldn't have to do this alone. We'll go in my car.

HALLIE: Thanks, everybody. I sure could use the support.

MARIE: Go ahead and go. We'll clean up and make sure everything is locked up. Give me a call later and let me know what happened.

Marie begins to straighten out cushions and picks up coffee mugs.

CAROL: We should have another meeting soon.

ANGIE: Next week—same time, same day, my place. See you later.

CELESTE: Bye.

MARIE: Good night, you all.

Hallie, Celeste, and Angie exit stage left. Marie continues to clean, and Carol picks up the garbage bag.

CAROL: I'll take the garbage out. I'll be right back.

Carol exits, and Marie stops what she is doing and sits down. She looks around to make sure she's alone. Then she takes out her cell phone and dials a number.

MARIE: Hello, hello, Rachel. It's Mom. I'm surprised you answered. I thought I'd just be talking to your machine. I know you don't like me to call you, but I have to 'cuz I'm your mom, and I want you to know that no matter how angry you are at me, I will always love you. I'll always be here for you. Hello? Hello?

Marie stands up and checks out the room to make sure she is done tidying up, and talks to herself, consoling herself as she does so.

Well, at least I said it this time before she hung up, and she did answer the phone this time. That's something different. I'll call her again on her birthday next week. Maybe this year I'll send a card.

Carol calls from the other room.

CAROL: Are you ready to go, Marie?

MARIE: Yah, I'll be right there.

Carol comes to the doorway and peeks in.

CAROL: I thought I heard you talking. Who were you talking to?

MARIE: Oh, nobody. I was just talking, wishing out loud.

Marie is tired as she gathers up her things and leaves the room, while the light slowly dims.

Blackout.

Responsibility to raise good sons

Survival Strengths

SCENE 6: WHAT OUR CHILDREN NEED TO HEAR

Three steps of a house (use milk crates) situated as in Scene 2. Three mothers sit: Sarah in centre, Marlene at stage right, and Haven at stage left. Each of the four storytellers enter from alternate sides of the stage wearing a white fringed cape. Each carries a rattle.

TAMARA:

> We are our mothers' daughters
> We are our children's mothers
> Our responsibility is huge
> To heal our own childhood wounds
> So that we don't pass on
> The abuses we suffered as children.

SHERRY:

> It's never too late
> To go back and to repair
> Damage that has been done
> With our silence
> Our cruel words
> Or our absence from their lives
> When they were little and helpless
> And needed us.

LORRAINE:

> There is no future without
> Our children . . .
> We cannot move forward
> Without lifting them up
> And carrying them with us
> When they fall.

PEGGY:

> As wounded women and mothers
> We must not rage at men
> Forgetting that our sons,
> Nephews, grandsons
> Will one day be men too.

After the storytellers are finished, they move in a semi-circle around the stage, and softly rattle as the mothers speak.

MARLENE: They grow up so quickly.

SARAH: One minute they were babies cuddled in my arms...

HAVEN:... and in the blink of an eye they were grown...

MARLENE:... and leaving home, determined never ever to be like you. They leave angry...

HAVEN:... and hurt, remembering every cruel word, every slap or punch. They don't want to remember, but they do.

Sarah moves to centre stage, and Tamara moves forward to shadow and support her.

SARAH: When my daughter died, all I could think of was all the words that I never got to say, all the gentle touches I wanted to give her.

If I had one more moment with my girl, I would have given her more love. I knew she was having a hard time, and I was never there for her when she needed me. If I knew she was going to leave, I would have done things differently.

If I only had a moment, I would say, "I'm so sorry for all those ugly things I said to you when you were little. Please forgive me for scaring you and making you feel unloved. It was never your fault. It was always mine. I took my grief and anger out on you, and you were innocent. You never deserved that, my precious, precious girl. Can you ever find it in your heart to forgive me?"

I always thought there'd be time, but there wasn't. Suddenly she was gone, and all I have left is silence and regret. You people, talk to your children now. We never know when the Creator will call. They need to hear what we have to say. They need to hear the truth.

Sarah sits back down, and Tamara stays close by for support.

MARLENE: The hardest thing to do is to talk to your child when they're mad at you. Sometimes I can't get past feeling rejected and abandoned when they turn their back and won't answer my calls and won't include me in their lives. I know those are all those feelings from my childhood haunting me again, and that I ought to rise above them and remember that I am the adult, but it's hard when I am feeling so much like a child again. I know it's not fair of me to expect my children to take care of my feelings and to parent me when they need parenting themselves.

I must take this wounded child that I am and heal her, and help her make peace with her mother so that I can be more there for my children when they need me, especially my adult children. I want them close to me, and I want them to have a better life than I did.

HAVEN: I am a single mother of five children. I left my relationship because I don't want my children to grow up with violence. I want my sons to learn to treat women with love and respect, and I want my daughters to know it is not okay to put up with violence. I want my children to see me being strong and independent. At the same time, I want them to see that I am not afraid to ask for help. There is so much that I want for my children. They need my love and encouragement. It is like watering a plant—nourishing their every need, listening and really hearing what they have to say, giving them duties that help them to grow, preparing my sons to be kind, gentle men, and my daughters to be strong, loving, compassionate women. It is such a big job being a mom—the most important job in the world.

Song "Blackbird."

Blackout.

SCENE 7: HONOURING OUR MOTHERS

Scene is the same as the end of Scene 3, with Anna standing with her back turned, and Carol sitting on the floor watching her saying,

CAROL: This is how I remember Mom, always looking back to somewhere in her past. She never, ever saw me. I was forever reaching for her, and she was never there.

Carol (the adult) approaches her mom. This time her steps are more sure, deliberate, and in her hand, in her eyes, in her heart she carries a love so strong that her mom can't move. She encircles her mom into her arms and draws her back. Each of the women enter with a gift: a comfortable chair, a beautiful blanket, a piece of colourful cloth, a cedar branch, a cape, a grandchild for her arms. The women surround and tend to the mother's every need. Women sing softly an honouring song for mothers.

SHERRY:
I am a survivor of family violence
I fight with tears, prayers to the Creator, love, lessons learned.
I call on the Creator for guidance & strength & courage & mercy.
I am first a woman, secondly a woman. I am a spiritual warrior.

Sarah leads honour song for women

THE END

EVERY WARRIOR'S SONG

SCENE 1: WHEN THE CIRCLE WAS STRONG (1900)

The stage is dark with the silhouettes of Indian people sitting in a circle. The characters are dressed in black, but each is wearing something traditional that is representative of the time period. The backstage acts as a screen for a film (or slides) that depict Aboriginal people the way they once were when the circle was strong, prior to the residential school experience.

As each of the scenes play, the characters come to life creating a vision of what life was like with their body and movement. The important themes are as follows: family interaction, childhood freedom, nature, spirituality, community, sense of wholeness.

The final scene is about death, a traditional burial which symbolizes loss. After the death scene, the lights dim and there is the sound of wind in a storm. People try to hold on to one another, but they are pushed here and there by the wind. As each character is tossed about, they cover their face with a neutral emotionless mask.

The next scenes on the screen are scenes of oppression: residential schools across the nation, the church, government, children in residential schools, alcohol abuse, violence.

Once again, the characters use the masks and movement to depict the losses that people are experiencing. The music is loud, but becomes quieter as Regina moves to centre stage. When she removes her mask, everything is silent. The other characters are frozen in their disconnectedness and isolation.

REGINA: I was a little girl living in the mountains with my brother and my grandmother when they took us away. All we did was play and pick berries. My granny loved us. She never knew how to scold or get angry. My brother and I, we'd sit on top of the mountain and eat all our berries and kye7e would say, "you're gonna get diarrhea." We'd laugh and she'd laugh too. She never knew how to say unkind words or to be mean. When we did wrong, she'd just give us a look and say this one word in our language and we'd behave. She had no reason to hit us or yell or call us names. When I was a child in the mountains, all I knew was love.

Regina moves from centre stage to stage right, and Joe moves to centre stage. He removes his mask.

JOE: They picked us up in cattle trucks. They weren't even clean. They smelled bad. They herded us up like animals and took us off to residential school. Kids were crying. Nobody prepared us, but I could tell by the look in my sla7a's and kye7e's eyes that they didn't want us to go. I wanted to be strong for them and the little ones, so I wouldn't cry. As we drove away, I watched them, that small group of parents and grandparents waving. They grew smaller and smaller until they disappeared, and still I wouldn't cry. Every September, when the season changed, it was like that.

Joe moves to stage left. He stands silently holding his mask.

REGINA: A big car came, and it had Indian Affairs written on it. I knew that because I could read some English by then. My grandmother got on in the front seat, and we jumped in the back. We weren't used to seeing cars like that, and we thought it was an adventure. We thought we were going berry-picking with that white lady. They took us to this building in town, and they told us to wait. My grandmother had to sign some papers. Then they put my brother in a taxi. They said he was going to Tranquille Hospital because he was mentally handicapped. I never knew what that meant back then. He was just my brother who liked to play. My granny took me in another cab to residential school. As soon as we knew we were going to be separated, we held on to each other. They had to pry us apart. I was just screaming and so was he.

Regina is silenced by her grief.

JOE: As soon as I got there, they cut my hair and took my clothes away. They took my protection bundle that I wore around my neck. They made fun of it and burned it with my clothes. They left me naked, and when I got into the barber chair, other boys started calling me names and making fun of me too. It hurt my feelings, but I knew not to cry. At first, I learned to fight. I was a real scrapper, until I realized that's exactly what they wanted us to do. They turned us on each other in vicious ways.

REGINA: They put me in this tub because they said I was dirty, and that I had to wash all the fleas off. Then I sat on this tall stool. My hair was really long then, and they just started chopping it off until it was real short. They gave me a number. I still remember that number today. I am number 13.

JOE: Right away I got beat for speaking Indian. I didn't know how to speak English. They used a conveyor belt to beat us on our hands and arms. Sometimes they used a yard stick. They'd beat us until we were bloody sometimes. I never forget this one instructor who beat us pretty bad. He got a charge out of beating up little kids. He wanted to hear us cry. I never let him see me cry. I think about him sometimes today. I think sometimes I'd like to look him up, but then it's probably better that I don't know where he is. I might kill him if I see him. Let him feel what it feels like to get beat.

REGINA: When I went into Intermediates, there was this janitor. He was a really tall guy. I don't know how I got into that. I feel so ashamed. When I got up to go to the washroom, he called me. I don't know why I followed him down to the laundry room. He had one of those places where you fold the clothes. The first time he just grabbed me and laid me down on it and started touching me all over. He told me not to tell nobody. This was our secret. No one should know. It happened to me like that for a long time, and I never told anybody.

JOE: Every morning we had porridge and a dry piece of bread. We'd walk past the supervisors' dining room, seeing huge platters of bacon and eggs and buttered toast. Oh, man, that smell was so good. Then I'd have to sit down to my bowl of mush that was so thick it was like glue. I'd have to sit there and pick out the mouse shit before I could eat it. Hunger, I could tell you about that, and how I learned to steal. We used to steal potatoes. We would roast them in the bonfire while we were raking leaves. We were so hungry, we'd burn our mouths eating those potatoes, half-burnt, half-raw. We'd shovel them into our mouths while they were still on fire, hoping we wouldn't get caught. We'd get whipped for stealing. They tasted so good.

REGINA: When I went into Seniors, the abuse was still happening to me. This time he came right into the dorm where I was sleeping. I don't know how anyone could sleep and not hear what was going on. My bed was right in the middle of the dorm. I chose that spot because I thought nothing could happen to me there. I never slept against the wall or in the corners. I always chose a spot right in the middle where it was safe, I thought.

Oh man, I woke up and I couldn't even scream because he had his hand covering my mouth. I couldn't even breathe for a second. He held me so I couldn't even bite him. What he did to me in the laundry room, he did that night upstairs in my bed. After he left, I was so scared I told my supervisor what happened. She told me I was lying, and I was just trying to cause problems for that guy. Everything that happened to us there—we were always told to be quiet, not to talk about it to anyone.

Not long after that, I remember waking up in the middle of the night and turning over, and he was there in the next bed with another girl. He was holding her down the same way he'd held me. (*Sigh, weeping*) I got up, and moved as fast as I could to the supervisor's door. I told her, "he's here.'" I remember saying that. She grabbed a club, and she went down to the dormitory, but he had already run out the side door. Once again, I was called a liar and a trouble maker.

That other girl, though, she was sitting up in bed crying, so I sat with her. We talked late into the night about everything. That's the first time I realized that it wasn't just happening to me. There were eight other girls. Ten of us altogether. From that time on, we promised to never let each other be alone or wander by ourselves. We promised to always be together, and to watch out for each other. The supervisors called us "the ten liars," but we didn't care.

Regina returns to her place with her back straight and her head held high. She is proud of the stand that these little young girls have taken. She replaces her mask.

JOE: I have no pictures or records of me when I was in school. It hurts me that I don't have anything to show for those years. It's like they didn't exist. I wish I could have a picture of myself in that school when I was a kid, or some papers saying I was there. It's hard to have nothing. It makes you feel like you're nothing.

Joe returns to his place on the stage, and puts his mask back on.

All the characters continue to stand away from each other and move their bodies to depict the pain, emptiness, loss, grief, isolation, fear that is told in these two stories. Through the dimming lights, all we can see are their white emotionless faces. A picture of the residential school takes up the entire space in the background.

Blackout.

SCENE 2: MEETING PLACE (1970)

Evening in an Indian bar in the city—a good place to hang out to beat the loneliness, and hopefully to find companionship or run into somebody from back home. It's also a place where illegal activity takes place, a place to sell stolen goods, or to score drugs. It's also a good place for a fight.

The scene opens into the dark smoky interior of the bar where we hear strains of music from the 1970s and ice clinking in glasses and other bar sounds. We see the silhouette of the players arranged together at centre stage. The only lights are from the jukebox at stage right.

The characters include: Tamara, a 17-year-old runaway who waits impatiently for her 40-year-old playboy boyfriend, Eddie, to arrive; Alex, who is Eddie's 22-year-old sidekick, an unemployed, wannabe singer with a drug problem; and Regina, a worn-out, once-attractive 55-year-old woman who has seen better days.

When the light brightens, each of the characters moves into their space. The entrance is at stage left. Regina is situated at a small round bar table with two chairs, near the entrance. Tamara leans against the bar close to where Regina is sitting, ready to run just in case she is checked for ID and has to make a getaway. There is an empty stool next to her that she saves for Eddie. Alex lounges against the jukebox playing chords on his guitar and singing along with the jukebox. He is waiting for Eddie too, and waiting for some action.

The door bursts open and Eddie is there. He is a hunk with long black hair. He used to hang around the fringes of the American Indian Movement, snagging chicks, before he went back to drinking. At 40 years old, he has never held down a steady job, and has never been in a long-term relationship. He is a party animal, experiments with drugs (marijuana, hallucinogenic), and cons and hustles his way through life.

He and Tamara have been enjoying a very brief whirlwind romance. He is starting to get careless, showing up late, taking her for granted. Tamara is not pleased, but not quite ready for a showdown just yet. She is tired of staring at the door, and sits leaning up against the bar. Eddie sneaks up behind her, and covers her eyes from behind. She reacts violently, pushing him away.

TAMARA: I told you not to sneak up on me like that. Damn it, Eddie.

Eddie grabs her and tries to hold her still. He laughs at her helplessness, but she breaks free.

Eddie grabs her again. He likes her feistiness, but he wants to make sure she knows who's in control.

EDDIE: So, you wanna fight, eh?

TAMARA: Stop it, Eddie. Just back off.

EDDIE: Come on, baby. I'm sorry I'm late.

TAMARA: You're always sorry lately.

EDDIE: You got a problem with that? I told you. Nobody runs my life but me.

TAMARA: You could have told me that before I got knocked up, asshole.

EDDIE: Who asked you to get knocked up? Sounds like it's your problem, isn't it?

Tamara turns away from him and tries to look tough, but is on the verge of tears. The old lady turns to look at her, and they lock eyes. An understanding passes between them, and Tamara, with great effort, stops her tears and turns to face Eddie.

TAMARA: Yeah, I guess it is my problem.

EDDIE: Come on, baby. I told you I'd help you out. It's not the end of the world.

Tamara allows him to kiss her, but she is not very responsive.

Eddie lays on the charm, and behind her back, he winks at Alex, and is aware of everyone who is watching. He fancies himself a real heartbreaker.

EDDIE: I brought you a present.

Eddie pulls a brown paper bag out of his jacket, and slides it across the bar at her. He is very pleased with himself.

It's something you really, really wanted. For our anniversary. We've been together six months today. Bet you thought I'd forget.

Tamara peaks into the bag, and lets out a shriek of excitement.

TAMARA: Oh, Eddie! It's the sweater, the red sweater.

She holds the sweater up against her, and poses for him, all happy and smiles.

I can't believe you did this.

EDDIE: Okay, that's enough. Put it back in the bag now.

Eddie glances nervously around the room. Tamara lowers the sweater and studies Eddie suspiciously.

TAMARA: How did you pay for this, Eddie?

EDDIE: Well, I didn't exactly pay for it, but you don't need to worry about that.

TAMARA: You lifted it, didn't you? Damn you, Eddie. You spoil everything. I don't want it if it's stolen.

Tamara shoves the sweater across the bar to him and turns away, angry again.

EDDIE: I went through a lot of trouble to get this for you. I could have got caught.

TAMARA: That's just it, Eddie. You could have got caught. You're on probation and I'm pregnant. I don't want to do this alone.

Eddie looks hurt, rejected. He has never been able to handle these kinds of situations very well. Usually he just leaves, but he really cares about Tamara.

TAMARA: I live my life in fear for you. You take too many chances, like you don't care.

EDDIE: But I do care, about you.

TAMARA: Do you, Eddie? Then why am I always worried that you'll do something stupid and go off to jail and I won't see you again?

EDDIE: Baby, you know what your problem is? You worry too much. I'm right here. I'll always be here, and if not, I'll always come back for you. I love you, baby. You know that.

TAMARA: No, I don't know that, and I'm afraid that I'll always be waiting for you to come back for me. That's no way to live.

She stands up, and pulls her jacket tight around her, and begins to walk away. Eddie grabs her arm and tries to stop her, but she pulls away.

Eddie holds the sweater up again in a desperate attempt to entice her back.

EDDIE: Come on, at least try it on. I want to see what you look like.

TAMARA: I don't want to, Eddie.

She shoves it away, and Eddie's mood suddenly turns ugly. He becomes menacing, dangerous.

EDDIE: So you're gonna be a bitch tonight, are you? I'll show you what I do with bitches.

Eddie raises his arm to hit her, but Alex moves quickly to stop him, catches his arm, and calms him down.

ALEX: Come on, Eddie. You don't want to do that. Just let her go. She'll cool off. Let's you and me go get high. I know a place where we can get some good blow.

Eddie backs off but still focuses on Tamara. The idea of getting high captures his attention.

EDDIE: You get out of my sight if you know what's good for you.

Tamara is shaken and afraid.

TAMARA: Can I have the keys to our room?

EDDIE: To my room? You can just wait until I get back.

Tamara moves toward the exit, and Eddie yells after her.

EDDIE: You'd better be here when I get back. Oh, and don't worry about that sweater. I'll give it to someone who appreciates it.

Tamara exits. Eddie looks around the bar and spots Regina.

EDDIE: Here, you want a sweater? It's yours. Get the damn thing out of my sight.

Alex guides his friend over to the bar.

EDDIE: Women, they're a pain in the ass.

ALEX: Aw, forget about it, Eddie. Come on, let me buy you a beer. Bartender, let's get some service here.

EDDIE: You buy me a beer? Now that's a switch. Since when did you ever buy me a beer?

Turning his pockets out, Alex searches around for some money.

ALEX: Well, you'd better grab it fast. The offer is about to expire. Where in the hell did all my money go? Hey partner, you got some money?

Eddie, disgusted, throws some money on the counter. Alex raises his beer for a cheer.

ALEX: Now what were we celebrating again?

EDDIE: My anniversary—Tamara and me, six months. That's a long time for me. Now I'm beginning to think I'm wasting my time.

ALEX: Yep, I think you can forget about that. How about we celebrate your freedom instead? Since it looks like that relationship's going nowhere fast.

Alex cracks up at his own joke.

EDDIE: What the hell is that supposed to mean?

ALEX: Lighten up, Eddie. I was just joking.

EDDIE: Asshole!

ALEX: Yeah, that's what some people call me, but I'm not a rich asshole. You got more money?

EDDIE: For what?

ALEX: The blow, man. It costs a lot of money to get high nowadays, but it's the best. A few lines, and you'll forget all your problems. In fact, you won't have any problems. That's how good it is.

Alex whips his guitar around and sings a few lines of a song about drugs and lost love ("Dazed and Confused").

EDDIE: Quit fooling around, Alex. I want to get high. I want to get totally messed up. I only got a few bucks though. But hey, I got something I can sell.

ALEX: Ah jeez, you're not gonna start selling your body again. Then we'll really be broke.

Alex cracks up at his own joke. Eddie is menacing.

EDDIE: You think that's funny, eh? Just wait until you go to jail. Pretty boy like you won't have no problem selling that body. They'll eat you right up.

ALEX: I ain't never gonna go to jail. Quit talking like that. You're scaring me.

Eddie pretends to spar with Alex, and gets him in a choke hold.

EDDIE: See how easy it is? Toughen up. Toughen up, little bro.

Alex struggles free. He's a little upset, but is not accustomed to standing up to Eddie, who is his hero.

EDDIE: Asshole. I wasn't even talking about that. I was talking about that sweater. I could sell the sweater.

ALEX: Hey Eddie, I get my feelings hurt when you call me names.

Alex clowns around, pretends to cry, and when he opens his eyes, Eddie is gone. Eddie has moved over to where Regina is still preening in front of the mirror, checking out how good she looks in the sweater.

EDDIE: You got any money, old lady? You gonna have to pay up or give it back.

She pulls the sweater possessively around her. She is not going to give it up without a fight.

EDDIE: Look, it was a mistake, okay? I didn't mean I was giving it to you. Nice sweaters like that is gonna cost some bucks.

She shakes her head, no, and tries to pull her coat on over it. Eddie tries to prevent her from putting the coat on, and they wrestle. Alex moves in and tries to separate them.

ALEX: Take it easy, Eddie. She's just an old lady and that bouncer's looking this way.

EDDIE: Come on, I need some money. At least give me some money.

ALEX: Yeah kye7e, I know you got your check on Wednesday. You must have some money.

REGINA: You gave it to me.

She looks around the bar for support.

REGINA: Everybody heard you say I could have it. You can't take it back now. I only have a little bit of money. Here.

Slowly she draws a handful of change out of her coat pocket, and sets it on the table, and then steps back. They both step forward to see what she has.

EDDIE: Shit, that ain't even enough for one round. Give me back that goddamn sweater now.

Eddie seriously starts to wrestle with her, but she hangs on, yelling out for help.

ALEX: Ah shit, Eddie. You're gonna get us kicked outta here. Here comes that bouncer. Come on, Eddie, let's go.

Alex drags Eddie to the door and they exit. The old lady slowly recovers from the attack.

REGINA: It's okay, folks. The show's over. I ran him out of here. Hey bartender, let's have another round for me. One more beer.

Regina takes off her coat and is making sure that the sweater did not get damaged in the struggle. She spots herself in the mirror again, and slowly begins to preen, thrilled at the way she looks. She begins to sing and dance, laughing and stomping her feet, and chucking in between.

REGINA:
    16 tons and what do you get?
    Another day older and deeper in debt
    St. Peter don't you call me, 'cuz I can't go
    I owe my soul to the company store.

VOICE #1 from Offstage: Turn up the jukebox.

VOICE #2 from Offstage: Shut up, you old bag.

VOICE #3 from Offstage: You're gonna scare away the customers.

Regina really begins to clown around, pretending she is boxing with her shadow.

REGINA:
    If you see me comin' better step-aside
    A lotta men didn't and a lotta men died
    One fist is iron the other is steel
    If the right one don't get you the left one will.

*Regina goes to the bar to get her beer, clowning and dancing all the
way. She returns to her table with her drink. Everybody ignores
Regina again. The bar noises return back to normal. She is old and
lonely, and usually nobody even bothers to talk to her anymore, so
she's learned how to entertain herself.*

*Light dims until all we see is the silhouette of Regina lost in her
own world.*

*Tamara enters and cautiously looks around. She takes her place at the
bar again, just as she was earlier, ready to run, ready for anything.
She spots the old lady in the sweater and smiles. Regina glances
back at her.*

TAMARA: The colour looks good on you.

Regina holds the sweater possessively around her.

I don't want it. It looks better on you.

Regina pushes an empty chair out and motions to Tamara to join her.

REGINA: He's no good.

TAMARA: I know that.

REGINA: Then why do you wait for him?

TAMARA: Because I don't have anywhere else to go, and because
I think I love him.

REGINA: Ah! What do you young people know about love?

TAMARA: Not a lot, but I can feel it. Have you ever been in
love, kye7e?

REGINA: I guess I was. I had six babies.

TAMARA: Is that what love's about, kye7e? Having babies?

REGINA: I don't know. Why are you asking me crazy questions?

TAMARA: I suppose it's because I don't have anybody else to ask.

REGINA: Well, don't expect answers from me.

Regina is clearly agitated.

After all I've been through in my life, what could I tell you? You could be me when I was your age, and look at me now.

TAMARA: So you don't see much hope for me?

REGINA: Now I didn't say that. I do know one thing though. The sooner you get away from him the better. He's bad news, even before you came along. I know that kind of man, in and out of jail. He'll never change. He's too old for you, and he's got too many problems. How old are you?

TAMARA: Seventeen. How old are you?

REGINA: Fifty-five last Tuesday. Aren't you too young to be in this place?

TAMARA: Yup, but they never ask me for I.D. Aren't you too old to be in this place?

REGINA: Don't get smart with me.

TAMARA: I'm just teasing you, kye7e.

REGINA: You're just trying to change the subject. You should try and find someone your own age, who doesn't drink and hang around bars.

TAMARA: Well, it's too late now. I'm gonna have this baby.

REGINA: It's never too late to change your life.

TAMARA: Did you ever think about changing your life when you were my age?

REGINA: Sure, I thought about it. I just didn't do anything about it. Anyway, we're talking about you, not me. I'm not the one with no place to go. Don't you have family around here?

TAMARA: They're all step-family. It's a long story. Besides, they all drink. I wouldn't know how to ask them for help.

REGINA: You're related to the Chief, aren't you? Why doesn't he help you?

TAMARA: He doesn't even know me.

REGINA: Well, here you are sitting on my doorstep like a little orphan. I guess I'll have to help you.

TAMARA: I can take care of myself.

REGINA: Sure you can. That's why I'm going to help you anyway. Here's my daughter's phone number. Her name is Morning Star Peters. She's the social worker on the Rez. Give her a call.

TAMARA: She's your daughter?

REGINA: It's better if you don't mention my name. She'll help you out, find you a place to live.

TAMARA: Don't you two get along? Wow, if she's a social worker, shouldn't she help everyone?

REGINA: She helps me. We just don't see eye to eye. We don't talk.

TAMARA: Wow, that's kind of sad.

REGINA: Why? Why is it sad? Lot of people on our Rez don't talk, and it's better that way.

TAMARA: But you're her mother.

REGINA: And I sent her to the same residential school I went to, even when I knew what was going on there. We both went through the same abuses. Why should she talk to me? There are some things in life you can't forgive. I understand that. I've never forgiven my mother either, so there.

TAMARA: But you gave her such a beautiful name, Morning Star. I wish that was my name.

REGINA: A pretty name for a pretty baby. She was my first one, and I gave them all pretty names before they were taken away from me. I had six babies, and I remember each one of them when they were born. That's all I could give them was pretty names. The rest of it was not so pretty.

TAMARA: Where were they taken? To residential school?

REGINA: Foster homes and adopted out. I don't know where they all ended up, but they're better off wherever they went.

TAMARA: They're never better off, because it's lonely, and it's strange, and you always want your mom. You always wonder how long it will be before you can go home. What did you do that was so bad for them to send you away?

REGINA: Bartender, another beer here. Why don't you have a beer? That'll help you forget.

TAMARA: It's not good for my baby, and I don't know if I want to forget.

REGINA: Ah, what have you got to forget? You're too young to have anything to forget.

TAMARA: When I was three my favourite uncle started to molest me. I still have nightmares, and I'm afraid of the dark. Nobody wants to talk about it in my family, and sometimes I think that's why I was sent away, so they won't have to remember. When I was seven, I watched my mom drown. I was too little to save her, and she was too drunk to save herself. This was after my daddy beat her up. She was trying to get away from him. Now all he does is drink.

My granny who practically raised me just died last year. They put us in foster homes because they said she was too old to care for us. I really miss her. I don't even know where my baby brother is or my sister. I ran away from my foster home because my foster dad wouldn't leave me alone. I hitchhiked all the way back here to be with my granny. Then she died. That's when I met Eddie. He's okay, but you're right about him. His nightmares are worse than mine.

REGINA: Everybody goes through hard times.

TAMARA: I know that, but talking about it helps. It's not that easy to forget. Drinking doesn't help me.

REGINA: Well, it's been helping me all these years, until you started digging all this stuff up.

TAMARA: I don't think I'll ever drink. I don't like the taste of it, and I don't like the way people act when they get drunk. My dad was a mean drunk. It's funny—he was so quiet when he was sober. My mom would drink until she passed out. No food, no hugs, no mom, no nothing. I don't want my baby to grow up like that.

REGINA: Well, you're smarter than most people to figure it out. It's best you don't start then. Once it takes hold there's no quitting.

TAMARA: You sound like my kye7e. That's what she would say.

REGINA: Well, you should listen to her. Did you listen to her when she was alive?

Tamara gets teary missing her granny.

TAMARA: All the time. I listened to everything she said. I was never scared when she was alive.

REGINA: Well, she's probably still around, still trying to help you.

TAMARA: I know she is. I can feel her sometimes.

Tell me one thing good about the residential school. Nobody tells me anything, and I want to know.

They sit for a silent moment while Regina strains to remember. Suddenly she stands up and preens, with a huge smile on her face.

REGINA: I used to be a dancer. My feet were quick back then.

She shows off her legs and feet.

I still got good dancing legs.

She begins to dance from memory, lost in her own world.

My favourite was the Mexican hat dance. I played the boy because I was tall.

She dances in a circle around a pretend Mexican sombrero. Tamara is enthralled.

We were the best. We even travelled to Mexico. That's how good we were. I knew all them dances, the Irish jig, the Scottish reel. We even won competitions against white kids. That's how good we were. How 'bout that?

She gets more energetic and almost knocks over the table. Tamara jumps up to help her regain her balance, and they collapse laughing in their chairs.

TAMARA: Wow! You can really move, kye7e.

REGINA: I always liked dancing. I wanted to be a dancer.

TAMARA: You could be a Pow-Wow dancer, a fancy dancer, or a jingle dancer.

REGINA: Not those kind of dances. We never did those kinds of dances. It wasn't allowed. Besides, when I said I wanted to be a dancer, I didn't mean Indian dancing. That's not dancing.

TAMARA: Why do you say that? It's our kind of dancing. They should have taught you Indian dancing too.

REGINA: They wouldn't even let us speak our own language. Why do you think they would let us dance Indian dancing?

TAMARA: You're right.

REGINA: Of course, I'm right.

TAMARA: Who taught you to dance, kye7e?

REGINA: That sister who was real mean. She'd strap our legs if we didn't move fast enough. Sister Mary Rose. She was a mean one. We had to practise, practise, practise. She stayed on top of us all the time. She was a mean one. Never make a mistake. We weren't allowed to hang around with the other kids, even my sister who was too dark to be a dancer. I had to stay away from her. Those were the rules.

No brothers or sisters allowed in that school.

TAMARA: How sad and lonely, just like foster home.

REGINA: I'd get so lonesome in school, homesick, hungry for the touch of my sister's hand, her smile, anything to not feel so alone. I'd take a chance and when I'd pass her in the hall I'd reach out to touch her. It's like it wasn't enough. I wanted to put my arms around her. She'd smile, and I'd smile, and then Whack! Right across the head, knock us right off our feet. We'd get yanked around and strapped. It was worth it though for just that one touch, a smile from someone who cared.

TAMARA: Oh, kye7e, how sad. Do you ever talk about that to her today?

REGINA: We don't talk. We gave up talking a long time ago.

TAMARA: That's the way my family is. I hardly know my aunties and uncles or cousins. Everybody is kind of distant and closed. They keep to themselves and keep their mouths shut. You should have seen them when I reported my uncle's sexual abuse. They all started fighting and blaming each other, and then they all quit talking. The only time we ever get together as a family is at funerals. I think maybe that's why I want this baby so much, even though I'm scared. I think maybe it will help me to not feel so alone.

REGINA: Sometimes having a baby when you're too young makes you feel more alone than ever. Besides, that's too much responsibility for a baby to have to help you not to feel alone. Babies just got to be.

TAMARA: Gee, I never thought about it like that, kye7e. I think I'm gonna have to start thinking more about my baby and less about me. That's gonna be hard for me to do because I am by myself. I don't think Eddie's gonna be much help.

REGINA: That's why you need to call Morning Star. You need to find somebody else to help, because he's not going to be around.

TAMARA: I just had an idea. Maybe you could be kye7e to my baby.

REGINA: You don't want a drunken grandma for your baby. You should find somebody who doesn't drink.

TAMARA: kye7e, after all that you've shared with me tonight, I think you would make a very good grandma for my baby. Besides, there is nobody else.

REGINA: If I'm going to be kye7e to your baby, I don't want you hanging around in this place anymore. This is not a good place for a baby to grow. It's too smoky in here, and the music's too loud, and people are crazy. The next time we visit, you come to my place at the Cecil Hotel. I mean it. I don't want you in here anymore.

TAMARA: Okay, kye7e. I won't hang around here anymore. You know what, kye7e? Eddie and I stay at the Cecil Hotel too. You and I are neighbours. I think the Creator is bringing us together.

REGINA: Hmm . . . It's not a very good place for a baby to grow.

TAMARA: Well, when the baby comes, I'll move to an apartment with a yard, and you can come stay with us. Wouldn't that be great, kye7e?

REGINA: I'd have to have a talk with your man. He's got a bad temper, and he'd have to learn not to hit people. I'll tell him that myself. He'd better straighten up. He's not a kid anymore. An old man like that, he should know better.

TAMARA: I know he'd listen to you when he's not drinking.

REGINA: I'm tired. I'm gonna go back to my room to sleep. You better go on home too.

TAMARA: I have to wait for Eddie to get back.

REGINA: You're not gonna be safe with him tonight. Take my keys to my room. You stay there tonight, and then we'll figure things out in the morning.

Regina gives her keys to Tamara.

It doesn't matter how late it is. If he gets mean to you, you come to my room.

You should come now, but I know you won't.

TAMARA: Do you want me to walk you home?

REGINA: Nah, I just cut across the alley. I walk myself home every night.

Regina gets up and prepares to leave. She is very touched by her connection to Tamara and how much they have shared.

Nobody ever takes time to listen to me like you did tonight. I didn't realize I had so much to say. Thank you for taking time to listen to an old lady talk. I'll be expecting you soon and we'll talk to Morning Star. We'll get you some help. Don't worry about it. Just worry about your baby.

TAMARA: Thank you, kye7e. I feel so much better knowing you're there.

REGINA: Are you sure you don't want your sweater back?

TAMARA: No, kye7e. It's not my sweater. It's yours. It looks beautiful on you.

Regina exits and Tamara goes to the jukebox and plays some music. She returns to her table to wait.

Two men enter the bar. The younger man, Joe Two Feathers, wears a ribbon shirt, blue jeans, and cowboy boots. He also wears a brown cowboy hat with an Eagle feather hanging from a beaded hatband. He is very proud and upright. He is accompanied by another man, Chief Philip Jack, who is dressed more conservatively. Joe is a member of the American Indian Movement. Philip is the Chief of the local band. They are both involved in a local roadblock and protest. They stand at the bar close to where Tamara is seated.

CHIEF: Let me buy you a beer. What do you want, a draft?

JOE: Nope, not for me. I'll have a Coke.

CHIEF: Oh, I keep forgetting. You don't drink.

Joe turns to take a look around the bar.

JOE: Not while it's killing my people. You ought to think about that.

CHIEF: Oh, what about the pot you guys smoke? That doesn't count, huh?

JOE: What did you ask me here for? Can we just talk about that?

CHIEF: Yeah, let's get down to business. We're all pretty edgy. The police are coming in tonight. That's what I've heard. They're gonna arrest all those fellas at the blockade, charge them with mischief. What do you think about that?

JOE: Let 'em come. We're not gonna back down. If this is what it takes to get them to listen to us, then this is what we'll have to do. From now on, we're standing up. No more begging on our knees.

CHIEF: I worry that somebody will get hurt though. What do you think about those women and children being there? You think we might get them to leave just to be on the safe side?

JOE: Ha! I'd like to see you try. This is their fight too. They won't leave. I know some of those women. I know they've been through rough times in residential school. I also know that some of their kids have been apprehended and put in white foster homes. They got their reasons for being there. And those grandmothers, do you think they're gonna back down? They'll be the last ones to leave. To tell the truth, I feel safer knowing they're there.

CHIEF: It shouldn't have to be like this. Damn! We shouldn't have to fight for every little scrap.

JOE: At least we're fighting on our feet now, not begging on our knees. We're fighting for our rights, our land, our language, culture, everything they took from us in residential schools. I'm fighting for my childhood. You won't see me backing down, no matter how many jails they put me in. They'll never silence me again. Ever.

CHIEF: Be cool, Joe. We don't wanna get too militant.

JOE: Militant! What the hell does that mean? Just another label they stick on us to justify what they do. They're the thieves, murderers, rapists, oppressors and the sooner you get that straight the better off you'll be.

CHIEF: Hey Joe, I'm on your side. I know exactly how you feel.

JOE: Do you? Do you, Chief? Do you know how I feel? Because I'm not the only one that feels this way.

CHIEF: I think you forget. I went to residential school, too. You don't see me crying around about it. Besides, I don't see what the hell that has to do with anything.

JOE: But did we have the same experience? I don't think so. You had your grandfather speak up for you. They were scared of him. I didn't have nobody. Things happened to me there that I could never tell you, or anybody, about. But I'll tell you one thing, as long as I'm alive, they're gonna pay. Don't kid yourself, Chief, residential school has everything to do with what is happening right now. It's called rage. You should try it, sometime.

CHIEF: I respect that, Joe. All I'm saying is that not everybody agrees with what we're doing. I'm getting a lot of pressure from other Leaders to back down and try and negotiate instead.

JOE: Well?

CHIEF: Well what?

JOE: Is that what you called me here to tell me? You wanna back down?

CHIEF: No, I just wanted to let you know that there are people who think that things can be solved peacefully, through negotiation.

JOE: Yeah, I know all about the White man's peaceful negotiation. It's the same crap they fed us in residential school. Teaching us kids to be civilized, while they acted like barbarians. And they called us savages.

CHIEF: Now Joe, you know that as Chief, it's up to me to consider all possibilities and make decisions that are best for all the People.

JOE: I hope you listen to the People while you're making those decisions.

CHIEF: I always take my direction from the People.

JOE: What about these people in here, Chief? Do you make decisions for them?

He motions with his lips around the bar.

JOE: What about that Elder who just left here? How do you know what she needs? And that young girl there, why isn't she home with her family? Why isn't somebody looking out for her interest? She's too young to be out here on her own in a place like this. What are you doing about that, Chief? I hope you listen as good as you talk.

At that moment Eddie bursts through the door. He is strung out and agitated. Alex has him by the arm and is trying to drag him back out through the door. Eddie is bigger and stronger though, and he pulls his arm away and Alex almost falls.

ALEX: Let's not go in here, Eddie. Come on, let's run.

EDDIE: You run. I just want to get me a drink.

ALEX: You don't need another drink. The police are gonna be all over this place.

EDDIE: What're you? My old lady? What are you squawking about? Bartender, give me a drink.

ALEX: You didn't stop to check her, Eddie. I did. I think she's dead, and I don't want to go to jail.

EDDIE: I'm not scared of no jail, free room and board for the winter. Those cops better not try and mess with me.

Eddie spots Tamara and he heads over to her. Then he remembers how drunk and loaded he is and feels ashamed.

Hi baby, are you waiting for me? We can go home now.

Tamara stands up and is transfixed by something she sees dangling out of Eddie's jacket. Fearful, she speaks up.

TAMARA: What's that in your coat, Eddie? What have you got?

EDDIE: It's nothing. It's just that sweater I got you. I know you said you didn't want it, but we could sell it and get something else.

TAMARA: How did you get that sweater, Eddie?

She takes it from him and notices that it is torn and has dirt stains.

Why is it torn? Alex, what happened? How did he get this sweater?

ALEX: I tried to stop him. Oh, God, we shouldn't even be in here. Come on, Eddie, let's go.

EDDIE: It's nothing. Really, it's nothing. I just gave her a little shove and she fell.

Sirens sound outside. Tamara screams. Eddie runs for the door, where he is arrested. Alex holds on to Tamara.

ALEX: Tamara, stay out of it. You can't afford to get involved. I'll get you out the back.

Alex pushes her toward a back exit. Tamara is hysterical.

EDDIE: Leave me alone, you son-of-a-bitch. I didn't do anything. Tamara, don't leave. Come back. Don't leave me.

Chaos, Sirens.

Blackout.

SCENE 3: RUNAWAYS

It is just before dawn. The setting is Regina's hotel room at the Cecil Hotel. The room is dark except for the flashing neon lights through the window.

Tamara and Alex have been hiding in the park all night. They are both cold and scared. Alex is high, and the drugs and his ordeal make him paranoid and jumpy.

Tamara enters first. Cautiously she tiptoes in, followed by the more noisy Alex, who does not want to be in the room of the dead woman.

ALEX: Turn on the lights. This place is creepy.

Alex reaches for the light switch, but Tamara moves quickly to stop him.

TAMARA: No, shush, just be quiet. We don't want anybody to know we're here. We shouldn't be here.

ALEX: Then why did we come here? I told you we shoulda stayed in the park.

Alex is suddenly startled by what he thinks is someone standing in the room, but it is a coat rack with clothing hanging from it.

Oh, man, I thought that was somebody standing there. Let's get the hell outta here.

Tamara crosses the room to show him there is nothing to be afraid of.

TAMARA: See, Alex, it's just a coat rack.

Alex bumps into the table and knocks some things to the floor.

Tamara moves quickly to his side to stop things from falling and to make sure he doesn't cause any other damage.

Shush, Alex, don't move.

ALEX: Well, I can't see. Turn on the light.

TAMARA: No, just sit down somewhere.

Alex stumbles around in the dark, then finds the bed and sits down. Tamara stands still and listens to make sure no one heard the noise that they are making.

ALEX: You said yourself we shouldn't even be here.

Alex examines the bed he is sitting on, and imagines the old lady lying there.

I feel spooky sitting on her bed. Do you believe in ghosts, Tamara?

He can't see Tamara and he is suddenly scared.

TAMARA, where in the hell are you?

TAMARA: I'm right here.

ALEX: Well, stand where I can see you.

TAMARA: Are you scared of the dark too, Alex?

ALEX: No, I just don't like to hang out in dead people's rooms in the middle of the night.

TAMARA: At least we're off the streets. Hanging out in the park wasn't such a great idea either. Why don't you close the drapes, and I'll turn on this small lamp here.

Alex moves over to the window to pull the drapes shut and Tamara turns on the lamp.

Alex sits back down on the bed, comforted by the light. He notices the television set beside the bed.

ALEX: Let's turn on the TV. We can catch the six o'clock news, see if there's anything happening yet.

TAMARA: Okay, but we still have to be quiet, let's keep the sound down.

Alex turns on the TV and they both sit on the bed to watch. It contains a commercial and other unrelated news.

ALEX: I'm tired.

Alex slumps over, as if he wants to sleep.

TAMARA: I'm tired too, and so cold.

She pulls a blanket over and wraps it around her, then she begins to cry softly to herself. Alex sits up and clumsily tries to comfort her, but he's not too good with women's tears.

ALEX: Hey, Tamara, don't cry. It'll be okay. Once we find out what's happening, then we can figure out what to do.

TAMARA: Did you know her at all?

ALEX: Nah, I just seen her in the bars. She hung out there all the time. I never spoke to her. She was just an old lady, an old drunk.

TAMARA: I knew her. I spoke to her. She was my friend. I'm gonna miss her. Where is that sweater?

Alex searches in his jacket pocket and pulls out the sweater.

ALEX: It's right here in my pocket.

TAMARA: Can I have it?

ALEX: Sure.

Alex hands her the sweater, and she cradles it in her arms.

TAMARA: It's probably the only beautiful thing she owned. Eddie should have let her have it. It was stupid to fight over a sweater.

ALEX: Ah man, Eddie was messed up. He was bombed, man. He didn't know what he was doing.

TAMARA: That's no excuse to hurt an old lady like that.

ALEX: Well, I guess he knows that now, 'cuz he's in big trouble.

Suddenly Tamara is riveted by what she sees on the TV screen.

TAMARA: Oh no, Alex, look! That's you on TV.

Alex jumps up to turn the sound up. He is stunned.

ALEX: Shit. Damn. Why am I on there? I didn't do nothin'.

TAMARA: Be quiet, Alex, so we can listen.

ANNOUNCER: Police are searching for Alex Abbot, an accomplice to the murder. Abbot is believed to be living in the area and could be dangerous. If anyone knows his whereabouts, please call the number on your screen. Identity of the 57-year-old Native woman is being held pending notification of next of kin.

Alex jumps up and begins pacing the room. He is very incensed by his fear. As he paces, he hits the wall in frustration.

ALEX: Now what am I gonna do? I'm not going to jail. I've never been to jail. I never even done nothin'. I'm not an accomplice. I even tried to stop him. What do they want from me?

TAMARA: Alex, you have to stop that. Alex, they probably just want to question you about what happened. You're probably their only witness.

Alex is not even hearing what she is saying as he continues to react.

Alex, come here and sit down.

Alex reacts to Tamara's calmness with anger, and even as he resists sitting down, he sits down.

ALEX: How can I sit down? My whole life is going down the toilet.

Tamara tries to calm him down, and speaks to him in a soothing voice like speaking to a child.

TAMARA: Alex, listen to me. Just try to calm down so we can think.

Alex buries his head in his lap, and then begins to thrash around.

ALEX: No, no, no, no.

Alex jumps up and begins pacing again. Tamara loses her patience with him.

TAMARA: Alex, if you don't settle down, someone is going to hear you, and they're going to call the police, and then you won't have any choices. You've got to be quiet. Listen to me.

Alex stops beside Tamara and listens, hoping she will have a solution.

ALEX: Okay, okay, you're right.

TAMARA: Eddie's your friend. He won't let them put you in jail. Think about it. When they ask him, he'll tell them you didn't have anything to do with it.

Alex becomes hopeful.

ALEX: You think so?

TAMARA: Of course, Alex, it makes sense. Come, sit down.

Alex sits down tentatively beside Tamara.

Now, we've got to figure out a way for you to turn yourself in.

Alex jumps back up again, agitated and angry that she would suggest such a thing.

ALEX: Turn myself in? Are you crazy? I'm not gonna turn myself in. I'm not stupid. You know how cops treat Indians. Even if Eddie told them the truth, they won't believe him. They like putting Indians in jail. The more Indians in jail, the better.

TAMARA: Well, maybe it's not such a great idea. It's just a suggestion. I'm just trying to help.

Tamara's attention is distracted again towards the TV.

TAMARA: Look, Alex, look what's happening. It's that blockade on the bridge.

Alex sits beside Tamara at the very edge and watches the TV.

ANNOUNCERS: Thirteen Native men and five women were arrested early this morning at the Pincher River Roadblock. Local Natives have been blocking the bridge for over two weeks, claiming that it runs through traditional territory. They are protesting unfair treatment by the Department of Indian and Northern Affairs. Well-known activist Joe Two Feathers had this to say:

Sounds of Protest songs and Indians yelling in the background. Alex stands up.

ALEX: What did I tell you? They got a bunch of Indians in jail now. That oughta make them happy.

TAMARA: Shush, I want to hear this.

VOICE OF JOE TWO FEATHERS: It's time for the government to wake up. Our people are not the problem. Our houses are overcrowded and falling apart. We have no jobs, just handouts. Our women and children are suffering. Where is all the money the government stole from us for our lands and our resources? They live like kings and we live like beggars in our own land. Where is the justice in that?

ANNOUNCER: The eighteen who were arrested are expected to be charged with mischief and released. Chief of the Pincher River Indian Band had this to say:

VOICE OF CHIEF PHILIP BEAR: Our people should not be arrested for speaking the truth. We only have to look around to see the conditions that we, as Indian people, live in: the poverty, the alcoholism, the abuses. Look at how many of our young people suicide, how many of our people are locked up in jail. I, as a Leader, cannot stand by and watch while my people suffer. If this is the only way to get the government's attention, then this is what we will have to do. I stand with my people.

TAMARA: Alex, they're all in there. Joe Two Feathers is in the same jail as Eddie. Maybe Joe could talk to him. Maybe he can help him out.

ALEX: Ha! Do you think they're gonna let any of those Indians near each other? They keep them all separated, especially Eddie, 'cuz he's a murderer. They probably have him in solitary confinement.

TAMARA: Well, it could make a difference, them all being there and them speaking out about prison. It could make a difference for you, Alex.

Alex is sarcastic toward Tamara's perceptions, and all he can see is darkness and despair.

ALEX: How could it make a difference? I could, maybe, go down there and join them all in jail? Indian prisoner number 20: Alex Abbot, the accomplice.

Alex walks away and turns away. He doesn't want to hear any more. He feels cold, isolated, alone.

Tamara continues to try to help him.

TAMARA: Maybe you could get our Chief to help you. He talked about our people in jail. He must care about that.

Alex turns back to face Tamara, but his shoulders are slumped in defeat.

ALEX: Ah, he's just saying that. Just politician talk. He can't do anything.

Tamara is annoyed by Alex's negative attitude at each of her suggestions.

TAMARA: How do you know unless you ask him? You are so bull-headed. I'm the only one coming up with suggestions here.

ALEX: We're accused of killing an Elder, Tamara. At least that's the way they'll look at it. They won't give a damn about us. We're not political prisoners. We're murderers.

Tamara is suddenly alert.

TAMARA: I thought you said it was an accident.

ALEX: It was, but who's gonna believe that? Yeah, we're both messed up, big time.

Alex sees a prescription bottle on the dresser, and as Tamara talks, he checks out the label, then opens the bottle, and shoves some pills in his mouth. He also spies a few pieces of costume jewellery, which he slips into his pocket. Tamara sees him but doesn't say anything immediately.

TAMARA: Well, I know Eddie is in deep trouble, but you? You have a chance, if you'll just let somebody help you.

Alex walks angrily up to Tamara, and yells at her.

ALEX: For Christ Sakes, Tamara! Who in the hell is gonna want to help me?

Tamara is afraid of his anger, but she stands up to him.

TAMARA: Okay. Okay. Don't yell at me. I'm just trying to help. You should quit taking drugs. It makes you all weird, and quit stealing from her.

She reaches out her hand, and he sets the jewellery but not the prescription bottle in her hand. Tamara sets the jewellery down on the table by the bed. Alex is remorseful, because he really does like Tamara, more than he should, since she is his best friend's girlfriend. He sits down beside her.

ALEX: I'm sorry. I didn't mean to yell. I'm just . . . I don't know.

TAMARA: Scared?

Alex is relieved that she understands.

ALEX: Yeah.

TAMARA: I'm scared too. That's why I'm going to ask for help.

ALEX: From who?

TAMARA: Morning Star Peters.

ALEX: Who's that?

TAMARA: The social worker on the Rez, but she's one of us. I know her 'cuz she's related to a friend of mine.

ALEX: So what're you gonna do? Just call her up?

TAMARA: Yeah, that's what I'll do, but I have to do it quick before I chicken out.

Tamara goes to the phone and searches through Regina's telephone directory. As she dials the number, Alex lies down across the bed. He is very tired.

ALEX: Tamara, do you think she could help me too?

TAMARA: I think she would. She's very nice, and she really cares about people.

Alex takes his shoes off and curls up into a ball on the bed.

TAMARA: Hello. Hello, could I speak to Morning Star Peters please? (*Pause*) I'm sorry for calling so early. This is Tamara Fisher. Do you remember me? (*Pause*) Oh good, I was afraid you wouldn't. I'm in town. (*Pause*) I ran away. It wasn't a very good situation. (*Pause*) This is a bad time for me to be calling, isn't it? (*Pause*) Yeah, I've had some bad news too. I need help. I'm scared. I offered to walk her home. I shoulda just done it. If I only had walked her home, this wouldn't have happened. I'm so scared. You see Eddie, he's in jail now. I'm at . . . I'm at the Cecil Hotel. I'm in your mom's room, and you're the only one I could think of to call.

Tamara breaks down, sobbing into the phone. Alex sits up in the bed and stares at her like she is mad.

Will you please come? Will you come now? Okay. Okay. I won't. Morning Star, please don't call the police, yet. Yes, I'll be okay 'til you get here. Bye.

ALEX: Tamara, what did you mean by *your mom's room?*

TAMARA: Morning Star is kye7e's daughter.

ALEX: Oh man, you're crazy? Right outta your mind! She'll call the police. Right now I'll bet she's on the phone calling the police. You didn't tell her I was here, did you? She doesn't know I'm here?

TAMARA: No, I didn't tell her. You heard everything I said. I didn't tell her anything like that.

Alex puts his shoes back on and begins to prepare to leave.

ALEX: Well, I'm taking off before she gets here.

TAMARA: Where are you gonna go, Alex? They're looking for you. At least with Morning Star, you have a chance. It's better if they don't pick you up, like you're a criminal. It's better if somebody from the Rez speaks for you. I still think you should call the Chief.

ALEX: I don't believe she'll want to help me if she thinks I killed her mother.

TAMARA: But you didn't, did you?

ALEX: No.

TAMARA: Well then, tell Morning Star. She'll understand.

Alex with another streak of cruelty, which seems to come up when he is scared.

ALEX: You are so stupid, Tamara. What makes you think she won't just ship you right back to that foster home?

TAMARA: I have to believe. It's all I got. And if she does, I'll know it's not because she wants to. She'll do everything she can not to have to. When you meet her you'll understand.

Alex heads over to the door.

ALEX: Well, I'm not sticking around to find out. When do you think she'll get here?

TAMARA: She'll be here any minute now.

Alex is by the window examining the ledge outside.

What are you doing, Alex?

Alex opens the window.

Alex, get away from the window. You're scaring me.

She tries to pull Alex away, but he pushes her and climbs onto the ledge.

ALEX: I'm not going to jail. I'm not going to jail.

TAMARA: No, Alex, please.

Tamara reaches her arm out to pull him back in as he falls forward. She screams and falls to the floor. Morning Star bangs on the door and calls for Tamara. Then silence and the AIM Song begins.

Blackout.

SCENE 4: PRISON TIME (1971)

Almost a year has passed since the murder of Regina Blackwater. Eddie has been convicted of manslaughter and is serving a seven-year sentence in a medium security facility. He has a lot of time to think about his life. Recently he has become involved with a Native Brotherhood in prison, and is learning traditional spiritual ways. He attends sweat lodges, and is presently completing a fast. He is waiting for his Spiritual Advisor, Martin High Bear, to arrive to help him to break his fast.

He sits cross-legged in the middle of a sparse room. There is one window high up on the wall to his left. This is the only window that allows natural light in. A spotlight lights the area immediately surrounding him. The rest of the stage is in darkness. As he sits, one by one, all those people who have impacted his life visit him in spirit.

He wears the neutral mask from Scene 1. He is well-protected. There is no visible emotion. Everything is shut down. The scene depicts isolation and a sense of being immobilized.

Tamara enters slowly, tentatively, from stage right. She is very pregnant. She moves to centre stage, and begins to read a letter that she has written to Eddie. As she reads, she crosses out words and scribbles in new ones, composing as she goes along, choosing her words carefully, still afraid of him.

(Love song—flute)

TAMARA: Dear Eddie, I can't take care of you anymore. If you could see me, you could see that I am barely able to take care of myself. I am tired of your rage. I hate it when you yell at me, and blame me for your problems. You blame everybody else but yourself. Our baby moves inside me. It's getting ready to be born. I'm scared. I have to learn how to be a mother real quick. I never had a mother, at least not the kind of mother that I want our baby to have. I can't visit you anymore. I hope you understand. Your prison walls depress me, and everything seems so hopeless. After all that's happened with kye7e and Alex, I feel I can't love you anymore. I don't understand love.

I don't understand how it could just disappear like that, but it has. I know you'll always be the father of my baby, but I'm going to have to say good-bye. I realize that all my energy needs to go to this baby. There is nothing left for you. Please don't try to contact me. I won't respond. I won't change my mind.

Tamara moves so that she passes by Eddie, but she does not acknowledge that she sees him. As she comes close to him, she opens her hand and allows the letter to flutter to the floor in front of him. She exits stage left. He picks it up, holds it to his face to try and catch the scent. He cradles it near his heart, and with a sound of anger and anguish he crumples it up and throws it away. He regains his composure, and we once again see his emotionless self. From the corner of his eye, he sees something flutter—the faint outline of a warrior dancing. When he turns to look directly in the dark, it is gone, whatever it was he saw.

First, we hear the sound of the wind, as in Scene 1. Alex enters from centre backstage. He moves to stage right and sits mirroring Eddie, as he did in life. He wears the same clothes that he wore on the night of his death. Nothing much has changed about his appearance. He still looks unkempt.

ALEX: *(Wind)* Eddie, look at me.

Eddie refuses and shakes his head, no. He holds his hand up to block out the vision.

I know you can see me, Eddie. I know you can hear me. I'm stuck here, Eddie, just like you. I can't go forward and I can't go backward. I don't know if I'll ever be able to move again. I wasn't trying to kill myself, but I wanted everything to stop. It happened so fast. I wanted to die, and then I wanted to live. By the time I changed my mind, it was too late. Goodbye dreams. Goodbye life. I told you I wanted to be a singer, Eddie. Remember that? You laughed at me. I wanted to play in a rock and roll band and become famous. I know I coulda done it. I was good. If it wasn't for the drugs, I mighta made something of myself, but now it's all gone. There's nothing left. Twenty-five years is not enough time to be somebody's lover, somebody's friend, somebody's husband, father, grandpa. I just wanted to be somebody, but it all ended too fast. I looked up to you, Eddie. You were my hero. I wanted to be just like you. I just wanted to be like you. That's all I wanted, was to be just like you. Like you, Eddie. Just like you.

Alex moves back into the darkness and is gone. Eddie puts his hands over the mask. He tries to remove it. He is overcome, and with a great effort, he straightens his shoulders and becomes immobile again, his grief trapped inside. He sees the vision of the warrior dancing again out of the corner of his eyes. Angrily, he turns to look, challenging it, and it disappears.

kye7e moves out of the darkness of stage right. She does not speak, but we hear a healing song and the drum. Eddie is not able to see her at all, but he feels her at times, and the feeling is unsettling for him. She is in a good place, and she emanates love and peacefulness. She wears a soft, white doeskin dress.

She walks on a mountain trail. The sun on her face. Her eyes drink in the beauty of the lush green plants and trees. The song is her healing song. It soothes her on her journey. She stops to pick berries and to eat them. She listens to the sounds of birds singing. She sees Eddie. She feels compassion for his suffering, and she moves to comfort him from the other side. Even though he doesn't know what spirits are around him, he tries to push them away. He has no vocabulary for love, compassion, forgiveness. As she comforts him, we hear a male voice speaking a passage from Chief Seattle's speech about the loved ones that have gone over to the other side.

CHIEF SEATTLE'S VOICE: "Our dead never forget the beautiful world that gave them being. They still love its winding rivers, its great mountains and its sequestered vales, and they ever yearn in tenderest affection over the lonely hearted living and often return to visit and comfort them."

Eddie takes off the mask, and sets it carefully onto a beautiful scarf, wraps it and sets it aside. kye7e continues on her journey, and exits stage left. Eddie stands up and moves within the tight space of his confines, as he paces, and we get a sense of the small world that he is forced to live within. He stops and stares into the darkness where he saw the dancer. There is nothing but shadows. There is the sound of the heavy steel door being opened. Eddie stops pacing and looks to see who is coming. Joe Two Feathers appears from stage left.

JOE TWO FEATHERS: Eddie, how you doing, man? I thought I'd come up and tell you that Martin got held up in a ceremony. He'll be about an hour late but he's still coming to help you to break your fast.

Eddie and Joe shake hands using a special symbolic handshake of brotherhood.

EDDIE: It's good to see you, bro. I've been just waiting it out, trying to be patient.

JOE: Yeah, well, I know what that's like. We didn't want you to think he wasn't coming.

EDDIE: I appreciate that.

JOE: How're you holding up?

EDDIE: It's a little rough, thinking too much.

JOE: Yeah, I know how it gets in here—walls moving in on you.

EDDIE: Yeah, I've been staring at that window, wishing I could fly away.

Eddie pushes the mood away, not wanting Joe to think he's feeling sorry for himself.

Other than that, everything's cool. How 'bout you?

JOE: I've been pretty busy. There's a lot happening in that world out there, and you know me, I like to be in the middle of things. We've been having a lot of demonstrations, sit-ins, roadblocks, you name it. It's time for the People to rise up.

EDDIE: You haven't been getting arrested again, have you?

JOE: Ha! Almost. But that doesn't scare me. We got to keep fighting for those traditional territories. We can't let them people encroach on sacred grounds. We got to hold them accountable for how our people have been treated. I got a lot of fight in me, and no jail is going to stop that.

EDDIE: Well, I admire you for it. I wish I could be out there fighting too.

JOE: You don't need to be out there. You're in here, and there's a lot for you to fight for, for our brothers in here.

EDDIE: Yeah, I suppose you're right.

JOE: I can tell you're not convinced though.

EDDIE: Maybe it's because we don't have any power in here.

JOE: Sure you do. It's all in here (*indicates his head and his heart*). Just got to get your spirit up—in time, Eddie, all in good time. At least you're on the right road now. Right?

Eddie is dubious.

EDDIE: Yeah, I suppose.

JOE: We shut down that residential school in Sechelt. Just walked right in. There was about twenty of us.

EDDIE: I had two sisters who went to that school.

JOE: Not a good scene. There's this priest who's been there for years. One of the brothers said he molested his little sister. Well, she's all grown up now, but that son-of-a- bitch really messed up her life—alcoholism, prostitution, suicide attempts, but she came with us that day. It felt good to watch her take back her power. She confronted them, told them how he used to invite little girls back to his house beside the school, to watch TV, he said. Come to find out, he's been doing that all along, with those supervisors just turning a blind eye. You can't tell me they didn't know what was going on. They didn't want to give him up. That coward was running around trying to hide. You know our songs are powerful.

A song of protest is heard—an American Indian movement song. It starts out from a distance and gets louder and louder. Joe joins in the singing. He has a good strong singing voice. There is power behind his words and his stance. We can almost see the scene he is describing. Eddie admires him, but he is afraid to sing, afraid to hear his own voice, afraid to feel the strength of the culture, but he is feeling something.

When we came in singing, they were just shaking. We told them we weren't leaving until they got rid of that priest, and if it meant shutting that whole place down, that's what we would do.

Eddie is elated by this story as he thinks about his own residential school experience and those that abused him.

EDDIE: Man, I wish I coulda been there. What did they do?

JOE: Ah! They just tried to patronize us, so we set up camp right by the road, and we wouldn't let anybody in. We kept an eye on those kids, and we told them they didn't have to put up with anything from those people. It was sad that some of those kids were scared of us. You know how prisoners of war are? They get so beaten down that they get afraid to speak out against their captors. Two days it took them to dismiss that priest. We watched him leave, made sure he was gone. I don't know where they send people like that though, and that worries me.

EDDIE: I wished you were around when I was a kid.

JOE: Well, that's why we have to stand up for our kids now. We know what it was like, being helpless. Anyway, I thought you'd like that story.

EDDIE: It's a good story.

JOE: A good story is like medicine. It'll keep you going for a while.

EDDIE: I'd sure like to learn to sing like you.

JOE: You just need to practise. Sing every chance you get. You get a lot of power from singing. It helps you to breathe, and I know in here, you really have to struggle to breathe. I'll bring you a hand drum next time I come.

EDDIE: Yeah man, that would be great. I've never had a drum.

JOE: Well, I should get going. They won't let Martin up here until I leave. Good luck for your fast. The hardest part is behind you. I'll be back to see you again soon.

Joe exits stage left to the same sound of metal scraping as the door closes behind him. Eddie sits cross-legged on the floor again. His demeanour is more relaxed. There is a softening of his face. He waits expectantly for Martin High Bear, the Elder. As he waits, he attempts to sing the song that Joe just sang. He feels self-conscious and wavers at first, but soon it is a good strong song. As he sings, the warrior dances. He wants to look, but he is afraid. He turns his back. He shivers. His voice wavers, but he continues to sing, staring at the door until Martin appears. Eddie stands up in respect.

MARTIN: Was that you singing? Don't let me disturb you. That sounded good.

Eddie is embarrassed.

EDDIE: Just practising. I didn't think anyone could hear me.

MARTIN: Don't be ashamed of your singing. You sing as loud as you can. That's when those good spirits come around. They like to hear you sing, and you jump up and dance too.

Martin sings and dances around the room.

You'll be able to feel them dancing with you.

He stops in front of Eddie and smiles at him with the kindest eyes that Eddie has ever seen. It is like a warm light washing over him and he is deeply moved.

It makes me happy to hear you sing.

EDDIE: Who are the spirits that you are talking about?

MARTIN: Ancestors that have gone before. They could be anybody.

EDDIE: Do you think some of those old warriors come back to dance, you know, like Crazy Horse or Geronimo?

MARTIN: Probably. I'm sure they do if they're needed. Is that who dances with you?

EDDIE: Nah. I was just asking. Joe was just here.

MARTIN: So that's who got you singing. That Joe, he makes everybody sing. He says there are no spectators when you sing. It's not a show. Everybody has to sing. He's pretty smart, getting all them spirits moving like that.

The old man laughs with delight. Then he spreads out a beautiful blanket, and lays out his sacred objects.

Let's sit down, grandson. This is not for show either. This is just between you and the Creator. You don't need to be anybody special to pray. Everybody has their own power.

Do you understand me?

EDDIE: Yeah, I just get afraid to make a mistake.

MARTIN: As long as you pray from your heart, only for good things, and have good thoughts, you can't go wrong. Every day. It's such a small thing to learn how to say "thank you" to the Creator. Soon it will become as natural to you as breathing. Do you believe that?

EDDIE: Yeah, I feel . . . that. Maybe sometime that's what's missing from my life.

MARTIN: Now you got it. That's what I'm talking about. And you know that song you were singing?

EDDIE: Yeah.

MARTIN: That's a way of praying too. There's all kinds of ways of praying. For example, when you look up there at that window, what do you see?

EDDIE: Light.

MARTIN: What kind of light?

EDDIE: Sunlight.

MARTIN: Describe it to me.

EDDIE: Well, in the morning, it's very bright, and it sends light right across to that other wall, and you can see through it. It looks warm.

MARTIN: And how does it make you feel?

EDDIE: Happy and sad.

MARTIN: Well, that's a prayer too, because you're telling the Creator something with your emotions about that beautiful gift he sent you. When you took the time to look at it and appreciate it, that was your way of saying "thank you." That's a good prayer.

Eddie smiles, pleased with himself again.

MARTIN: This has been a long fast for you. Four days, four nights, and tonight it's time to celebrate. This is also your first time, right?

EDDIE: Yes, it is.

MARTIN: How are you finding it?

EDDIE: I'm feeling pretty weak, but I'm having strong dreams. I think I see things, but I don't know if they're really there. Sometimes I get scared, but it's a good kind of scared. I've been wanting to do this for a while.

MARTIN: Everything has a message. It may not make much sense now, but later on it will become more clear. Tell me about what things you get scared about.

EDDIE: I get angry or sad. I feel that very strong sometimes, and I know I'm supposed to only have good thoughts, so I push it away, but it keeps coming back.

MARTIN: But those emotions are natural. Everybody has them. Our job is to figure out where they come from, so they don't take over our spirit. The important lesson is to learn how not to use those angry feelings, or your fear of feeling sad, to hurt anyone or yourself. When you push them away, they will always come back. If you face them, you might have a different result. Tell me about your anger. Who were you angry at today?

EDDIE: I don't know if I can talk about that. It's just hard to talk about.

MARTIN: That's the job that I'm talking about. It's a hard job. I understand. Where do you feel your anger when it comes?

Eddie indicates the pit of his stomach, and he is beginning to feel angry, a natural emotion for him.

EDDIE: Right here.

MARTIN: I saw your young friend the other day, Tamara.

Eddie straightens up and reaches for the mask, and holds it to his chest defensively.

MARTIN: She's such a good mother to that baby. She was playing with him in the park, and he was laughing out loud, just being a kid. She's very protective, and she hugs him a lot. What do you think about that?

EDDIE: (*Eddie sneers*) Good for her.

MARTIN: But aren't you happy for that child?

EDDIE: I guess so.

MARTIN: Or are you too angry at Tamara to care?

Eddie is cornered and moves the mask further up his chest. He is ready to run.

EDDIE: She's nothing special. She's like all the women I've ever known, including that woman who was supposed to be my mom. All of them run out on you, take off as soon as you're down and out.

MARTIN: That's good. You're allowing yourself to feel the anger. Don't forget to breathe. Tell me about your mom. What was it like being her kid?

Eddie is a little ashamed of having this outburst in front of Martin, whom he respects and reveres.

He continues to cradle the mask.

EDDIE: She dumped me in the residential school. She got my grandpa to bring me there. I was four years old. They didn't tell me. I just thought we were going for a visit. He said to go with that nun, while he talked to the priest. I didn't want to go, but I always listened to my grandpa. I was playing upstairs. After a while, I wondered how come he didn't come to get me. I went over to the window, and I saw him walking away. I banged on the window and yelled, "sla7a, sla7a come back," but he kept going. I was scared, but I figured he just forgot me. I figured as soon as he got home, and Mom saw I was missing, she'd come right back to get me, but she didn't. She's never been there for me when I've needed her.

MARTIN: Is that what it feels like with Tamara?

EDDIE: Yeah.

MARTIN: But she's there for your child. She'll never leave him. I want you to think about that. Those are sad memories. Very sad. That must have been very difficult for you. Four years old, you were just a baby, and you still needed your mom, didn't you?

EDDIE: I got over it.

MARTIN: Did you? Well, that's good. Do you want to pray a little bit? Do you think this would be a good time to do that or not?

Eddie is relieved in the change of subject.

EDDIE: Yeah, I'd like to pray.

MARTIN: How 'bout if we pray for children to be safe. That would be a good thing to pray for, I think. Don't you?

EDDIE: Sure, that sounds good.

MARTIN: Why don't you start? Maybe you could pray that your son always be safe, and that his mother always be close beside him, at least until he's old enough to be on his own? What do you think of that?

EDDIE: Yeah, I suppose I could do that.

MARTIN: This is where that lesson comes in, about only having good thoughts when you pray. That's why it's a good thing to let off steam before you pray, so it doesn't get all caught up in there.

Eddie is nervous about the prayer and unsure of himself, but he relinquishes the mask and sets it aside.

MARTIN: While you pray, I will take this rattle and sing a song for children. This is a happy song for children.

Eddie puts on a serious face, but Martin sings the Mickey Mouse Minnie Mouse song for children, which makes Eddie laugh. They both have a good laugh.

MARTIN: You see, it doesn't have to always be serious. Laughter is good medicine too.

Martin begins to sing again, taking up the drum this time.

This is a big sacrifice that you make to fast these four days. The Spirits see your tears, and they know you are sincere. The Creator hears your prayers. That little boy that you once were came here tonight asking for help. He is carrying a lot of pain. Whatever it was he needed back then—his mother, to feel loved and nurtured, to be safe—you can help him now with your prayers.

At this revelation Eddie begins to cry, silently at first and then huge sobs as he remembers his crime against the old lady. Martin sits silent until his cries subside. He hands him some Kleenex and simulates taking up the smudge and feather and guiding the smoke around him as he sings.

Maybe someday you can forgive yourself.

EDDIE: I don't know if I can. I told myself I only pushed her a little and it was an accident that she fell and hit her head. She killed herself, stupid old woman, but I know that isn't true. There was rage in my heart that night. I pushed her hard, and kicked her when she was down. She reminded me of all the women who never protected me when I was a kid. I was full of drugs and booze, and I felt sorry for myself. It was my fault. It was all my fault.

Eddie sits silent for a moment. Tears fall silently from his face.

I have no more excuses. There is no forgiveness.

MARTIN: It is good to face the truth, but you are so hard on yourself, grandson.

EDDIE: My life is empty. I have no one. Tamara is gone.

MARTIN: Your relationship with Tamara ends, but your relationship with your son continues.

EDDIE: It's the same old story. Whenever I care for somebody they leave me.

MARTIN: What is the worst thing about being alone?

EDDIE: Having nothing to live for, being empty.

MARTIN: When you are alone you get to face yourself with no distractions. You were empty, and expected her to fill you up when you met her. That's too big a responsibility for a young girl, alone, and trying to raise a son. Besides, that's your job to fill yourself up.

EDDIE: (*Defensively*) I wanted us to raise him together.

MARTIN: But that's not possible, is it, grandson?

EDDIE: She could have at least waited until I got out.

MARTIN: I want you to think about what you just said. You want her to take care of your feelings, to be responsible for making you feel good for another five or six years? In the meantime, who takes care of her feelings, who is responsible for her?

EDDIE: I can't seem to do anything right. I'm useless.

MARTIN: Where is your compassion? Where is your mercy? Your love for yourself?

How can you love someone else when you have so little love for yourself? How can you ask someone else to love you when you have no love for yourself? Think about it. What is there about you to love?

EDDIE: Nothing, I guess.

MARTIN: That is your job then.

I'm going to go pick up my other bundle. I have something in there for you. I want you to smudge again, and to take sips of this water.

Don't drink too much or you'll get sick. I'll bring the fruit when I come back, and you can break your fast.

Martin exits. Eddie does what he has been instructed to do, and then he sits waiting. From the corner of his eye, he can see the warrior dancing again, but he is afraid to look. Slowly, he turns his head, but the warrior does not disappear this time.

EDDIE: Who are you?

WARRIOR: I am the warrior that has been dancing in your head. The one who was your childhood hero. The one you believed in when you used to believe in yourself. Can you remember who that was?

In this version, Eddie uses his fantasy of War Chief Geronimo, but any childhood super hero warrior could be used (trickster).

EDDIE: I've been thinking about you. How you've always been my hero, even when I was a child and all Indians were bad, even when Hollywood made a clown out of you. You were still my hero. You were everything I believed a true Indian man should be. And all my life, everything that you were, Great War Chief Geronimo, I was not. How is it that you come to visit me now when I am so pitiful? What could you tell me that could make any difference in my empty life? I am nothing. I am nobody. I am dirt underneath your feet. My life is shit, so what do you want with me?

Geronimo stands suddenly and lets out a huge war whoop, a chilling sound, victorious and powerful. Eddie is shaken into silence, his descent down into his own private hell broken by this powerful energy. Geronimo paces around the small space.

GERONIMO: Why do you stay here? Why don't you leave this place?

EDDIE: Because I can't. There are locks, and bars on the windows.

GERONIMO: (*Fiercely*) They are nothing compared to what you have in here. (*heart*) But for you there is nothing in here, but a prison. Is that so?

EDDIE: No, I don't think so.

GERONIMO: But isn't that what you were telling me in that great speech that you held me captive with?

EDDIE: I was just feeling weak right now because of what I'm going through. I'm not sure what I was saying.

GERONIMO: Words have power. They can build a prison inside you if you are not careful, especially now, when you are at your strongest. You just think you're weak.

EDDIE: I don't understand?

GERONIMO: You've allowed yourself to grow soft, my grandson.

EDDIE: Sure, I want to leave. Don't you think I'd leave, if I could? Who would want to stay in a place like this? If I could walk out that door, I would.

GERONIMO: And how long would you stay out there before you came back?

EDDIE: You're right. I always seem to end up back here.

GERONIMO: It's because you've grown comfortable with the scraps that the white man throws you. You are like a starving animal. You have nothing in here (*indicates his heart*) to sustain yourself. What has happened to your warrior spirit?

EDDIE: I don't know. I don't think I've ever had one. From as far back as I can remember, I've been in prison.

GERONIMO: You had one when you were born.

EDDIE: Well, then, I don't know what's happened to it. It's just gone. I have no memory of it.

GERONIMO: Do you want it back? Do you want to be a warrior? Do you want to lead your people out of this prison?

EDDIE: With all my heart. I'm tired of being a prisoner. My life as it is, is not worth living. I know I can do better. I just don't know how.

GERONIMO: You know how. You're just not used to making a stand. A warrior doesn't retreat. He must be willing to stake himself down to the ground, and fight to the death for what he believes in. I see, though, that you are not running anymore, and you have stopped hiding behind that mask. There is hope for you. Your body is still in prison, but your spirit is breaking free. Now comes the real battle. I am here to stand beside you. We will fight this enemy together. If you believe you were given this life for something better, I am here to listen.

Geronimo sits comfortably and waits for Eddie to speak. There is a small awkward silence as Eddie realizes that Geronimo is waiting for him to speak. Eddie stands up and faces the small window and looks toward where he knows the blue sky is. He sits back down in a position where he can see the window, and he gazes at it as he speaks.

EDDIE: I've never talked about this to anyone before. I don't know if I can talk about it now.

Eddie glances back at Geronimo, who remains stoic and listening. He returns his attention back to the window.

When I was very little, I knew another window in another prison just like that one. It was longer and wider, but it also represented freedom to me. I'd sit on the window sill and hide behind the drapes. I'd curl right up against the window, and nobody would know I was there. That's how small I was. I'd see the blue sky and dream of escape. I'd watch the birds fly, and wish I could be a bird so I could fly too. I'd stare at the sun and watch the clouds, and I'd think that is the same sun and clouds that my mother sees when she looks out of her window at home.

My favourite dream was about the river. I knew it was the same river that ran by my house. I'd think if only I could lie in it and float, it could carry me home. I'd close my eyes and imagine my mother's surprise. She'd be so happy. She'd hug me and hold me, and she'd never allow me to return to that school. That was my life at residential school from the time I was four until I was 16. I dreamed of escape. That was my prison.

I missed my mom and dad. I wondered why they never came to see me. I know they started drinking more, and they'd even forget to pick me up for holidays. I'd wait and wait with my bags packed while other kids left, but nobody came for me. Eventually, I learned never to expect too much. That way I wouldn't get disappointed.

I don't know how old I was when I started to be afraid to sleep at night. But I remember lying in bed, feeling terror, struggling to keep my eyes opened, waiting for something awful to happen. I'd watch other boys taken to the priest's room at night. I could hear them crying. One night it was my turn. You couldn't say no. That's the way it was. I was sick with fear and shaking when he yanked me up and pushed me ahead of him into that room. I thought of screaming for help, but I knew no one would come.

He undressed me. He touched me in shameful ways. He forced his penis in my mouth and made me perform oral sex. I was sick and tried to pull away, but he held me by my neck and wouldn't let me stop. I couldn't believe what was happening to me. Then he put his penis into my behind. The pain was unbearable. I tried to scream, but he held his hand over my mouth. I could barely walk. Then he told me to get back to bed and to quit acting like a big baby. I crawled right to the centre of my bed, and tried to disappear.

I wanted my mother so badly that night. I thought if I wished really hard, she'd know and she'd come. She never came.

The next day, the other boys made fun of the way I walked. Every night for five years I waited for my turn. There was no escaping from that prison.

Eddie gets up and returns to his original position beside the blanket facing Geronimo. Tears are flowing freely down his face, and he makes no attempt to cover them up.

Prison, that's my home now. It's all I know.

GERONIMO: A child who can dream, and a man who can cry, is no prisoner.

EDDIE: But after a while, I kept banging my head against that window. I couldn't fly. The window became bars, and I still couldn't fly, so I quit dreaming.

GERONIMO: Back when you were a child you couldn't escape so you dreamed of freedom. Now when you are an adult you can escape but you won't. You are no longer that helpless child. Look at all that you are. You are strong in your body. You have a good mind, and a spirit that is struggling to survive, but your heart is wounded because for all these years you've kept all that pus inside. Your mother didn't come because she couldn't, not because she didn't want to. All these years you've kept her away, even while you are longing for her. Your prison is in here (*indicates his head*). Go back to that window.

Eddie gets up and returns to his spot at the window.

Look again at that blue sky. See if you can see your mother coming for you in the shape of an eagle. She knows how to fly now. You take hold of her and you fly away.

Eddie begins to cry for his mother.

EDDIE: Mom, Mom, I need you, Mom. I knew you would come for me.

Geronimo exits and Martin re-enters. He carries a special bundle and lays it on the blanket, and then goes and kneels down beside Eddie.

MARTIN: I see the spirits are working. It is a good thing to see your tears. Don't hold them back.

He opens his arms and Eddie allows himself to be cradled. When his sobbing subsides, Martin leads him back to the blanket. He gives him the Eagle feather to hold.

You don't have to tell me what you saw in your vision. That is between you and your Creator. However, if there is anything that you don't understand I could try to help. Is there anything you would like to know?

EDDIE: How did Geronimo die?

MARTIN: Ah, now his is a great story. A true War Chief. Some Apaches say he never surrendered to death. On his deathbed he sang a song, and he told the spirits in his song, "I am waiting . . . I am waiting for the change." So you see, it wasn't the end for him. It was just another beginning.

Blackout.

SCENE 5: CONCLUSION

The conclusion uses movement and words to bring the circle back together again as a continuation of the circle coming apart in Scene 1.

In this scene, the drum symbolizes the core foundation of the circle and the culture. The sound of the drum calls the People back to the circle. In the circle they must face each other with truth by removing their masks and telling something from their heart. This scene uses dance, song, words, and the actors who are all the children of residential school survivors. The unmasking of the actors to tell a truth about their lives and how residential school has impacted them symbolizes what happens in a circle when people are sharing and healing. The final song is a song of protest, a song of standing up, speaking up, and fighting injustice.

ACTOR (JOE TWO FEATHERS): I don't understand why my dad beat me so bad. If I made a sound, he beat me harder, so I learned to take pain without making a sound. He's a residential school survivor. He was beaten too. I don't understand how someone who was put through so much pain could turn around and do that to someone else. I'll never do that to my kids. I realize now that all I ever wanted from him was love, and when I was a kid, he couldn't give that to me. I've worked hard to take off this mask and realize what it means to love myself. I want to soar like an eagle and be free. I deserve to be loved. I deserve to be happy.

ACTOR (ALEX): There's so much behind this mask. I don't know if I'll be able to get through it in a lifetime. It's like this huge mountain piled up, and I'm walking around it, around and around, wondering what to tackle first. As a child, there was no innocence. I felt shame for even existing. Rejection came from everywhere, total and complete. I grew up in foster homes. The foster homes I knew were just like the residential schools I've heard about, the same abuses, rejection, and oppression. I grew up with no love. I live day-to-day, and try not to have too many expectations. This mask helps me to survive. I take it off now and then, and it feels good.

ACTOR (REGINA): I was silenced by fear when I was a child. I got beaten into silence by those people who were supposed to love and protect me. When I got sexually abused, I couldn't tell anybody. I had to put on this mask and that's how I survived. You should see all that's hidden behind here, all the tears, the wasted years, the rage, the shame. Sometimes, I can still feel that scared little kid in there, hunched over, her head down, still thinking it's her fault. That's when I take the mask off, and I fight through the wall to get her free. Both my mom and dad went to residential school. They never talk about it. I don't know that they ever will. We're all so cut off, separated, isolated, but I'm fighting for a voice, a yell so loud it will bring all those walls down. (*Warrior woman's yell*)

ACTOR (CHIEF, MARTIN): There's a secret behind my mask that I've always kept well-hidden. I was sexually abused by a female relative, and later on by a male. There was no one there to tell me it wasn't my fault or that it was not right what these people did. There was no one there to comfort or to help me through all that shame and confusion. When I began to abuse female relatives, I chose to stop. Those memories still cause me pain today. It's risky to talk about it, but I know it's important. I must break through the shame from my own abuse. I take off the mask, and I feel hope. Telling the truth about myself helps me to heal.

ACTOR (TAMARA): I am completely alone behind this mask. No one can come near. I trust no one. I let people in only so far, then I move on. My mom, my aunties, and my granny are all sexual abuse survivors, and most of my relatives are residential school survivors. I know my dad beat my mom and that frightens me. I promised myself that would never happen to me. No one to break my heart, no one to make me cry, no one to say good-bye. It feels safe in here, but it's lonely. My greatest fear is that I'll wake up and I'm thirty, still alone, still afraid to try. But I'm going to take a chance. I'm going to take this mask off because I don't want to be alone anymore.

ACTOR (EDDIE): Wake up! Did I scare you? Did I make you laugh? Because that's what I do when I get scared, and I get scared whenever I start to feel. That's when my clown spirit comes out and saves me just in the nick of time. I've spent most of my life hiding behind this mask, telling jokes. I haven't had an intimate relationship in my life. Intimacy means trusting someone with my heart, and I trust no one. I cringe when women say "we need to have a talk." They talk. I squirm. Then the relationship ends. I'm alone again and feel sad, so I put this mask on and pretend I don't care. I learned that from my mom. She was a residential school survivor. She had a hard time hugging me. She'd stiffen up and push me away, and I felt like she didn't care. Behind this mask, I'm scared, but I do care. I want to be able to give someone my heart.

STORIES

THAT GREY
BUILDING

The grey cement building stood back from the road, making an eerie shadow against the twilight sky. The eyes closed, boarded up a long time ago. It was out of place there. Always had been. When they closed it down finally, it was as though they all just walked away and left it lifeless. Then someone who couldn't stand the staring vacant eyes boarded them up.

"That grey building was once like a prison to me. It still looks like a prison," my mother said, indicating the boarded-up old residential school that sat in the middle of the village on her reserve in the Kootenays. "So many children died there. It robbed me of my childhood. We saw things in that place that no child should ever have to see. That place, and that other," she tossed her head, contemptuously indicating the whitewashed church that sat directly across the road from the school, "will probably still be here long after I'm gone." Indian houses fell apart in five years, but not those places. In every reserve you travel to, the church is usually the only original building still standing.

"Nowadays, the only time anyone ever goes to church is when someone dies. Now the priest will come down only once a month to conduct mass. Everyone will be falling down drunk all week, but somehow they manage to make it to mass. What has the church ever done for my people?" Uneasily, I listen to the bitterness creep into my mother's voice. "They never taught us anything about survival in those schools, but they sure taught us how to pray and how to suffer." Then suddenly she is silent. Sadly silent. What happened, Mom? What went on in those schools? I asked and felt a tightening in my throat, a sadness, a loneliness passed from my mother to me.

I turned off the main road to my grandmother's house. I sensed that my mother did not want to see her right then. I headed up into the mountains, and for a long time we rode in silence, enjoying the healing beauty of the land. It was early summer and everything was fresh and green. In that part of the mountain there were still a lot of empty spaces. This was the way it must have been before the settlers came, I thought. What memories this land must hold for her, and how it must have changed. I glanced over at my mother and her face had settled into a silent calm. The storm passed on for the meantime, but I could tell she was remembering something.

"From the time I was a small baby, my grandparents carried me with them when they travelled," my mother began, quietly talking. "We used to ride through here on horseback before there were any roads. I used to ride double, behind my grandmother on horseback from the time that I was barely able to walk. My parents were always busy working the land. That's the way it was back then, the grandparents always took care of the younger children. They were our teachers. My grandmother used to teach me all the time, even when I was a baby. She never used to get angry at me like my mother sometimes did. All the time she would be explaining to me, telling me stories, teaching me the proper way to do things and why things had to be done in a certain way. Whenever we travelled, all along the way, my grandmother would stop the horse to show me something. The land was like a storybook to her. She knew every inch of it and had a great love and respect for the land. To love the land is the most important lesson she ever taught me."

And it's the most important lesson you've ever taught me too, I thought.

"My grandmother, your great-grandmother," she said to me, "was a very strong and powerful woman. She never allowed anyone to push her around." As my mother spoke, I could feel the tension easing out of her and the tone of her voice became stronger. "The first few times when we had to go into town to buy supplies, those white storekeepers would make fun of the way she used to talk. She spoke barely any English but she sure could tell those white people off in Indian. Eventually they learned to leave her alone. If she ever saw them picking on an Indian she'd be right there, never allowing them to get away with it. She didn't have much respect for white people and she never trusted them at all.

"'This is our land,' she would always tell me, 'every inch of it has been given to us by the Creator. Since the beginning of time Indian people have lived between these mountains. This is where the Creator put us,' she'd say, then she would stop the horse and make me get down and walk with her on the land. 'It has always been our job, since the beginning of time, to take care of this land, and of every single living thing that was put here on it. Every Indian person knows that we are the caretakers for this land, and that is what you must teach your children and your children's children. Our people must never forget that this is our land. Someday, many people will try to tell you and your children that this is not your land. You must promise me that you will never believe them, and that you will never allow your children to believe. Without the land, an Indian is nothing.'

"I was just a small child when she told me those things," my mother said, "and ever since then, almost everything that she ever told me has happened." As she spoke I came around a bend in the road that opened onto a spectacular view of the valley where my grandmother lived, and something silently omnipotent passed from my mother to me. "Whenever I start feeling weak, I always come back to the land to regain my strength. The land is where our strength comes from," she said.

We began to feel hungry, so I pulled the car over beside some trees, and we made a picnic of baloney sandwiches. "Indian steak," my mother calls it. After we'd finished eating, we lay down in the grassy coolness to relax. I was almost dozing off to sleep when my mother began talking again.

"One day we were on horse and buggy riding up in that direction," she pointed off in the distance, "we always used to go up there to pick huckleberries. There's a flat field over that ridge and that's where the farm houses start. Civilization," she said sarcastically. "When we came over that ridge, right away I saw something that had never been there before. As we rode toward it, I kept glancing nervously at my grandmother because I knew that she was not going to let that fence strung across the middle of the field with the big No Trespassing sign on it force her to turn back. The minute she spotted the sign, she cracked the whip, and urged the horses on. When we got to the gate, she told me to get down and open it so we could pass through. I was very, very frightened, but I didn't dare disobey. In the distance I saw a rider approaching very fast on horseback, and I knew I had to get the gate opened before he got there. I was struggling with the gate and all the while that white man was shouting abuses at me in English, which my grandmother could not understand. He was very angry, calling us every dirty thing he could think of. My grandmother was shouting back at him in Indian, insulting him in a horrible way, using words that I'd never heard her use before. I think she even threw in the few English swear words that she knew, she was so angry. The horses were already halfway through the gate when he got there, and he raised his whip trying desperately to drive them backwards, while my grandmother urged them forward. At the moment, when she was almost through the gate, she pulled her rifle out from underneath the seat, aimed it at the white man, and started yelling at me to get back into the wagon. I think she took the white man by surprise. He didn't dare reach for his rifle, because I think he probably could tell by the look in my grandmother's eyes that she would not hesitate to use the rifle that she had aimed at his head. He stopped advancing, but continued to shout at us as we rode away.

"My grandmother told me to tell her what he was saying. I didn't want to repeat some of those words to my grandmother, but I did tell her that he said that we were trespassing on private property, and we were never to pass through his land ever again. My grandmother got very angry and started hurling curses back over her shoulder. She was so angry I was afraid that she might turn back to shoot him anyway, but finally she calmed down and became very silent as we continued our ride up into the mountains. The sun was already down and I was thinking that soon we would have to make camp, when finally, she spoke again.

"'Never forget that,' she said gravely. 'It's exactly as I told you it would happen. There will come a time when you and your children will have to fight for this land. Never be afraid to fight for what you know is right. That white man, he knows that land he put a fence around and claims as his own is our land. I know it's our land and you know it's our land. We never sold it to him, and we never gave it away to that white man. He stole it. Remember everything, because someday they will tell lies. They will try to convince your children that we gave it up without a struggle.'

"We continued on for a while longer, and I went back over that whole day, over and over again, trying to remember every detail. When we came to a fresh spring, we began to make camp. I was about seven years old at that time," my mother said. "We let the horses loose from the buggy and I got busy gathering firewood, while my grandmother hooked up the lean-to tent. We built up the fire and began to prepare the evening meal. We expected that soon my grandfather would arrive. He always travelled a little behind us, so he could hunt for game along the way. He would eat with us, then play games with me and tell me stories before I went to bed. In the morning he was always gone before I got up. That night he came very late. I was already in bed, and I lay listening to their voices going on, very low, very quiet, very serious, late into the night. It seemed strange to me that there was no laughter by the campfire that night, and I believe that was the first time in my short life that I began to be afraid. After that night we never spoke about that incident again.

"Our days were always full of hard work and many adventures for me. Every day my grandmother continued to teach me. She always spoke to me about the spirits that watched over us. Each morning she would wake up just before sunrise, so that she could welcome the new day, in the proper way. I would listen to her as she moved around getting ready, unpacking her sacred things. Then, just as the sun barely touched the corner of the mountain, she would begin. I could smell the smudge filling up the space in our tent, and with my eyes closed I could watch her purifying herself, then brushing the sacred smoke all around me, asking Nupika, the great spirit, to keep me safe. She always talked to the spirits like they were old friends, and offered them tobacco. I always felt so safe and protected under the pile of blankets that she would tuck around me, before she went down to the spring for her morning swim. She always told me that water was a powerful spirit, and jumping into the cold water every morning is what gave her her strength. I'd stay a long time in bed listening to her voice soothing, and gently rising and falling with the beauty of our language." My mother paused, remembering, then continued, "There are no words in English to express what she would tell to the spirits.

"'The language is so important for our survival,' she would say to me, 'You must teach your children to speak the language. When you pray in your own language, it is the most powerful thing because the spirits know that the prayers are coming from your heart, and it makes it easier for them to listen.'"

My mother became quiet again. We packed everything back into the car, and rode in silence through a long narrow valley that was surrounded by tall clay cliffs with rutted-out trenches that ran down the length of them. I stopped the car to take a better look and my mother started speaking again.

"I will always regret that I was unable to teach my children to speak the language. I wanted to, but times were so difficult when you were all little. I could never even teach you about Nupika until now. All my grandmother's teachings, I was never able to pass that on until now. Maybe if I had never gone to that school my life might have been different and I could have chosen a different path for my children." She lapsed back into silence. Hurtful silence.

"You did the best that you could," I said. "Those times were really hard when we were growing up. Anyway, I'm glad you're teaching me these things now. I do get a lot of strength from the stories you tell me. Tell me more about the school?" I wanted to coax her out of her melancholy mood.

"That was the turning point in my life," she said. "After that, it was as though I had no control over my life anymore." She looked so lost and so very sad. I wanted to put my arms around her and make her stop talking because I knew how much it hurt her to remember, but instead I sat very still, willing her to continue.

"I remember I was about eight years old when the priest came to speak to my parents. My grandparents were also there. I'd already heard some talk about the new residential school from some of the other children. I never wanted to go there and I never believed that my grandparents would allow them to take me. I had never been anywhere without my grandparents before, and if they couldn't come with me, I had no intention of going. After the priest sat down, everyone, including myself, sat down too. He cleared his throat and suggested that it might be better if I went outside to play. I stood up and looked at my grandmother, but she pulled me back down beside her, and nothing more was said about that. 'The reason I've come,' he began, 'is about the child. We have put her down on the list to begin school at the next session, which will begin in two weeks.' Afraid, I moved closer to my grandmother for reassurance. 'What is he saying?' she asked my mother sharply. While my mother translated, she cut in harshly, 'Tell him she's not going to that place.' Abruptly, she stood up and took me out of the room. We heard them talking in the next room for a long time. I hung onto my grandmother. 'I'm not going to have to go, am I?' I asked. 'No,' she replied. 'I'll speak to your grandfather. He won't let them take you.' When the priest left my mother came into the room and told my grandmother that I would have to report to the school by the end of two weeks. If I didn't go, the priest said that my parents and grandparents could be punished for breaking the law. 'Whose law?' my grandmother spat. 'It's not our law to allow them to take our children.'

"The atmosphere was tense all evening. My grandmother was angry at my mother for not standing up to the priest. I was afraid and that night I prayed very hard to Nupika not to let them take me away. Early the next morning my grandmother was up and packing the horses. She told me to get up, and gave me very specific instructions on how I was to prepare myself for the day. I had to go down to the river to bathe in the cold water. I sensed the urgency in her and followed her directions exactly. Before the sun had barely made it into the sky, we started out toward the tallest mountain, my grandmother, my grandfather, and me. Before we left, my grandmother gave me a strong, bitter tea to drink. 'You will eat nothing until we camp tonight,' she said gently, 'You must be very strong today.' We travelled all that day, going up and up and up into the heart of the tallest mountain, and I wasn't afraid anymore. I was very happy because I knew how much my grandparents loved me.

"We stayed up in the mountain much longer than the two weeks. All day long we worked side by side, and my grandmother shared with me all of the secrets of her great wisdom. She showed me where to look for the healing bark and roots, how to pick them, and how to prepare them for storage. I rose early in the morning, before the sun barely touched the corner of the mountain, and I bathed with my grandmother. Together we thanked the Creator for giving us another new day to live. We never spoke at all about the school and we never talked about how long we would stay up in the mountain.

"One day my grandfather came back from hunting, and he told us that he'd seen signs of horses on the mountain, but he never took the time to see who they belonged to. He came directly back to camp. He and my grandmother began to quickly gather up our belongings. She bundled me up on the horse, and we travelled all night to the other side of the mountain. After that, we kept moving. Every other day we would make a new campsite, but they found us anyway. One night, four RCMP officers walked into our camp. They told my grandparents if they didn't bring me down to the school, they would have to go to jail. My grandmother sat silent, defeated, and all night long she held me tight, trying to make me believe that everything would turn out alright. For me it was like the end of the world. I felt as though I were about to lose something very, very precious, and I was powerless to stop it from happening.

"All the way down to the village the next day, I cried and begged and pleaded and argued with my grandmother. That was the first time that I had ever argued with her. I refused to see that she was powerless too. Finally, my grandmother stopped the horse and told me to get down. She dismounted, and sat me down beside her underneath some trees, and began to try to comfort me. I will always remember every word that that old woman said to me. Years later, I would often wonder if it might not have been better if we had known then what to expect. Then my grandmother could have prepared me in a much different way.

"'It is good that you are going to that school,' my grandmother said. 'You will learn many things that I am unable to teach you. Look closely at your granny. I cannot read or write or speak the white man's language. When I have to go into town to buy the things we need, it is hard for me to make people understand, and they laugh and make fun of me. I don't want that to happen to you. At that school, you will learn all of these things, and when you finish, you will be able to get a good job in a store or in an office. You won't have to be poor and struggling like your granny. Times are changing now, and soon we will have to learn new ways to survive. Maybe this school will teach you these new ways.'

"That next day my grandmother brought me down to the place where the priest had instructed my parents to meet him. My grandmother kissed me and whispered some words of encouragement. She slipped a small buckskin bundle in my hand, and instructed me to keep it close to me at all times, for protection. I turned and walked slowly down the road, hugging my protection bundle and the clothing that my grandmother had packed for me close against my chest to cover up that awful aching in my heart. My eyes were aching too, but for my grandmother's sake I would not allow myself to cry. When I turned to wave to her for the last time, it took all my strength to keep from running back to the safety of her arms. In all my young years she was the only safety I'd ever known. Another girl, Theresa, and her younger cousin, Mary, came to join me. Theresa was a year older than me. She took my hand and turned to wave at my grandmother, and together we walked towards the wagon.

"There were about seven or eight of us latecomers that day. We joined hands, and, squeezing tightly, we walked the remainder of the way to where the priest stood waiting with a self-satisfied, indulgent expression on his smiling, reddish face. I had to turn my face away, for suddenly I was consumed with a hatred that threatened to choke me. Then, as I turned my head, I caught a glimpse of my granny who couldn't read or write, and who wanted so desperately to believe that the school would teach me something good. And I knew that for her sake, I would always have to try harder to understand."

THERESA

Mary knew for sure now that this was a bad place to be. Over the last six months, ever since she first came to the residential school, she always tried so bravely to feel like it was a good place. Now fear and the shock of Theresa's death made her spirit grow so very weak inside of her. Even now, as she called out to the spirits of the grandfathers to help her, to give her strength and understanding, there was only cold, empty silence around her. Deserted, all she heard was the quiet swish, swish of the placid-faced sisters as they glided past the doorway, oblivious to her torment that was going on inside.

She remembered being dragged down the stairs and through the corridors, crying, kicking, screaming, and raging at them to listen— because she knew she saw those hands that pushed Theresa down that flight of stairs. For only a moment, she stood stunned, until she heard the loud crack of Theresa's head striking the cement floor below. Then her eyes connected with the cold, cruel, angry, angry eyes of Sister Luke, and her heart stopped, before she could almost feel her own small body flying through the air, and banging against the cement stairs. She felt arms and hands, subduing and pulling at her, forcing her to be quiet. All the while she knew that Sister Luke was wanting to do to her what she had done to Theresa.

For three days they kept Mary locked in the small prayer room off the rectory. Each night, alone, she suffered with a fear that she'd never known in all of her nine years before. There were strange spirits here—menacing, unfriendly ones, whose language she did not understand. They followed her into her sleep, and brought evil, terrifying images that drove her from her bed. All night she walked back and forth across the checkered floor. Then towards morning, soon after falling into an exhausted sleep, the sister came to tell her to get up. She immediately knelt on the icy, hard floor that the nun pointed to. Then for two hours until breakfast she prayed in English, out loud, with her rosary. "Praying for your soul," the sister called it.

The English words, always strange on her tongue, alien to her ears, stuck in her throat, and they seemed somehow ridiculous. For Mary there was no comfort, but she'd learned soon after coming to the residential school that the sisters and the priest liked listening to those words—over and over again, the same words, first thing in the morning before they were barely awake, during morning mass, before lunch, during afternoon prayer, before supper, during evening mass, and finally for the last time, at night, before they were allowed to climb into their warm beds. The nuns and the priest drew strength from those words. They were comforted, reassured, but to Mary they were only words, a punishment for her crime, for telling lies, for allowing her eyes to betray her on the stairway that day.

After the lengthy prayer, the sister got up and left, and another came in with her breakfast tray: lumpy, cold porridge that also stuck in her throat. Disheartened, she pushed the tray away, and sat perched at the edge of the cot, facing the open doorway, and waited. She closed her eyes and listened to sounds of the girls in the sewing room down the hall, sounds of the food trolleys in the kitchen, pots and pans being slammed around, and voices and laughter of the boys going out to the fields for their morning work, but none of the sounds were for her, Mary. It was as though she'd disappeared too. Silently, one tear, then another rolled down her cheek and disappeared beneath her chin that rested on her drawn-up knees. Silently, she mourned the loss of Theresa, her dearest and most trusted friend.

Theresa, who was part of every childhood memory, was gone, and Mary, overwhelmed by the empty space inside, sobbed silently, tiny little animal hiccoughs and gulps that she forced back into her throat.

They were only a year apart and inseparable. Because Theresa was the older one, she decided very early that tiny cousin Mary was to be her responsibility. After that, whenever the grown-ups and the other children rushed on ahead, Theresa always waited for Mary to catch up. When life was one enormous, frightening monster, it was Theresa who faced it head on, tore its monstrous head off and showed Mary that there never was anything to be frightened of. Mary believed that Theresa was frightened of nothing. She wouldn't allow the priest and sisters to intimidate her. When she knew she was right, she stood her ground no matter what punishment they threatened her with. She totally perplexed them, and quite often, they didn't know what to do with her, for she had an uncanny ability of keeping them slightly off-balance. She would cut right through their arguments, patiently reasoning with them until they became so worked up that they often resorted to physical violence, or, exasperated, they sometimes just walked away. Mary and Theresa, whispering and giggling later on in bed, imagined that the priest and nuns probably had some pretty interesting conversations with God about her.

Back at home the People called Theresa the old woman, because they saw the old woman whose Indian name she had inherited in the words that she spoke. In the small mannerisms, the way she laughed, and the way she carried herself, she was a leader, and the People recognized and respected it. It is true that the People believed that when a name is passed to a child, that child will grow to possess the characteristics, the personality, and temperament of the person who carried it before. Theresa accepted this and wore the name with pride. But when she got to the school that was so different from their home, all of those characteristics that were so much a part of her, her bluntness and outspokenness, became almost a hindrance. Indian children were supposed to be meek and silent. The first, most important lesson was to love, fear, and respect God, the priest, and the nuns, in that order.

Theresa presented a challenge because she questioned everything. She wanted to know why they were not allowed to speak in their own language anymore. "If I forget my language, how will I talk to my grandmother, and to all the old people who do not know how to speak English?" she questioned. Every chance she got, she spoke in Indian and urged Mary to do the same. No matter how many times they whipped her or how many meals they deprived her of, she adamantly refused to forget, and because she influenced the other girls, the sisters took every opportunity to isolate her.

Once during a morning classroom lesson, Sister Augustine suggested that perhaps they were having a difficult time understanding the lesson, because Indians were not as smart as white people, and it couldn't be helped. They were always saying things like that. It was a way they used of humiliating the children into accepting the new ways as quickly as possible. Mary hated the way those remarks made her feel—as if they were wounding the flesh around something very fragile inside, and she had no way to ward off the blows. When they said things like, "Indians are dirty, stupid," the hurt went right into her heart and stayed there. She knew they weren't true, but she felt helpless and sad all the same.

"Do you know how to skin a deer?" piped Theresa from the back of the room where she usually sat.

Sister Augustine, unnerved and taken aback, replied, "Of course not."

"I do," said Theresa, "and I know how to cut and dry the meat. My grandmother taught me. I even know how to tan the hides. I could survive all summer up in the mountains by myself if I had to," she quickly concluded.

"That will be enough!" snapped Sister Augustine, quickly escorting Theresa from the room.

Mary didn't see Theresa for the rest of that day or the next. When she was finally allowed to return to the dormitory, she looked tired and subdued, but Mary could see the reflection of that familiar deter-mination still in Theresa's eyes. Mary knew then that they would never be able to break that spirit of the old people that was in her. No matter what they did to her, that spirit would be with her until she died, and suddenly a coldness crept around Mary's heart. It kept tight-ening until she could feel the pain. She could see Theresa lying so still and broken. She moved closer and could see that her lips were blue.

The nuns told the children that it was wrong to have such fanta-sies and superstitions or to be influenced by them. It was a sin to talk to the spirits or to perform the rituals that had been taught to them by their grandmothers. Mary couldn't stop the visions from happen-ing. She knew that they were sent as a warning, but sometimes bad things could be prevented from happening. The old people had the power to stop a death if it was not that person's time to go back to the Creator. But Mary knew that it was a sin to think like that, so she said nothing, did nothing, and now Theresa was dead. Mary sat rocking, dry-eyed. She couldn't cry anymore. There were no more tears, but a pain that she kept pushing back settled somewhere deep inside her and turned into a dull ache.

Cramped and cold, she stood up to move around the small room. She walked over to the doorway and peeked out into the corridor. Two of the sisters walked by, eyes averted. Neither of them spoke to her. She made a game of it, trying to stare them down, attempting to force them to make eye contact with her, but each time they acted as though she did not exist. Mary began to enjoy it, to enjoy the silence and the sense of freedom that her new invisibility offered her. All she'd ever really wanted from them was for them to leave her alone.

She went back to the bed and lay across it, staring at the ceiling. If she could lie very still and very silent, she knew the grandfathers would be able to help her. If she could empty her mind, let go of the despair and that feeling of hopelessness, they would come to her.

She recalled that time when she received the news that her grand-mother was very ill. News seldom came from the village. The nuns did not allow it. It was old Alex who came from her village, who helped out around the school, who told her. Mary was desperate with fear and worry, for in her dreams she could see her granny, lying so still, weakly coughing up the blood. Theresa told Mary to make a food offering to Nupika. Somehow she must find the small plant that grows in the fields, and a piece of yellow cloth, and this too she must leave for the spirits. Mary did this. Then the sisters caught her singing the song to call the spirits. They put her in front of the big classroom, and with all the children present, they strapped her until her hands bled and she could not help but cry out. Later Theresa found her sobbing in the dormitory. "You must never stop believing in Nupika, no matter what they do or say to you," she said passionately, fervently. "Promise me, Mary. In the end it will only be Nupika who will be able to help us." She stroked Mary's hair and soothed her, making her sit up, wiping her eyes. "It is true what our grandmothers tell us, that there is nothing that Nupika cannot do. You must believe that." She bent to peer deep into Mary's eyes. "Your granny is going to be alright," she said.

It was that memory of Theresa that brought the warmth back into Mary's heart. Theresa was always talking to her and the other girls like that, every chance she got. It was as though she knew she would not be around much longer, so she worked quickly and took many chances. Just as rapidly as the sisters worked to tear the Indianness out of them, Theresa worked with the same amount of determination to restore it. In the sewing room, Theresa always talked to those who sat closest to her, quietly, so the supervising sister wouldn't hear.

"You must never let them make you ashamed to be an Indian," she'd begin. "It is lies, what they tell us in here. When they tell you those things, you must think back and remember how our people live. You must remember the goodness in our people and how happy you were before you came to this place. All they have taught us here is how to work hard, like slaves, and how to pray in English to their God. They want us to forget Nupika because they know that is where we get our strength from and they want us to be weak. No punishment could ever be as bad as forgetting who you are," Theresa emphasized, then lapsed into silence, but her words lay there in the space around them filling those who were beginning to weaken, with shame.

Theresa was always sticking up for the other girls. She was not one bit scared of those sisters. Being tall for her age, she often had to physically force herself between the child and the sister who was attacking her, which enraged the sisters more than ever. It was this courage that enabled Theresa to gain the respect and admiration of all the other girls. Even the older girls felt a loyalty to her and no matter how the sisters attempted to isolate her and to dissuade her followers, they could never gain even one convert. It was easy to see that the sisters preferred to keep the girls at odds with one another, by instigating rivalry among them by singling out favourites. Even these "favourites" had a certain degree of loyalty to Theresa. She wasn't even afraid of the priest who terrified some of the other girls. Theresa often had a difficult time concealing her contempt for him.

"He would like us to think he is the 'God' that they speak about," she often told Mary, "but he's not. He's nothing but a dirty old man," she'd sneer.

Mary had already heard some of the stories about the priest and the older girls, and knew what Theresa was referring to. But it was Sister Luke that Theresa clashed with more often than the others.

No one liked Sister Luke. She was mean. A tiny, diminutive creature who appeared to be lost in the miles of black and white veils that were her nun's habit. She was always yelling and screaming, especially at the very little girls. She terrified them, and seemed to thoroughly enjoy it when she made them cry. The girls never doubted that Sister Luke abhorred Indians. When Mary and Theresa first came to the school, it was Sister Luke who had the misfortune of stripping and searching Theresa.

Mary remembered vividly how they'd travelled all day and part way into the night, before finally arriving at the enormous, grey building that was the Indian Residential School. They were all very tired and hungry. However, they were not allowed to eat or sleep for several hours yet.

They were immediately ushered to a huge, brightly-lit room with showers lining one wall and sinks along the other. They were instructed to strip, and put all their clothing and travelling bundles in a pile in the middle of the floor. The sisters acted like they were afraid to come near them. When all their clothing was in the pile, two sisters scooped it up into plastic bags to be either washed or burned. It was here that Theresa was to begin her struggle with the sisters that was to continue until her death.

After their clothing was removed, the other sisters began examining them for anything else they might have on their person. Before leaving home, Theresa had been given a "protection bundle" by her grandmother. This she wore around her neck attached with a length of moose hide. Sister Luke spotted it and told her to remove it. Theresa refused. Sister Luke reached over to yank it from her neck, but Theresa grabbed her hand and wouldn't let it go. Theresa was used to working with her hands. She had very strong hands, and she was not a small girl. Mary saw the pain that contorted Sister Luke's face, before she exploded into rage. It took four sisters to catch Theresa and hold her down while Sister Luke removed the precious bundle, and then it took several more to pull Sister Luke off Theresa, who managed to take a good chunk out of Sister Luke's arm before they were pulled apart. Sister Luke never forgave Theresa for that incident, but was careful never to confront her directly again. Whenever Sister Luke went after one of the smaller girls, she was always careful that she was out of sight and earshot of Theresa.

Mary wondered what had sparked the incident on the stairway that day. All she could recall was seeing them there, Theresa at the edge of the step, two steps below Sister Luke. She couldn't see Sister Luke's face from where she stood, but she looked tall and menacing, arms flailing, towering over Theresa. Theresa moved and looked as though she were trying to get around her to the top of the steps, but Sister wouldn't let her pass. There was someone else there too. Mary couldn't remember, out of the corner of her eyes, who was standing in the doorway to the office. It happened so quickly. Mary could remember trying to yell at Theresa to be careful, and in that same moment she saw Sister Luke grip the handrail with one hand and push Theresa with the other, bracing herself, using all her strength.

It hurt Mary's head to remember when all she wanted to do was forget. Mary fell asleep and began to dream. She dreamed about that time, it seemed such a long time ago, before she came to the residential school. She dreamed about her grandmother and her grandfather and about being happy. She dreamed about that time that her family, Theresa's family, and all the old people from the village went to visit the old camping grounds. She imagined the scent of the smudge and could hear Nupikas talking to her, above the trickle of the springs. They were telling her such beautiful things and Mary was so very, very happy.

"Mary, get up." The sound of the sister's voice jarred Mary back into reality. She didn't want to wake up, but she sat up quickly and tried to rub the sleep from her eyes. "Mother Superior wants to talk to you. You must come with me now." It was Sister Ann, who was usually kinder than the other sisters. Mary liked Sister Ann. "How are you feeling?" she asked Mary. Mary indicated that she was okay, then asked her when she would be allowed to return to the dormitory. Sister Ann shushed her gently and told her she could not answer any of her questions, that the Mother Superior would tell her everything. "Why am I being punished?" she asked. "I didn't do anything wrong." Sister Ann crossed over to the doorway, and after checking to make sure no one was coming, she pulled Mary very close to her and in a very low, firm tone, she spoke.

"You must never repeat what you think you saw on the stairway that day. Never," said Sister Ann. "It is as though it never happened. Promise me, Mary, that you will act as though it never happened."

"But I did see . . ." Mary began to protest, but something in Sister Ann's eyes and the urgency in her voice stopped her. There were tears in Sister's eyes and this Mary could not bear. "Promise me," she repeated. Slowly Mary nodded her head.

Mary had to walk up the long stairway to get to Mother Superior's office. She stood stiffly at the bottom of the steps, wanting but not being able to look at the spot where Theresa had lain broken and hurt. Sister Ann put her arms around her shoulders and hugged her, gently urging her up the steps. When they got to Mother Superior's office the first person Mary saw was Sister Luke, and her first impulse was to turn and run. Sister Ann had a firm grip on her shoulder and turned her back around. "Mary." She said her name so softly, like a prayer, that Mary responded by walking the rest of the way up to Mother Superior's desk.

"Well, Mary, are you feeling better today?" she asked.

Mary nodded.

"We're very happy to hear that. We've been worried about you, you've been so very sick. We understand how much you are going to miss Theresa. We're all going to miss her because we all loved her very much. But Theresa is so very lucky because she is with God now." She smiled at Mary, studying her face very carefully.

Mary nodded again.

"I am thinking of allowing you to return to the dormitory with the other girls. Would you like that?"

Again, Mary nodded.

"There won't be any need to talk about your illness with the other girls. You won't talk about it, will you, Mary?"

Mary shook her head.

"You're a good girl, Mary. Well then, it's settled. You can return to the dormitory this evening."

It was very late, long after "lights out," before someone finally came for Mary. Anxiously and cautiously, lest she change her mind, Mary followed the looming, black figure of Sister Catherine down the maze of shadowy corridors, back to the girls' dorm. Up the three short steps and through the swinging doors, Mary almost had to run to keep up to Sister's quick pace. The only sound was the noise of Sister's shoes, click, clack, click on the hard, polished floors. They entered the sleeping dorm, moving rapidly between the rows of beds. Sister stood by while Mary threw off her clothes, slipped into her nightgown, then slid into the narrow cot, pulling the blankets up close around her.

"Goodnight, Sister Catherine," she whispered into the dark.

Sister was already gone. Mary lay on one side, staring after her, carefully keeping her eyes averted to avoid looking at that painfully empty bed that stood next to hers. Soon weariness and relief at being back in familiar surroundings made her fall quickly into a very deep and dreamless sleep.

The brightness of the overhead lights woke her. It was always still dark outside when Sister came, clapping her hands, firing off her usual morning instructions, and prodding those who liked to lie a few moments in the bed. Mary jumped out of bed and immediately knelt down on the icy floor, ready to recite the morning prayer. She was determined to leave a good impression on her first day back. Conscious of the curious gaze of those nearest her, she kept her eyes focussed on the crucifix that hung over the doorway to the hall— back straight, hands clasped, words clearly enunciated, as they were instructed to, she began to pray. Soon the coldness spread up from the floorboards, up through Mary's knees until she had to lean slightly forward against the bed, and clutch her elbows close to her body to prevent them from shaking. Some mornings Sister Dominic barely skimmed over the most important prayers, but on this particular morning, probably to mark the occasion of Mary's return, she carried on longer than usual. Mary had long forgotten the meaning of the words, but she knew them perfectly, by heart.

After prayer, the children automatically lined up in the aisle. Only five at a time were permitted into the bathroom. They weren't allowed to speak or to look around the room. Mary kept her eyes straight ahead, staring at the back of the girl's head that stood ahead of her in line. After she scrubbed her face and hands with the harsh-smelling soap, Mary dressed, straightened her bed and joined the others in the line in front of the cafeteria. All duties were carried out in total silence. In the cafeteria, she sat next to Julia and Marceline, who whispered to one another when Sister wasn't looking, but no one whispered to Mary. She ate the bowl of lumpy porridge because she was hungry, but she pushed the piece of dried-up bread away, and someone reached out and quickly retrieved it. As she ate she carefully picked out the tiny black pellets of mouse shit and hid them under her bowl. Mary remembered the first time that she noticed the waste in her bowl of food. She was horrified and tried to tell the sister. Sister was furious and hauled Mary up in front of the room where she had to stand until everyone had left. Sister explained to the others that Mary was ungrateful. Mary and the other children soon learned that it was better not to complain.

From breakfast, every morning, the children went to morning mass. Mary sat in the third row, on the left, where she usually sat and waited for the sermon to begin. The priest began to talk about the virtues of honesty, and the evilness of spreading lies. Mary felt uncomfortable when she realized that he was directing his sermon at her. He was looking right at her, and her face felt hot. She lowered her head, for by this time everyone was looking at her. She wished desperately to leave the room, but no one dared even move while the priest spoke. They think I made that whole thing up about Theresa, thought Mary. Maybe I did? Mary was confused and didn't know what to think. The priest and nuns did that. They made it so that you could never be right if you didn't think what they wanted you to think. Everyone knew that the priest and the sisters were always right. Mary wanted to hide her face, to bury it in her lap, but she sat with her back straight and stared at the crucifix on the altar above the priest's head.

In the classroom, no one spoke to Mary and no one wanted to sit next to her. She sat off by herself and tried to keep her mind on the lesson. Sister Ann, who taught the lesson, was kind to her, tried to draw her in, but Mary refused. Later, during bible reading, Marceline came and sat beside her. They didn't speak, but it was comforting to have her there. Marceline was from the same village and was the same age as Mary.

The afternoon was spent doing chores. It was Mary's turn to work in the kitchen. First, she had to help the older girls get the pots of white, watery-looking "Chicken a la King" they called it, ready for the evening meal. Sister showed them how to make the sauce so that it was not too lumpy. Then little piles of chopped-up, boiled chicken and vegetable were carefully measured out and added. Mary helped sift through half a sack of rice, picking out as much of the waste material as possible. No matter how many times they went through the rice, it was impossible to get rid of all the lumps of dirt and excrement before Sister hurried them along.

Later in the afternoon, they began to prepare the meal for the supervisors. It was considered a special privilege to prepare food for the priest, but it was a task that Mary did not much enjoy. Sister Marguerite supervised very strictly so that they could not pilfer even one taste of the fluffy, creamy mashed potatoes with the precious scoops of butter, inserted to melt over the top. The tantalizing smell of grilled pork chops was so overpowering and tempting that sometimes if Sister turned away for a moment they were able to taste the scrapings from the bottom of the pan. Mary helped to set the tables with white tablecloths, real china and silverware. The three tables for the sisters and the priest were situated halfway down the cafeteria, surrounded by the children's tables—bleak, wooden without tablecloths, tin plates instead of china, and one spoon. Mary carried a platter of meat through the crowded room, while the children sat down to their pre-served, cold plates of Chicken a la King. She saw the hungry looks on the faces of the smaller children, a look that they hadn't yet learned to conceal. She set the steaming platter down in front of the priest first, then waited to pass it down the table. She kept her eyes straight ahead on a spot on the far wall, careful not to stare at the sisters or the food. Staring was a sin. Wishing for something that did not belong to you was an even greater sin. Mary emptied her mind, so she would not think of the emptiness inside her stomach.

Hunger was never a part of their lives before coming to the school. Now, it was all they ever thought about. It seeped into every conversation. It became part of every activity, and it even followed them into their dreams. Most of Mary's life before the school had been carefully divided up as to season, between gathering food, preparing it for the long winters, and sharing it at the many winter feasts and gatherings. Food was for sharing, for enjoying, and for offering to the spirits. Now, the lack of it seemed to drain the spirit right out of their bodies. Stealing became part of the ritual. Mary had finally reached the end of the table, and by then there were four pieces of meat left on the platter. The remainder, she knew, would go either into the garbage or to the priest's "favourites." If Mary was lucky, one of the trusted ones would share a piece with her. For, in spite of everything, they still knew how to share. Few of the girls ever coveted anything entirely for themselves. Even stolen goods were carefully divided up. Mary knew that extra loaves of bread were baked and purposely left on kitchen windowsills for the boys who worked hard out in the fields. Mary rarely saw the boys, but she heard the other girls talking about them.

The inadequate food and the harsh conditions had already taken their toll that year. Nine children, including Theresa, had died of various ailments. They caught colds often, and someone was always complaining of a sore throat. No real doctors came to examine them. If they got seriously ill, the sisters did the best they could to nurse them back to health, but they never sent any of the children home until they were dead or almost dead.

Mary began to feel the symptoms of that dreaded sore throat, and soon her neck was so swollen that she could barely swallow anything. Even water was excruciatingly painful to consume. When Theresa had seen how ill she was, she immediately took charge and managed to nurse her back to health. Theresa would slip down to the river to pick and prepare the healing herbs that she held in a steaming cup to Mary's lips and ordered her to drink. Despite the agony, Mary allowed her to slip bits of the pounded up roots into her mouth, which she slowly chewed, allowing the healing juices to trickle down her throat. She slipped in and out of consciousness, imagining that the priest came into the room and was moving her around. Then Theresa came and made him stop. Theresa would not allow her to eat any of the cafeteria food while she was recovering, bringing her other things instead. Theresa never did trust the food from the cafeteria.

"It's that food," she'd say, "I know that is what's making us sick. If only we were able to eat the food from home, we'd never be sick."

Instead she brought Mary pieces of waᶜkna (dried elk meat) with saskatoon berries pounded into it. She would sneak into the nuns' rooms and steal fresh fruit. Soon Mary began to regain her strength and the swelling disappeared. Mary never doubted that had it not been for Theresa, she too would have died like the others. It frightened Mary to realize, now that Theresa was gone, how much she had depended on her. It was as though Theresa had always stood between her and all the wickedness of their new world. Now she was left unprotected, vulnerable, an easy prey, a frightened rabbit with coyotes howling all around her—weak, because she was so afraid. She stood on a stool, bent over the steaming sinks, scraping pots and pans, with tears and sweat streaming down her face. Alone. Afraid.

Soon that day passed, then another, and another, all routinely the same. The silence became a buffer zone around Mary. Silence and obedience became her protectors. She listened to the conversations around her, but never commented. She was respectful to the sisters, carefully followed rules, and tried as much as possible to stay far away from the priest, with his all-knowing, probing eyes. She only spoke to him, to anyone, to God, in confession. Now her only sins were her thoughts, which she tried desperately to discipline, so that she would not have to share them with the priest. She went to communion often. She listened carefully to the sisters' detailed instructions on how the host was to be received, and was petrified with fear each time the priest placed the thin, round, white wafer of Christ's body into her mouth. She held it securely with her tongue to the roof of her mouth, away from the teeth, lest she accidentally bite into it, and the blood of Christ would come streaming out of her mouth. Then everyone would know the extent of her sins. Sometimes it got stuck to the roof of Mary's mouth, which kept her in agony until it melted away. Still she went to confession and communion often. She tried hard to be a good Christian, but when thoughts of Nupika came to her, she got caught between the two, until bitterly, then angrily she blamed first, Nupika, then God, for her predicament. She became consumed with guilt, fear, doubt, uncertainty, confusion, until it was easier to believe in nothing. Hadn't both Nupika and God abandoned her?

At night she lay alone in the darkness thinking about Theresa. Soon it would be time to go home for the holidays, without Theresa. She was afraid if she left she would be leaving Theresa here, alone. Thoughts of Theresa walking up and down the empty halls searching for Mary made her sad, so she pretended that Theresa was already at home, waiting for her. She counted up all the things that were waiting at home for her and visualized them in her mind, exactly as she'd left them. Eyes closed, she wished with all her heart, fervently, that her return would be as though she'd never left. She could picture the horse-shaped tree that she used to ride on, by the laneway to her granny's house, her mother forever racing across the field on horse-back. She'd be greeted by all the dogs that hung around her granny's house. They would rush at her, yapping and excited. She would sit down at her granny's wooden table, and Granny would bring her a huge, steaming plate of elk meat and roots, tempting her with the marrow-filled bones that she loved so much. Mary moved dreamily, curling up in a warm ball. Soon, it would happen soon, then all this would be behind her. She never dared to think about home in such detail before. Before it was close enough to be almost real. On nights when memories made her this warm, she dreamed about Nupika. She couldn't light the smudge here, but sometimes she imagined she could smell it.

That night she dreamed all night about her granny. They were camped on the high plain, up in the mountains. She was lying in the tent that her granny had erected, among a pile of skins, warm and listening. She couldn't see her, but she could feel her close by. She could hear the sounds of a creek laughing, running and playing among a grove of swaying, creaking trees. "Mary," her granny was calling to her, coaxing her to get up.

"We have so much work to do today," she said. "There is so much preparation."

Mary stood outside the tent, facing the mountain. Her grandmother's voice came out of the darkness behind her.

"You must walk along the creek, toward the mountain," her grandmother continued. "You will come to a place where the cottonwood and willow grow. There you will build a sweat lodge. You will use ten good, strong willow poles that you will find along the creek. When you have completed the lodge, you will continue to walk along the creek to the mountain edge, where you will find a pile of smooth rocks. Those you must carry back to the lodge."

Mary worked hard all morning, trying to get everything ready before the first sun came over the mountain. She laid the last rock into the pile of circled rocks, as she was taught, then lit the fire around it. She sat down by the stream to wait, concentrating on the voices around her. Soon all the wood burned away, leaving the glowing rocks in the centre, and Mary knew it was time. She went to open the flap of the sweat lodge, and then she saw her granny for the first time. She looked strong and happy, her face radiant and smiling. She motioned Mary to bring in the rocks. One by one, balanced between two strong branches, Mary laid seven rocks into the pit that she'd dug into the centre of the sweat. Then she entered and closed the flap tightly behind her, so none of the light of the world could follow her in, so the darkness could not escape. She moved over to the opposite side, facing her granny, who spoke to her gently in the rising and falling tone of the People's language. Mary understood her perfectly and answered her in perfect words that came right from her heart. The steam rose up, enclosing Mary's body, and she could feel the sweat pouring out of her, drawing all the misery and sickness out. A song that she could remember hearing the old people sing rose out of someplace deep inside. She sang loud and clear until she could feel the spirits all around. As she sang, her granny told her stories about the

People. Ancient stories, full of wisdom and knowledge. Mary brought in the remainder of the rocks, then lay across the sweet-smelling cedar branches. She listened to her grandmother's words filling up the space around her, and inside her so that she wasn't hungry anymore. She wasn't cold. She wasn't afraid.

Suddenly she woke to find the sister and several of the girls standing around her bed. Sister was prodding her with the smooth pointer stick she always carried with her. Mary quickly got up from the bed. Sister didn't say a word, but stared at her in a strange way. She motioned everyone to get ready for morning prayer and instructed Mary to lead it. Mary recited, loudly and clearly, the words of the prayer. She hardly had to think, for she knew them perfectly by heart, but her mind was far away on a plain, high up in the mountains, where she knew Nupika and the People had not forgotten her.

Afterwards, as she jostled her way up to an empty sink, Marceline bumped into her and whispered, "You were singing in your sleep. It was so beautiful what you were singing. It even frightened Sister. Did you see the look on her face?" Marceline smiled at her in a warm and sisterly way, the way Theresa used to smile at her. "You must have been talking to Nupika in your sleep," she teased, then quickly retreated away from her.

Then Mary realized that Marceline had been speaking to her in Indian. Nervously she looked around to make sure none of the sisters were standing nearby ready to pounce on them. All morning Mary thought about her dream, and about Marceline speaking to her so warmly in Indian. She hadn't realized until that moment how terribly lonesome she had been.

Automatically she carried out her duties, in silence, carefully, two hours in the sewing room, two hours in the classroom, and an hour in the church, unable to shake the dream from her mind. She didn't want to forget it, and wished the night to come swiftly, so she could lie alone to remember in peace. The day passed quickly, as Mary knew all the days would, until she was among her people again. Carefully she moved, fearful of making even one mistake that might inadvertently disrupt the delicate balance of the forces that controlled her life. She wasn't sure, but she thought it was possible that the sisters or the priest could make her stay behind, if there were any reason that they wanted her to. She still lay on one side in her bed to avoid looking at Theresa's empty bed. One night she felt someone tugging on the blankets behind her, and slowly she turned to look over her shoulder.

"Move over," Marceline whispered as she climbed into Mary's bed, readjusting the covers over their heads so no one could hear them talking.

"I have to tell you something. It's about Theresa. It's something I heard from the older girls, who heard it from old Alex. You know old Alex who works in the barns sometimes? Not too long ago he came back from our village. He said Theresa was sent home in a bag with a note attached saying that she'd died of pneumonia. He was there when Theresa's mother was preparing the body. First her mother noticed the bruises on her body, and as she felt around she noticed that Theresa's neck was broken. All the old ladies came and examined her until they knew for certain that her neck was definitely broken. All that night they sat up discussing what should be done. Early the next morning, Theresa's mother, her grandmother, and another of the elderly ladies went into town to make a report to the police, but who would listen to an old Indian woman who couldn't even speak English? Nobody would listen to her. They said she was crazy and chased her out of town. There was nothing that could be done, so they buried her. Somehow, they knew you were there, Mary, and they are afraid for you. You must be silent, your granny says."

Faintly, Mary realized how much she had hoped that she wouldn't have to return to the school, that somehow, after she went home for the holidays, her granny would be able to help her, after she knew the truth. Now Mary realized that her people were as helpless as she.

THE LETTER

I don't remember when Danny and I first became friends. Maybe it wasn't until grade two, because I spent a long time being lonely before she became my friend. Danny, the letter, and that lonely time is what I remember the most about school.

For a long time I never went out into the schoolyard to play. The noise frightened me and I knew I would end up standing by myself in that great big yard, because nobody ever wanted to play with me. Instead I'd wander up and down the empty halls to the bathroom, back to the classroom, and up to the long windows by the entrance, and stand there watching them play, wishing the long lunch hour would end. One day Mr. Hewer discovered me there. After that, during lunch he would come out to talk to me, trying to coax me out into the yard. Mr. Hewer was nice, but I wished he'd go away. Finally, as a last resort, he called one of the girls over and told her to take me out to play. She looked uncomfortable, but didn't dare disobey. I was embarrassed and somehow ashamed. She brought me to the group of skipping girls and said, "Mr. Hewer said she has to play with us." I didn't know what to do. Mr. Hewer watched for a while. I stood fidgeting, trying to look like I was having a good time. After he left, they moved their game a little away from me and soon I was standing alone again, hoping the bell would ring. After that I started spending my lunch hours in the bathroom, hiding in the stalls whenever I heard someone coming. I know that went on for a long time, but when I was a little girl everything went on for a long time.

In retrospect, I don't believe I was overly sensitive in thinking they didn't want to play with me. I was, after all, one of the first Indian kids from the reserve to come to their school. Nothing in their experience would have helped them to know how to act with me. There was very little interaction between the Indian and white community. What they knew of Indians was what little they read about in books, what their parents told them, or derived from the glimpses they got of us, when we came to town on weekends to shop. Before I went to school I barely knew they existed, and I doubt if any of them had ever set foot on a reservation. There were other things, too, that set us apart. My timidity was an excruciatingly painful thing. I was ready to take flight at a moment's notice, my body forever tense and waiting. As a child, my mind was full of unimaginable disasters.

We were sent to school to learn how to live like white people. Times were changing and there was no place for us Indians anymore. I think my father really believed if we learned how to talk, to dress, and to act like them, there would be a place for us in their world. My father was one of the first ones on our reserve who saw the changes that were coming. He never considered sending us, with the other Indian kids from our reserve, to the residential school in Kamloops.

I couldn't understand why I had to go to school. I didn't want to go. I refused to speak a word to anyone. I would just sit and wait until we would go home again. It was not only difficult to read the words in the books they gave us; it was more difficult to understand what they meant. I didn't know anyone except my brother and I was so lonely and scared. I don't recall exactly when I started to be ashamed of who I was. Ashamed of the clothes I wore. Ashamed of my skin, because it was brown instead of white like everyone else's. I don't know when, but I know it happened.

This sense of shame at being an Indian grew until it permeated my whole life. It was not only in the school. More and more it became a part of my own people—an attitude that developed and spread. My awareness grew out of the attitudes of some of my relatives who treated us badly because we were dark-skinned and acted so Indian, while my lighter-skinned cousins were admired and paraded around in their store-bought clothes. Ours were always second-, third-, and even fourth-hand, we were so poor.

My beautiful, young aunts would come to visit. They always brought their latest white boyfriends with them, showing them off like some first prize. Mostly they were broken-down old men with red faces from too much alcohol. I didn't like the way they smelled, and I didn't like the way they would hug me when they were drunk. Most of all, I didn't like the way they treated my mother, like they thought they were better than she was. They created dissension between my mother and father.

I think my mother may have attempted at times to instil a sense of Indian pride in us, but she must have felt like she was fighting a losing battle. Years later, she told us that when she came to live with my father, the Secwepemc people had already lost most of their Indian ways. They didn't like to hear her talking about the Indian ways that the Ktunaxa people still practised. She reminded them of the things they were trying so hard to forget.

My mother said when we were babies our granny and aunties never liked to babysit us because we looked too much like Indians. One day they offered to take my brother Bobby to town with them. They were spending a long time in the bedroom getting him ready, so finally my mother went in to see what the problem was. At this point in the story, the anger she still carries with her often emerges. "There they were," she said, "dumping a bottle of talcum powder all over your brother trying to make him look white."

There were always so many problems in our home. Even though my father worked hard and steady at the sawmill, we were always poor. Clarence Wright, who owned the sawmill, also owned a butcher shop in Kamloops. Every Saturday night he'd come by our house with a big sack of leftover scraps from his week of butchering. The meat was often slightly spoilt, but we were grateful for it and ate it anyway. There was no way to keep the mice out of the flour and oatmeal bins. I remember sifting through them, trying to pick out their waste from our food, and we ate that too, because there wasn't anything else. We were better off than most of the families on the reserve, yet it was a constant struggle to keep us clothed and fed, and to keep shoes on our feet in the wintertime. It wasn't until I started school that I realized how poor we were, and that being poor was not acceptable. There were poor white kids too, but to be poor and to be Indian was about as low as you could go.

I became aware at a very early age of complex adult problems, and this contributed to my serious nature. Sometimes I think I didn't know how to play. During my childhood, my mother spent extended periods of time in the hospital because of a troublesome injury in her hip. This injury plagued her most of her life. Other times she and my father would have horrible, drunken, weekend fights, and then she'd go away for a long time. I was the oldest girl, and while she was away there was so much work, too much responsibility, almost too much for me to bear.

Danny, as I remember, was always one of the most popular girls in the school. She had a very loud voice. A tall, blond girl, full of laughter and sunshine, gregarious, with never a shortage of friends. She was kind to everyone. Her real friends she chose carefully. One day she decided I was to be her friend. From that day on I was rarely left out of anything. I was not permitted to dissolve into the background, for she would literally reach out, put her arm around my shoulder and say, "You must come too, Vera. It'll be so much fun," daring anyone, with her eyes, to disagree. For a long time, it was Danny, the Stelter twins, who lived on the farm next to Danny, and me. In school, we did everything together. School and home were two distinctly separate places, each occupying a separate corner of my life. I felt uneasy when either came into contact with the other, though they never often did.

I have only one recollection of my mother ever coming to the school. Maybe she came other times, but only that one time stands out clearly in my mind. It was at a Christmas party, and I guess it never occurred to me that she would come. The party had just begun, and most of the other mothers were already there. She came through the door slowly, smiling at everyone. She introduced herself and sat down with the others. She looked so pretty and vulnerable, yet proud sitting there among all those white ladies. I'd never seen my mother look like that before. Some faint thing fluttered inside me, and I went up and hugged her. I was so excited to see her there. I wanted everyone to know she was mine. Later that evening she remarked to my father, "Vera was so friendly to me at her school today. She was so happy to see me. She never acts like that around here." I always thought that was a strange remark to make. I was never aware of how we reacted with one another. I think she moved in and out of my life so often, I was afraid to show her I loved her.

I never invited Danny to my home. She would have been out of place there. I'd ride with my dad down to the farm area, the flats, they called it, to buy vegetables in the summer. I'd see her house among the trees, way down at the end of a long dirt road, beside the river. Her house looked big on the outside, and I imagined that inside, it was much like the pictures I'd seen in magazines. I can't remember if I was ashamed of my house. I just knew instinctively she'd be out of place. For instance, where would she sit in our cluttered room full of broken-down, second-hand furniture? I couldn't picture her anywhere there. If I were to invite her for dinner, none of our plates matched and there were only enough chairs for us. Someone would have to stand up. She probably didn't eat the same food we did. It would have been awkward for both of us, and the subject never came up. She was my school friend. I never talked about my personal life and she never asked.

Some Saturdays we went to movies together, whenever I didn't have to babysit my brothers and sisters, or whenever my father would permit me to go. He was very strict and there was a lot of work to do at home, especially on the weekends. He never allowed me to hang around the street corners in town, like other Indian kids my age, but sometimes he let me go to a movie with Danny. I think he liked me to be friends with Danny because she was a good girl from a nice white family. Her parents were well known and respected in the community.

Wherever we went we were surrounded by her friends, and I think they got used to me hanging around, because I began to feel comfortable, like I belonged. Every once in a while, I'd still feel the coolness from new kids that joined our group. It wasn't anything particular that they did, but I could detect it. Because I'd known so much rejection by this time, I became quite adept at detecting it. They were nice to me to my face, but I knew the ones who didn't carry good thoughts of me in their head. Danny never seemed to notice or perhaps she just ignored it. If I tried to exclude myself when one of these kids was around, she'd insist that I accompany them. I was so shy, I didn't like to push myself on people, and I think if it weren't for Danny always reaching out to me, I still wouldn't have had any friends.

Sometimes I did well in school, but mostly my grades were average. I had to struggle to grasp the material because there wasn't anything that I could relate the subject matter to in my life. Also, I didn't have a lot of free time to do homework or often I didn't have a quiet space. I remember times that my dad would insist that I study, but it didn't seem to fit anywhere in our household. In the classroom, I hated it when questions were directed at me, or when attention was focused on me. I'd cringe whenever Indians were mentioned in Social Studies class. Every time that happened, all eyes, including the teacher's, would turn to look at my brother and me, like we were real live specimens. I'd just want to crawl under my desk and die. Those books made Indians sound so stupid, so primitive, as did most of the material at the time. I think some teachers were pretty ignorant and prejudiced too. They'd read the material over slowly and make cruel remarks, enjoying it if they managed to get a laugh out of the class. When my brother was in the classroom, he never allowed these remarks to pass. He'd get into heavy discussions with the teacher, but for some reason I just couldn't. When he wasn't there, I'd feel miserable and sad in my silence.

My friendship with Danny lasted years. During the summer holidays, we didn't see much of each other. I'd run into her in town a few times or I would catch a glimpse of her and the twins when we went down to get vegetables. Summertime was the time to gather food, and we were always busy. Whenever she was there, my mother dried, canned, pickled and smoked whatever she could get her hands on, preparing for the long winter ahead. She dried wild berries on the roof of our house, and what the squirrels and birds didn't carry off, she put away in the food cellar in the back. She constructed a smokehouse for the fish, and spent long hours in our kitchen canning jars and jars of fruit, vegetables, deer meat, and salmon. My father and brother went hunting, and she'd take the deer hides to work them until they were soft and white. She'd put them away to make moccasins and gloves to sell, later when she had more time. She was very talented. She did beautiful beadwork that brought in extra money to help us through the hard times. I loved the freedom of summer, but we had to work so hard. Everyone had to do their share. We were not allowed to just play. Because of my friendship with Danny, towards the end of summer, I always looked forward to getting back into school.

As we got older and social activities outside of school began to increase, it got difficult for Danny not to exclude me. There were weekend parties I couldn't be invited to, but I accepted this. There were limits that I'd already imposed upon my life. The lines were very clear. I don't think I ever wanted to go to those parties, but I began to long for something. There were times when the confines of my world made me restless for more. I'd go walking in the hills behind our house and cry because there were so many things I could never do, so many places I could never go, so many people I could never know. I would cry from sheer frustration. I dreamed of living in a nice house like Danny's. I dreamed of nice clothes. I wanted so many things that I believed would elevate me out of the darkness I was in.

I wanted to be like Danny. I wanted to go somewhere where I didn't have to be an Indian anymore.

By the time I was in grade six there were quite a few Indians coming to school from my reserve. Although we were from the same reserve, we barely knew one another, because they lived on the village side, across the river from where I lived. My father never brought us to the village often. I think he had clear ideas of how he wanted to raise us, and he kept us isolated for a reason. He was an extreme disciplinarian. He punished us severely and often enough for me to be always a little afraid of him. He encouraged us to have white friends, and while he didn't discourage me from having Indian friends, he specifically forbade me to hang around with most of the Indian girls from our reserve. He said they would all end up getting pregnant before they married, because they were allowed to run wild. That isn't what he wanted for me. He said if I ever got pregnant before I was married, he would throw me out into the streets, that I would no longer be his daughter. He made me afraid to even look at a man. My father had such big plans for us. He wanted so much more for us than was possible at the time. What we wanted for ourselves was never important.

When the Indian kids started coming to our school, I didn't go out of my way to be friends with them. I had my white friends. I had already begun to adopt an attitude toward my people. The more Indian they looked and acted, the more I avoided them. Danny was kind to everyone though, and it wasn't long before she knew them all. Sometimes I felt jealous and so confused. I had no one to talk to about these feelings, so I carried them around inside me like some ugly little secret.

Danny, the Stelter twins, and I still hung around together, most of the time. During lunch time, I had to go down to the post office to pick up the mail. Sometimes they'd come with me. We'd walk halfway through town where the post office was, and if someone had money we'd stop at Jack Maw's store on the corner to get candy before we went back to school. One day, as I pulled out the stack of envelopes from our box, I noticed a letter addressed to me. They all crowded around, because we weren't accustomed to receiving any mail. There was no return address on the envelope, and I didn't recognize the handwriting. I opened it and held the pages up so they could see. "Why don't you hang around your own kind?" the letter began. "We don't like you hanging around with us. Why don't you stick with Indians like yourself?" Quickly I lowered the paper, folded it, and shoved it in my pocket. "What did it say? Who was it from?" they asked. I was relieved that no one saw the words, and I made up something about being late for class. I had this ugly feeling inside like something awful was about to happen, but I knew how to cover my feelings really well. I rushed to the bathroom when we got back to school, and hiding in the stall I used to hide in so many years before, I took the crumbled page out of my pocket. It was painful to look at it, but I had to know what it said. I wanted to know who it was from. "Why don't you stay away from Danny?" the letter continued, "if you stayed away from her, she'd have more friends. Nobody likes you around. Why can't you take a bath? You stink. All Indians stink." It had no signature. I tore it into a million pieces and flushed it down the toilet, but it stayed there in my mind. I couldn't erase it. I wanted to cry, but the school bell rang. Then all the memories of that achy lonely time came flooding back and engulfed me in waves of sorrow and shame.

Taking a bath and washing clothes were all-day projects around our house. On Saturdays, we carried endless buckets of water from the river, over the railroad tracks, across the highway to our house. My mother kept the wood stove burning all day, heating the water as she washed us and all our clothes. That was my job when she wasn't there. In the middle of winter, when the trail was slippery and the river iced over, we melted tubs of snow instead. We washed quickly, so as many of us as possible could wash before the water got cold.

I spent a long time wondering which one of Danny's friends wrote that letter. I suspected everyone. I hung around with the Indian kids, or kept to myself and watched Danny from a distance. She still tried to include me, but most of the time I absolutely refused. One of the

Indian girls dared me to steal a clock from McLeod's Hardware, and I got caught. Clarence Wright was also the judge in the nearby town of Chase, and after consulting my father he made me go to the courthouse. He talked to me a long time and told me I wasn't allowed to go to town again by myself. I felt like a criminal. I was so ashamed. My father made me give him back my mailbox key and whipped me. He told me I shamed him, and everyone in town would know his daughter was a thief. My mother stood outside in the dark for a long time staring at the night. The Indians ridiculed me at school because I got caught.

After that there are only fragments in my memory. I blocked it out, whatever came later, and don't remember anything until the summer when I was fifteen. My mother took us all with her to Washington to pick strawberries. My father stayed home alone because he had to work. A white man brought a big bus to pick a bunch of us up to take us to work on his farm. It was fun, just Mom and us. She never made us work very hard, and she let me buy clothes with my money. She let me walk to town with the other girls, to go to movies on Saturday afternoons. That is when I had my first boyfriend. She still kept an eye on me, but she let us go for walks and hold hands, and she was nice to him. When we came back home, my father was angry all the time. He ridiculed my mother and treated her very badly. I never knew what it was about, but he acted like he hated her. She told him she was going to leave, and this time she was never coming back. He'd been drinking for a couple of days, and he told her to go ahead, but that she should take her brats with her. I heard him say that. When he left the house, I went into my mother's room. She was crying and packing her bags. "Don't leave us here, Mom," I said. "He doesn't like us either. When you're gone, he whips us all the time." My mother broke down, crying loudly. "But I don't have any money. How would I take care of you," she said. I ran to my room and dug out the money I'd made from strawberry picking, and instructed my brothers and sisters to do the same. We gave all our money to her and she stopped crying. "Okay," she said. "I have friends in Chilliwack. We can go there. Help the kids pack their bags. Hurry and don't take too much."

On the way up to the train station, I was so excited. I couldn't believe that I was finally going to leave, for good. I never wanted to come back. It was like an answer to my prayers. I didn't know exactly where Chilliwack was, but I knew I would like it there. We waited at the train station all afternoon, and just before the train came, I ran to the telephone. I looked through the telephone book for Danny's number and called her. "I'm leaving," I said, "I'm going with my mother to live in Chilliwack." It had been a long time since I talked to her, but she was happy to hear from me. "My mother and father had a big fight, and they're separating, and my mother's taking us with her," I explained. She sympathized and said, "I'm going to miss you." Nobody ever told me they were going to miss me with such sincerity. And I knew when I looked back someday, she'd be the only person I'd ever miss, from my childhood, from that town, from my memories.

THE ABYSS

EDITORS' NOTE
"The Abyss" was first published in *Residential Schools: The Stolen Years*, edited by Linda Jaine, Saskatoon: University Extension Press, Extension Division, University of Saskatchewan, 1993, 107–116.

PREFACE

"The Abyss," from which the play Strength of Indian Women *was written, is based on the stories of residential school as told to me by my mother. Just before my mother died she disclosed, to my sisters and me, the sexual abuse she suffered in residential school. I believe it broke my mother's heart to realize that all my sisters, many of my nieces, and at least one brother had been sexually abused. She blamed herself for not being able to protect us and for not being able to help us when we were suffering.*

Our father was also physically, emotionally, and possibly sexually abused, although he never disclosed this information. He was often a violent man.

My younger two sisters and two brothers spent several years in Port Alberni Residential School. Although my older brother and I didn't attend residential school, we didn't really escape it either as it visited us every day of our childhood through the replaying over and over of our parents' childhood trauma and grief which they never had the opportunity to resolve in their lifetimes.

It is important to recognize that the residential school experience was different for each successive generation. For some people it was a good experience, but for the majority of our people it was tremendously destructive and that destruction impacts on present and future generations.

For me, the opportunity to write this story helps to purge, and helps to heal my relationship with my mother. When I read this story over I still cry because I grieve for the gentle man in my father who was never allowed to grow, and I grieve for my mother who never had the loving relationships she deserved, nor the opportunity to be the mother I knew she could have been. I grieve for myself, and all those others of my generation who lost childhoods and adulthoods to incest and sexual abuse. Thank you for giving me a place to let this story go.

THE ABYSS

Mom gathered the pictures out of the old cookie tin that she kept underneath the armchair, and she spread them out in front of her on the coffee table. She pushed them about, bent, intent upon her search. The one she chose she held up close to her eye, peering at it, then she held it out for me to see.

"Tell me what it is," she said. "I can't see nothing with these old eyes."

"It's a bunch of girls," I told her, "lots of them, standing in front of a big grey building. There's a priest standing there with them."

"That's the one," she said, "St. Ignatius Residential School still standing there today. All our cheap houses falling down, but that place still stands there, reminding us."

She took the picture from me, and slowly, carefully, lifted herself from the chair, and moved away toward the window where it was light.

"How old do you think these girls are?" she asked.

"They look like they're about eight or nine," I responded.

"How many are there?"

"Maybe fifty or more."

She leaned up against the window sill, took off her glasses, and once again held the picture up close to her good eye, squinting at it.

"Aahhh," she cried out in recognition, "I was looking all over for this picture since the last time you were here. I wanted you to see it. Look at all them little girls. There's me, that pretty one," she laughed.

I went to her, put my arm around her shoulders, and bent close to see who she was pointing at. I noticed how frail she was. She wasn't well, I knew, and I worried to myself.

"The one with the nice haircut, huh?" I commented.

"That's my bowl cut," she said, "I still wear my hair like that when I get tired of braiding it. Lookit, and we're all wearing the same dress too. That old itchy, woolly thing, it was so ugly."

"How old were you when this picture was taken?" I asked.

"Let's see, that was way back in—must have been somewhere around 1929, or '30, somewhere round there, when I was nine. That was a long time ago. You know, out of all these girls, there must be only a handful of us still alive today. Most of them died, pretty violent too, alcohol, suicide, sickness.

"This one here, Annie, she was murdered in the city. I remember when she went off to the city, and I remember when they brought her back. And this one here, Julia, her husband used to beat her up whenever he got drunk. He was always drunk. One day he beat her so bad she went into a coma and never woke up. She left six babies and they scattered to the wind. I don't know where those babies are today.

"Laura, this one, she committed suicide when she was just young; and this one here," she pointed to a tall, thin girl who stared defiantly into the camera, "Boy, she sure was a troublemaker, ended up getting hit by a train, was out drinking. I used to have problems with her, but still I felt bad when she died. She was so young.

"You know this one here, don't you?" she asked. "Lucy Sam. She sat next to you at the memorial feast for Antoine; remember she held your hand? She was lonely, and she said you reminded her of her daughter, Angeline, the one who got killed in that car wreck last winter."

"Oh yeah, I remember," I said. "She had the scar over her eye and there was something wrong with her arm. I asked you about that, I remember."

"Joe Sam did that to her. He was a violent man. He nearly took that eye out, and he broke that arm so many times it never would heal straight anymore." Mom slumped over in weariness, and as I led her back to the armchair, she continued to talk. "Still, she stayed with him and had fourteen babies. Most of them are dead now. I think she's only got one son left. Life sure has been hard on her, but still she carries on."

I helped Mom onto the chair and plumped pillows all around her and put one under her feet.

"I guess all you can do is carry on," she sighed.

Then I took the crocheted comforter and tucked it around her shoulders. Soon she was fast asleep, her head leaning back, her mouth falling open, the lines on her face relaxing. The picture fell from her hand onto her lap. I sat watching her, wondering about her life, thinking about Lucy.

"Lucy used to be one of the prettiest girls in that school when she was young," Mom had told me. "She was a nice girl too. Everybody liked Lucy. Especially that priest," Mom said with disgust.

It had been a humbling experience for me, sitting there with Lucy all that night, letting her hold my hand. When she finally left in the early hours of the morning, she'd thanked me, stroking my hair, and telling Mom how lucky she was to have such a nice daughter. I could tell Mom was proud, and it made me feel good because I knew I'd made her happy, and had made Lucy happy too.

"Lucy was pregnant when she'd left that school," Mom told me. "No one knew for sure who did it, but everyone suspected it was the priest. That marriage to Joe was arranged by her family. It was the only thing they could think to do at that time. He was a widower with small children, and she was pregnant with no husband."

"It wasn't easy in those days for a woman to get by on her own. There was no welfare, no way she could support herself. Still, they could have had a good life, if only he hadn't drank so much, and if he hadn't been so jealous and so angry. He couldn't forget about that one baby that wasn't his. That baby died anyway, just like all her others. Still he wouldn't forget. She always loved his babies, those that weren't hers, and took such good care of them. She sure took it hard whenever one of her babies died. She was a good mother, she loved babies.

"I don't know what made that man so mean. Must have been somebody hurt him really bad when he was little. The way they used to beat those boys in that school, it's a wonder they didn't all turn out mean."

Mom told me Lucy spends all her time in the graveyard, pulling weeds and planting flowers all around those little plots. On special occasions she even puts flowers on Joe's grave. When I think of her, that's how I picture her, moving among those wooded rows of crosses, all stooped over with weariness and age. When I think of her stroking and patting my hand so tenderly all through that long night, my throat gets achy with unshed tears.

In the chair, Mom stirs. She doesn't open her eyes, but asks for a "cup a' tea, with lots of sugar and cream."

I'm glad to have something to do. When I come back with two steaming mugs of tea, she has the lamp on and is holding the picture up again, studying it with her good eye.

"This girl, here, used to be my best friend," she said. "Her name was Agnes. She came from somewhere over there in the East. She was a long way from home. They used to do that, take them so far away from their people. When that happened they couldn't go home for their holidays. I'd feel so sorry for those ones who had to stay behind.

"I'll always remember Agnes standing up there at that window, staring out at me, waving away, whenever I'd leave to go home. I used to want to take her with me, but I knew my folks didn't have much, and I just couldn't ask them. But I'd bring her treats when I came back, an apple and some oranges. Those were real luxuries in the school.

"When Agnes was thirteen she ran away. She never even told me she was going, but I knew how unhappy she was. She told me once that when all us kids would go home and only a few of them were left there, that the priest wouldn't leave them alone. I never liked him. He did awful things to us."

"To you, Mom?" I asked. "He did things to you, too?"

"Yeah," she muttered angrily, "to all of us. I'll tell you about that sometime, but now I want to talk about Agnes. What they did to her."

"They were pretty tough on kids who ran away, weren't they," I commented, wanting her to go on.

"If they were caught, it was pretty bad for them," she responded. "There were four others who ran away with Agnes. They were all those ones from the East. They'd planned it for a long time, saving up lots of food. They almost made it over the mountains, but some of the men from the village went after them and, of course, they caught up to them. They talked them into coming back. I never got over that, our own people brought them back.

"They made us clear away the tables and chairs in the cafeteria, and rang the bell for everyone to come and watch. They brought the runaways in one at a time. The Sisters held those little girls down so they wouldn't get away. They took turns whipping them. When one would get tired, another would step in. They kept whipping them until they made them cry, and even then some of them wouldn't stop.

"We didn't want to watch that, we tried to look away, turn our heads away, but those Sisters standing amongst us forced us to raise our eyes and look. The whole top of my dress was soaked in tears.

"I'll never forget them for what they did to my friend Agnes. They whipped her the longest because they said she was the ring-leader, and because she wouldn't cry. They kept yelling at her, 'Cry! Cry! Cry!', and she wouldn't cry. I wanted to beg her to cry so they would stop. Then I noticed a trickle of blood running down her leg and when she fell it smeared all over the floor. She had started on her period, started bleeding, and still they wouldn't stop. They propped her back up, and the blood was all over her legs, and all over the floor and still they wouldn't stop. They broke her that day. She was never the same after that.

"My friend, Agnes, she killed herself with the booze. She took off to the city straight from school. Never even went home. I saw her down in Vancouver once. Somebody told me she was around there, down on the skids. So I went down there to look for her. I thought maybe I could help her out. She was pretty bad. She just wanted money, so I gave her my last few dollars. I figured it would go to good use, if it could help her forget. There wasn't much I could do for her by then. I felt real bad. Then I heard she got hit by a car, and died not too long after that. She was my best friend, I couldn't have made it through that school without her."

Mom sat for some time, silent tears rolling down her face. When I tried to comfort her, she waved me away. Then, when she finally spoke, there was a great bewildered hurt and sadness in her voice that I recognized immediately; it touched me inside my emptiness, in that never-ending lonely space deep within my heart. I realized then that I could never touch my mother in such a way that could relieve the despair that had settled around her like a dark cloud, a long time ago, in the same way that she could never relieve my loneliness for her.

"I've often wondered why I'm still living and all these other women are dead." She stared at the picture bitterly, and the bitterness crept into her voice, causing me to draw back. "I've asked that over and over again and there is never any answer."

Then she began to tell her story. The story that I had waited over forty years to hear.

"The priest he tried to destroy me too, but I wouldn't let him." She slunk down into the chair and spoke from memory the words that were painful for her to share. I sat very still, afraid to move, lest she stop speaking. She'd always been so careful not to tell me too much. Trying to protect me, I guess, but I needed to know.

"We used to get sick a lot, us girls," she said. "There were no doctors who would look at us back then. Whenever we got sick we'd just have to go to bed and wait it out. Some of those Sisters would experiment on us, try different things to get us well. None of it worked though, we'd just have to wait it out. Some girls weren't strong enough to make it. They were always sending somebody home in those body bags.

"One time, one of the girls from my village died, and they put her in a bag and slung her over the back of a horse. They had to tie her down so she wouldn't slide off. They made me and this other girl take her back home. It took all day to get there. We were just little girls, and I remember we were riding through the bushes and we got into a fit of giggles because the other girl said, 'Lookit, Molly's head is bouncin' up and down. I wonder what she's thinking.' Molly was the name of the girl who died. Gee, we must have been crazy just laughing at her like that. There were these men who came along from the village and they really bawled us out.

"There was this one dorm where all the sick kids had to go. Anyone who got sick got sent there. One day my neck swole up so big I could hardly swallow, and Sister sent me to bed in that dorm. When I got to the room, I noticed there was another little girl there. Her name was Sarah. I tried to talk to her but she told me to pretend I was asleep or else someone would come and bother us.

"'When he comes,' she said, 'just keep pretending you're asleep. Sometimes he just goes away.'

"I didn't know who she was talking about, but I pretended to sleep, until I got so tired I almost did fall asleep. Then I heard someone talking. I peeked out and it was Father Millar.

"'I've come to visit you again, Sarah,' he said. 'Who's this in the other bed? Oh, it's Sousette. What a nice surprise. I think I'll visit with her first.'

"I kept my eyes tightly closed, hoping he'd go away. I felt the weight of him on the bed as he knelt down. At first I thought he was going to pray over me, so I just lay there. Then I felt his hand underneath the covers, touching me down there. I tried to push his hand away, really I tried, but he told me, 'No, no Sousette, you just lay still.'

"He kept feeling around and I kept pushing his hand away. I started to cry because I didn't want him doing that. I was so scared. I couldn't stop crying. Finally he got mad and got up and said, 'I'll go over to Sarah. Sarah's not scared. She's not a crybaby like you.'

"I shut my eyes tight and tried not to listen to what he was doing. It made me so sick to hear that, and Sarah, she didn't say a word, didn't make a sound, didn't even cry. I think he did that to her a lot. She was always sick, always in the dorm. She finally died too. That must have been a relief for her. She suffered so much.

"After that, whenever I got sick I wouldn't go into that dorm. I'd get my coat and whatever other coats I could find and I'd pile them up in the bathroom. That's where I'd sleep. It sure was cold in there, but I didn't care. It was better than going through that with Father. I couldn't stop him forever though. One day he just did what he wanted with me, and oh how I've hated him for that. I've hated God too.

"In my whole life I've never known a gentle man. They've all been mean and rough just like Father. I've never known what it's like to be loved by a gentle man."

She dropped her head back as if all her strength had gone from her. She reached out and took my hand in hers. I opened my mouth to speak, and closed it again. I wondered what she would think if she knew that I too, as a child, had been abused; that I too, have never known a gentle man. I wanted so much to tell her, but I couldn't. Instead, we sat in silent sorrow, apart, separated by the secrecy and isolation of our memories—imprisoned there.

Quite suddenly she turned and smiled so sweetly at me. "You'll tell me some day," she whispered.

Then the light flickered and faded from her eyes and she was gone.

POETRY

THE STORM

It was one of those rainy Vancouver nights
That she sat by the window to write
Allowing her eyes to stray now and then
Out towards the bay where she caught
Glimpses of it faintly against the storm
Movement like music straining in her mind
The marimba, the drum, the violin
Coming together in a crescendo
Of sound and light.

In the distance, a bell
The ticking of a clock on the wall
Announces two a.m.
Deliberately she holds back
Wills herself not to respond
Hears faint rasping noises
In desperation she races down
The staircase, descends
The steps two-at-a-time
Wrestles the door against the storm
Reaches for him in the dark.

I barely made it into the bay, he said,

The winds were so strong
I saw your light and I came.
He was wet, wounded, collapsing into her.

She struggled to stay inside her dream
Slowly opened her eyes
Was blinded by the cool cruel dawn

Knew for certain he was gone

All night long she dreamt
Of sunny corn-filled fields
Of comfortable contented women
In colourful skirts.

She'd never go to meet him again
He'd never make it back
To get her this time
He was forever gone
Blown away in last night's storm.

The sun blazing through the window
Forced her to witness her emptiness
The imprint of him
Pressed against her heart.

On her sofa
A straw hat
Damp from
Last night's rain
Abandoned
Forgotten there.
She reached inside her bedside drawer
Drew out the sharpest pair of scissors
She could find
One-by-one she plucked her eyes out
And threw them into the bay.

In grief and darkness
She felt her way to her desk
And there began to write
The eulogy of her soul.

Ah, the secrets are being swept ashore **again**
In great crashing waves they come

Pressing down upon me
Insinuating themselves
Into every corner of my being.
My body betrays me,
Remembering all those shameful places
Where my mind refuses to go.

I want to die, to drown in it
To be carried away
To a place where nobody
Knows my name
But that cruel ocean won't claim me
Instead she spits me out naked
Gasping on shore
Gasping for breath
Gasping for life.

I know I cannot hide behind those secrets anymore
I can't bear this life of loneliness

The isolation that separates me
Because I think I am different
And all those shameful secrets
Are all my doing
I'm ashamed to live
While they, dead or dying,

Carry the horrible secret to their grave
Trusting I will do the same
I am, after all, the dutiful daughter,
The loyal niece,
keeper of the secrets,
the family pride.

I know I must tell them or perish
If I don't tell them I shall die
But I'd rather cut out my tongue.

A woman without a tongue has no safe place in this world
She is expected to be silent

Devoid of emotion
Obedient
Kneeling at the feet of men
A woman who knows her place
Is following behind
Lying beneath
Legs spread
Mouth opened
Ready to receive
That insidious embrace
That tongue down the throat
Without protest
Feigning pleasure
Not grief.

No one can crawl inside the heart of a woman without a tongue
A woman without a tongue has to pretend she has no heart.

What I know about life, about love, I could crush you with it.
(I know too much about life

And too little about love)
I have loved people without them ever knowing it
I have loved them from a distant place
On the periphery of their lives
Where I've always placed myself
A safe distance away
So I am not a burden
And love can't get to me
Past that wall of secrets
That surrounds me
I have loved you.

My brother and I grew up with ghosts
who moved things, opened and shut doors,
tapped on windows, and waited
for children to be alone.

My brother saw them as normal.
They had a relationship
that I never understood,
he could see them, talk to them—
I could feel them but I was so scared.
I couldn't breathe,
            couldn't see,
                        couldn't move,
clenched my fists and stomach into knots
until I was sick.

He'd say:
            "I saw so-and-so
            sitting in our chair last night;
            I called his name but
            he wouldn't answer
            and then he disappeared."

"So-and-so" was always
somebody who was dead.

He wasn't teasing when we sat on the front steps in the dark,
a six-year-old and a five-year-old,
he was serious when he'd say:
            "I can see them coming up the road again,

like floating light, they're headed straight for us.
There's nothing to be afraid of."

But I was already inside the door
begging him to come in,
but he wanted to speak to them
he was curious
and had this gift
he wanted to explore.

Nobody talked openly about ghosts
except in whispers,
caught between civilization and superstition
from the past, they admonished my brother
            not to talk about things
                        that only he could see.

He had to tell someone
so he told me.

I listened through fear that took hold early
and grew with each passing year
I got used to it—ghosts, life, people and my brother's stories.

Then one night they came full force
when mom and dad left us to go drinking.

            They tried to steal my little brother
            who was the weakest because he was a baby.
            They were relentless.
            They stayed all night
            going round and round the house,
            our dog Tippy barking, then whimpering
            wanting to protect us

until my brother called him to come inside.
We cowered under blankets
and listened to the old man next door
speaking Secwepemc,
singing songs to make them go away.

Mom and dad came home at daybreak.
The old man met them by the road.
I felt the fear in their whispered conversations.
They stayed home after that
for as long as they could, united;
until another drunken brawl
caused them to quickly come apart;
to forget all about us
and ghosts in the night.

They kept coming, the ghosts,
the predators, the ghosts
and then the predators again.
I don't know which I feared the most?

As soon as I was old enough to leave
I moved away to the city where neon lights
and sirens offered me a comfort and safety
that the darkness and silence never could.

L.A. OBSESSION SONG

You long to live forever
Should I never let you down,
Waiting in the wings of life
In a fading wedding gown.
Would I give up all my youth
While age waits by my door?
But you know I'll go on waiting
Or what else should I live for?
To wrap myself round you
To cloak you from the cold;
To later lie discarded
Alone and growing old.
You swear you'll always need me
To hold your head up high
To swear I truly love you
With no single reason why.
To see your face forever
In tattered magazines
To see the shallow truth
Behind your lifelong dreams,
To see you give forever
'til there's nothing left for me
but this thing that I can give you
this love that sets you free.
Then I'll give you all my dreams,
And I'll give you all my life
I'll forever be your lover
I'll never be your wife.
I'll be the sweetest love song
That you can call your own,
I'll be your silent shadow

So you never walk alone.
Yet . . .
This madness drives me on
To learning silent sighs
To aching unfulfillment
To escaping helpless cries
To know I can't forget you
No use to even try
To admit I truly love you
With no single reason why.

ADDICTIONS

Do you know how wonderful it feels
To share early morning
Running and laughing in the rain?
If you knew how much I loved you
You'd forget about your pain.

Is there such a thing as happiness
That isn't lost in pain?
Is there such a thing as happiness
That never disappears?

I could never hope to erase
All that sadness in your eyes
It's hidden behind your laughter
Behind your bad disguise.

I hate to see your pain
While I'm loving you so much
If you knew how much I loved you
Would you recognize my touch?
Have you ever known a love
That asks no guarantee
If I gave you such a love
Could you give it back to me?

When I'm banging on your door
And you're never, ever home,
When I'm drunk and tired and lonesome
And 3 a.m. alone
When I didn't find who I wanted
And realized you weren't there

And wondering if I wanted you
Enough to make you care
And worrying and wondering
Most of all where you were?

LIES

He's not going to tell me the truth
I knew it the moment I set eyes on him.
God, he was handsome to look at
And lies slipped easily off
His tongue
Onto my aching, waking body,
Wounding me with
Tiny, ache formations
Across my back,
Paining and pleasuring me
All the same.
Woven dreams
Enrapturing me
In smooth and silky
Half-truths,
Omissions
And innuendoes.

He is well-practiced at his art
And I at 32 was still a girl
Waiting for all my dreams
To come true.

LIFE ABUSE OF GIRLS

Lying on the cold, hard floor,
Thrown against the wall
Landing like a hard stone
Crawling back for more
Can't get enough of you

Prisoner of war
At your mercy
I would do anything for you
Please don't leave
me.

I want you to see me.
Look at me
Your back is like
A knife to my heart
I am drowning in
Desperate seas of saliva
And tears. Why?
Why won't you love me?

THE WOMAN I COULD BE

I'm an endangered species, you know;
An empty flattened vessel,
A receptacle for all your weaknesses.
My arms reach outward
      To encircle the wounded
            To love, to nurture, to protect.

My self vulnerable, terrified, defeated
By your eyes,
      Your mouth,
            Your fists.

An angry, selfish, macho-man like you,
You think you don't need the love
A creature like me
      Gives

            And gives

                  And gives.
I have a burning,
A bubbling inside
A stirring that unfulfilled
Grows more conspicuous everyday.

A need to move out
            From the shadow of you
A need to take back my arms,
            To move away from the war,
               To reach inward
                    To soothe, to protect
The frightened child inside;
To heal her wounds,

To nurture her
Until she grows strong enough to terrify
A man like you.

Could you love the woman I could be,
Or are you stuck on abusing
The child in me?

FOOLS

Your words like ice picks
Chip away at my heart

Forcing aside
The only defences I have

You think
Love lives here

What a fool you are

LONELINESS

It's the loneliness I fear the most
That's why I can't leave,
The loneliness,
It creeps up all around me
Especially at night.
It's so thick I can feel it.
Where did it come from?
Was I born with it?
Inherited it from my mother?

I remember mom on hot summer nights
Sitting on the steps of the house
Watching the cars go by on the highway
Like watching her life slip away—waiting,
Always waiting for dad to come home.

I remember dad
He always came home angry,
Oh, but he wasn't always like that,
But he never spoke to her either.
I was just a kid when mom finally left for good,
I guess she just got tired of waiting.
How she struggled and struggled to keep us together,
Welfare lines, worry lines on her face
And always, always that loneliness.
I'd lie and watch her from my bed at night
Sitting at the kitchen table with her bottle
Staring out the window—
Waiting for the darkness to begin.
All the while I'd be praying,
Hoping that this was the night

She'd just go on to bed
When it got dark.

But then she'd get up
And go over and get the mirror,
It was just a broken piece of glass—
She'd balance it between two books
And the sugar canister
Then she would stare into it
For a long time, touching her face
here and there, touching those lines.
Then she would put on her lipstick
From the one good tube she never allowed
My sister or I to play with,
Then she would comb her hair,
She had such long, beautiful hair.
Oh God, those eyes,
She had such sad, lonely eyes.
I've tried to forget them
But sometimes I catch glimpses
Of those same desperate, grieving eyes
When I'm pacing around the house,
Waiting—
Waiting
For him to come home.
I'd try not to let him see them,
I'd turn away, cover them up,
"You stop looking at me like that," he'd say.

She'd always come to the door
Before she left, and I'd keep
My eyes tightly closed
So she wouldn't know
I was awake—

As soon as the door would close,
I'd jump out of bed
And run to the window
To watch her looking so alone
On that dark road.
I knew she was going to the bar—
I wanted to stop her—
Wanted to run after her,

"Mom, please don't leave us, don't go,
Mom, please stay home with us."

ABUSED MOTHERS, WOUNDED FATHERS

I kept my mother and father longer than most Indians my age,
I was 41 when she died and 42 when he slipped away;
Yet, sometimes I despair how I wasted all that time,
I never really got to know them
until long after they'd gone.

Even from a distance I think I always knew my mother loved me,
I used to wonder about my dad though
being as close to him as I was, it was hard to tell.

It must have been hard on them how I stayed away,
kept all shut up inside, never married,
never gave them grandbabies to redeem themselves on.
I heard Dad tell it once, how he figured it was his fault
how I grew to mistrust the world.
It makes me ache inside to think about it.
Sometimes I wake in the middle of the night
and I tell them things I never told them in life,
it's easier for me to talk to them
when they can't answer back.

Mom and Dad grew up in residential school,
there wasn't much love in those places.
When I lie very still,
close my eyes,
I picture them as children
five and six years old;
I take them up into my arms,
hold them tightly,
rock them gently,
kiss them all over their faces

the way babies ought to be kissed,
because I know there was no one
to do that for them back then.
It's somehow soothing to me.

Someone told me once
that when my dad was a boy
he used to get beaten
until he was bloody.

HUNGER

My dad was strong,
he was tougher than anyone I ever knew;
I could tell when he was hurting though,
by the fury in his eyes.

Sometimes he would yell.
he would yell and scare us kids
with his rage,
he would hit us and yell.

It wasn't until years later
that I understood,
he was just being that little kid again,
only this time he was fighting back.
We were casualties of that senseless war.

"I'm going to write a book,"
I told my dad,
"about residential school."

"Good," he replied,
"You come by some afternoon

I could tell you all about it."

I arrived on Sunday
with half-a-dozen blank tapes
and a notepad.

"So," I asked,
"What was it like in residential school,
Testing, testing 1-2-3."

"We were hungry," he replied,
"we used to steal potatoes," he chuckled.
"We were so hungry we'd burn our mouths
eating those potatoes

half burnt, half raw, covered with dirt,
we'd shovel them into our mouths
while they were still on fire
hoping we wouldn't get caught,
we'd get whipped for stealing,
they tasted so good.
I don't think you could ever understand
that kind of hunger,
you kids today, you have everything."

Us kids, used to have to eat
every single bit of food on our plate,
we'd get beaten if we didn't.

There was so much anger at our table,
it was hard to swallow
past the fear in our throats.

"I couldn't speak English," he whispered,
"I spoke Indian and I got whipped,
I got whipped a lot."

Tears from my father's eyes
Rolled silently from his face.

I couldn't go to him
I sat frozen like a statue
by his grief.

Silently
I packed my recorder,
blank tapes, notepad,
and I left him there
to sort out his feelings
for himself.

I never interviewed him
about residential school
ever, ever again.

THE CATHOLIC CHURCH

My mom used to be vicious at the Catholic Church.
She would call those priests and nuns right down into the ground.
There was a time she would not set foot inside a church.
At funerals she directed her prayers to Nupika from the front steps
Peering now and then into the darkness waiting for service to end.

The only time people go to church around here is when they die.
They walk 10 miles in the cold just to church when someone dies.
When I die don't ever bring me to that place.

I used to hate the church too although I never knew why.
I guess I hated them because I loved my mother.

Every time we passed by that vacant, grey structure
That once was St. Eugene's Indian Residential School
I could feel my mother's anger, brittle and hard,
Exploding beside me, shattering sharp like broken glass.

She never cried like my father, she told it to me straight
And hard-edged, embittered and enraged so I became afraid.

That ugly, grey building was once like prison to me.
That ugly place still standing there,
All our cheap DIA houses falling down
But that place still stands reminding us
Someone ought to burn it down.

Fearful that she just might do that one day I'd distract her,
Make her change her mind; say something to make her laugh.
I loved to listen to my mother laugh.
She had a good sense of humour,

An offbeat way of viewing the world
That's what got her by all those tough times.

Ought to burn that place down too,
She'd say as she tossed her head toward the neatly-spired,
Whitewashed Catholic Church that still dominates
The centre of her village today.

DEADLY LEGACY

There was sexual abuse in our family,
as a child all adults were suspect,
I was especially afraid of old people
I stayed scared until I was 40-years-old.
I had no memory before nine years of age,
placed no importance on memories that were sad.
Suddenly, they emerged
in frightful pieces of physical
and soul-destroying pain.

I thought I'd caused it,
was sure it was my fault,
felt alone,
shared it with my mother;
her whole being turned its back,
covered its ears,
closed its eyes,
and said:
                    "No."
My sisters,
brother,
nieces cried out,
nephew committed suicide
and then she listened.

The pain in her voice
soothed the aching wounds
in my heart.
                    "I always wanted lots of children,"
                    she said,
                    "because I grew up alone.

I grew up in the residential school,
they never taught me
how to take care of my babies,
that's why you and your sisters
had to suffer, because I didn't know
how to protect you.
I'm so sorry you had to suffer like that."

"It's okay mom,"
I said,
"now it's going to be okay."

Soon after that she died.
In all my life
that was my mom's
greatest gift to me.
She freed me up inside
to learn to forgive her
and to love her
in a more truthful way.

My mom was abused, sexually,
by a priest in residential school,
she never told us that
until just before she died.

KEEPING SECRETS

> I know everything there is to know
> about keeping secrets

It's taken a lifetime
for me to make peace
with my mother
a lifetime
for my mother
to make peace
with her mother

> I know everything there is to know
> about keeping secrets

"I was sexually abused
by a priest in residential
school, you weren't there
to stop it," my mother said.

"How could I?"
my grandmother replied,
"the same thing
happened to me."

In all her 87 years
not once had she hinted
that such a thing
could ever happen.

> I know everything there is to know
> about keeping secrets

I have secrets in
every part of my body,
secrets too painful to tell
secrets difficult to reconcile
an empty, vast, wasteland inside
that no amount of healing
can fill

      I know everything there is to know
      about keeping secrets

FORGIVENESS

After my mom spoke of the abuse
I saw her change,
become softer

quit quite suddenly
attacking the church,
began to go inside
to sit with the People.

"People need something
to believe in," she said,
"God is the same Creator
I pray to, we must respect
one another's beliefs.

When I die
bring me to the church,
it'll be easier
for the People that way,

The Creator is everywhere,
it won't make a difference
to me when I am gone,
but the People need
something to believe in."

WHEN I FIRST CAME TO KNOW MYSELF

When I first came to know myself,
My mother said, "I was only three years old
And travelling up in the mountains
With my grandparents. My grandfather
And grandmother loved me
Very much and took me
Everywhere with them
And taught me everything.
At that time I knew my place
In the world
I knew where I came from
And where I was going.
Everything was clear to me,
That is when I first came to know myself.
Then the priest came
And took me from my people
And I lost everything.
I came to know myself again later in life
I quit drinking and it all came back to me,
My grandparents' teachings."

> "When I first came to know myself,"
> I said, "I was already a woman
> Almost 40 years old, until then I had
> No knowledge. I had no place in the world,
> And I knew nothing about my people.
> When I first came to know myself
> I was sitting inside the sweat lodge
> Praying with my mother
> Listening to her gentle voice
> Speaking in her language to the spirits

Greeting them as though they were
Old friends come to visit.
It is very dark and the air
Is thick with cedar,
I sat bent with tears
Streaming down my face,
Crying because I felt so safe
And for the first time in my life
I felt clean. That is the time
When I first came to know myself."

WHEN MY SISTER & I DANCE

When my sister & I dance
To the sacred drum
We take a long time to prepare.

Our dresses are special
Ktunaxa dresses.
We wear them only when
There are good feelings
Surrounding us
When we hear
The gentle sounds
Of our people's language
Between the drums
And laughter.

Hers is elk,
Tanned, smoked and stitched together
With great care
By our grandmother Kupe
Decorated with iyute and shells
She carries the pride
Of our people
In the rhythm of her footsteps
In the to and fro
Motion
Of fringe across her shoulders.

Mine is pure white deerhide
Made for me by my mother
When I was 15-years-old.
This dress and I have travelled

A long way together,
As far away as the city
And back,
There are tear stains
From those times
I've held its softness
To my cheek
And wondered
Who am I?

Now it is as though
I'm putting it on
For the first time.
We decorate our hair
With quills and beaded ornaments
Laid over rabbit skin hair ties.

Each hair smoothed
Straight back
In neatly arranged
Dark Indian braids
Caught at the ends
With long, narrow strips
Of buckskin
Wrapped round and round.

I wear the beautiful shell
Breastplate
That Derek made
And the black velvet
Beaded shoulder cape
That once belonged
To Kupe.

My sister wears Kupe's beads
And always borrows my winter shawl.

We both wear high-topped moccasins
And carry
Eagle-feather fans
That we cherish.

Carefully we inspect one another
Checking to ensure nothing
Will fall when we dance.
When we are ready
We walk proudly out to the floor.

We were already young women
The first time we danced.
We were shy, self-conscious
Didn't know what to do with our hands.
Too soon from the city
We worried more about the things
Around us
And knew nothing
Of what lay dormant inside.

Our mother,
So wise with age,
So gentle with words
Spoke to us:

> "Never mind who might be watching you,
> You are not there for them. Remember
> When you dance you are building your road,
> The circle you follow is your life's journey.
> When you dance, pray for a good, strong road ahead.

Pray for all the bad things
To be taken from your path.
Dance hard.
Nupika likes Indians to dance hard.
Sing loud,
That makes Nupika happy.
The spirits will hear your prayers.
Never be ashamed that you are Indian,
Be proud."

When my sister and I dance,
Our feet barely touch the ground.
The only sounds we hear
Are the drums
And the voices
Rising up
From the hearts
Of our people.

Some songs are so powerful
They make my heart
Beat like the drum,
I hold the eagle feathers high
Feel the rush of the wind
Beneath its wings
Lifting my spirit
To that place
Closest to the sky.
My feet barely touch the ground
When the sacred circle
And I are one.

It is at these times
That I truly know
Who I am
Why there is life inside
Where it flows to
And from where it came.

When my sister and I dance
We move in perfect harmony
To the four directions
We give thanks

Thank you to the north
Thank you to the east
Thank you to the south
Thank you to the west

Thank you
For bringing us back home
For bringing us back to life again.

She said with a smile through the tears of her grief
"As a girl I was so quick I could catch fish with my hands."

Before the darkness, before the pain,
"I was so light I could catch fish with my hands."
Tiny feet dancing among stone and sand,
music of water push against graceful hand,
face uplifted to warm summer sky
laughter echoes off trees that sigh
at her beauty, her grace, her child sweet innocence,
Not scaring fish
but enticing them
to jump into her outstretched arms
entranced by her joy, her sparkle,
her love-filled eyes.
Before monsters came
before darkness
she really could
catch fish with her hands.

Determined now,
Resolute
she stands
too weary to run
she faces the dark
invites the sun
believes again
that she really can
catch fish with her hands,
believes.

TWO BROTHERS

Two brothers playing
Hide-and-go-seek
Chasing each other across sandy beach
Laughing and shouting into the wind
Never dreaming that this could end.

Two brothers taken to foster homes
Mom and dad they took a bad turn
The babies are gone out into the world
With no one to protect them from the storm.

But little brother
I never stopped loving you

Big brother
You were always my hero.

Two brothers in a cold dark world
Shuffled about in foster homes
Sometimes together but coming apart
Two brothers with one broken heart.

Bad things happen to children who laugh
To children who play and run too fast.
Bad things happen to children who love
To children who cry
To children who dream
To children who sigh
Shouts turn to whispers then fade away
Shouts turn to whispers then fade away
One day soon there's nothing to say.

Little brother gets beat
Little brother he cries
But there's nobody there
So he holds it inside.

Big brother gets abused
And pretends it's okay
He gets angry a lot
And learns to survive.

Two brothers
Two numbers
As they shuffle the deck.

But little brother
I never stopped loving you

Big brother
You were always my hero.

One day in a healing circle they meet
Two grown men with sorrow
Etched on their faces
Hard men to get close to
Hard men to know
Uncover a memory so distant and sweet
Of laughter and running
Across sandy beach
Memories of pain
And hands that let go
Through grief reach out
Become brothers again
Through laughter and tears
Let each other know

But little brother
I never stopped loving you

Big brother
You were always my hero.

LA GUERRA

What do I know about war,
Grandmothers and babies being killed
Massacres, blood, permeating fear?

I know about love.
I've known safe places
In spite of where I've been.

"those puta soldiers kill everything..."

and I can't imagine what it felt like
to watch, helpless.

What do I know about the war
That rages on in your mind
That spills out into my life.
I'm so scared of you sometimes.

"My family, todos, everything wiped out,
my babies gone I don't know where."

I who have never experienced
A close death, what do I know
About being empty, alone?

I want to run, hide, to find a safe place
Far away from you, but then
I want to stay, to be the one
To rub that fear out of your mind
The one to save us both
The inevitable death of war
Should we decide to stay.

He stumbles along in the park,
Clutches his pain to his heart,
Tight, hoards it there
Wild-eyed, drunk;
Moves unsteadily
Disoriented among merry-makers,
Powell Street Festival celebrants,
Musical invaders,
Feasters of delicacies,
Samplers of culture,
Repulsed by his stench;
His dirty, unkempt, uncared-for,
Un-loved, dis-spirited,
Empty self.

They shield the eyes of their babies,
Childhood ought not to see,
With their bodies,
Uneasy, downward glances,
Eyes break contact, disguise disdain,
The line of their backs tell it all,
Pretend he's not there.

The master of ceremonies has arrived,
Boisterous and bold like a clown,
He bows low, falls into the grass.
Unsteadily he rises
Greets his guests one-by-one,
His glazed, bloodshot eyes stare out
From pockmarked, saggy gray,

Brown like the earth,
Brown like my skin.

Face outward, toothless grin,
Delighted by the company
Their rudeness lost on him.
Gently he is nudged aside,
Greatly he protests
Arms flapping
Struggling to stand his ground.

This is my land,
Go back where you come from.

He is lifted by both arms and moved
To an unused corner, a reservation
Within the territory
He stands resigned,
Disappointment in his eyes,
Eyeing the cool, green grass,
Falls down, face first into it
And lies very still.

The child and I who once abhorred him,
Rejected him, turned our back too
In shame:

Drunk Indian
Indian drunk,

Study him now, curiously,
Without awkwardness,
Wonder what he dreams
Relative, ancestor, forgotten warrior,

Weary lines, broken teeth, bruised lips
Clenched in despair
Or ecstasy.

Wonder how,
Now that we know the secret,
How we managed to escape?

INHERITANCE

It never ceases to amaze me
when I see that soup line-up
down on Powell
how I managed not to end up there
considering where I've been.

Of course I am grateful
that my father was so strict
never allowed me to look at a boy
told me that's where babies came from
as though babies were
evil sinful things
that only happened to bad girls.

      "If it ever happens to you
      and you're not married," he said,
      "don't ever come home
      I would be too ashamed."

Of course I am grateful
that my mother was never there;
she taught me how to be
resourceful,
      industrious,
          alone,
she gave me her babies
so I wouldn't have to have
any of my own.

      "If a man hits you,
      leave him," she said,

"if he hits you once
he'll always hit you
again and again and again."

I've always left
never stayed long enough
for a man
to put his marks on me.

She came to a realization in late spring
In the melting snow
In the beautiful valley
Of Qu'appelle
Her sense of purpose
Disintegrated.

Another lonely room
A solitary meal
The singleness of her bed
Her empty heart
Let go.

All the years
She'd toiled relentless
Waiting for life to begin;
During this season
She'd placed great hope
But could see nothing coming
In the distance
Only a past looming behind.

In reality it had already come,
In a flash was gone
Wasted, squandered
In reckless youth

What stirred inside?
What came to life?

Erupted in rage
For that child who knew desire
Too soon.

Like china pieces
She wrapped all womanly desires
Into silk scraps,
Gathered up her dreams,
Packed all evidence
Of past regrets
Into each crevice of her heart,
And through the opened door
Escaped with her secrets
Into the night.

NEVER EVER TELL

It was such a big deal before I told anyone,
                    The biggest, darkest secret
                              In the whole wide world.

Like something coiled evil in the dark,
Paralyzed with fear that I was.

He warned me
Burnt it into my eyes
NEVER EVER TELL.

It came out slowly
                    Like broken pieces of glass shards
                              Across my tongue,
Spewed forth
From the vomit
In my soul.

After that
Each time I spoke of it
I wept in shame, fear, rage and grief
Until one day
                    Magically
                              It was gone.

The fears became regrets
For the life
That never was
And soon that disappeared too,

It was then
That it became
No big deal.

I should have spoke of it sooner
Instead of holding it for so long,
All that time
      It was me
            Waiting there
                 In the dark.

These red and grey brick buildings
Have an air of permanence
Built to last, by settlers
Who decided to stay.
They've been here
100 years and more
Inhabited by relatives
       Of relatives
           Of relatives
Their hallways and staircases
Boardrooms and offices
Overcrowded by the ghosts
Of my ancestors' oppressors
Who squashed the spirit out of them
One-brick-at-a-time
Its mortared foundation
Echoes the cries
Of all that is lost
And what has been gained
Through sheer will
And determination to survive
But still they speak to me
Of sadness and loneliness.
I am lost in this place
Of law makers and thieves.

THE TRUTH ABOUT COLONIZATION

Brown-skinned people are enslaved
to add colour to white people's lives.
Oppressed, to create bureaucracies
to administer poverty, grief,
delinquency, and shame.

To give white people a worthwhile cause
to carry forward into the next century,
all those Indigenous, Aboriginal, Natives
who dared survive life
inside the boxed cage
created by greed.

Brown-skinned peoples' true history erased,
Title and Rights denied
to make way for vivid, romanticized,
more appealing convenient tales
of the noble savage
who fought and lost,
valiantly, to the great white
founding forefathers
of this stolen land.

Indians as backdrops to the grand exploits
of explorers, discoverers, colony-builders
of a history that only just began in 1492
on this ancient homeland
of our ancestors.

Brown-skinned children stolen,
      stripped, torn-down,
      ripped apart, emptied out,
      fashioned into colonizing tools
      of self-hatred.
Taught to be ashamed to be brown
      by a brown-skinned colonial education
          that instils in us the belief
            that white is right;
That brown-skinned people
belong at the end of the line
to ensure colonizers, settlers
and all future generations
      maintain privilege
          in this colonized world.
Brown-skinned people's sacred
ceremonial beliefs,
      objects,
          medicines,
            rituals,
stolen, filtered, processed, packaged, sold,
swallowed up by a New Age Movement
of lost souls searching
for something better than Christianity
to believe in:

      Waya waya waya ho
      twist and shift its spirit to fit
      Waya ho waya ho waya ho
      bought at quick fix magic shops
      with explicit instructions of
      "how to," for a price,
      become a medicine man overnight,
      a pipe-carrier, shaman.

They adorn mantels and makeshift altars
with feathers, beads, smudge bowls, offerings
for white people to comment on, and to play with.

Brown-skinned people survive.
Knowledge of our true history
strengthen our ties to
mother earth, to father sky,
to our beliefs and to
all future generations.

We work hard to resist
the evils of genocide,
We refuse to die,

We make supreme sacrifices
in prisons across the land,

We birth activist babies
who raise up their fists in unity,
give the warriors' cry,
There is no end to resistance
and that is the truth about colonization.

JUSTICE

I am a product of colonization
In this land called Canada
I am the result of cultural oppression
By church and government
I am a survivor of forced assimilation
And genocide
I am First Nations, Aboriginal, and Indigenous
Person of this land.

Yet, I do not speak the language
Of my ancestors
I know little about the customs and traditions
Of my people
I have never fasted up in the mountain
I have no song, nor dance
No Indian name to define me
And for most of my life
I could honestly say
I don't know who I am.
When I look around my world
I see my people
In this land of riches
Confined to small spaces
Forced to fight everyday to protect
Traditional territory
Living lives of poverty
Similar to third worlds
I find my rage stirring inside me
I feel robbed
A sense of injustice.

When I look around my world
I see the hearts and backs of my people
Breaking beneath burdens
Of unresolved grief
Nightmarish memories
Of childhood trauma
Residential school, foster
And adoptive homes, TB sanatoriums
Generation-to-generation
Physical, emotional, spiritual, sexual
Abuse and shame
I feel the rage stirring inside me.

When I allow my ears to listen
To voices of other people of this land
Who have no mercy
No love, no compassion, no understanding
Of its unjust history
Who come for freedom, opportunity,
Adventure, riches,
I feel my rage stirring inside me,
Who stand on the graves of my ancestors
And carelessly say:
"why can't those Indians get it together?
They live off our tax money you know."
I feel my rage stirring inside me
Camouflage for powerlessness and shame
Anaesthesia for grief
A sense of injustice.

I feel unsafe in the white world
To speak my views out loud
Or to share my culture

Uneasy, mistrustful,
Afraid those white people
Will steal the very words I speak, steal the
Ceremonies,
The sacred circle, sacred stories, songs and dances,
Wear our names
Copy our art and sell it
I get nervous when they write things down
So I tell them straight
"you can't write it down."
I fight hard inside myself
To see the human beings that they are.

I am a product of colonization
The result of cultural oppression
A survivor of genocide
I carry the burden
Of all the unresolved grief
Of my ancestors
In my heart, on my shoulders, in my gut.

In this lifetime
I have committed myself
To fight for Justice.
My brother tells me
"*It is injustice that is our enemy, not white people,
remember we are fighting on the same side as
Geronimo, Mandela, Gandhi and King.*"
We take responsibility for our rage
We fight on the same side
For justice.

BERIC

Your letters
like a mirror
force me to look in

to see myself

They draw my eyes
away from my
despondent staring
into empty horizons
after pointless pools of
dark dark waters

that I think I am

Your words are
like milestones in my life
reminding me of its worth

A life lived with purpose
If I could regain my words
I have another story
I could tell

I could be myself again
instead of this sick person
waiting for the end

your belief in me
is like a light
much stronger than mine.

CHRISTMAS INSIDE OF ME

I have a Christmas tree
inside of me
all decorated up
with stars, glitter,
and twinkling lights
waiting to give
all of the gifts of my life
that I can't take with me
when I go;
a Christmas tree inside of me
waiting to receive
all the gifts that you
and life have to offer.

I have a turkey dinner
with all the aromas, textures
tastes of Christmases past
spread across my table of joy
and music of conversation
in my ears all that
my heart remembers . . .
"pass the gravy, please"
punctuated by laughter,
"mmm the cranberries taste so good,"
interrupted by sounds of children
running in new hand-made moccasins
carrying new toys too excited to eat,
"can we have more stuffing here?
and a spoon of mashed potatoes
and a brussels sprout or two . . .
don't forget we have dessert."

I have endless memories
of Christmas dinners
carefully packed away
and cherished.

Such memories have no end
I could make Christmas dinner
when I am 100 years old
and in my sleep
when my star
shines its brightest.

SPRING FEVER

Today the sun came
shining through the cold,
relentless it barged
through every space and crack
around the blinds.

Even with my eyes tight shut
it kept right on playing with me.

I growled like a bear,
turned away, rolled over,
then over again,
burrowed my eyes
into the sheets,
hung stubbornly onto sleep
and grumbled:

"Oh quit, you're only teasing me.
I know the minute I get up

get dressed
get raring to go

You'll disappear,
just like you always do
behind the nearest
vapid dark cloud
that seduces you
and then where will I be?"

Ooh that old Sun, he wouldn't quit
he just went right on
making sweet love to me.

MEGCENETKWE

This babe that nestled in our arms
Restored all hope,
Revived all dreams,
Rekindled our belief
that the world was a better place
because you were in it
If only you could stay
Megcenetkwe
Keep us innocent and sweet
Teach us the mysteries of life
Never leave our side

But you are the messenger
Who brought us together
In one great love,
Who touched our lives so
Briefly and profoundly
Left so suddenly
Our hearts broke
In the bittersweet tempest
Of our grief how can we not
Be thankful
For the pleasure
of warming ourselves
Against your sacred sweet light.

DYING

I climb a tall, steep mountain, thick with fallen logs and
treacherous underbrush that snake around my ankles and drag me down
with each step. I want to reach the top so I can breathe. I carry a
heavy pack that bears down on my shoulders and causes my breath to
come in short gasps, I claw at the earth and stagger, unbalanced by
the weight of my burden. It is so simple to remove it, just unhook
the strap and drop it and keep moving forward. My steps so light
until I realize that if I reach the top without the solid weight of
my beliefs, my convictions, all efforts will be futile. I retrace
my steps and search anxiously for my pack. Fear turns to panic, I'm
losing my balance, losing my sense of direction, falling down instead
of up, losing, losing, losing . . .

Something pushes at my chest, knocks the breath from me and
my eyes fly open to bottles, machines, and concerned white faces in
uniforms so bright they hurt my eyes. I feel rage tear the tubes out
of my arm, yank the breathing cup off my face. "I can reach the top
of the mountain on my own, I don't need your help." They always try
to help but they just get in the way. They force me to breathe,
force me to live with tubes that pump drugs and nourishment through
my veins, force me. "Kill me now," I think, "all these years you've
been trying to kill me, so kill me now." It becomes a mantra that
undoes me, for it is the anger and hatred of oppression and white
people, I'm sure, that keeps me alive. "Kill me now, kill me now,
kill me now."

It's a long lonely vigil, waiting for death when you've
exhausted all your resources, and pushed all love away. I'm like
those Blues songs I play through the nights when I can't sleep. "I
don't know why, but I'm feeling so sad, I long to try something I've

never had," Billie Holiday, or the deep husky tones of Etta James'
"Feelin' Uneasy." I've memorized those tunes and they play over and
over until my head aches. I keep beat with my left foot and the
sound of the IV dripping through the tubes. I can feel the
disappointment at the foolishness of my life settle in the creases on
my face. I won't look at the view out the window; I'll stare at the
wall instead. "It's depression" the do-gooders conclude as they talk
over, under and around me as if I weren't there. They send a social
worker and it becomes a battle of wills between her chatter and my
silence. I refuse to let anyone off the hook; no one will get one
drop of kindness out of me while I wait for death.

I am in this state for days before help arrives. She stands
timidly at the door, with a bouquet of wild flowers that match her
dress, and a basket of blueberries, no doubt, wild as well. She is
familiar, her eyes like mine, her lips, her awkwardness, her youth,
were all once me. I try to say her name, but my memory won't work
and my throat has dried up. I haven't used my voice in days and it
cracks roughly when I attempt to say her name. I'm afraid I will
frighten her away, so I beckon her to come forward, come close to
me.

She is tearful as she bends to kiss me and stroke my hair. In that
moment I feel love enter the room and I am uneasy but grateful for
its presence. She holds the flowers up to my nose, I close my eyes
to smell them so I can imagine the field or the mountainside that
they came from, then she slips a blueberry into my mouth and I
smile. I can feel that smile spread across my face, fill me up
inside then begin to pour out of my eyes just as the nurse enters the
room. My whole face wants to greet her with my usual grimace and
tell her "fuck off" but I can't. I can't be angry with this angel in
the room.

"Aren't we lucky to have such a pretty visitor today?" she gushes. I keep a slight smile plastered on my face and the words, "fuck off," on the tip of my tongue when our eyes connect. "You have to get out of bed, can't lay around," she says as she raises the head of the bed and I slump forward like a rag doll. "The doctor's orders, she'll recover quicker," she says to my visitor. I want to punch her but I can't reach around behind me as she pushes me forward, then turns me to the side, and pulls me up. I decide the minute she lets me go I'll make myself fall so she'll leave me alone and let me die.

Before she lets go I feel another set of arms go around me and pull me close. "I'll take care of her," she says, "please, let me. You must be very busy and I have lots of time." I feel myself leaning into her, enjoying the feeling of her embrace, "Besides, we have a lot of catching up to do," she says, turning us both away from the nurse, who quickly leaves the room. I feel a little bad about being so miserable but it's a feeling I have and I can't let it go. It's part dream, part real but I can't tell where one ends and the other begins. I have imagined her for over 40 years now, as a baby, then an adolescent, and now a grown woman. I keep saying her name like a prayer that falls from my lips in my most desperate times. Simone Ann, I whisper, my baby, my child, my girl. I believe she's come to take me home, back over to the other side where I can have peace, where my body will stop aching and where I can breathe. She takes me into the bathroom, sits me on a stool and gently she washes my face. She hums a comforting tune that I recognize from my youth. Tenderly she washes me all over, and clips my nails. Her smile is like a warm glow of sunshine on my skin and I bask in it with so much joy. She brushes, and then plaits my hair close to my head. Every now and then she stops what she is doing and rocks me, holds me close, I can feel love seeping into my bones. I am thrilled to be a mother, cherished by a daughter, this child I birthed who has

come to take me home. After my bath she returns me to a freshly re-
made bed, tucks me in ever so carefully and I fall into a deep sleep.

When I finally wake it is as though days, or weeks or months have
passed, perhaps even years of peaceful sleep. It is the best that
I've had in a long time. No dreams, no worries, no sudden startling
responses in my body. The first thing I notice is that my knees no
longer ache. I can also turn my head without pain. I test it, bend
my knees and straighten them, no pain; turn my head sideways and then
back and forth, no pain. It feels so incredibly delicious to wake up
with no pain.

She stands near the door I feel her leaving me. I am
heartbroken and reach out my arms to her. She shakes her head and
blows kisses instead. It's not your time, she says. There is too
much work to do, and then she is gone. I can still feel the taste of
wild blueberries in my mouth; still smell the scent of wildflowers on
my skin. I get up out of bed and walk up and down the corridors
until the doctor comes to release me. I am well enough to enter the
world again. I have recovered, whatever illness was there is now in
remission, and I am free to continue on with life. There are no more
thoughts of dying, only living a longer life and I accept that.

AFTERWORDS

1. Sophie Williams (Marceline's grandmother) and Marceline's mother Mary Paul (a.k.a. Kupi).

2. Monica Luke and Sophie Williams.
3. Sophie Williams, third from left, next to husband Seymour Williams.

4. Auntie Helen and Marceline Paul.

5. Marceline Paul (top row, forth from the right).
6. Marceline Paul Manuel (fourth row from bottom, far left). Photo courtesy of Constance Brissenden, and first supplied by Vera Manuel for the 1998 publication of *Strength of Indian Women*.

7. Marceline and Mary Paul.
8. Marceline and Vera.

9. A young Vera.
10. Emalene and Vera in California.

11. Bobby Manuel and Marceline Manuel.
12. Marceline Dancing.

13. Emalene and Vera. Photograph by Duncan Murdoch.

NARRATIVE ACTS OF TRUTH AND RECONCILIATION: TEACHING THE HEALING PLAYS OF VERA MANUEL[1]

MICHELLE COUPAL

> *We might decide that stories are necessary*
> *to holding the universe together.*
> Arlene (Emalene) Manuel, 2017

In its Call to Action number 62.i. (2015), the Truth and Reconciliation Commission of Canada (TRC) appeals to all levels of government to consult and collaborate with survivors, Indigenous peoples, and educators to "make age-appropriate curriculum on residential schools, Treaties, and Aboriginal peoples' historical and contemporary contributions to Canada a mandatory education requirement for Kindergarten to Grade Twelve students" (*Final Report* 331). Secwepemc and Ktunaxa writer Vera Manuel's plays—*Strength of Indian Women, Song of the Circle, Journey Through the Past to the Future, Echoes of Our Mothers' Past,* and *Every Warrior's Song*—are particularly well-suited for teaching students at both secondary and post-secondary levels about the history and legacies of residential schools. The plays presented here are deeply engaged with narrative acts of testimony, pedagogy, healing, and, indeed, truth and reconciliation. Manuel wrote the bulk of her plays in the late 1980s and throughout the 1990s, before the word "reconciliation" entered the public domain. For her, reconciliation had to do with the reconciling of Indigenous peoples with each other and in their communities, when dealing with the legacies of the Indian residential school system. Residential schools were not benign places where students were educated but rather colonial institutions of cultural genocide that wrenched generations of Indigenous children from their families, communities, and land to "teach" them to adopt European customs, religious beliefs, languages, and epistemologies. The losses of Indigenous knowledge systems, languages, community, and family relationships are present and pressing as Indigenous communities seek to reclaim, rebuild, and celebrate resurgent interconnections between language, land, spiritual beliefs, and traditional knowledges. The plays collected in this volume seek to foreground the truth of Canada's colonial violence that targeted Indigenous peoples. Together, the plays are like medicine bundles for Indigenous peoples of Turtle Island living the exploitations of colonial power and healing from wounds created by a history of assimilative policies and practices in Canada.

DECOLONIZING THEATRE THROUGH STORY

I have taught the play, *Strength of Indian Women*, a number of times over the past five years.[2] I have always taught it as a piece of "dramatherapy," written as such by Manuel, who was a practising dramatherapist and healer committed to the use of theatre, poetry, story sharing, and writing as medicine for individuals and communities. In a "kitchen table dialogue" between Emalene Manuel and me on the topic of *Strength of Indian Women*,[3] I asked Emalene how Vera became a dramatherapist and how she employed dramatherapy in her plays. I was struck by Emalene's response. She said, and I am paraphrasing, "We used the term 'dramatherapy' because it was the only available word for what we were doing at the time. I think what we were really trying to do was to *decolonize theatre*" (my emphasis).

In the plays of Vera Manuel, decolonizing theatre is imbricated in the centrality of stories to Indigenous lives, their circulation in communities, and the transformational powers that stories have in teaching audiences about Indian residential schools and their aftermath. While plays are generically considered to be fictional, Manuel scuffs the boundaries of the genre by staging disclosures by Indigenous people about colonial trauma. Decolonizing theatre, then, is intimately connected with the work of stories, and the work of telling the truth about Indigenous lives and Canada's history. For Vera Manuel, this project was always a personal one. Manuel's parents, George Manuel (Secwepemc) and Marceline Paul (Ktunaxa), and some of Vera's siblings attended residential schools in British Columbia. This legacy of residential schooling, as Vera Manuel is quoted as saying in the 2012 TRC document, *They Came for the Children,* "visited us every day of our childhood through the replaying over and over of our parents' childhood trauma and grief which they never had the opportunity to resolve in their lifetimes" (79).

Just as Manuel's words have become part of public testimony, through the historical document published by the TRC, so too have her plays. In this way, Manuel's theatre practice pushes at the boundaries between fiction and testimony, story and fact.[4] Sam McKegney makes the claim that creative forms of residential school narratives, "offer profound complications to the historical record as it stands, commenting not only on how residential schooling is remembered but also on how its legacy ought to be reacted to, its transgressions addressed, and its survivors (and their communities) empowered" (17). Manuel's work similarly complicates the historical record, in part, by adding to this public history storied versions of truths regarding Indian residential schools and their consequences. In her foreword to *Strength of Indian Women*, Manuel emphasizes the play's grounding in truth: "Stories about the abuse and helplessness of little children in residential school are true stories. Because of this, they are the most difficult to write. I didn't make up the stories told in *Strength of Indian Women*. They came from pictures my mother painted for me with her words, words that helped me to see her as a little girl for the first time."

The plays contained in this collection, then, are creative forms of therapeutic testimony. They offer up a course of healing through the telling of difficult personal and shared histories, through the acting out of the healing process, and, importantly, through the reclamation of traditional Indigenous cultural practices. Manuel uses theatre to create a therapeutic space of community healing that can serve as a way to approach and teach Indigenous understandings of trauma and healing. As Jo-Ann Episkenew (Métis) contends, "Contemporary Indigenous literature serves two transformative functions—healing Indigenous people and advancing social justice in settler society— both components in the process of decolonization" (2009, 15). In circulating stories of being a child in the residential school system, Manuel's plays implicate Indigenous and settler audiences and readers as witnesses and participants in the project of social justice.

Now that Manuel's plays, stories, and poems are in print, the question becomes, how should this much needed, yet often difficult material be taught?[5] This introduction provides educators with preliminary suggestions for bringing the work of Vera Manuel into the classroom, and provides students with a starting point when entering into a relationship with the stories shared by Manuel through her characters. I articulate the ways in which Manuel's theatrical productions enact testimonial discourse through their staging and content. I do so primarily through the first play in this collection, *Strength of*

Indian Women. The scope of this essay does not allow a close reading of all of Manuel's plays, so my choice is representative of her established tropes, strategies, and therapeutic processes. I also chose this play because I have had the privilege of teaching it, as it was previously published by Living Traditions (1998). *Strength of Indian Women* is arguably one of the most teachable texts dealing with Indian residential school traumas and legacies available today. It is one of the few residential school fictions that commits itself to a multi-generational community of women. Further, while the play dramatizes testimonial-style disclosures of four Elders about their experiences at residential school, these moments of testimony (by characters) and witness (by audience members or readers) are followed by healing through the reclamation of Indigenous ceremonies and traditions. Manuel's decolonized theatre is thus embedded within her storyline through a process of narrating a series of events, testimonial disclosures of abuse or violence, followed by healing through community, spiritual beliefs, and ceremonies.

Although this is not my focus, Manuel also explores the traumatic impacts of residential school on Indigenous men in both *Journey Through the Past to the Future* and *Every Warrior's Song.* The traditional role of Indigenous men as protectors of their communities and the wounding that occurs when their role in their communities is lost are negotiated in *Journey Through the Past to the Future.* The play moves from an idyllic community where children are sacred and loved, to the imposition of residential schooling, and finally to the re-creation of community sparked by the unearthing of items thought to be lost: a button blanket, drum, sacred items, and traditional medicines. The play ends with the restoration of lost language and "Women's Warrior Song," a song gifted to the People by Martina Pierre of the Lil'wat First Nation circa 1990 and now regularly sung at gatherings meant to honour Indigenous women.

In *Every Warrior's Song,* the central therapeutic moment occurs near the end of the play, notably through the character of Eddie, whose experiences at a residential school have led to patterns of self-harm and violence against women. Eddie, who is in prison for the murder of an Indigenous woman, is guided through ceremony by an Elder who has also survived residential school and helps Eddie acknowledge his past behaviour. Through talk and the telling of his story, Eddie makes a direct connection to the spirit world, which results in a reconnection to his emotions. Through a connection with spirit and emotion, Eddie transcends his literal and symbolic imprisonment and begins the healing journey.

TEACHING *STRENGTH OF INDIAN WOMEN*
THE IMPORTANCE OF POSITIONING

I have had success with what I am calling positioning exercises in Indigenous literature classrooms at the university level. A customary Indigenous protocol of introduction is to provide one's community affiliation and a sense of the land from which one comes. For example, I am a member of the Bonnechere Algonquin First Nation, with familial ties to Black Bay in the Petawawa area where the Algonquin side of my family resided. The other side of my family is French, from northern Ontario, and before that Quebec, and before that France. I am Indigenous to this land on my mother's side and a settler to this land on my father's side. As an Indigenous scholar, I also need to acknowledge my complicity in colonialism through the French settler side of my family. In this way, I work to open a discussion in the classroom about colonial history in Canada, and the importance of acknowledging our involvement in that history, while always looking forward to hopeful change in the future for Indigenous peoples and for our relationships with settlers. Non-Indigenous and Indigenous educators need to articulate where they stand as pedagogues so that they might model for students a positional approach to Indigenous stories. This approach demands critical self-reflexivity and a willingness to enter into a relationship with Indigenous material on its own terms.

In "Treaties, Truths, and Transgressive Pedagogies: Re-Imagining Indigenous Presence in the Classroom," Margaret Kovach (Plains Cree, Saulteaux) argues that, "Educators, in literature and in primary voice, speak of interrogating their own sense of complicity and guilt of being players in the oppression of Indigenous peoples. To move through the critically reflective affective dimension is part of the process and because it has been heard before it does not mean it is finished work. As Elder knowledge tells us when it comes to the heart we talk until the talking is done. Transgressive pedagogies, which at their core are relational pedagogies, move nowhere without this work" (2013, 118–119). Kovach suggests here a pedagogical imperative to work through one's own complicity in settler and Indigenous history. I encourage all educators working with Indian residential school literatures, or any material dealing with Indigenous content, to critically reflect upon the grounds they stand on—how they got there and whose lands they occupy—to mindfully express their position, and to encourage students to do the same.

Positioning oneself in relation to Indigenous issues requires ethical engagement with the literature under study. Kovach suggests that "Non-Indigenous educators may so fear being offensive that avoidance of Indigenous questions becomes the 'moral' way of avoiding addressing the Indigenous-settler relationship" (118). In the post-TRC age, avoidance is no longer an ethical option. Non-Indigenous educators may have difficulty with material and epistemologies that can bump up against their own ways of thinking. These moments of cultural incomprehension can, in fact, lead to the incorporation of new knowledges and strategies for teaching unfamiliar material.

After I introduce and position myself, I encourage students to similarly position themselves through writing prompts. These are designed to elicit articulations of their ancestry, settler or immigrant history, and, more holistically, the feelings, spiritual beliefs, and the knowledge they bring to their readings. I do this with the view of fostering a place for them to stand on, which can be especially difficult for non-Indigenous students. Whether they are Indigenous or non-Indigenous, teachers and students can share their ancestry and alliances, bridge their differences, and enter into conversation with textual material that is sometimes difficult. Positioning encourages a relational articulation of alliance to the literature rather than a potentially othering one. I usually conduct a series of positioning exercises: the first before the material is read, the second after reading is complete, and the final one at the end of class discussion. I have found that for non-Indigenous students, their positioning usually shifts during the process toward more nuanced understandings of and approaches to the texts. Depending on the class and its size, these exercises can be done as private self-reflective writing or as pieces that are shared with the whole group.

The principles of storywork, as articulated by Stó:lō scholar Jo-ann Archibald, can be incorporated into the classroom: in the first instance, as examples of Indigenous ways of making meaning through stories, and in the second, as part of positioning exercises which ask students to approach the text holistically. Storyteller Ellen Rice White (Snuneymuxw First Nation) explains, "'I work with stories and I try and tell teachers that the story isn't telling the children what to think or feel, but it's giving them the space to think and feel'" (quoted in Archibald 2008, 134). Thinking *and* feeling mark a turn from traditional Western pedagogies, which tend to emphasize cognition, to Indigenous pedagogies that embrace holistic (mind, body, spirit) approaches to stories. Tanana Athabascan scholar Dian Million suggests that emotional knowledge "fuels the real discursive shift around the histories and stories of residential schooling. One of the most important features of these stories is their existence as alternative truths, as alternate historical views" (64). Thinking and feeling one's way through stories, which are also histories, means understanding the complicity between story and history, which can lead to the creation of new narratives about Indigenous and non-Indigenous relationships.

I further encourage students to not just think about their relationship to the writer but also to think about the Indigenous community that is represented in the text. Responsibility to community is essential to any artistic, pedagogical, and scholarly approach to Indian residential schools. While Manuel's ancestry is Secwepemc and

Ktunaxa, it was her Ktunaxa mother, Marceline Paul, who gave her spiritual guidance later in life. Marceline Paul attended St. Eugene residential school in Cranbrook, British Columbia and the Ktunaxa words (*Nupika*—the spirits and *Titti*—Grandmother) used in the play gesture back to her community. Still, Manuel includes a stage direction at the end of the play allowing actors to substitute their own language in place of Ktunaxa words, which suggests that Manuel intended the play to be inclusive and relevant to other Indigenous peoples and nations. Even so, her welcome is especially extended to Indigenous women and this play is entirely peopled by women, as is *Echoes of Our Mothers' Past*. It is to this community of women that the responsibility for sensitive and ethical approaches is owed: the women who survived St. Eugene Residential School, and the children who did not; the actors portraying the characters in the play; communities of Indigenous women who saw the play performed in the 1990s; Marceline Paul and her mother, Mary Paul; and Vera Manuel, her sisters, and all of the Manuel women who share this history. As teachers, students, and readers, we need to honour the strength of these warrior[6] women.

READING *STRENGTH OF INDIAN WOMEN*: TESTIMONY, STORY, AND HEALING

> All of you went through so much. Someone should
> write about it. They should make a movie about
> how you survived. I feel real proud sitting here
> among you. You're just like old warriors.
> (*Strength of Indian Women*, 66)

First staged at the Firehall Theatre in Vancouver's downtown eastside in January of 1992, Manuel's *Strength of Indian Women* was performed by a cast of Indigenous women in an area known for its poverty, crime, violence, drug use, and sex trade, but also and importantly for its activism. On the heels of the inaugural performance of

Manuel's play came the second annual Women's Memorial March in the same neighbourhood on Valentine's Day 1992 commemorating murdered and missing Indigenous women. Manuel's play focuses on the disclosures and legacies of abuses suffered at residential school by a group of Indigenous women. One of these Elders, Agnes, recounts the night her friend and fellow residential school survivor, Annie, was murdered in Vancouver where the two worked as sex workers. Agnes tells her story because, as she says, "It could just as easily have been me that got killed. Somebody has to talk about it. Somebody has to tell the truth about what happened to all those little girls" (54). As Manuel emphasizes in her foreword to the play, the stories she tells are true ones that need a public stage. The presence, then, of Indigenous women on stage telling what are true stories of child abuse and the aftereffects of residential schooling—which led Agnes and Annie to life on the streets as sex workers—alongside a real-life commemorative protest of missing and murdered Indigenous women pushes at the limits of the play's fictional form by staging its personal, public, and political import beyond the lives of the characters. This first staging of the play is thus a form of public, dramatic testimony to residential school survival while it concomitantly connects the audience as witnesses. For those audience members who are also survivors of residential school or have family members who are, the play enacts therapeutic disclosure of abuses followed by healing through the community of women who share their stories and through the reclamation of traditional Indigenous practices.

By emphasizing the play's grounding in lived reality and truth, Manuel invites her audience and readers to apprehend the play as testimony to the stories her mother told her about residential school and to her own experiences as a child of residential school survivors. *Strength of Indian Women* came out of a short story Manuel wrote called "The Abyss."[7] She discloses, in her preface to "The Abyss," the sexual abuse that she, all of her sisters, and at least one of her brothers suffered as children. Before she died, Marceline Paul disclosed a story of her own sexual abuse in residential school to her daughters.

Like Sousette in the play, Manuel's mother *"blamed herself for not being able to protect us and for not being able to help us when we were suffering"* ("The Abyss" 239). In that preface, Manuel says that her father was also physically, emotionally, and possibly sexually abused, although he never disclosed the abuse. He was, according to Manuel, often violent (239). For Manuel, writing "The Abyss" helped her "to purge" and "to heal" her relationship with her mother (240).

Strength of Indian Women was similarly "pure therapy" ("Letting Go of Trauma"). Not just seeking therapy for herself, Manuel was very aware of the therapeutic potential of *Strength of Indian Women* for her audience and for Indigenous communities. As a therapist, Manuel also understood the importance of creating an ethical and safe place for exchanging stories of trauma that always have the potential to retraumatize listeners.[8] As she says in her foreword to the play, "A tremendous responsibility is attached to telling the unresolved grief stories of First Nations' people. Words have power; they cause us to feel the emotions of the story they are telling. . . . The responsibility we hold in passing on these stories is to role model a healthy lifestyle for our children, who are always watching us for direction. When we share our life stories, we must create a safe place for those who come to listen, in order not to hurt ourselves or others" (76). At a public reading of the play on 17 May 2007 in Wisconsin, the director, Emalene Manuel, recommended that counsellors and spiritual advisors be in attendance because of the potential issues that the play may raise for Oneida tribal members in the audience (Benton 2007). In her analysis of Manuel's play, Episkenew suggests that "Many Indigenous people who either attended residential school themselves or are the children and grandchildren of those who did recognize these stories as truth" (164). That recognition by audience members marks a significant connection through stories to testimony but that identification also has the potential to open up past wounds for those listening.

Christy Stanlake describes her experience attending a staged reading of *Strength of Indian Women* at a conference at Miami University in Oxford, Ohio in 1999. Stanlake (2009) recounts that when Vera Manuel arrived for the first rehearsal, she was "shocked" to discover that the students reading the play were mostly non-Native and "insisted that Native Americans play all the roles" (160). The choice of exclusively employing Native American actors was more than a personal preference for Manuel. Stanlake argues that the play "is a gathering of histories by 'unofficial historians' who serve as both characters in the play and as witnesses—for each other and for the audience" (160). Stanlake suggests that the presence of Indigenous women on stage, even though they come from different communities, has a layering effect, where their own family stories are added to those of the characters: "These performers delivered the testimonies of the elders, while their bodies bore simultaneous witness to the possibility of boarding-school experiences beyond the scope of Manuel's characters. Indeed, during the post-performance discussion, each woman who had read for the play mentioned how she was connected to additional accounts of boarding-school atrocities. This splintering encouraged a further multiplication of narratives, an even wider circle of communal truth" (160). The opening up of a "wider circle of communal truth" represents an important moment of testimonial discursive exchange and connection through shared stories.

The presence of Indigenous women on stage telling stories that Indigenous (and possibly non-Indigenous) audience members would recognize as true contributes to the real-life testimonial aesthetic of the play, particularly when one considers that Vera Manuel and her sister Emalene would sometimes participate as actors. In both published versions of the play (1998, 2018), two photographs appear below the title. These pictures are significant editorial markers of the first printed version of the play and warrant attention. One of those photographs is a 1998 production picture of Emalene playing Sousette with Vera as Lucy (see Photo 13). Audience members who attended such a performance would have witnessed true stories of the

Manuels being replayed by family members. For the sisters, performing their family stories for an audience would have the therapeutic potential that comes with testimony in the presence of witnesses, where the traumas can be heard and acknowledged. As Vera Manuel describes it, "I put myself in therapy, in group therapy, and worked with my younger sister Arlene. We worked a lot together on this stuff and then it just naturally led me into the work that I do today" (Interview). The play, then, becomes part of their therapeutic journey as a family, and it does so through the act of storytelling. Manuel further explains, "Our greatest learning is through our storytelling, when people sit around in the circle and start talking about their lives and other people learn from their experience, and it's very, very powerful" (Interview). Bringing her role as healer to the stage, Manuel creates what I would call a theatre of group therapy.

The second photograph below the title is of children flanked by nuns standing in front of a residential school. Less obvious is the priest who stands beside the nuns near the right-hand corner. The notes to the play indicate that the "historic photo" was supplied by Vera Manuel (see Photo 6). Both *Strength of Indian Women* and the short story "The Abyss" open with a mother and her daughter looking at a photograph of the mother as a child posing with all the other children in front of the residential school she attended. In both texts, the wording explaining the picture is almost identical and in both the daughter describes the photo to the mother, who is having trouble with her eyesight: "It's a bunch of little girls. Lots of them, standing in front of a big grey building. There's a priest and a nun standing there with them" (*Strength of Indian Women* 30).[9] The almost exact repetition of the scene and dialogue brings a verisimilitude to the exchange between mother and daughter and to the picture. Interestingly, the name of the residential school is fictionalized as St. Ignatius Residential School in "The Abyss," whereas in *Strength of Indian Women,* the school that both Manuel's mother and grandmother attended is named: St. Eugene Residential School. The shift from earlier fictionalizing to outright naming of the school suggests Manuel's move toward a more direct form of truth-sharing. Note, however, that the archival photograph of little girls, nuns, and a priest standing in front of a residential school, provided by Manuel for the print publication, does not include the date of the picture or name of the school. The slippage between fact and fiction here reveals how literature can function as an alternate form of testimony. It provided a vehicle for Manuel to disclose a family legacy of abuses without having to endure the further trauma of filing a criminal complaint against the abusing priest and/or the residential school. Written well before the public TRC testimonials, the play provided a stage for safe disclosure otherwise not available.

The photograph of the school, whether it's St. Eugene's or not, is interesting when one considers the primacy of the photograph to the play. The play opens with Sousette looking for the picture, which she shows to her daughter, Eva. The photograph sparks Sousette's memories of residential school and serves as a visual springboard for the ensuing discussion with Eva about her experiences and also the experiences of her friends, Lucy, Mariah, and Agnes. The first memory that Sousette shares with Eva is Lucy's sexual abuse by the priest at the school. Lucy becomes pregnant but the baby dies. As Sousette says, "Not just Lucy. Other girls had babies, too. Lots of babies buried behind the school, buried in the schoolyard" (32). As this first scene draws to a close, Sousette picks up the photograph again and according to the stage direction, "As she speaks, the light fades, and a slide of the picture of the girls in the school lights up on the back wall" (33). Indeed, the photograph lights up the back of the stage at various moments throughout the play.

The play is structured by the testimonies of Sousette and the other Elders within the context of Sousette's granddaughter Suzie's traditional coming-of-age celebration. Suzie is thirteen years old. The play takes place over the three days of preparation in advance of the feast. While Suzie is at the lodge for her two days of fasting prior to the ceremony, the women tell their stories of abuse at residential school. Sousette explains to Eva, Suzie's mother, that: "I talked to the others.

We decided you need to know everything, about the school and about us. You need to know because of Suzie. It's her history too" (32). The upcoming ceremony anchors the play in hope and healing through the recuperation of the traditional Indigenous ceremony of becoming a woman through the next generation, represented by Suzie. Sousette and Eva look at a picture of Sousette wearing the buckskin dress that Suzie will also wear for her ceremony. The dress was sewn together by Sousette's grandmother, with beads and shells, and made from skins of deer hunted by her grandfather. The dress is a potent symbol of traditional and healthy family practices prior to the imposition of residential schooling. Eva's coming-of-age as a woman was not celebrated because, as Sousette explains to Eva, "People were afraid of Indian ways back then" (35). In the play, "Indian ways" come together with individual stories to form a collective story that is also a testimony and an act of healing.

In *Strength of Indian Women*, then, testimony to childhood trauma does not conform to the Western model of an individual recounting of past horrors to a singular witness, the therapist. Instead, there is a gathering of voices as the individual stories of the Elders come together as a collective to convey their full history. The women both testify to and witness each other's stories, with the audience as a community of witnesses. Christy Stanlake argues that Manuel's play models the "reciprocal relationship between the stories of a community and the story of an individual" (131). The relational aspect of traumatic testimony, in that each person is connected to every other person in a community, is an essential feature of Manuel's approach to the trauma story and healing. For the most part, the remainder of the play is structured by the group of women telling their stories by taking centre stage under a spotlight and speaking directly to the audience. The light shining down on the speaker, while the other characters sit on the couch and pay attention, evokes a scene of testimony and witnessing, within the safety and comfort of Sousette's home. For Christy Stanlake, "The personal stories told by each woman adhere to a form of witnessing, in which the play's conventions of realism break while each woman stands alone center stage to deliver her story directly to the audience" (112). The stage brings the testimony out of the private sphere of the home into the public sphere of the community. For Sousette's daughter Eva, this represents the first time that she is a witness to the history of her mother and aunties, a history which is also her own. Sparked by the photograph of the Elders as little girls at residential school, Eva wants to learn more about their experiences from her mother, Sousette, and from her friends. Lucy, however, is reluctant to speak: "There's some things that I shouldn't tell you" (42). Sousette intervenes by telling Lucy that Eva has a right to know their history, and she insists that Lucy tell Eva about the sexual abuse by the priest at the school. Sousette's insistence upon the importance of Lucy's childhood traumas to Sousette's daughter's understanding of the school system underscores the importance of community to residential school legacy discourse.

As a Gregorian chant begins to play, Lucy takes centre stage. The liturgical chant evokes connections to lugubrious priests—here ritualistically preying upon young Indigenous girls—while the sacred music of the Roman Catholic Church is radically and ironically supplanted by the testimonial of an Indigenous Elder. Under the spotlight, Lucy discloses a scene of molestation by the priest. Agnes finds her throwing up behind the stairs after the assault and the two (with some of their friends) decide to run away from the school. She also talks about being caught and brought back, as Lucy says, by her "own people" (44). For Lucy, this is a devastating betrayal, the disclosing of which exhausts and silences her. Sousette takes centre stage when Lucy can no longer continue, which emphasizes that it takes a community of women to tell the story. Sousette fills in the gap for Lucy by discussing the beating she witnessed of Lucy and Agnes, by the nuns, when the girls were brought back. This act of witnessing by Sousette provides Lucy with the strength and support she needs to continue: "*Lucy stands to deliver the rest of her story with all the power she needs to conjure up the image and to destroy it*" (45; original emphasis). Signalling an act of collective healing whereby the women tell their stories to release the pain of their past, this stage direction is intended for the cast members rather than the audience by suggesting a cathartic posture for the actor. The monologues then quickly diverge from individual testimony and healing to group testimony and witness. Lucy thus moves from her own abuses to testifying to those of Agnes, who was beaten more severely than the rest of them because she was seen as the "ringleader." Just as Sousette witnessed Lucy's trauma, here Lucy bears witness to Agnes's. Following a relentless beating made worse because of Agnes's refusal to cry, according to the stage direction, Lucy feels "broken herself, at this moment" and says, "They broke her that day" (45). The picture of the girls at residential school lights up again as Sousette rejoins their individual experiences into a collective one: "They broke her body, they broke her heart, but they never broke her spirit. Agnes's spirit lives inside each one of us" (45). As Episkenew asserts, "characteristic of most Indigenous literature from Canada, rather than an individual, the community in *Strength of Indian Women* is the protagonist" (166). In this play, all of the women reciprocally share and testify to each other's traumas. They do so as a group for the next generation, represented by Eva, for the generation following her, represented by Suzie, and for the present-day community of witnesses sitting in the audience.

Of all the Elders, Mariah has the most fraught relationship with the act of testimony to past traumas. The last of the group of Elders to arrive at Sousette's house for the ceremony, Mariah has had a history of silences, including being silenced by Lucy, who has retained girlhood antagonism toward her because of Mariah's perceived privileges at the residential school. Mariah's testimony to the group of women thus marks a significant break in her pattern of silence and represents the possibility of healing both for Mariah and for the friendships between the Elders. Manuel believes that for healing to occur, one must acknowledge past traumas and grieve lost childhoods. This is hard work, which is why, as Manuel says, "people don't go there. They slam on the brakes when they are feeling vulnerable and the tears come, but I think that's really key in healing. Remembering things that have happened from the past and allowing ourselves to have those feelings, tears, anger, and grief about what happen[ed]s, so that we can move past it and we can start changing those behaviours" (Interview).

Silent witnessing has been the hallmark of Mariah's traumas. Accordingly, she begins her testimony by saying that she has been afraid to speak her whole life. Mariah has been othered by both Indigenous and non-Indigenous communities. She has lived "on the edge of two worlds," fitting into neither the white nor Indigenous communities easily (56). She reveals she was taunted by residential school classmates as the "teacher's pet" while in the white world, she was called a "squaw" and a "Pocahontas" (57). Her light skin, however, gave her the advantage of appearing less Indigenous than the other girls at school in the eyes of the priest and nuns. Mariah was granted special privileges both because she looked non-Indigenous and because she remained silent, yet this came at the cost to her identity. As Mariah says, "because I was so good at saying nothin' I became one of them" (58). Indeed, as she continues her testimony to the group of women, her refrain is "I said nothin'" (57, 58). Mariah describes how she silently watched a nun throw a girl down two flights of cement steps for speaking her own language (57). She also had said nothing when she heard girls being taken away by the priest at night. She silently witnessed a girl in the school delivering a baby and then watched that baby's burial in the school cemetery (58). Mariah's is a tragedy of silence. As she says, "My screams were silent and my agony all consumin'" (58). The community of women, particularly Lucy, are able to understand through Mariah's disclosure that silence itself is traumatic when one is burdened with the act of witnessing the pain of others. Mariah is also importantly given a stage upon which to begin her own healing journey by way of talking for the first time about her life of silent witnessing. The ethics of responsible witnessing are foregrounded through Mariah's story, which imparts to the audience and readers the burden that comes with being a spectator to trauma. Mariah's testimony to the trauma of silence thus has the potential to foment the audience out of silence and into action for Indigenous empowerment and justice.

At this point in the play, all of the Elders have taken centre stage to disclose past traumas or, in Mariah's case, the trauma associated with being a silent witness. Together, their stories have accrued layers of meaning that exceed the limits of any one woman's story. The final testimonial disclosures complete the story of the women through the testimonies of Sousette and Eva to the intergenerational legacy of residential school abuses. The institutional, loveless environment of residential schools has produced generations of children deprived of healthy models of parenting and appropriate loving relationships. The spotlight first shines on Eva as she recounts her memory of a past conversation she had with her mother, Sousette, at a point in time when Sousette did not acknowledge her own traumas:

> Do you remember how you used to beat me, Mom? Do you even remember the bruises? Do you remember the ugly things you used to call me, and all the times you left me alone? I wouldn't have cared, if only you loved me. Do you even know what that means, love? Every time I go to hug you, you stiffen up. Do you know that you do that, Mom? Do you know how that makes me feel? And now I'm doing the same thing to Suzie. I push her away, Mom. I call her stupid, and I hit her, and I don't want to. / Tell me again that residential school was good for you. (60)

Episkenew discusses the pattern of abuse that is passed along to Eva because of Sousette's lack of parenting skills: "Suzie, although two generations removed from the residential school experience, is still a victim of its violence and barbarity. Violence breeds shame, and shame breeds more violence. This is the despicable legacy of the colonial regime's policy of 'Indian' residential schools, and without healing that legacy will be passed down from one generation of Indigenous people to the next" (168). The promise of healing, through a change in the patterns of behaviour, is represented through the unfolding new relationship between Sousette and Eva. Sousette tells Eva that she loves her, something that she has been unable to do in the past. When Sousette finally stands up in the centre of the stage to testify, she tells her group of friends and her daughter Eva about the times when she and another girl were sexually abused by Father LeBlanc in the infirmary. The purpose of this disclosure is not to dwell on the sexual abuse itself, although its disclosure is important for Sousette's own healing. The focus is on how this abuse, shared by many survivors of residential school, prevented Sousette from being a good parent to Eva, and before this, Sousette's own mother from being a good parent to her. Sousette reveals, "Then other women began to speak up. Even my mother, before she died, said the same thing happened to her. And my Eva, I couldn't protect her. I was too busy running away" (66). In a moment of mother-daughter reconciliation and healing, Sousette rocks Eva in her arms, tells her that she loves her, and asks for her forgiveness.

The enactment of healing familial relationships damaged by the brutal assimilative practices of colonialism—represented in the play by the primary system of control over Indigenous peoples, the residential schools—marks a significant discursive strategy to promote wellness in Indigenous communities. Crucial to this endeavour is the recovery of Indigenous traditions and practices, represented in the play by Suzie's coming-of-age ceremony. Stanlake connects this ceremony to the transformational power of storytelling: "as Suzie undergoes a ceremonial transformation into womanhood, the audience observes a dramatic portrayal of how storytelling creates a transformation within the women's community" (112). Thus, as Suzie fasts and cleanses herself in advance of her ceremony, the Elders, in a parallel journey, tell their stories to similarly purge themselves as they, too, mark a transformation to healing. Their storytelling also gestures towards reconciliation as they move from shame and silence to a community of prideful voices. Their chance of healing and reconciliation lies foremost with Suzie. As Agnes says, "Suzie will turn the whole world right side up again, the way it was meant to be, and we'll celebrate" (66). All of the women help Suzie into her ceremonial dress as Suzie describes her visions at the lodge. The deer that came to her great-grandfather, when he was hunting for the skins making up her dress, visited her and told her that she would have a long life and that her own daughter would wear the dress (67). With the promise of a new legacy of Indigenous values, customs, and empowerment for women, Sousette, Eva, Agnes, Lucy, Mariah, and Suzie all leave together for the ceremony, as an honour song begins (69). In the play, Manuel honours the strength and endurance of the community of women, while she also directly honours her own mother. One of the gifts given to Suzie before the ceremony takes place is a blanket from her great-grandmother Marceline, the first name of Manuel's own mother.

Eva says to her mother and Aunties, "All of you went through so much. Someone should write about it. They should make a movie about how you survived. I feel real proud sitting here among you. You're just like old warriors" (66). Eva's valorization of the strength of the women Elders and her call to spread the word of their survival through media, such as film, mirrors the performative work of the play itself and Manuel's commemoration of her own family history and survival. As heart-wrenching as this play is, it is also fundamentally a healing artistic enterprise that offers its writer, actors, audience, and, through the printed version, readers the opportunity for therapeutic transformation, through the powerful models for change represented by the three generations of women in this play. *Strength of Indian Women* thus emphasizes the communal and participatory elements of healing trauma and the importance of telling one's story both individually and as a collective, to family and community members.

EMBEDDED TEACHINGS: VERA MANUEL'S RECOVERED SHORT STORIES

DEANNA REDER

This anthology adds to Vera Manuel's legacy by bringing to publication a series of high profile plays that have been long unavailable to the public, as well as a selection of poems that Manuel herself helped curate. Also, along with the previously published story "The Abyss," this collection brings to print three unknown and unpublished short stories, written in 1987, that confirm Vera Manuel as a leading voice of her generation. Well before contemporary revelations of sexual and psychological abuse in residential schools were publicly acknowledged, Manuel not only demonstrated, in these stories, her profound understanding of the impact of these abuses but also suggested a route to healing. She proposed a method that relies on intergenerational respect, on a clear-eyed assessment of the damaged familial and cultural ties, on the importance of telling one's story, and on the appreciation of the role of the body in remembering.

Much of Manuel's method is evidenced in the work that was performed when she was alive. Her only published and most famous play, *Strength of Indian Women*, clearly presents her practice as a dramatherapist who worked with a generation of Indigenous women to find healing through composing and sharing their own stories.[1] Also, in her poetry, published in a variety of venues over the years, Manuel reveals her understanding of second-generation trauma and postmemory, even before Marianne Hirsch coined the term.[2] Now that we are able to read these three new stories, we can see just how ahead of her time Manuel was in her understanding of the effects of residential school abuse and colonization, and how effective her methods of healing continue to be.

Keep in mind that Native American scholar Dian Million, in *Therapeutic Nations: Healing in an Age of Indigenous Human Rights* (2013), considers the difficulties for Indigenous people at that time to access "conduits of power for 'truth-telling'" (94). Million quotes from a 1991 address given by Chief Bev Sellars of Soda Creek First Nation, at the First National Conference on Residential Schools, held in Vancouver in June of that year: "When we did get the courage to tell our stories, people thought we were lying, or even if we were telling the truth that it must have been our fault these things happened" (quoted in Million 2013, 94). Million writes about the inability of Indigenous communities to speak out against their oppressors[3] and credits feminist activists for helping the public understand the importance of discussing often taboo topics, like domestic abuse and incest, in order to condemn them as crimes. In particular, Million dates 1988 as a watershed moment when several key texts were published that allowed Indigenous people to be able to "name their family atrocities using language connected to social justice movements" (89). She notes specifically the conversations sparked by the publication of Christine A. Courtois's *Healing the Incest Wound*; Tony Martens, Brenda Daily, and Maggie Hodgson's *The Spirit Weeps,*

Characteristics and Dynamics of Incest and Child Sexual Abuse, With a Native Perspective; and Maria Yellow Horse Brave Heart and Lemyra M. DeBruyn's "Healing the Dysfunctional Indian Family" (1988). Bev Sellars substantiates Million's analysis when, in her 1991 address, she cites the recent interest in these histories by media venues like the talk show *Shirley*. It devoted an episode to residential school experiences (29 March 1991). Sellars continues:

> *The Fifth Estate* and other television programs did stories on residential schools, newspapers from across the country wanted a story, and a couple of books were written as well. Our secrets were being told and for many of us we were forced to remember in detail things that we had tried so hard to forget but were still being tormented by in our unspoken memories. We all knew the horrors that went on in these schools, not only with our generation but our parents' and grandparents' generations as well, and the stories being told now are just the tip of the iceberg. (quoted in Furniss 1995, 124)

It is significant to emphasize that Vera Manuel's short stories predate Million's 1988 "watershed moment." Manuel's work was pathbreaking. It is difficult to do much more than speculate how it is that Manuel was so exceptionally perceptive and eloquent, able to consider the corrosive effects of colonization and residential school trauma on Indigenous peoples so early. She was also one of the first to create methods of healing through her writing and storytelling.

Part of the reason undoubtedly lies in the fact that Vera Manuel was a member of a prominent First Nations family. Once her Ktunaxa mother, Marceline Paul, was able to come to terms with the abuse she had suffered herself, she became a highly respected cultural leader and valued mentor to her daughters. Likewise, her Secwepemc father, George Manuel, held a series of leadership roles both nationally and internationally from 1959 until his passing thirty years later.[4] He coined the term "The Fourth World" to describe Indigenous societies struggling under colonization and was the one to first propose the Universal Declaration on the Rights of Indigenous Peoples.[5] In addition, Vera Manuel's sisters and brothers are high-profile activists, artists, educators, and cultural workers. Best-known are possibly her sister Doreen Manuel, a filmmaker, and her brother Arthur Manuel (1951–2017), an Indigenous activist who worked internationally and wrote *Unsettling Canada: A National Wake-Up Call* (2015) and *The Reconciliation Manifesto: Recovering the Land, Rebuilding the Economy* (2017). Although they became influential leaders, members of the Manuel family suffered abuse at a variety of residential schools throughout British Columbia. Her mother attended St. Eugene Residential School in Cranbrook. Her father attended a residential school in Kamloops and then, once he had contracted tuberculosis, he ended up in Coqualeetza Indian Hospital in Chilliwack. And while Vera and some of her siblings went to local public schools, her brother Arthur attended British Columbia residential schools in Kamloops, Cranbrook, as well as St. Mary's in the town of Mission, in the Fraser Valley. It is not surprising then that much of Vera's work as an artist is founded on an intimate knowledge of the suffering brought on by colonial institutions. However, the successes of her art and her healing vision are based in more than simply being a witness to trauma. First, she was able to conduct therapeutic work with her mother and her sister Emalene that grounded her inter-generationally and gave her the insight to see beyond the damage done to her parents and community; such insight opened the door for her to accept and forgive the abuses she suffered. Next, Manuel was able to articulate her experiences of abuse using Indigenous storytelling through the venue of theatre. While theatre performance is generally secular in context, Vera Manuel incorporated spiritual exercises, like drumming and singing, alongside other acts of public storytelling. In a 2004 interview with Tahltan artist Peter Morin for *Redwire*, she discusses the opportunity to be creative in therapy "especially with our people, because we come from a history of oral tradition and we're very visual" (Interview).

In that same interview she also describes her first play, *Song of the Circle,* that includes much of her personal story:

> There was so much shame about the things that happened in my life that I didn't want it to come out; and I remember the first play and seeing all my secrets on the stage and thinking, "I wonder if these people know that this is all about me?"... It was really well received ... I remember attending this conference in Kamloops; it was the twentieth anniversary of the UBCIC conference, and my father was still alive then, and they were going to honour him at this conference. They asked me to bring this play and they didn't really know what it was about, so I managed to bring this play. And they brought him out and put him in the first row. I was really nervous about that.... During the break I went to go talk to my dad, just to see what his reaction was. He told me, "My only regret was that your mother wasn't alive to see this. She would be so proud of you." And I thought he really understood, part of him really understood. (Interview)

This personal experience of being able to successfully share her story with her family and community helped her understand the opportunities for healing using art. She was then able to help future creative collaborators (for example, women who attended her dramatherapy workshops) to articulate the unspeakable that terrorized them.

One of her strengths was her faith in the stories of other survivors and hence her ability to document abuses that were not legible to dominant society. Indeed, some of these abuses are still hard for mainstream Canadians to process. For example, towards the end of *Strength of Indian Women* one of the survivors, Sousette, tells the others that after her years at residential school she had met someone who had worked at the local flour mill. This person told her that he was instructed to doctor the flour intended for the residential school by including a cup of a mysterious white substance to every sack—the friend remembered getting fired when he asked what that substance was. In the play, the women around the table theorize its effects on them, as they remember how the food at the school made them sick.

It was not until 2013 that historian Ian Mosby revealed findings that support the suspicions of Manuel's characters. Mosby reported that government-approved researchers conducted nutrition experiments on selected residential school inmates in the 1940s and 1950s. For example, Mosby discusses an experiment begun in the 1940s, by Lionel Pett, in which students at an unidentified residential school were fed a special flour that could not be legally sold in Canada because it broke laws against food additives. Mosby summarizes Pett's 1952 report that recounted "a set of unfortunate results. Rather than an improvement in nutritional status, the students at the experimental school saw their blood haemoglobin levels decline . . ." (Mosby 2013, 164).

In a 2014 blog, Mosby reflects on the media attention that his research garnered, first from survivors whose experience was validated by his research, and second from a shocked Canadian public: "the confirmation of what had long been known by these survivors—that they were part of some kind of scientific experiment—had unleashed a flood of additional questions yet to be answered. It is, in many ways, a depressing commentary on contemporary Canadian society that such stories were not taken seriously by the government or the media until they were published in an academic journal by a white, male, settler historian." Yet over two decades earlier, Manuel took these stories seriously, including the ones regarding the adulteration of flour at residential schools. In the author's note to her one published play she comments: "I didn't make up the stories told in *Strength of Indian Women*. They came from pictures my mother painted for me with her words, words that helped me see her as a little girl for the first time" (25). Manuel was able to listen to her mother and believe her, which allowed her to listen to and believe other Indigenous people. She understood the function of state and church deception and the residential schools' curriculum of shame, violence, and worthlessness.

She understood the ceremonial actions of witnessing that exist in Secwepemc and Ktunaxa ceremony that can be replicated in secular theatrical performances and the subsequent healing power of performance and of respect.

While theatre offers a special context in which to tell stories, some of the same attitudes in her scripts are evident in Manuel's three previously unpublished short stories. Each is marked by the respect for the strength of her people, even as she speaks baldly about the obliterating forces that they faced. Manuel's short stories acknowledge the spiritual health and power of her ancestors even as they demonstrate the effects of trauma caused by land theft, lies, abuse, and murders that were key tools used to colonize her people and land.

The value of her writing, besides her beautiful phrasing and intimate dialogue, is her understanding of the function of humiliation, shame, and self-hatred instilled in Indigenous students by these schools long before residential school abuses were brought to mainstream Canada's attention. Not surprisingly, then, even thirty years after they were first composed, Manuel's short stories remain relevant, especially now that the Truth and Reconciliation Commission of Canada has delivered its final recommendations.

These short stories are written to validate the emotional, physical, and spiritual experiences of residential school survivors and their children and grandchildren. Manuel wants to portray her characters as remarkable yet overwhelmed by powerful and psychologically undermining forces. Both "That Grey Building" and "Theresa" are about strong, beautiful, resourceful, defiant women who are overpowered by the state and the church.

In the first story, the narrator's great-grandmother confronts a white settler who has erected fences and claimed Ktunaxa territory as his private property; she openly defies him and reminds her granddaughter that this seizure of unceded land is theft. She emphasizes to her granddaughter that "We never sold it to him, and we never gave it away to that whiteman. He stole it. Remember everything, because someday they will tell lies" (203).

Later in "That Grey Building," the grandmother tries to stop her granddaughter from being abducted and sent to residential school, by taking the girl into the mountains. After they are followed and eventually detained by the RCMP, the grandmother and the grandfather surrender, and the grandmother tries to comfort the child by telling her that school will teach her how to read and write so that the little girl "won't have to be poor and struggling like [her] granny" (207).

This story is told in a variety of voices, with the youngest voice being a second-generation survivor. This second-generation narrator shares stories told to her by her mother, who was the first in their family to be forced to attend residential school and who relates her own grandmother's attempt to protect her. And the mother of the narrator is an astute critic. When the daughter chauffeurs her mother around the countryside, and the two of them drive past what is likely the former St. Eugene Residential School, the mother states: "That grey building was once like a prison to me. It still looks like a prison" (199). In Geoffrey Carr's 2009 analysis of St. Eugene Residential School's architecture, he supports the mother's description: "Referring to these carceral spaces as 'schools' flattens the particular nature of these institutions by applying a euphemism that often implies salubrity and self-improvement. Instead I propose alternate terminology that self-consciously intervenes in the received nomenclature and social memory of this violent colonial past" (112). While the narrator's mother thinks of the old school as a prison, Carr suggests that residential institutions be called "engines or factories of modern colonialism" (112).[6] The mother in the story would agree with Carr's renaming; she herself laments "So many children died there. It robbed me of my childhood. We saw things in that place that no child should ever have to see" (199). And later she adds: "They never taught us anything about survival in those schools, but they sure taught us how to pray and how to suffer" (200). The narrator's mother is able to see how her generation was systematically confined, abused, traumatized, and sometimes killed—without ever being educated to live and work in general society. This was intentional so her community would be less able to fight the takeover of their land and societies.

In "That Grey Building," Vera Manuel provides the antidote to these brutal, painful, dehumanizing experiences when the narrator's mother remembers the relationship her female ancestors had with their territory:

> My grandmother used to teach me all the time, even when
> I was a baby. She never used to get angry at me like my mother
> sometimes did. All the time she would be explaining to me,
> telling me stories, teaching me the proper way to do things
> and why things had to be done in a certain way. Whenever we
> travelled, all along the way, my grandmother would stop the
> horse to show me something. The land was like a storybook to
> her. She knew every inch of it and had a great love and respect
> for the land. To love the land is the most important lesson she
> ever taught me. (200–201)

The narrator adds, "And it's the most important lesson you've ever taught me too, I thought" (201).

This alternative, immeasurably superior Indigenous pedagogy, this development of appreciation for, expertise about, literacy in, and emotions towards the land, and this affirmation of familial relationships defies the brutal, dehumanizing lessons of the colonial project, which focused on taking the land and debasing its owners.

In the story "Theresa," residential school inmate Theresa is called "the old woman" by her people because they recognized, in her outspokenness and courage, the memory of a respected, deceased former leader. Theresa's confidence in the beliefs of her ancestors and her objections to humiliating treatment make her an opponent of the school: "Just as rapidly as the sisters worked to tear the Indianness out of [the students], Theresa worked with the same amount of determination to restore it" (214). One of Theresa's key reminders is that students need to be proud of who they are: "You must never let them make you ashamed to be an Indian," she'd begin. "It is lies, what they tell us in here" (214).

Manuel gives an example of the effects of this shame as she describes the character Mary who cannot help but absorb the humiliating comments meted out to all of them: "Mary hated the way those remarks made her feel—as if they were wounding the flesh around something very fragile inside, and she had no way to ward off the blows. When they said things like, 'Indians are dirty, stupid,' the hurt went right into her heart and stayed there. She knew they weren't true, but she felt helpless and sad all the same" (212). Theresa's reaction, however, is open defiance. When Sister Augustine tells her class that "Indians [are] not as smart as white people" (212), Theresa responds by asking "Do you know how to skin a deer?" (212). Making the point that she and her people have knowledge and skills that the nuns do not, Theresa reminds herself and her classmates that these degrading statements are lies.

It is Theresa's cousin Mary who witnesses Theresa's final confrontation, when a nun pushes Theresa down the stairs and kills her. Mary then records a conspiracy to silence her, as she is put in seclusion from the other children, and alternately told not to "tell lies" and warned not to talk about what she saw. When a message from her family is passed on through another girl at the school, Mary is advised to keep quiet in order to stay safe. While Manuel demonstrates the string of outright lies that colonization is based upon—that the land no longer belongs to Indigenous people, that they do not have the ability to educate and raise their own children, and that Indigenous people are intellectually inferior—she is also illustrating how degrading comments and murderous actions are on the same continuum of abuse suffered by residential school survivors.

The third story, "The Letter," is about a First Nations girl named Vera who, along with her brother, is the first in her community to attend an otherwise all-white school, and the story shows the generational effects of racism at work. At the school, Vera is befriended and protected by Danny, one of the school's most popular girls. Vera is emotionally sensitive, able to determine the hostility around her, and physically sickened by the misrepresentations of Indigenous people in the school curriculum. She admits that she is uneasy when other First Nations children begin to attend her school and states: "I had already begun to adopt an attitude toward my people. The more Indian they looked and acted, the more I avoided them" (235). Having learned the racial logics in her community, she practises the same actions of social exclusion that initially kept her isolated.

When she is sent an anonymous, insulting letter that suggests she abandon her friendship with Danny, she quickly retreats, in a way that at first seems timid and docile. However, Vera has to navigate a landscape riddled with threats. She decides to end her friendship with Danny to avoid contempt and its threat of violence—resentment that could materialize into something nastier than a letter.

At the story's resolution, the character of Vera describes how her mother, after enduring ridicule and bad treatment from her husband, Vera's father, decides to leave him but does not have enough money to take her children with her. Vera convinces her mother that she and her siblings can contribute with their summer earnings to the escape and her mother relents and tells them to pack lightly. Just as they are about to leave, Vera is elated and makes a good-bye call to Danny and their parting is warm. Free from the school and an abusive father, Vera is able to make amends.

It is not easy to determine why Vera Manuel did not publish these stories at the time or why she did not publish more work generally. The only short story she ever published in her lifetime was "The Abyss," a story that is very similar to her only published play, both published in 1990s and both out of print.[7] Some hints might come from her work in the theatre. Because Manuel staged her plays in therapeutic contexts to suit the community she was serving, she was less concerned about organizing performances in mainstream play-houses. And as her role as a dramatherapist expanded, she began to involve the women who shared their stories with her in the actual composition of the plays. In fact, one of the reasons we didn't include several of the jointly written plays in this publication are the complication such creative process brings in identifying authorship and in gaining permissions for publication.[8] It might be that, given Manuel's dedication to her dramatherapy as well as her failing health towards the end of her life, finding time for other writing or typical literary venues for her work were of secondary interest to her.

But it is clear that Manuel had hoped to write and publish more. At the end of the 2004 interview, Morin asked what would be her next step. Manuel replied: "To finish my novel. I want to move into writing novels and books. I love writing plays but they have a limited life. I want to write a novel, and it will be hanging around here after I am long gone, that teaches people something; passes on some of the knowledge and information that's been given to me. I think that we do need more novels and books written by our own people." With her community work, her need to make a living, and her subsequent illness, Manuel was never able to complete her novel. But this collection is hopefully one step closer toward fulfilling her goals.

"THROUGH POETRY A COMMUNITY IS BROUGHT TOGETHER": VERA MANUEL'S POETRY, POETRY ACTIVISM, AND POETICS

JOANNE ARNOTT

Vera Manuel's poetry is held deep in our hearts. Her words vibrate with the sounds and rhythms of her life—from Ktunaxa territory to Los Angeles, to Secwepemc territory to Vancouver, to Davis

Inlet, to Tyendinaga, to a small café on Davie Street. The energy and noise of the street, the green hush of birch forests, loving voices of friends, family, lovers, and even the acid anger of haters—all heard and felt in her poetry. And her words pulse with the music of her life—Pow-wow, R & B, Blues, Etta James, Bob Dylan, Keith Secola. She loved music.

Vera's words embody generations of oral tradition, embody story, the "lyric," resistance and renewal and celebration. And her words are her voice, a voice I can still hear. Vera once said she resisted being published because she felt her words, her poetry should be experienced out loud, spoken, whispered, voiced—heard by the People, with the People. I always felt the love of thousands of ancestors surrounding her as she read. She laughed when I called her Maya Angelou's Indigenous sister. But they shared hope in their voices, their words.

We all share a sadness of missing her, of missing that before. But we are strengthened by the words. Her words live on in paper, in recordings and in our memories—memories that know no time.

I was a friend, a sister, a colleague—shared an office, shared work, shared dreams and secrets. We would talk for hours on the phone, rambling everywhere about our lives. I can still taste the good food she made. I can still recall her kindness to my family; we are still nurtured by that love—nitânis, nicicimak, nîcisânak, nikawiy.

She knew great loss and sorrow. She knew the bitterness of colonization, of genocide. She never lost hope for her Nations and her family. She never lost hope for any who struggled. I try every day to be a better Indigenous woman, to bring more good and art and story to this world, guided by her words, by her art, her stories. Kinanâskomitin. I am grateful for you.

LORETTA TODD, 2018

In a café on Granville Island, Vancouver, 2008, a full house gathered to receive oral presentations of a new anthology of British Columbia poets. It was the launch for *Rocksalt: An Anthology of Contemporary BC Poetry* (Mother Tongue), and the first time I heard Vera perform her work in person. Vera arrived with her sister Emalene, and her little dog, and we all settled in to listen to the performances.

When Vera's turn came, she walked slowly to the microphone. She lifted her two hands together, and in a slow, precise rhythm, called the room to quiet and the ancestors in, striking one stone against the other. With the world fully focussed, she presented "The Catholic Church." Simple, powerful, resonant, and complete, her poem was very well received.

Vera's strengths were not only as a writer and a healer, but also as a performer. Drawing on her experience and research, she embodied the truths she had to teach and share. One of the roots to the development of her unique process in healing arts was the decision by her father, George Manuel, to invite Maria Campbell to come to their community in the 1970s, to teach writing and healing. Through this apprenticeship and with others to follow, Vera went on to make a life's work. She lived in Vancouver for many years, studying history, Indigenous culture, and writing at University of British Columbia (UBC), and writing at Langara College, and she apprenticed with healers like Jane Middelton-Moz.[1] Although she wrote poetry from a young age, it was in her later years that poetry came into focus as a central avenue for making sense of the world and for building community. As Todd puts it, "She had an ability to speak truths in a way that opens up dialogue rather than shuts down minds" (unpublished notes 2017).

As a member of World Poetry (WP), she was a featured poet at their coffee houses and on the World Poetry Café radio program (CFRO 100.5 FM). This community-based organization, with local and international facets, was founded to create a space for poets of all languages and traditions to come together, and in this context, Vera thrived. In 2006, her work was acknowledged with a World Poetry Lifetime Achievement Award.

In the same period that the Granville Island reading took place, Vera joined forces with Loretta Todd and others to develop a gathering under the auspices of Aboriginal Media Lab[2] and the grunt gallery, to acknowledge, honour, and celebrate the long history of Indigenous poetry in British Columbia.[3] The Strong Words conference was held at the Chinese Cultural Centre on East Pender Street in Vancouver, on 22 November 2008. As Artist-in-Residence for Aboriginal Media Lab, Vera researched the history of resistance to colonization and the creative self-expression of Indigenous people in British Columbia and across Turtle Island, in poetic voice, to the present day.

In her research notes, she articulates specific assertions or poetics that hold true for many writers, although not all. While some poetics call for greater emphasis on language sensitivity or for disruptive approaches to meaning and sense, Vera's poetics are about affirming embodiment and emotion, and acknowledging the emotional impacts of history, including historical amnesia and erasure. As Loretta Todd observed, "Vera's words embody generations of oral tradition, embody story, the 'lyric', resistance and dialogue. And her words are her voice, a voice I can still hear" (personal communication 2017). Vera wrote: "Poetry and poetic expression is an important element in expressing Aboriginal lived experience because it reaches people through the heart, and often through the spiritual aspects of our lives. Poetry speaks the truth because it originates from the emotional landscape of the heart and the soul; a poem can easily strip a person of defences leaving them vulnerable to the emotions it evokes. Genocide has impacted greatly on Aboriginal people's lives; generational trauma related to genocide has created silence, emotional numbing, and isolation." At the Strong Words gathering, Vera sat on a panel to present the highlights of her research, "Words that Move & Tell Truths." Joining her on this panel were two of Canada's better-known Indigenous authors, Maria Campbell and Lee Maracle. Each panelist spoke in turn to the issues of how oral and written traditions have collided, through the processes of encroaching European settlement and often brutal suppression (colonization) of Indigenous people, individually and collectively. Each spoke, from her own experiences and perspective, to how we can make sense of these collisions in ways that allow creative existence and thriving in the present, and for future generations.

An important element of the gathering was the "Honouring Our Poets" section, focused on the legacy of E. Pauline Johnson, Chief Dan George, and George Clutesi. Phillip Kevin Paul introduced a biography of each poet, followed by readings from their works. Stefany Mathias and others read from Pauline Johnson's poetry. Chief Dan George and George Clutesi's works were recited by various readers, including family members. As part of the celebration of Chief Dan George, his grandson Gabe George shared stories and a most profound, spirit-healing, revitalizing song by Chief Dan George's eldest son, Bob George. The process of bringing attention to the words and works of writers who came before us arrives with a notable teaching, emphasizing relatedness and continuity, affirming living memory, the power of the spoken word as a vehicle for transmission. Other aspects of Vera's poetics that relate to the importance of this section of the gathering is illuminated in Vera's research notes:

> Poetry provides a space to express the sacred through language, song, movement in an honourable and respectful way. When we listen to speeches by past great orators and wisdom keepers ... the way they speak from their heart is like poetry. This is what has survived, the magic of storytelling, passing on teachings in a way that people will listen, understand, and feel connected. Through poetry a community is brought together.

Other sections of the gathering showcased contemporary poets, spoken-word artists, rappers, and singer-songwriters, a vital demonstration of the current flourishing.

In the months following the Strong Words gathering, a dozen local writers established the Aboriginal Writers Collective West

Coast (AWCWC). AWCWC met regularly for a few years, writing together and hosting many events and gatherings. Vera introduced me to Ariadne Sawyer, co-founder with Alejandro Mujica-Olea of World Poetry (WP), and asked us to collaborate on a series of poetry events featuring Indigenous poets. The two groups collaborated on a number of events in the years following. Russell Wallace was a key organizer of many of these events.

AWCWC collaborated with a number of other arts and literary groups, including Talking Stick Festival, Asian Canadian Writers' Workshop, Gallery Gachet, and with educational institutions, primarily Native Education College, and Simon Fraser University. In 2011 we created an art show and a book, *Salish Seas: An Anthology of Text + Image*, which included two of Vera's poems and two poems by Chief William K'H Halserten Sepass.[4]

Vera joined an online writers group of Indigenous women that I hosted, Storytellersplayspace. Through sharing work and conversation online, Vera and I decided to collaborate on a collection of her poetry, the result of which has been included in this volume. This established habit of communing and communicating online grew into a blog, *Vera Manuel Tribute*, initiated after Vera's death. Intended to honour Vera and to preserve an archive of the many aspects of her work, the tribute page received assistance and support from many people. I worked most closely with Emalene Manuel, consulting on the blog, and later we joined forces with Michelle Coupal, Deanna Reder, and The People and The Text project.

Vera's poetry is deceptively simple, usually narrative, and generally emotionally evocative. Some are closer to song, some resonate with oratorical finesse, and some are conversational. Many are autobiographical. Others seek to embody experiences shared with the author by other people, gestures of affirmation and witnessing. What is important to note for the reader is that the text was intended to be presented orally, and that may be the best way to receive and fully access the text, to fully absorb the spoken word and song qualities of the work.[5]

As Vera's poetry publications came much later than her playwriting, there is little critical response to her poetry, specifically. I find the intensity of her most polished work is effective as text, communicating spirit, emotion, idea, and intent as powerfully as that written by masters of the form. Vera's artist statement, where she sets out her goals and influences as a poet, was first published in *Rocksalt* and is shared with permission:

WHERE POETRY COMES FROM

Poetry became my way of telling a story about subjects too painful to talk about within my family, community, tribal groups and nation. Poetry gave me license to say out loud everything that others were afraid to tell. an Elder told me once that "poetry is a gentle way of talking about painful things."

For years I used my poetry as a tool to help people to heal and never thought to publish it or to use it for any other purpose. As long as the words that came to me could help to open doors for others to get at their feelings and their own words that is all I cared about.

Both my parents and most people of their generation were residential school survivors. My father also spent a significant portion of his adolescence in a TB hospital. When I was a child no one talked about the past, but I grew up in a home full of silence, shame, violence, incest, and rage. The way I survived was to keep silent like everyone else, but I always wrote poetry. When I look back on it now I realize I was not as silent as I thought, between the lines the stories are all there. Poetry helped me to find the words to tell, to connect, and to resist my tendency to isolate. In the telling I have gained many allies. Poetry is a powerful source of healing.

My father was an orator who could hold the attention of huge groups of people with his passion and commitment to the land. My mother was a storyteller who passed on knowledge about the Kootenai culture and land. Their gift was their ability to speak from the heart where poetry comes from.[6]

APPENDIX

Indians and Residential school: a study of the breakdown of
a culture

History 404

Vera Manuel

26 April 1987

INDIANS AND RESIDENTIAL SCHOOL: A STUDY OF THE BREAKDOWN OF A CULTURE

VERA MANUEL

SUBMITTED 26 APRIL 1987 AS AN ESSAY FOR A FOURTH YEAR HISTORY CLASS. THIS ESSAY, WRITTEN BY VERA MANUEL WHEN SHE WAS AN UNDERGRADUATE STUDENT, PREDATES NATIONAL DISCUSSIONS OF THE DAMAGE OF RESIDENTIAL SCHOOLS.

INTRODUCTION

The way that I felt about the residential school is that during the first nine years of my life I was a happy child. I remember laughing, walking in the woods and feeling very close to my grandparents and I felt loved. I had control of my life. Then I went to residential school and my whole world fell apart. I lost everything at such a young age and I became nothing.

I felt all that I loved, my grandparents, my parents, they had
all abandoned me.

My grandparents, they sent me to the residential school because
the RCMP threatened to put them in jail if they didn't. My
grandmother said that maybe it would not be such a bad thing
because I would get an education; I would learn some skills so
I could get a job that would enable me to take care of myself.
When I was 16 they let me out of the school and I came back
to the reserve and I didn't know nothing. I was 16 but I was
still like a nine-year-old child. That was the upbringing in the
residential school, they took over your whole life, they didn't
even want you to think for yourself and then when they were
finished with you, they threw you back out into the world
without even telling you how to survive. I guess that's why a
lot of my people killed themselves with booze, they didn't have
anything to replace it with. Me, I had my grandparents and they
told me that they were going to have to train me all over again.
They taught me how to tan hides and how to do beadwork
and for years that was the only trade I had, I couldn't get a job,
I wasn't trained for anything.[1]

Marceline Paul,
Kootenay elder,
Drug and Alcohol Counsellor,
Bonaparte Indian Band

From an Indian perspective there is very little written about the resi-
dential school experience to give a clear indication of its historical
impact upon the lives of Indian people. Most Indian people carry

---

1   Marceline Paul, Kootenay Elder, Drug and Alcohol Counsellor, Bonaparte Indian
Band, 1987. Vera Manuel's original endnotes have been slightly revised and reformatted
for publication.

this experience only in their memory and are reluctant to talk about it, often because it was a painful experience that they would rather forget. This silence over approximately four generations, and the reasons for it, are an indication that the experience has had a most profound effect. The idea that Indian people had to go through this experience at such an early age is interesting to contemplate; because what it actually was, was a mortification process not unlike the experience that prisoners go through when they are incarcerated. Loss of freedom to speak their own language; to practise their own culture; to pray in their own way; to be with their own people; and the loss of pride and self esteem that came with the teachings that were designed to replace their own. The result of this experience has affected Indian people right through to today and has contributed to some of the more negative aspects found in Indian communities, such as: alcohol and drug abuse, violent deaths, high infant mortality rates, sexual abuse, etc.

By 1961 the Indian population had reached the all-time low of 180,000 in Canada, and then it rose to 300,000 by 1979 and continued to slowly but steadily increase thereafter.

In the 1960s, 50–60% of Indian health problems were alcohol related.

In the 1960s, violent deaths among Indians were 3–4 times the national average.

By 1961 the strength and stability of family units appeared to be eroding, as evidenced by increased divorce rates, births outside marriage, children in care, adoption of Indian children by non-Indians, and juvenile delinquency.

By the 1960s social assistance and welfare use increased from slightly more than 1/3 to slightly more than 1/2 within 10 years due to lack of adequate training and high unemployment rates on reserves.

Indians incarcerated in penitentiaries and jails was 3 times their proportion of the total population.

Each generation has responded to and been affected by residential school in a different way. The first generation during the mid 1800s had more freedom of choice than later generations. For example, they had a choice as to whether or not they wanted to attend and they were able to maintain stronger ties with their families. They were also equipped with strong traditional training and therefore their cultural identity was intact and very much in evidence before they went into the schools. The parents of these children had more involvement and therefore more control over the lives of their children in these schools. The second generation, during the latter 1800s to early 1900s, were faced with more stringent rules and a stronger conviction on the part of the missionaries to separate Indian children from their parents. This second generation was just as resistant as the first but the schools were becoming more organized and more powerful and worked more closely with the government whose policies were always aimed at the assimilation of Indian people. One of the main forms this resistance took was evident in the poor attendance records of the students. Parents kept their children out of school and children constantly ran away. In 1894 the government passed a law making Indian children attend school.[2] The third generation was forced to attend residential school with the threat of imprisonment for parents who refused to comply. Rules became even more stringent and punishment more severe.[3]

---

2   John Munro, Minister of Indian and Northern Affairs, *Indian Conditions: A Survey* (Ottawa: Indian Affairs and Northern Development, 1980), 4–9.

3   Millie Poplar, "Assimilation Through Education," Union of British Columbia Indian Chiefs, paper to educate people on Master Tuition Agreement.

We were strapped for everything. We were strapped if we were caught speaking our own language, but I kept speaking my own language anyway, that's how I managed to keep it. A lot of us didn't care if we were punished, we couldn't just give in to them all the time. There were a lot of times when we had to keep silence and if we were caught speaking when we weren't supposed to we were strapped. We learned to steal food because we were so hungry all the time and then we were strapped if we got caught. The nuns used to cut the crust edges off their bread and this would be thrown in the garbage, sometimes someone would grab a handful and stick it in their mouth and for this they were punished.[4]

As the relationship between the administration and community continued to deteriorate there is an indication that there was also greater resistance on the part of parents and students. From 1917 on the priests had to actively recruit pupils and many parents refused to enrol their children. "Each year principals complained of parental un-cooperativeness, defiance and indifference. Unless cajoled and threatened few parents brought their children to the school."[5] Many Indian children ran away and returned to their communities where they were apprehended and returned to the school for punishment.

Many of this third generation, with continued resistance, managed to retain the language, culture and much of their own spirituality intact within themselves, but were unable to pass it on to the next generation; for it was the fourth generation after the experience of the residential school first began that was the one to lose the language, the spirituality and most of the culture, because they were never taught. This was the generation that had no identity; that lost touch with the teachings of the elders because they could not speak the language; their own spirituality lost to them and unable

4   Marceline Paul.
5   Jo-Anne Fiske, "And Then We Prayed Again: Carrier Women, Colonialism, and Mission Schools" (MA thesis, University of British Columbia, 1981), 54.

to fully grasp the Christian religion, they were left with nothing to believe in; and all that remained of the culture was a few songs and dances, some of the traditional foods, the drum, and a few pieces of art and traditional clothing. By about the 1950s and '60s conditions on the reservations had deteriorated to a point where almost nothing was being passed on to future generations. Alcoholism caused the destruction of family and home so that by this time residential schools became havens for neglected, unwanted children.

THE MISSIONARIES AND THE GOVERNMENT
The Oblates that came to the interior of British Columbia from Oregon to Christianize and civilize Native people saw the change to an agrarian lifestyle as a positive step for them. If Indians were settled into communities they would be easier to convert and easier to control. The migratory lifestyle that Indians lived was viewed as inherently wrong.[6] The government of British Columbia would have also seen this as a more desirable lifestyle in compliance with the demands of incoming settlers. It was shortly after Confederation that church and state joined forces to consolidate their ideas of implementing industrial schools. The federal government viewed these schools as essential to teaching Indians an agrarian lifestyle and "ultimately to assimilation into a 'superior' European society."[7] Like other denominations the Oblates felt it was necessary to separate the children from their home so they could more easily teach them to be good Christian young people on the European model.[8] Initially Indian people were not willing to just hand their children over. While they did not object to the new educational opportunities for their children, they had not visualized being separated from

---

6   Celia Vayro, "Invasion and Resistance: Native Perspective of the Kamloops Indian Residential School" (MA thesis, University of British Columbia, 1968), 31.

7   Ibid., 32.

8   Margaret Whitehead, *The Cariboo Mission: A History of the Oblates* (Victoria: Sono Nis Press, 1981), 111.

them. They wanted the new learning to be a supplement rather than a replacement for traditional education.[9]

A report which was the basis for future Indian education policies was released by the Government of Canada in 1847. It is a clear example of cultural oppression becoming written policy. The idea of the superiority of the European culture is evident by the statement of the need "... to raise them (the Indians) to the level of the whites,"[10] and the pressure to take the land out of Indian hands. Indians were to remain under the control of the Crown, efforts to Christianize and settle Indians into communities was to continue, and schools that practised manual labour were to be established under the control of missionaries. Also in the discussions was the suggestion that there was a definite need to minimize as much as possible the influence of parents on the children.[11]

> Parents resented both the long separation from their children and their inability to visit them at will. Parents were considered by the school administrators to be a nuisance, an interference to routine. Visiting hours were limited to two and one half hours per week and all visits were under supervision. No one other than parents or guardians were permitted on school premises, thus older siblings were cut off from the rest of the family. Parents could enter only the chapel and the visiting parlour. These humiliations were not suffered in silence. But the Oblates, rather than negotiating more satisfactory arrangements, grew to be more rigid and harsh.[12]

The attitudes of the Department of Indian Affairs regarding the separation of Indian children from their parents in order to educate them is reflected in this submission by the Honourable Clifford Sifton, Superintendent General of Indian Affairs in 1902:

---

9 Ibid., 113.
10 Vayro, "Invasion and Resistance," 32–3.
11 Fiske, "And Then We Prayed Again," 53–4.
12 Ibid.

As a civilizing factor the advantage of the removal of the pupils from the retrogressive influence of home life is shared pretty equally by the industrial and boarding schools, although the latter are generally situated on or near the reserves with a view to overcoming the strong objection manifested by the parents to the removal of their children to any great distance . . . The pagans outside the sphere of civilization are disposed to regard education as an attempt to erect a barrier between them and their children.[13]

As more and more settlers came into the province, Indians were finding themselves with less and less, including less control over their own lives. They had suffered loss of land, loss of traditional tribal government, loss of social patterns, and a loss of lifestyle dependent only on nature; now they were also expected to give up their children.[14] This was something that they were never able to fully accept through the first three generations. Children played a vital role in the community. It was through the children that the elders were able to pass on their knowledge to ensure that it was retained for future generations. With the children gone the elders lost their role as teachers and children were no longer learning that which was vital to their survival, which of course was exactly what church and government intended. In 1885, S.B. Lucas, Acting Agent of Peace Mills Agency, expressed the prevailing view that

The aim of all these institutes (schools) is to train the Indian to give up his old ways, and to settle among his white brethren on equal terms and with equal advantages.[15]

In 1985 the Department of Indian Affairs saw integration as a way in which Britain could cease to be responsible for Indians:

---

13 Department of Indian Affairs, *Annual Report, 1902–03*, xxvii–xxviii.
14 Whitehead, *The Cariboo Mission*, 122.
15 Department of Indian Affairs, *Annual Report, 1885*, 167.

... if it were possible to gather in all the Indian children and retain them for a certain period, there would be produced a generation of English-speaking Indians, accustomed to ways of civilized life, which might then be the dominant body among themselves, capable of holding its own with its white neighbors; and thus would be brought about a rapidly decreasing expenditure until the same should forever cease, and the Indian problem would have been solved.[16]

A statement made in 1920 by Deputy Superintendent General Duncan Campbell Scott to the House of Commons is a clear indication that the position of the government to eliminate Indian cultures had not changed:

... Our object is to continue until there is not a single Indian in Canada that has not been absorbed into the body politic and there is no Indian question, and no Indian department, that is the whole object of this bill.[17]

THE INDIANS

George Manuel, a Shuswap leader and elder, wrote in his book *The Fourth World*, "All areas of our lives which were not occupied by the Indian agent were governed by the priest."[18] The role of the government was to implement policy and to give direction as to the future of Indian people. The responsibility to put this into practice was given over to the church. Both church and government were convinced that they were both acting in the best interest of the Indians. Neither saw any value in the way that Indian people lived before the Europeans came; ethnocentric, they believed that they were doing the Indians a favour by teaching them the only form of education that they knew:

---

16 Department of Indian Affairs, *Annual Report, 1895*, xxiv.
17 Campbell Scott, quoted in Vayro, "Invasion and Resistance," 36.
18 George Manuel and Michael Posluns, *The Fourth World: An Indian Reality* (Toronto, Collier-Macmillan, 1974), 63.

. . . a tightly controlled, frequently harsh, educational regime imported from Europe. Schools operated under strict controls. School staff expected order, instant obedience, total attentiveness, and disciplined behaviour. If a child failed to act according to the expected norm, or exhibited behavioural problems, the answer was punishment. This system of education, applied in all schools, public, private, and parochial, had the support of parents who themselves had experienced the same. This European system was applied at the Mission without any consideration being given to cultural clash.[19]

No consideration was ever made to alter the system to accommodate children brought up in a totally different culture. Indian children's lives were much different in that they concentrated on enjoying the present, and their elders taught them to exercise personal freedom of choice. They were used to freedom, not confinement, and their former teachers were members of the extended family group whose closeness they were used to. They were seldom, if ever, physically punished and could not understand the use of corporal punishment:[20]

It was the priests who introduced lashings to my people, and they practiced it for awhile. When someone did the least little thing wrong the priest told my people that that person would have to be punished publicly and they would lash him. It was an ugly way to be, it was not the way of my people and it taught my people how to hate.[21]

From the beginning the education system was carefully planned so as to alter Indian values. And equally as important as the altering of Indian values was the way in which this was achieved by humiliation, degradation, force; Indian children were made to feel as though

---

19 Whitehead, *The Cariboo Mission*, 122.
20 Ibid.
21 Marceline Paul.

being an Indian was a sinful thing. There is some suggestion in historical accounts that teaching Indians to speak English was a good thing, because it gave Indians a common language; and that was the only way that Indians could learn the non-Indian symbols. Most Indians when questioned about their residential school experience will say, "We were forbidden to speak our own language. We were made to feel that it was wrong, because we were punished so severely for speaking in our own way." "Anything that we did that was Indian was sinful."

> I was punished quite a bit because I spoke my language . . . I was put in a corner and punished and sometimes, I was just given bread and water . . . or they'd try to embarrass us and they'd put us in front of the whole class.[22]

> I remember sometimes I'd be talking to one of my friends in Indian and all of a sudden one of the priests would come with the strap. It was like they could hear everything. They used to whip us pretty hard when they heard us speaking Indian and they would make fun of us, ridicule us.[23]

> I used to get strapped for speaking Kootenay, but I couldn't stop speaking it. My grandparents couldn't speak English, if I forgot my language how would I be able to speak to them when I went home. Whenever the priests and nuns would punish me I was so full of resentment and anger and that made me more determined than ever. I still have my language today. No matter how much they strapped me they could never beat it out of me.[24]

Public humiliation was the worst punishment for the children. Traditionally in the Indian community public humiliation and ostracization were often used as a strong social control. In the residential

---

22 Celia Vayro, "Invasion and Resistance," 106.
23 George Manuel, Shuswap leader and Elder.
24 Marceline Paul.

schools public strappings were given frequently to combine public humiliation with corporal punishment:

> I got in trouble for chewing gum.... It was such a minor, minor thing in my view. But I was taken into the playroom. ... She was a lay person. She took down my pants right in front of everybody.... Can't remember whether she used her hand to spank me or whether she used a ruler or a strap ... but I remember being punished.[25]

The curriculum taught to Indian children contained only the information necessary to change Indian children into literate English-speaking Christian farmers, craftspeople, or manual labourers. The following Department of Indian Affairs Annual Report on the curricula of the Kamloops Indian Residential School is typical of most Industrial schools. This report is for 1902–03 and varies very little throughout the former and following years.

CLASSROOM WORK:

boys: 8:45 am–12 pm, weekdays except Sat.
    4:45 pm–6:15pm
girls: 2 pm–5 pm, ½ hour study in pm.

Religious instruction is given daily for half an hour. Morning and evening prayers are said in common. On Sunday the pupils assemble three times in the chapel and one hour is devoted to the learning of hymns and to the explanation of the Gospel.[26]

There appear to be two points of view among Indians regarding quality of education: Some former students like Marceline Paul are adamant that the education was inferior, even to their own, and provided them with no tools when they got out of the school. They

25 Vayro, "Invasion and Resistance," 107.
26 Department of Indian Affairs, *Annual Report, 1902–03*, 415–16.

are critical because the schools were too regimented and repressive that students were ill-prepared for the real world when they got out:

> They made us believe that we would be able to survive in the white world with the skills that they were providing us with. But they didn't give us an education that we could use to get a job. We were taught how to work hard, most of our time was spent at back-breaking chores and most of our time was spent praying. I recall we had only three hours in the classroom and an hour of that was spent learning catechism and singing hymns. Boy they sure taught us how to pray. When we got out we couldn't fit into the white world and then neither could we fit back into the Indian world, we had lost so much, we were stuck somewhere in the middle. It took me years to find my way back to my people, back to the ways that gave me the strength I needed to survive, my spirituality. And what about my children. I was so confused when I left the school I never taught my children when they were young the things they needed to know.[27]

Some, however, claim that despite 'all that' they learned to enjoy it. 'It was painful, but 'good', 'taught (them) to work hard without complaining, to get up early and get a job' ... [A]ll expressed mixed feelings ... but even those who are bitter admit that they acquired practical skills and are grateful for them.[28]

The following are excerpts from the Department of Indian Affairs Sessional Paper on the Kootenay Industrial School in Cranbrook, B.C., 1900–01.

---

27 Marceline Paul.
28 Fiske, "And Then We Prayed Again," 56.

Land – . . . we have rented one hundred and twenty acres in order that the children could receive a more thorough training in farming, as this knowledge is considered one of the most essential parts of their education.

Attendance – average attendance for the year was fifty-four.

Farm and Garden – The boys receive instruction in farming and gardening, working each day under the supervision of the foreman.

Industries taught – The work for the boys consists chiefly in gardening, farming, clearing land and sawing and splitting wood.

Carpentering – . . . repairing premises . . . building fences.

Shoemaking – mending shoes and harnesses.

Girls Industrial work – mend clothes, darn, dress making and fancy work, cook, bake, house-clean, laundry and dairy work.

Moral and Religious Training – 1/2 hour is devoted to the explaining of Christian doctrine, besides many short instructions are given to inculcate in them the principles of honesty and morality.[29]

In reviewing the Department of Indian Affairs Reports it is evident that boys and girls were trained specifically for an agrarian and Christian lifestyle. The effort to totally transform the lifestyle, the values and beliefs, the spirituality, the language, customs and traditions of Indian people over a few generations into European citizens was an utter failure that has never been properly dealt with

---

29   Department of Indian Affairs, *Annual Report 1900–01*, 425–26.

and still causes repercussion to today. Within the last ten years there has been a gradual move by Indian people themselves to unravel their painful history to get at the crux of the problems that are destroying their people. One of the problems that comes up time and time again is the residential school experience. At first all you hear is the common complaints such as: "all I remember is being hungry all the time."[30] "I remember the loneliness, I felt abandoned."[31] "They made me ashamed of being an Indian, I don't remember exactly when, but I know it happened."[32] Later you hear of more serious problems that most are reluctant to talk about but claim happened time and time again, that of sexual abuse of girls and boys or children who were constant troublemakers, rebellious ones being murdered. Slowly these painful memories are being unravelled and many Indian people concerned with the high drug and alcohol rate among Indians are hoping that the residential school experience when all told will someday provide some of the keys to the problems and from the answers will come some of the solutions.

> I was in a workshop not long ago when the subject of sexual abuse came up. One by one everyone in the room related a bad experience that they'd had, but I didn't say anything. It was so long ago and I thought it wasn't important. Later over lunch I told one of my classmates about the time in the residential school when I was sent to the dormitory to lie down because I was sick. There was another [girl] already there when I came in. We weren't suppose to talk but she whispered to me that she was glad I'd come because she was afraid of Father Patterson who came in when the other students left to go for a walk and messed around with her. We heard someone coming and we pretended to be asleep, he came around to my bed and started touching me and I began to cry and he got mad . . . after that

---

30 George Manuel.
31 Marceline Paul.
32 Mary Michell, Kootenay Elder.

whenever I got sick I piled a bunch of coats in one of the lavatory stalls and slept in there. After I told my story to my classmate she told me that it was very important for me to talk about that experience because I was probably not the only one that it had happened to. That's one of the things that we had to do was talk about the things that happened to our people to try and find the reasons why . . .[33]

WORKS CITED

Barman, Jean, Yvonee Hébert, and Don McCaskill. *Indian Education in Canada, Volume 2: The Challenge.* Vancouver: UBC Press, 1987.

Department of Indian Affairs. *Annual Report, 1885.* Ottawa: Maclean, Roger, and Company, 1886.

———. *Annual Report, 1895.* Ottawa: S. E. Dawson, Printer to the King's Most Excellent Majesty, 1896.

———. *Annual Report, 1900–01.* Ottawa: S. E. Dawson, Printer to the King's Most Excellent Majesty, 1901.

———. *Annual Report, 1902–03.* Ottawa: S. E. Dawson, Printer to the King's Most Excellent Majesty, 1903.

———. *Indian Conditions: A Survey.* Ottawa: Indian Affairs and Northern Development, 1980.

———. *Indian Education Paper: Phase I.* Education and Social Service Branch, published under John Munro. Ottawa: Indian Affairs and Northern Development, 1982.

Fiske, Jo-Anne. "And Then We Prayed Again: Carrier Women, Colonialism and Mission School." MA thesis, University of British Columbia, 1981.

Getty, Ian L., and Antoine S. Lussier, eds. *As Long as the Sun Shines and Water Flows: A Reader in Canadian Native Studies.* Vancouver: UBC Press, 1983.

King, A. Richard. *The School At Mopass: A Problem of Identity.* New York: Holt, Rinehart and Winston, 1967.

La Flesche, Francis. *The Middle Five: Indian Schoolboys of the Omaha Tribe.* Madison: University of Wisconsin Press, 1963.

Prucha, Francis Paul. *The Churches and the Indian Schools, 1888–1912.* Lincoln: University of Nebraska Press, 1979.

Vayro, Celia. "Invasion and Resistance: Native Perspectives of the Kamloops Indian Residential School." MA thesis, University of British Columbia, 1986.

---

33 Marceline Paul.

Webster Grant, John. *Moon of Wintertime: Missionaries and the Indians of Canada in Encounter since 1534.* Toronto: University of Toronto Press, 1984.

Whitehead, Margaret. *The Cariboo Mission: A History of the Oblates.* Victoria, BC: Sono Nis Press, 1981.

NOTES

EDITORS' NOTE

1   I was also motivated by an experience in graduate school when I attended one of Manuel's jointly authored plays, *Missing Lives*, and in subsequent conversations with the Helping Spirit Lodge Society, where copies of the plays were shared with me.

2   These group-authored plays are not included in this collection but will be released once efforts to contact all the authors are made.

NARRATIVE ACTS OF TRUTH AND RECONCILIATION: TEACHING THE HEALING PLAYS OF VERA MANUEL

1   For my friend, Jo-Ann Episkenew, one of the strongest Indigenous women I have ever known, who put a copy of *Strength of Indian Women* into my hands many years ago and insisted (with that "I'm-not-kidding-about-this" look in her eyes) that I read it.

2   At the time of writing this, the only published play of Vera Manuel was *Strength of Indian Women*, hence my choice to teach it. I see tremendous value in teaching all of the plays, stories, and poems collected in this volume, and encourage educators to bring these important works into the classroom.

3   Kitchen table dialogues are informal conversations between friends or colleagues, usually in the comfort of one's home. We adapted this format as a pedagogical tool for use in the classroom. Emalene Manuel and I had this conversation in front of students in a course run by Deanna Reder and Sophie McCall. The course was titled, "Indigenous Writing since 1867: Once Neglected, Now Celebrated." The dialogue was held in Vancouver at Simon Fraser University on 7 June 2017.

4   See also, Michelle Coupal, "Teaching Indigenous Literature as Testimony: Porcupines and China Dolls and the Testimonial Imaginary," in *Learn Teach Challenge: Approaching Indigenous Literatures*, edited by Deanna Reder and Linda M. Morra (Waterloo, ON: Wilfrid Laurier UP, 2016), 477–86.

5   Deanna Reder (Cree-Métis) and Linda Morra—riffing on Helen Hoy's 2001, *How Should I Read These?*—astutely asked all scholars of Indigenous literatures—"how shall we teach these?"—at a conference at Simon Fraser University in 2014.

6   In her 2017 capstone project for her Master of Education, Arlene (Emalene) Manuel posits a "warrior epistemology" as a way of understanding what she calls her "resurgent family genealogy," which she sees as a "warrior training ground" (22). The Manuel women come from a long line of activists that Emalene calls "warriors."

7   "The Abyss" is included in this collection. See pages 239–47.

8   Vera Manuel began writing plays and poetry at the same time that she was also conducting group therapy workshops. She eventually brought writing and therapy together. As she says, "they were like two separate things I was doing and it kept me really busy, and then all of a sudden they both started coming together; it felt so natural, such a natural fit for me to start taking my poetry into the workshops. And I would get to see what a strong impact it had on people to get them to open up about their stories" (Interview).

9   In "The Abyss" the lines read as follows: "'It's a bunch of girls . . . lots of them, standing in front of a big grey building. There's a priest standing there with them'" (240).

EMBEDDED TEACHINGS: VERA MANUEL'S
RECOVERED SHORT STORIES

1   *Strength of Indian Women* is one of the first and still one of the most accessible texts on residential school history, and, although long out of print, is still taught in classrooms as far away from Canada as Poland.

2   Several of Vera Manuel's poems were published, including in various editions of *Gatherings*, an annual volume released by Theytus Press (1990–) that was regularly the first to print the work of many emerging Indigenous writers in Canada.

3   Million tracks conversations in the post–Second World War era about the damage to Indigenous peoples that was caused by colonization. She studies the transformation of the discussion from focusing on Indigenous alienation and social disintegration— the anomie—of the Canadian Indian and Canada's resultant "Indian problem" to the notion of the victim, the societal acknowledgement of abuse, and the theories about trauma in the late 1980s.

4   George Manuel was president of the North American Indian Brotherhood from 1959 to 1960, chief of what was then known as the Shuswap Indian band from 1960 to 1966, the chief of the National Indian Brotherhood from 1970 to 1976, the first president of the World Council on Indigenous Peoples from 1975 to 1981, and the president of the Union of British Columbia Indian Chiefs from 1979 to 1981, and credited with organizing the Indian Constitutional Express.

5   For more information, see the biography on Manuel posted on the University of British Columbia Indigenous Foundations website: https://indigenousfoundations.arts.ubc.ca/george_manuel/.

6   Carr then draws on a the concept of non-place, as discussed by Marc Augé as a place of transit like airports or shopping malls that are not inhabited by anyone, and further defined by Italian theorist Georgio Agamben and exemplified by non-places like concentration camps and refugee camps, which are the unarticulated foundation of

modern power allowing states to keep out non-citizens. While I find Carr's analysis of St. Eugene's architecture to be helpful in highlighting that its design reinforces the logic of colonialism, I find the discussion of non-place to overshadow Indigenous discussions and experiences of it as a place of trauma. I don't think Carr is trying to diminish Indigenous experience but I find it distracting.

7   In *Residential Schools: The Stolen Years* (Saskatoon: University Extension Press, University of Saskatchewan, 1993), a slim volume edited by Linda L. Jaine and one of the first publications on the residential school experience

8   We hope to tackle this project in the future in partnership with these joint authors.

"THROUGH POETRY A COMMUNITY IS BROUGHT TOGETHER": VERA MANUEL'S POETRY, POETRY ACTIVISM, AND POETICS

1   This information was contained in Vera Manuel's Writing Resume and Biz Resume, n.d.

2   Also called the Aboriginal History Media Arts Lab.

3   Much of the discussion of this event was originally published in my essay "Strong Words," in the Spring 2011 issue of *Yellow Medicine Review*, with the exception of my discussion of Vera's poetics and quoted material.

4   See Aboriginal Writers Collective West Coast, History and Mandate, 2015, in Joanne Arnott's possession.

5   An oral performance of Vera's "Justice" was included in *Redwire Magazine*'s cd/online offering, *Our Voice is Our Weapon and Our Bullets are the Truth*. "Survivor" is a video-poem directed by Doreen Manuel, with soundscape by Sandy Scofield. At least one of Vera's poems was set to music as a song, published and performed by Wayne Lavalee. Vera also worked with Sandy Scofield to set a number of her poems in soundscapes, with Manuel orating. The following information comes from the *Redwire* biography and other sources: Her poetry and plays are included in several anthologies. Her poetry is specifically included in *The World Poetry Anthology* (WPP2002), *Rocksalt: An Anthology of BC Poetry* (Salt Spring Island, BC: Mother Tongue, 2008), Aboriginal Writers Collective West Coast's *Salish Seas: An Anthology of Text + Image* (Nanaimo, BC: Aboriginal Writers Collective West Coast, 2011), and in Barry Peterson and Blaise Enright's *111 West Coast Literary Portraits* (Salt Spring Island, BC: Mother Tongue, 2012), alongside a portrait taken in 2005. Her work was published in periodicals, such as *Gatherings: The En'owkin Journal of First North American Peoples* and *The Capilano Review*.

6   From the entry on Vera Manuel in *Rocksalt*, 2008. Used with permission of Mother Tongue Publishing.

BIBLIOGRAPHY

Archibald, Jo-ann. *Indigenous Storywork: Educating the Heart, Mind, Body, and Spirit.* Vancouver: University of British Columbia Press, 2008.

Arnott, Joanne. Aboriginal Writers Collective West Coast, History, and Mandate. Vancouver: 2015.

———. "Strong Words." *Yellow Medicine Review*, Spring 2011.

———. *Vera Manuel Tribute* (blog), 2010. http://veramanueltribute.blogspot.com.

Benton, Sherrole. "'Strength of Indian Women' Premiers May 17." *Kalihwisaks: She looks for News* (Official Newspaper of the Oneida Nation of Wisconsin), 26 April 2007. https://oneida-nsn.gov/dl-file.php?file=2018/05/04-Kalihwisaks042607.pdf.

Carr, Geoffrey. "*Atopoi* of the Modern: Revisiting the Place of the Indian Residential School." *ESC: English Studies in Canada* 35, no. 1 (2009): 109–35.

Coupal, Michelle. "Teaching Literature as Testimony: *Porcupines and China Dolls* and the Testimonial Imaginary." In *Learn, Teach, Challenge: Approaching Indigenous Literatures*, edited by Deanna Reder and Linda M. Morra, 477–86. Waterloo, ON: Wilfrid Laurier University Press, 2016.

Courtois, Christine A. *Healing the Incest Wound: Adult Survivors in Therapy.* New York: Norton, 1988.

Episkenew, Jo-Ann. *Taking Back Our Spirits: Indigenous Literature, Public Policy, and Healing.* Winnipeg: University of Manitoba Press, 2009.

Furniss, Elizabeth. *Victims of Benevolence: The Dark Legacy of the Williams Lake Residential School.* Vancouver: Arsenal Pulp Press, 1995.

Hoy, Helen. *How Should I Read These?: Native Women Writers in Canada.* Toronto: University of Toronto Press, 2001.

Kovach, Margaret. "Treaties, Truths, and Transgressive Pedagogies: Re-Imagining Indigenous Presence in the Classroom." *Socialist Studies* 9, no. 1 (2013): 109–27.

Manuel, Arlene [Emalene]. "An Ethnographic Film Research Project: Warrior Epistemologies and 'Akaminki.'" Capstone project for M. Ed., University of British Columbia, 2017.

Manuel, Arthur, and Grand Chief Ronald M. Derrickson. *The Reconciliation Manifesto: Recovering the Land, Rebuilding the Economy*. Toronto : James Lorimer and Company, 2017.

————. *Unsettling Canada: A National Wake-up Call*. Toronto: Between the Lines, 2015.

Manuel, Doreen. *Survivor*. Running Wolf Production. http://www.runningwolf.ca/credits/ (accessed on 3 September 2018).

Manuel, George, and Michael Posluns. *The Fourth World: An Indian Reality*. Don Mills, ON: Collier-MacMillan, 1974.

Manuel, Vera. "The Abyss." In *Residential Schools: The Stolen Years*, edited by Linda Jaine, 107–16. Saskatoon: University Extension Press, Extension Division, University of Saskatchewan, 1993.

————. Interview by Peter Morin. "Letting go of Trauma On and Off Stage." *Redwire*. https://users.resist.ca/www.redwiremag.com/lettinggooftrauma.htm (accessed 11 February 2018).

————. "Justice," Track 13 on *Our Voice is Our Weapon and Our Bullets are the Truth*. *Redwire*. http://redwiremagazine.com/site/redwire/music (accessed 11 February 2018).

————. *Strength of Indian Women*. In *Two Plays About Residential School*, 75–119. Vancouver: Living Traditions, 1998.

————. Strong Words Conference Research Notes. 2008.

————. Strong Words Conference Poetry Article Draft. 2009.

————. "Vera Manuel" *Rocksalt: An Anthology of Contemporary BC Poetry*, 150–151. Edited by Mona Fertig and Harold Rhenish. Salt Spring Island, BC: Mother Tongue Publishing, 2008.

Martens, Tony, Brenda Daily, and Maggie Hodgson. *Characteristics and Dynamics of Incest and Child Sexual Abuse with a Native Perspective*. Edmonton: Nechi Institute, 1988.

McFarlane, Peter. *Brotherhood to Nationhood: George Manuel and the Making of the Modern Indian Movement*. Toronto: Between the Lines, 1993.

McKegney, Sam. *Magic Weapons: Aboriginal Writers Remaking Community after Residential School*. Winnipeg: University of Manitoba Press, 2007.

Miami University Libraries. (n.d.). Walter Havighurst Special Collections and Archives. spec.lib.miamioh.edu/home (accessed on 11 February 2018).

Million, Dian. "Felt Theory: An Indigenous Feminist Approach to Affect and History." *Wicazo Sa Review* 24, no. 2 (2009): 53–76.

————. *Therapeutic Nations: Healing in an Age of Indigenous Human Rights*. Tucson: University of Arizona Press, 2013.

Morton, Stephen. *Gayatri Chakravorty Spivak*. London: Routledge, 2003.

Mosby, Ian. "Administering Colonial Science: Nutrition Research and Human Biomedical Experimentation in Aboriginal Communities and Residential Schools, 1942–1952." *Histoire Social/Social History* 46, no. 91 (2013): 145–72.

————. "Of History and Headlines: Reflections of an Accidental Public Historian." http://activehistory.ca/2014/04/of-history-and-headlines-reflections-of-an-accidental-public-historian/ (accessed 3 September 2018).

Stanlake, Christy. *Indigenous American Drama: A Critical Perspective*. New York: Cambridge University Press, 2009.

Todd, Loretta. "Thinking of Vera Manuel—Some Words from Loretta Todd." Unpublished notes, 2017.

————. Personal communication, 2017. Truth and Reconciliation Commission of Canada. *Final Report of the Truth and Reconciliation Commission of Canada: Honouring the Truth, Reconciling the Future*. Vol. 1. Toronto: Lorimer, 2015.

————. *They Came for the Children*. Winnipeg: Truth and Reconciliation Commission of Canada, 2012. http://www.myrobust.com/websites/trcinstitution/File/2039_T&R_eng_web[1].pdf (accessed on 11 February 2018).

Yellow Horse Brave Heart, Maria, and Lemyra M. DeBruyn. "Healing the Dysfunctional Indian Family." Paper presented at the National Indian Health Board Conference, 1988.